DEEP
NAKED

RILEY HILL

Other Books
by Riley Hill

Skin Slickers
Book II in the Naked Worlds
Series. The sci-fi paranormal
adventure intensifies as Crystal
is kidnapped by aliens.

Crystal's Skull
Book III in the Naked Worlds
Series. An alien artifact may
mean the end of the world.

Split River
A Mystery/Suspense novel set on
Sauvie Island in the
Pacific Northwest

Bone Pile
A Collection of Macabre
Short Stories set in Arizona

DEEP
NAKED

RILEY HILL

RIVERHOUSE LIT

Published by Riverhouse Lit
Dewey, Arizona USA

© Copyright 2013, 2018 Riley Hill
Registered Work: All Rights Reserved
Registration TX 7-922-509

Cover Artwork by Damon Za
Book Design by Desert Bloom SW
www.desertbloomsw.com

~

Although this work of fiction uses real names and places, the settings, characters, and occurrences are completely fictional and figments of the author's imagination.

LCCN 2013911771

ISBN-13: 978-1490503059
ISBN-10: 1490503056

Acknowledgments

With love and gratitude to
Carl Grimsman
who has both inspired and prodded me
as well as served as my guide
across uncharted oceans

Special consideration to
Stormey Goddard for her valuable research

~

Deep respect for my relatives of olde: Olof August Widmark (1824-1878), renowned Swedish fiddler; and Fredrik (*Svinstu*) Lindroth (1812-1853), the family wizard. This book was inspired by their true-life adventures and Olof's training with the *Näcken*. The portion of Olof's music which was not burned by his granddaughter is currently held in The Royal Academy of Music Library. It is my hope that in whichever dimension they are, my relatives will receive these writings with the wink and love with which they are intended.   –Riley Hill *for my father*

CONTENTS

PART I

NIGHT OF THE NÄCKEN

Part II

BLOOD WICKET

PART III

CRACKING SKY

PART I

NIGHT

OF THE

NÄCKEN

1

DARK VISIONS

For Crystal Carson the change began at dusk, with the color of music streaming through her head, and a tune she longed to play on her violin whistling through her lips. She skipped down brick steps leading from Tish's house to her bicycle and straddled it. Lifting her face into a cooling breeze, a stray droplet from a cloud or errant sprinkler landed on her cheek. She wiped it. An odd thought crossed her mind: *All change begins with water.*

Closing her eyes, she inhaled the scent of newly mown grass from the neighbor's yard and hung suspended in the peace of late summer.

As she raised her foot to the pedal, a tendril of confused energy from over her shoulder wormed its way into the rhythm of her song, mid-whistle. Her lips softened, becoming inert.

Clouds shifted across the sky, singling her out as though drawn by her upturned face. A bass rumble from the stomach of some unnamed beast echoed across the horizon as her eyes opened to a darkening of the air. More water droplets began pelting her.

An electrified presence emerged from the front-yard spruce to force its way through her cells into her body. The amorphous shape engulfed her — both violet and white molecules vibrated erratically, assaulting her with urgency. Her heart rat-a-tatted as fear shot from her stomach to her throat.

Raising herself to the seat, she strained her thighs and calves, pumping fast to outrun the shadow that now chased her. The dark mass flowed above her head and filtered through the trees, *whish*ing along with her. Within the mass, shaped and twisted into a caricature of horror, was the face of her best friend, Tish. *Crystal! Help me!* rasped the voice like crumbled leaves.

Compelled by fear, Crystal tensed her muscles and pumped for all she was worth. Her fingers white-knuckled on the handlebars, she kept her eyes straight ahead, refusing to look — to see if it was really there.

As it darted behind every car, bush, and mailbox, she sped her bike up five streets toward her home, where she knew her mother baked cookies and her father listened to the evening news.

Arriving winded, she rushed her bike into the rack and sprinted to the back door. The darkness seemed to blanket and come to rest in the peach tree.

Pausing, she breathed deeply to calm herself, gripping the solid wood of the door frame, and relaxed her features to appear pleasant. "Hi, Mom. Hi, Dad," she said as she entered the kitchen. "Smells good. What's for dinner?" She had never before been afraid of the dark, and at seventeen was ashamed to mention it.

In the morning, Crystal swallowed the remnants of a glass of water and pressed it to her bedroom door. Twisting her neck, she placed her ear on the butt end of the glass to magnify the sound of what was being said in the hallway. Still glazed with sleep, her eyes spanned across the faux Tiffany light fixture, a remnant of some earlier time period; her computer; and her huge poster of *Donna the Buffalo*. The glow from the window diffused light over her violin, hanging by its neck from a wooden holder her father had crafted for it.

"I'm not sure it's right," said her mother. A pause. "Well, she already has lessons." Another pause. "Oh, Sarah. I really wish you hadn't done that until you spoke with me and Richard. That's an awful lot of money — I know she's your favorite niece, but . . ."

The sound of Crystal's own pulse obliterated the rest of her mother's words, leaving her to wonder. So Aunt Sarah was giving her a present this year. Crystal giggled to herself. Maybe another Kreskin game? Tarot cards? Maybe she could arrange to not be here when her aunt came.

Pulling on her top, Crystal squeezed her breasts in under the fabric. She was growing again. Would she never stop? Maybe she had enough money to get a new blouse today at the mall. After she used the kiosk to look for jobs, she and Tish could hang out.

Dressed and pert in a tight creamy top and shorts, Crystal slipped on some sandals and pulled her hair into a thick ponytail. It was already starting to heat up in their small house and the mall air conditioning would feel really good today.

Into her ear piercings, she slipped pearl and copper earrings. Pausing to assess her ring collection, she then looked at her fiddle. If she wore rings her fingers would swell into sausages, and later when she practiced her dexterity would be poor. She skipped the rings.

Springing down the stairs, she paused at the kitchen to snare an apple before heading out the door.

"Hey, Squeaky. Where are you off to?" asked her dad, lifting his forehead over the paper.

"Mall," she said between crunches. Crystal smiled at her father's use of the nickname he had given her when she first took up fiddle. She hadn't heard it in a while.

"Need the car?"

"Nope. Bikes. Going green today."

"I think your mother wants to talk to you."

Crystal looked at the dishes in the sink and crinkled her eyebrows. "Dad, does it have to be now? I'm going to be late."

Her father set down the *Times* and drew his lips into a thin curl under amused eyes.

Crystal winced. She knew he knew she fibbed. There was always a bit of what he referred to as "womanly tension" between her and her mother.

"Probably better to get it out of the way, don't you think?" He sipped from a coffee mug.

"I guess." Crystal took another bite, chewed and swallowed. "Where is she?"

"Out back."

Crystal eyed the backyard through the window, where her mother kneeled among growing vegetables. Looking at the curve of her mother's back as she bent over the food left Crystal feeling a little mean and sad.

"Oh. Okay." Caught, she took a breath. "See you later."

Gliding along the back walkway toward her mother, Crystal sensed a strange presence overcome her. A shadow shifted toward her from the peach tree and her skin prickled as though someone were watching her. Her neck jerked, she inhaled and glanced at the tree. *The thing from last night?* Truly, there was only sunlight filtering through leaves.

"Good morning, Mom."

Her mother looked up, her cheeks pink from the exertion of digging. Amusement toyed with her lips from a thought or feeling she had been entertaining before Crystal interrupted her. "Hi, honey. Did you see all these tomatoes on these bushes?"

"There are a lot."

"We're going to have spaghetti all through next winter! I really like these Heirlooms."

"Dad said you wanted to see me."

"Oh, yes." Her mother's attention focused on her. "You're all dressed. Where are you off to?"

"Tish and I are going to the mall."

"This early?"

"We're going to hang out first at Tish's house and look for a job for me on *craigslist*."

"Well, that sounds fine." She spotted a weed and plucked it.

"So what was it?"

"What?"

"What you wanted to see me about?"

"Oh. Your aunt phoned and — I don't want you to get upset about this — but she has a present this year for your birthday."

Crystal had already gleaned this much from the eavesdropped conversation, but she groaned anyway.

"That isn't nice." Her mother squinted up at her.

"But Mom, she's weird." Crystal hadn't meant to whine and wished she hadn't spoken. She just wanted to get out of there.

"I know what you think, but your aunt had it hard. She never got over losing — "

"I know, I know. Her baby. But gads. That was a million years ago."

"Cris!" Her mother's eyes darkened. "Some losses a person never gets over."

Crystal knew this to be true. She knocked her shoe on some dry grass and apologized. "Is she coming over?"

Her mother lightened. "No, I don't think so. It isn't that kind of present. I wasn't sure what to tell her."

"What? What is it? A reading with Madame Zelda?" Crystal bit her lip when the words slipped out.

Crystal's mother cocked an eyebrow and suppressed a smile, then stood and brushed off her knees. "There's some camp in the Appalachians she heard about. I don't know why she thought you'd . . ."

Crystal's jaw dropped and her eyes widened. "You're kidding, right? Beans Camp? Did she say 'Beans'?"

"I'm not sure . . . I think so. Is this good?"

Crystal's gut wrenched. "Oh, Mom. It's good. It's good." Then a ripple of nausea muted her enthusiasm. What if her mother had it wrong? She didn't want to get too excited. It was expensive; over a thousand dollars for the week. This couldn't be true.

"What is this place?" her mother seemed puzzled and a little hurt. Already they were scrimping to give her music lessons.

"It's a nationally known camp. There are incredible musicians from all over the country that come and give you group lessons. It's intense. All you do all week is play!" Crystal read regret in her mother's look and tried to repress her enthusiasm.

Her mother was quiet for a moment. "Well, you should call her. I didn't get all the particulars." She picked up the hand tools and rake and began walking toward the house. Crystal followed a step behind her.

"Can't you call her for me?" Her voice trembled and sounded like a little girl's. Embarrassed, Crystal cleared her throat.

Her mother stopped and turned. "Now, Cris. It's only polite for you to thank her yourself." She continued toward the house.

Crystal was silent as her jaw tightened. *Rats!* Talking to her aunt might be harder than not going to camp. She weighed the two for a moment, unsure if she could force herself to make the call.

But when she considered not going, the energy that had been lurking in the tree eddied over her again, and her nausea intensified. She was beginning to feel genuinely ill. Fluey. She fought it down.

Left on her own, Crystal stared at her mother's back. Like always, she seemed distant, just out of reach. As though they lived on two different planets. Pulling her bike from the rack, she mounted. She needed to talk to Tish before making the call.

♪

On the other side of the world, eighteen hours ahead in time, Fredrik of Now snorted, waking himself up in the middle of the night. He'd been having one of his *true* dreams. From his cramped position in the fireplace chair, he opened his eyes and unfurrowed his brow, working to grasp the last of the images.

His buttocks shifted in the worn dent of leather and the chair, which had been his grandfather's before him, creaked. He stretched his tall Nordic form, hands outreached, toes pointing, and yawned wide-mouthed. Settling back, he scrunched his chin into the nest of his beard, closed his eyes and reached into the substance from which thought is composed. Who was it he had seen?

His mind's eye sifted through dimensions to a relative somewhere in time and space. Her presence was cool and loving. Her face loomed before him as though summoned, and he laughed a muted and airy sound at the spiked hair coiled atop her head and dancing, bright eyes. Her name whispered from what he referred to in secret as "the voices in the wind." *Sarahhhh.*

A chill of excitement coursed through his blood. As he thrust a *feeler* out to her, it penetrated her skull and lodged somewhere near her thalamus. *She was open to him!* This meant he could join with her — send and receive thoughts. He probed lightly so as not to alarm her and sensed her partial awareness of his presence when she channeled his thought patterns.

Through her eyes he scanned for what had drawn him.

For an instant, through Sarah's mind, he glimpsed the pale form of a young woman. Her abilities were unusual, even for their lineage, but it was clear they were not yet developed. Worse, she seemed to be fighting them.

He slapped the arm of the chair, and dust arose. *How had he not seen her before?* She could be the one, *the one,* to help with the forthcoming events, possibly carrying the strength to connect to the other side; to provide the exact element of energy needed to effect the Great Change.

His blood sizzled and worked through his veins — hard for an old man to take — and he pressed his hand to his chest. After all this time, he may have found her. Tears spread the hand-crafted chairs and rugs in the living room into a distorted painting.

As he stared into the dim air above his head, he probed harder. Sarah, seated at a table in a bright room with strange furnishings, opened a little more to him. He sensed, through Sarah, that the young woman was weak, yet was just beginning to turn. Confused, she had no control of her powers and didn't know what they were.

Why hadn't they trained her? As though called, an image of her formed next to his mantle.

Time had been turned on its head for millennia. How could this weak girl carry the energy to set right such important events? Looking at the set of her jaw, he also caught a flash in her eye. She held a secret, a connection to a force *beyond*. He sensed a strong ability to envision, and the potential to direct her will beyond what he could do, if she only knew how. Envisioning alone was not enough. He rubbed the leather cover of the book resting on his lap—his sacred book, the *Tales of All Time*.

All change begins with water, he thought. She would need the power found there. She would need to come to him for training. There was much she needed to know. He patted the book. He would do what he could to aid her, but she must come soon.

As usual he had little control over coming events. The planets were aligning all on their own. The *possibility* for change—the Great Change—was coming. But, if the girl failed to arrive, or failed to manifest the energy, they would still be trapped, moving closer to the eternal *Now*. All life would cease for all time and eternity.

What could he do? For a wizard, when it came to large manifestations of the world, he had little power. But if he could explain it to her, make her see . . . and if the universe was willing, she might be able to help.

Shrugging, he picked up a poker and bore the tip into a log in the fireplace. Sparks rewarded him.

2

UNWANTED GIFTS

As Crystal pulled up on her bike, Tish bounded out of the older-style suburban house sporting a whole new look. Her hair was still black, but set in a Keyshia Cole style short do.

"Oh! You look fabulous!" Crystal tried to make her voice upbeat, but she still felt sick. Friends for ten years, Crystal had seen Tish with more hairstyles, fingernail paintings, and tasteful piercings than anyone else she knew. Tish's flair for style and athletic prowess in basketball offset the otherwise rude comments she would have garnered at school for being a science geek. Tish had her game buddies, but neither girl fully fit in, and both were both glad high school was behind them.

Tish beamed, her hand going to her hair.

As Tish closed the door to join her, Crystal recalled the strange vision of the night before. Seeing her friend's smiling face made her stomach uneasy. A slight buzzing seemed to hover around her forehead.

"Why would I want to do that?" Crystal asked.

"What? Do what?"

Crystal watched as her friend mounted her bike. "What you just said. Go hang out at Jerry's."

Tish paused and stared at her. "What is *wrong* with you? I didn't say that!" Then she grinned. "I might have been thinking it, though." She began pedaling.

"Wait, I need to tell you — " she started, but Tish was already up the street.

Crystal followed on her bike, perplexed. She'd clearly heard Tish, and if direction was any indication, Jerry's house was exactly where they were headed. Tish obviously had plans other than going to the mall or looking for work.

Sun spots flickering through the trees danced on the back of Tish's colorful blouse as Crystal followed her up the street. "What?" she called out.

"What?" said Tish over her shoulder.

"Help you do what?"

"What? What did you say?"

"Help you do what?" Crystal tried to shout so her friend could hear.

"I don't need any help."

Crystal shook her head, annoyed. "Never mind!"

She kept pedaling behind Tish as a sense crept in on her of some darkness and someone watching, like earlier in the garden. Nausea shimmied up her body and she stopped. Standing still, she straddled her bike while Tish continued up the street.

A reeling sensation flowed over her as she heard voices, very faint, from far away. She had to concentrate to make out the words. *What is she then? Näcken . . . we don't know . . . when will she be here . . . not in time . . . Vingåker . . .*

Some words were garbled. A tone vibrated like nesting bugs from a nearby Rose of Sharon. The tone *was* the bush. Her eyes slipped upward toward the sky as it hummed toward her, then swept downward as the earth groaned at 7.85 hertz. A pressure crossed her forehead, she leaned over and vomited apple and bile into the gutter.

Crystal stood with her head hanging as sudden chills prickled her skin.

Tish returned, wide-eyed on her bike. "Oh, Cris! What happened?" She dismounted and placed her hand on her friend's back. "Are you okay?"

"*Ungh.* I don't know. I think I'm sick."

"We better get you back home."

Crystal thought of home, of bed, and felt better. Then she thought of her mother's request that she call her aunt. "I don't want to go home yet."

"What is it?" Tish's brown eyes bored into her own.

Crystal looked up and wiped her mouth with the back of her arm.

"Ugh. Gross." She spat. "You know my Aunt Sarah?"

"The Tarot card spooky aunt?"

Cris nodded, then frowned. "Yeah. You know how she gives me the creeps. Well, I'm supposed to call her."

Tish couldn't hide her sigh of impatience. "So, just hold your breath and call her. Talk fast. Why are you supposed to call her?"

Crystal glanced around to see if anyone was within earshot.

"She's giving me a really nice gift for my birthday and I don't know if I want it. There might be strings attached."

Tish stared at her friend and one hand moved to her hip.

"Then just refuse it. What is it?"

Crystal assessed her friend's attitude, expressed with her stance. She still felt nauseous. "It's a week at Beans."

"Beans? That fiddle camp you're always talking about?"

"Yes. The one. Darn! I want to go! But first off I don't know how she knows about it. She's not into music that I know of. And secondly, how would she even know that I wanted to go? Like she read my mind. I'm completely creeped out."

Tish chuckled. "You're scared she read your mind? Seriously?"

"Look—you don't know how odd she is. She's always trying to get me to be a witch."

"Well why don't you?"

"Why don't I what?"

"Be a witch? Maybe you could wiggle your nose and get us free passes to the movies."

"Huh?" Crystal stared. "I wouldn't know how to be a witch. And even if I were a witch, I wouldn't be a witch, because aren't they supposed to be evil? Like they run around with 'the horny man.'"

Tish guffawed. "The Horned Man."

"How do you know so much about it?"

"I had a spooky aunt, too. *Muhahaha.*" Tish grinned, then her face went serious. "But you really don't like her, huh?"

Crystal felt another wash of nausea and wished she hadn't brought it up. Could she really explain this to Tish? "It's not a dislike, exactly. She's just—strange. Also, she's the reason my folks won't let me have a cell phone. She says they cause cancer and she thinks Big Brother will follow me around and implant thoughts in my head through it. I tell you, she's really nuts."

Tish held up a hand. "I don't know why your parents would believe her. Anyway, can't you just ignore that? Get the present!"

Crystal looked at the ground.

"It's *Beans*." Tish cocked an eyebrow and tilted her head. "Look, just pretend to be nice to your aunt. Accepting a gift doesn't obligate you, does it?"

Crystal sighed and rubbed her arms, holding her bike between her thighs. "I just don't want her coming any closer."

She couldn't explain it to Tish without sounding like an idiot. Sarah went places — in her mind — and touched on areas she was not ready for. She *was* afraid Sarah could read her mind. And even what she said about cell phones . . . The thought that others might control her thoughts was beyond horrifying to her. Further, outside of the magic stuff, her aunt was always talking about recycling, the earth mother, the welfare of abused animals, and God. Even though she was all for most of these, Crystal just wanted to be a girl — just a normal girl. She didn't want to think about spooky, or dark, or even light things. She just wanted to ride her bike, play her fiddle, figure out how to go to college, and let the world go on around her. And then, someday, she'd meet a guy, get married, have kids and . . .

"Where did you go?" Tish's face loomed before her, drawing Crystal back.

"Probably outer space." Crystal stared at the grasses growing nearby, turning brown already. "I guess I'm being a baby."

"So, are you going to do it?"

"I'm still not quite sure, but I do think I should get home and take some Pepto."

The friends parted and Crystal pedaled back home, walked her bike into the back yard and set it up at the rack. When she moved toward the house, without meaning to she found herself avoiding the peach tree.

As she entered the back door, Crystal heard her aunt's ear-splitting cackle coming from the living room. *Rats! Too late to run!* For sure they had heard her come in. This was confirmed by her mother's voice calling, with a tinge of desperation.

"Cris? Is that you?"

Crystal sighed. "Me, Mom."

"Come here, please."

"Busy right now." She looked around at the kitchen counters, hoping to find an excuse to be busy, but the dishes were done.

"Your aunt is here to see you."

There was no way out of it. Crystal walked down a dim hall to the living room archway. Her aunt's florid face loomed before her, like a train at the far end of a tunnel, watching her come. A toothy grin from some evil genie was plastered across her head. Eyes alight with life and happiness shown under hair stuck into a high ponytail, like a cockatoo crown. Nausea started to return, but was instantly replaced by a defense mechanism as Aunt Sarah giggled a hello.

"Honey. Honey. Sit down a minute." Sarah patted a spot on the couch next to her.

Crystal smiled weakly and sat in a chair near her mother.

"Hello, Aunt Sarah."

"Did your mother tell you what I got you for your birthday?"

"Yes, she did. Thanks so much, Aunt Sarah. It was very generous of you."

"I just kind of guessed it would be the right choice. I mean, this is a very special birthday. Your eighteenth, right?" Sarah glanced at Emma and a significant look passed between them. "You've wanted to go, haven't you?"

Crystal ran her hand over the brocade arm of the chair and looked down at an imaginary speck on the floor. "Yes. Very much. But how did you know?"

Sarah laughed—a sound like a cawing raven. "Oh, you're funny. When you kitty-sat for me while I was on vacation you left a bookmark in one of my magazines. You'd actually doodled a fiddle next to the ad for the camp."

Crystal's body relaxed and she breathed a deep, quiet sigh.

"You didn't think I'd read your mind, did you?" Sarah giggled and cawed again.

Crystal stood. "Well thanks again, Aunt Sarah." Crystal moved toward her aunt, intending to give her a hug, which she knew her aunt expected. And, with the generous gift, how could she deny this one small gesture? But there was a barrier in the air around her aunt—a repulsion barrier—that she almost literally bounced off. A wavering inertia gripped her feet. She forced her way through, but as she neared her aunt time seemed to slow down. The voices she'd heard earlier that morning returned in an excited chatter. A gray film moved over the room. Nausea. Closer. Her aunt's face. Her breath. Crystal was afraid she was going to hurl. Right there on her aunt's ratty sweater. On her aunt's greasy face. On that hideous mole on her neck.

For a moment she drifted in a glossy light, a place composed of sound waves. Gentle, flowing. The next thing Crystal knew, her mother and aunt were standing over her.

"Crystal, are you all right?" Her mother's worried face was right over hers.

"Huh? What happened?"

"You went down, girl." Her aunt's voice.

"Let's get you up to bed. Here, Sarah, help me with her."

"No! No. I mean I can do it."

Back in her bed, Crystal felt herself dropping like a wooden feather into a well. Like Alice in Wonderland, spinning. She fought it, resisting the fall. She wanted to stay in the light. To dance on the surface. To be young, free, healthy. But a magnetic force she'd never felt before was drawing her. Its power moved up through her body as though it were consuming her. Deep vibrations were accessing her cells, activating forces beyond her. At last, she let go and felt herself plummeting downward into a deep, indigo sleep.

As she awakened, Crystal lingered in a half-slumber state and, for just a moment, realized she'd been having a conversation with . . . *someone* . . . with *many voices* . . . in a place of her dreams. Drawing herself free, she tried to remember what the voices had said and what visions she may have had, but they dissolved like spider silk, leaving her feeling empty and alone.

It was night in her room, but a bowl of cold chicken broth was on her nightstand, so her mother must have been in earlier. Her clock said 3:13—she'd been asleep nearly seventeen hours!

A golden figure stood next to her violin, and she stretched and smiled at it. Warmth and goodness radiated through her as she glanced around at the shadows on her wall and ceiling from the grinning, crescent moon playing with clouds outside her window. Sudden awareness jolted her. *A golden figure?* She looked back at the instrument. Hard. No one.

The hallucination had been so perfect that she thought for a moment she was delirious. But whatever had overcome her before, the illness, had completely disappeared and she felt healthy and, mostly, *ravenous*.

Slipping from under her blanket, Crystal moved wraithlike down the hall to the kitchen. She held the fridge handle with tension so it wouldn't pop open too loudly, and peeked inside. Some cooked chicken on a platter. Leftover salad in a bowl. A carton of milk. *Oh boy!* She loved her mother's chicken. Pulling a leg from the plate, she put it to her lips to take a bite. Reeling from the smell of it, she held it at arm's length. It smelled . . . *dead*. She sniffed at it and her gorge rose. It looked okay, plump and breaded with Italian parmesan breadcrumbs, and it had just been cooked that night. But it smelled like death, like dead flesh. *Why would she ever want to eat something dead?*

Putting it back on the plate, she removed the salad and glared at it. An aura pulsed around it — of dying light. *How very strange*, she thought, *the salad has an aura and I can see it*. She knew she would prefer one freshly picked, as it would be radiant with energy, but at least there was still light for her to — to what? *Consume!* came the unbidden answer.

Seemingly from the same place as the earlier voices, a flood of impressions about what to eat and what not to eat pressed and thrust against her consciousness. Her gut clenched and she internally fought the attack of information as though it were physical. As it beckoned her to clarity, she rejected it. As it insisted, it felt as though the side of her head opened up revealing a previously hidden perception: the perception of the *tone of things*. The music of the greens called to her in delicate shades and playful lights.

She was about to put the salad back, believing she must still be sick, when her body seemed to take over. From a distance, she watched her left hand grip hard on the bowl. Then her right hand plunged, picking up a gob of salad leaves and cuttings, and cramming it into her mouth. It was barely chewed before she packed in another fistful. Her eyes began to tear and she snorted to breathe as she gagged herself with the food. What was wrong with her? *Out of control!*

The fluorescents clicked on and she continued to munch. With lettuce leaves protruding from her mouth, she turned to see her mother watching her, bleary eyed.

"Oh, honey," Emma said softly. "I'm so sorry."

Crystal moved to the sink and spat the salad into the disposal. *Sorry?* What was she sorry about? But then she didn't care, as she began crying, holding the offending hand in the air before her. And her mother held her in her arms as though she were a little girl again, shushing her. Crystal cried, the wheels in her head spinning around. She was still sick. Yeah, that was it. Sick.

Or she'd gone insane.

Emma helped her back into bed and stroked her hair. Crystal didn't know what to say or ask about her behavior. Embarrassed to have cried in front of her mother, she pretended tiredness and closed her eyes. A few minutes later, her mother left.

Opening her eyes, she watched the moon, a lopsided, sinister grin outside her window. Only a few minutes ago the light play with the clouds had been beautiful. Now, shadows skipped like demons across her wall. She glanced at her violin, longing to connect with it. To play notes to soothe herself. For just a moment it occurred to her that she might be able to play the tones of the salad. Of other things. Unbidden, a deep yearning overcame her.

Closing her eyes, Crystal focused on the rhythm of her breath to stop herself from thinking. Soon, she was asleep again — this time in an agitated slumber.

3

HARPS, ELVES & LOVES

Whipped by the wind, rain slashed in a herringbone pattern against the glass of the kitchen window. As Crystal ran water into the tea pot, lightning flashed through the open curtains, blinding her. The summer storm had sucked the heat from the room, making it feel damp and unhappy. Setting the kettle on the stove, she sped to close the curtains.

Tish and she had planned a last get-together before she left for camp and before Tish began her training as a lab assistant at the local college. But looking out at the slosh of gray on the sidewalks and flooding in the street, Crystal couldn't muster the joy to visit her friend. So she was just as pleased when her doorbell rang and Tish, in a fully-hooded down coat, stood on her porch with streamers drizzling from her head and shoulders.

"Let me in, I'm burning up."

Crystal opened the door. "Why the thick coat?" She took the jacket while Tish shook out her hair.

"Who expected rain this time of year? My fall slicker was packed away. This was in the living room closet."

"Right," she responded. "Want some cocoa?"

"Nah. I'm too fat already. Wait. Yes. It's those durn HAARP guys, you know, that's doing it. Where's your mom?"

"She took off to the employment agency."

Crystal headed for the cupboard and the heated tea-kettle. "Did you say 'harp guys'? Guys playing harps? I don't get it."

"No. You do know what HAARP is, don't you?"

Crystal shook her head as Tish sighed. "Girl, you need to keep up on science more."

"Me? I'm not scientist. You're the science one of us."

"Hah. Don't I wish. My job will only be part-time. But it is really exciting. I'll have access to all the equipment in the science lab." Tish beamed.

Crystal smiled at her friend's enthusiasm and stirred in the cocoa packets. "So what does playing a harp have to do with science?"

Tish sighed. "Can we use your computer?" Crystal nodded, then handed her friend a steaming mug. They went to her room and she pulled a side chair over so they could share the system and both see the screen.

Tish set down her cup. "Observe and learn," she said.

Pulling up *Google*, she typed in *HAARP* and took the first entry that popped up. It was from *Wikipedia*.

Crystal read what was on the screen and smirked at her friend. "Very funny. This sounds like conspiracy theory."

"It's in *Wiki*. It must be true."

She read a little more. "This sounds crazy. You mean to tell me that we have gadgets on this planet that are bouncing waves around our atmosphere —"

"Ionosphere."

"Okay, off our *ionosphere*. People actually are trying to control the weather, without knowing what they're doing?"

Tish nodded, her face serious. She sipped cocoa, leaving a smear on her lip. "Worse. Because it affects brainwaves, some people believe it's used as a military weapon—for mind control."

Crystal raised her eyebrows and suppressed a grin behind a sip of chocolate. "How did you ever get into this? In science class?"

"Not really. We were studying sound waves, and the subject of ELFs came up and—"

Crystal giggled. "Elfs? You study elves in science?"

Tish puffed up. "To you laymen, that would be Extremely Low Frequency waves—*ELF*. You know, like right before you wake up, when you're half asleep? Those are alpha waves. People say you can access your subconscious then. And meditation can get you down to even lower frequencies. Theta waves."

Crystal looked to the side and thought of her experience with the golden being in her room and the voices. Could these events have been brought about by these waves? She thought of asking Tish, then discarded the idea. It was too weird.

"Anyway, we were discussing frequencies and a boy brought up HAARP. The teacher sort of made fun of him, and it made me mad, so I decided to look it up. There's tons of information about it on the internet, and it's been going on for decades."

"Yeah, but it sounds so—"

"Conspiracy theory? Crazy?"

Crystal nodded and walked over to her bed. "Or like magic."

"Well, one man's magic is another man's science." Tish raised her nose a little.

Crystal bent one leg under her and sat down. "Let's sit here. It's more comfy." She put her mug on the nightstand as Tish joined her on the bed. "So, anyway, you think this weather is caused by ELFs?"

"I was just making a joke, but who knows? There's been so much going wrong with our environment lately. It can't all be due to human pollution. There're the solar explosions — CMEs — poles shifting, melting ice caps . . ."

"Hey, you're depressing me." Crystal looked out her window at the blackening sky.

"I'm just saying, it's not normal to have these changes all at once. And with HAARP messing with the weather — who knows?"

Crystal was silent.

"So you've been studying sound frequencies? By the way, there's chocolate on your lip."

Tish wiped her lip. "All sorts of waves. But yeah, sonics."

"Well then, maybe you could help me reach a perfect high 'e' on my fiddle. I always get a scritch."

Tish shook her head. "Now we are *way* outside of my field. Music theory and I don't mesh that well."

The girls finished their cocoa and vowed to celebrate Crystal's birthday when she returned from camp.

♪

The next day, as Crystal opened a suitcase onto the floor, her mother knocked then entered her room.

Holding out a package to Crystal, she smiled. "Happy almost birthday, honey."

The padded envelope had come through the mail and appeared to have been opened. Crystal peeled off the rest of the packaging, then stared disbelieving.

"This is for emergencies only — it's a satellite phone," her mother said. A note of apology rang in her voice as she added, "I hope you don't mind, but it is used. I got it off E-Bay."

Crystal was ecstatic. "Mom! Thank you!" She stared at the phone. "But . . . what about what Aunt Sarah says?"

Her mother looked amused. "I *am* the older sister. Besides, I didn't want you so far away with no way to get ahold of us if you needed."

Crystal thanked her again and hugged her. Even if the phone had limited, prepaid minutes, it was a much nicer gift than she had expected and made her feel part of the human race. *At last!*

"I preprogrammed some numbers for you. I didn't think you'd have time before you left. You better charge it, though."

Her mother stood watching her as she bent to plug in the phone to charge for a couple hours while she packed.

She stood and returned her mother's steady gaze, then broke her eyes away. "I guess I'd better get packing." She shifted toward the bed.

"Crystal. There's something I need to tell you." Her mother stood perfectly still, hands hanging loose at her sides, sea-colored eyes matching her dress.

"*Uh*, okay. What?" She looked around the room and glanced at the clock. She was conscious that her mother had used her *formal* name. This could not be good.

"It could take a while. I thought that I could drive you to camp and we could talk on the way."

Oh no! Crystal's body tensed. She was looking forward to the drive with her happy-go-lucky dad . . . maybe singing songs in the car. Not some big heavy birthday coming-of-age conversation for eight hours.

"Well, I think Dad was looking forward to it . . ."

"Looking forward to what?" Her father's voice broke through the doorway, where he stood holding a duffle and another bag. "Here are those bags I promised. Now, what kind of trouble am I in?"

"Oh, Dad! Mom said she wanted to drive me, but I thought you were really looking forward to it . . ." Her blue eyes captured her father's brown ones, and she willed him to understand.

He entered the room and set down the bags. He shifted between looking at her mother, who gazed at him with fondness and a cool certainty, and Crystal, who projected *please* in almost screaming telepathy.

"What's this about, Emma?" he asked.

"I need to have a discussion with Crystal, and it might take a while." Emma had not moved. She seemed captured in an air of quietude, remote. *On that other planet again.*

He glanced again at Crystal, then back to his wife.

"Can it wait? Can it wait until she gets back? I think I promised her some father-daughter time."

Her mother gazed at Crystal, the look carrying a sadness, but her voice was pleasant. "Yes. I suppose," she said.

"I hope you don't mind. Besides, don't you have some resumes out? Some people might call . . ." Crystal trailed off.

"Right," her mother uttered, turned on her heel, and left the room.

Crystal mouthed "thank you" to her father, then let out a big whoosh of air as he left to join his wife.

Along with her regular outfits, Crystal stuffed two bags with "just-in-case" clothing, including a new, white ruffle dress she had purchased with hope for the spring hop, but never got the chance to wear. Sometimes camps and festivals had a final performance, and students would all dress up to perform for each other. It was the only dress she owned, since she preferred jeans.

Her birthday would come while she was at the fiddle

camp and this suited her fine; she didn't want the fuss about turning eighteen that her mother was certain to give and the idea of sitting through a cheery cake with Aunt Sarah's prattle sounded dull.

She and her mother had not spoken about the Night of the Living Salad (as she had started calling it in her head), and she'd taken pains to distance herself. Occasionally her mother would glance at her, or start to approach her as though she wanted to talk, but Crystal had managed to slip her grasp each time.

Right now especially, she didn't want her mother knowing what was going on with her. Some gnawing sense told her it had to do with the weirdness of her mother's entire family. And until Crystal could sort out her feelings she didn't want to share it. She hadn't even told Tish.

No other friends were bound to contact her for her birthday. Like Tish, she was a loner, not fitting into any of the cliques or groups of girls in school. Tish didn't fit because of her scientific brain, and Crystal because she played her violin so much. Her music took her places that other kids her age just didn't seem to go. Plus, the type of music she played was not classical, so she didn't even fit in that well with the kids in orchestra.

She'd taught herself to play at an early age, preferring fiddling over being with others. Unless, of course, they were in a folk music jam. There, she seemed to fit. There she could really cut loose, feel free, and be herself. Inventing tunes, following her muse, was her lifeblood.

Picking up some toiletries from her dresser, she stuffed them into a makeup bag. Then she pulled her violin case from beneath her bed and opened it on a chair. Plucking the instrument from the peg on the wall, she held it to the daylight and admired its shape and crafts-man-ship. She sniffed the curled grain of the back, and enjoyed the scent of rosin, wood, and violin varnish.

Getting her bow from the hanger, she tightened it and fitted the instrument under her chin. *Ahhh.* Now she felt complete. It was as though she had an unborn twin shaped just like a violin. Nothing made her feel whole and complete like having her instrument connected to her body.

Crystal closed her eyes and allowed the room to fall into a realm she called, to herself, the *nothing zone.* Her thoughts, outside traffic sounds, the birds, the ticking of the clock slowed, muted, and disappeared. Remaining were her, her fiddle, and a sense of *magnificence,* just beyond. From here, from this place of purity, she could play.

She drew the bow hair across the strings, then paused to tune one of them. Again she drew the bow, closed her eyes, and drifted with the sweet notes. She allowed herself to make up random tunes: fast, then pensive, then fueled by fire.

As she drifted upward into another world with the notes, she sensed something *glorious* just ahead. If only she could reach it. She felt lifted into a whorl of white energy, as though a hole had opened in her bedroom ceiling and allowed her soul to exit. Letting loose her preconceptions, she allowed her fingers to fly — free, unencumbered — they knew where to go. They knew how to seek, to attain the —

A knocking rattled her door and she ceased with a wrench. She stood still for a few seconds, her head pounding. *What the heck was that? Where had she been?* She opened her bedroom door to see her father.

"You ready to go, Squeaky?"

His brown hair had turned gray at the temples and he wore a quirky grin. A lump of tenderness shifted in Crystal's throat while she looked at him. Her father's shirt-tail was half in and half out of his trousers, and a piece of toilet paper was stuck to his neck where he had cut himself shaving. His glasses were askew, with the temple tip a half-inch above his ear holding the glasses to his face by the side of his head.

"I love you, Dad," she said. She put her violin in the case and hugged him. "I have those bags over there and one here. Plus my fiddle."

"Whoa! It's only a week. What are you doing, packing food?" He chuckled and Crystal grinned back at him.

"Are you sure you won't let me drive myself? I am almost eighteen, you know."

"I know, honey, but your mother and I discussed it. We can't afford to be without the second car. What if she got a job?"

Crystal acquiesced, lifted her fiddle and one bag, and followed her father out.

Driving to the camp in the Appalachian range would take over eight hours, but in the Aerostar at least it would be comfortable. Thoughts that she might receive a car of her own for her birthday had vanished when Crystal's mother lost her secretarial job to the poor economy. Not many positions were available in their small Ohio town, and any openings tended to get filled by friends of the owners.

Crystal slipped her hand into her pocket and palmed her new cell phone. She couldn't wait to use it to call Tish and tell her about the camp. It hardly felt bigger than a credit card, but she hadn't had one of those before, either.

She thought again about her mother trying to talk to her. Why hadn't she let her? She was almost an adult, yet she continued to push her away. This uneasiness she was feeling . . . could her mother have some sense of it? Tish seemed so close with her mom. Why couldn't she be more like Tish?

She shuddered. She didn't know what Mom wanted, and she couldn't allow herself to care. At least not today. It was probably some speech about turning eighteen, growing up, or some other notion that was liable to be tedious and embarrassing. She'd rather associate herself, at least in her own mind, with her father's side of the family.

A reflection in the passenger window showed that her lips were pursed and she was frowning. She straightened out her face and tried to put on a pleasant look.

The trees and miles went by, green, white, green, gray, green . . . Crystal floated into reverie. When she first noticed the voices slipping into in her mind, she looked to her father to see if the radio was turned on. It wasn't. Her father never listened to the radio.

Putting her hands over her ears, she tried to obstruct them. Even though faint, the sing-songiness grated in her head. She focused on the road to block them out.

"What are you doing to your ears?"

"They need to pop," she lied.

After a few hundred miles they stopped at a gas station and, as her father pumped gas, Crystal headed for the restroom. A sign over the door said OUT OF ORDER. "Oh, great," Crystal mumbled aloud.

Looking around and seeing no other patrons, she sidled to the men's restroom. No such sign was on its door. Screwing up her face, preparing for the worst, she gripped the handle and pulled.

The door opened hard as someone exited. She staggered backward, slipped on the gravel, and the man — or boy — jumped out and grabbed her arm to stop her from falling.

She caught herself and looked up into concerned eyes. *It's him! It's him!* the voices chatted excitedly and Crystal went numb as his hand, warm and dry, slid up her arm to her elbow.

"Are you all right?" Tall, lean but strong. The fingers grasping her biceps were firm enough to grip a guitar, or a cello. Brown skin. Violet (she swore they were violet) eyes. Minted breath. About twenty. Her thighs clenched together. Gads. She needed to go *bad*.

"I'm fine," she answered. They both said *sorry* at the same time, then chuckled. Upstate New York accent. They looked at each other again.

"See you later," he said, and moved away in long, easy strides. How tall was he? Way taller than her. They'd look weird together. He looked GQ. She must look like a road-rumpled hick from the sticks.

She turned and entered the room, holding her breath. Her head was buzzing, but now not just with the voices. Her heart was beating a staccato rhythm. What did he mean *see you later*? She tried to shake off the thoughts. They'd never see each other again. It was a chance encounter, and the electricity . . . there had been electricity, hadn't there? Maybe it was just her urgency to get into the restroom. She'd put it out of her mind.

But the voices wouldn't let her.

4

CAMP IN THE WOODS

The last hour driving in the Blue Ridge Mountains, the sky darkened into shadow and the climb steepened. No street lamps brightened the dirt road upwards, but a fattening moon shed a little light through the forest. The unpaved road had put the Aerostar through her paces, but at least they'd be on time to catch some dinner. In spite of the camp name, Crystal really hoped they weren't having beans.

She reached into the back seat to grab her coat, which she opened over her knees to put on once she arrived and stepped into the air. Craning her neck, she looked across the seats toward her fiddle, secured in the back part of the van. She hoped it hadn't become too cold on the way there.

She pulled the coat up to her throat, cradling her jaw, and found her thoughts drifting to the boy she had bumped into earlier. Replaying the event made her giggle, and her father glanced over at her, then back to the road.

Having had only one boyfriend, and that was over a year ago, Crystal felt ill-equipped to handle the throb of infatuation toward a stranger — especially infatuation at first sight.

At last the car crunched into a broad turn-around at the end of the road. Conscious of the little makeup she was wearing, Crystal took a peek in the visor mirror and popped a breath mint.

Out the side window emerged a clearing, and nestled at its back, along a ridge of pines, smoke issued from the chimney of a long log cabin. Clustered to the side sat several smaller cabins, which continued to scatter up through the trees at intervals. One of those would be hers to share with a roommate. It was too dark to see more just then. The main log house was lit and Crystal supposed they'd go in there.

"You ready?" asked her father.

"Oh, yeah." Crystal wrinkled her nose at him. "Geez, Dad. You want a breath mint?" He accepted one, then they let their legs reach out of the van. Crystal dropped to the ground and hurried to rub her butt before anyone came out of the log home to see them. Her father stretched openly and yawned widely. Crystal cringed. She loved her dad, but she didn't want anyone to see him being . . . so much himself.

A man with a large girth and western hat waddled across the clearing to greet them. He held out his hand to Crystal's father and, with a practiced smile, drawled "Welcome to Beans."

"I'm assuming you're Crystal Carson," he said to Crystal.

"Yes — *uh*, Cris."

"I'm Mason. Mason Weeks, that's me," said the man. "And this here is my daughter Wanda."

Wanda, who seemed a little older than Crystal,

stepped forward from behind him and said, "Nice to meet y'all." She offered her hand to each of them, then turned conspiratorially to Crystal, whose eyes were fixated on the girl's carefree and huge blondness. A slight, cold breeze sighed through the forest and her tresses danced with the wild abandon of naturally curly hair.

"Why don't us girls go on up to the house and let these men — "she winked at Crystal's father " —finish their man business. They can bring up your bags."

Crystal nodded assent. She liked the girl immediately and felt a rush of comfort. The West Virginian hospitality was not lost on her and she felt like they could be friends — at least as long as camp lasted.

A pile of sheets with feet moved across the yard, and Wanda stopped it to introduce Pete, who was in charge of laundry for the camp. Crystal watched amused, as he set down his load, nearly as tall as he was. He held out a bony hand and offered a shy "hello." He seemed like the kind of boy she'd see as a whiz in her computer class at school.

"Don't let his looks fool you," said Wanda after he left. "He's much stronger than you'd think. And that boy plays a mean fiddle!"

Excited voices and laughter ricocheted through the air as she followed Wanda into the house and then into a large open area with long tables set up for diners. Around the perimeter of the room were several more tables with red and white plastic cloths. These tables were laden with picked-over hot plates of ribs, chicken wings, potato salad, green salad, and other vittles designed to fill the bellies of hungry musicians. Someone had pulled out a mandolin and was plunking on it to the applause and laughter of those seated. Most appeared to have finished eating.

"I'm glad there's some left," Wanda said. "We keep the spread open longer on the first day as folks always drive in late."

The buffet looked good, but as soon as Crystal smelled the meat, the old feeling of nausea moved across her.

"*Uh*, is there a vegetarian table?" she asked Wanda.

Wanda, who was in the middle of explaining how great the ribs were and that they had come from Mr. Bee, the porker she'd helped to raise, looked at her like she was crazy.

"You don't eat meat, honey?"

"Oh. Sure. Just tonight I feel like eating light."

Wanda relaxed and let out a breath. "Oh, *whoo*! For a minute there I thought you might be one of them veee-gans. We ain't had any of them before and I wouldn't know what to do with one. But now that I see you're regular, there's a nice salad at the far end. I think it's got bacon in it, so at least you can have a little meat."

Crystal nodded slightly as she mentally made a note to pick out the bacon. She'd need to be discreet during meals, apparently, if her aversion to cooked flesh continued.

Wanda took her arm and pulled her up onto some pallets covered by a rug that served as a stage in the room. "Listen, y'all," she boomed with a voice not needing a microphone, "This here is Crystal—Cris. She's our newest player." Everyone applauded and yelled out welcomes as Crystal felt her cheeks turn crimson. She raised her hand weakly at the crowd and then she and Wanda got in line to get food. Crystal saw her dad across the room still talking or listening to Mr. Weeks. She waved at him, wishing she could go sit by him. All of a sudden it all felt overwhelming. Maybe she was just tired.

"Are any of the teachers in this room?" she asked Wanda.

Wanda scanned the faces. "No, they're probably all in the dining room with my mama. Except for Olaf, of course. He always eats in his room." Wanda blanched, then started, as though she'd let a secret slip.

"Olaf? Olaf *Widmark* is here?"

"Well, yes. But *shhh*, we don't *ever* announce it. He only takes two or three students a year and we don't want the others to get jealous. We never know when or if he's going to show up. Or who he's going to pick, for that matter."

"Well, I'd like to know. How does he pick them?"

Wanda laughed. "I don't know. Maybe he uses a crystal ball."

Crystal laughed, too. Stories abounded about the world-class player from the old country. Stories about magic and secret rituals. But he was the best player in the world as far as she and many other fiddle players believed. To have a chance — even remote — to see him play in person, or better, to be *taught* by him left her speechless. She wished she knew how he chose his players.

After dinner, Crystal gave her father a kiss goodbye as she probably wouldn't see him before he took off in the morning. Then Wanda took her to one of the small cabins nestled in the trees.

Inside, it smelled like wood smoke and furniture polish. A girl about her age was reading a book while seated on one of the cots next to a lantern supported by a crate. Crystal's bags had been set adjacent to one of three cots. At the far end of the cozy room, were two small dressers and a bench, which held a fiddle case. Wanda introduced her to Barbara, the owner of the fiddle, who would be her roommate for the duration of her stay.

"You get your choice of a bunk," Wanda said, nodding toward the empty beds. "A couple of sisters cancelled at the last moment, so you lucked out and just get one roommate.

Crystal smiled at Barbara, who returned the smile

with a dull glance.

"Where's the bathroom?" Crystal asked, looking around.

"Get on the trail and go out and down yonder. There's an outhouse. You can use that for — you know. Every other day we take turns showering at the house. There's four bathrooms in there, but over a hundred students, so only take about three minutes as all the water is from a well.

Crystal chuckled, then realized Wanda was serious. Three minutes? She couldn't even get her hair wet in three minutes. This was more like camping than she had anticipated. Wanda provided her with a brochure, showing the itinerary for the week and house rules.

After Wanda left, she and Barbara chatted for a moment—just long enough to know they didn't click and that Barbara had a more expensive violin. Then Barbara went back to her reading, leaving Crystal to get her belongings set up.

Deciding to have a look around, Crystal dug out her coat and penlight. She flipped her hand *goodbye* at Barbara, who ignored her and continued to read. She left the cabin.

The night air smacked her face; it had gone from cool to chilly. Anticipating the temperature this far up in the mountains, she had brought her warmest coat. She snuggled into it, then put on her gloves and beanie. Insisting it was still summer, albeit late summer, wouldn't make it any warmer.

The lights were off at the main house, and only a few cabins flickered with firelight. Laughter, whoops, and *Orange Blossom Special*, played by several fiddlers at breakneck speed, issued from one cabin.

Crystal walked into the clearing in front of the cabin and looked up. The Milky Way flowed like sequins across a velvet sky. The air crackled in her lungs, as she was filled with life and solitude. Then, lights blinded her as a car pulled into the clearing, and she stepped out of the way. Whoever this latecomer was would be going hungry, unless they had an open-kitchen policy.

Crystal didn't really want to talk to anyone, but she was in the awkward position of having been in the car's headlights. If she took off then, it might look like she was being unfriendly. Then again, it wasn't her job to greet guests. She decided to hold her ground just long enough to greet the person, then go get Mr. Weeks if necessary.

The tall man-boy she had collided with at the service station exited the driver's side of the Explorer. He stretched his arms above his head and whooped full-throated. "This is fantastic!

"Hi. My name is Glenn," he said holding out his hand.

"Cris." She took his hand and their energies met. He looked at her more closely.

"Hey, you're that girl I bumped into at the station, right?"

"I think so." She smiled. *He remembered!*

"So you're a player, too?"

She nodded as he looked around at the yard. "Maybe you can show me around . . ." He still hadn't released her hand, and Crystal tugged slightly to reclaim it.

Wanda, who had been watching them from the shadows, stepped forward.

"Hi y'all," she said jovially. "Welcome to Beans."

With his attention drawn away, Crystal decided to leave. Her stomach was jumping. She wasn't sure she liked how long he'd held her hand. Plus, she couldn't help but stare. He was the handsomest guy she'd ever seen, outside of a magazine model. And he seemed so warm and natural. An energy exuded from him. *Star quality.* He'd never go for someone like her. While Wanda went through her spiel, Crystal stepped away.

"Hey, wait," Glenn called, interrupting Wanda. "Can

we get together later?" His voice was clear and direct.

Heart-thud. "I'm going to bed now. It's been a day. Maybe tomorrow." Crystal couldn't believe it, nor could she believe how easily she had said "no" when she wanted to jump up in the air and shout *Are you kidding! I'll stay up all night if I have to!*

What was wrong with her? Nerves, excitement. She wasn't boy-crazy and he seemed pretty forward to her. Ignoring her attraction, she took pleasure in having retained her self-control.

She wasn't sure she could sleep at all, but a combination of the long day traveling and environmental stimulation pushed her into a pleasant underworld for the night.

Her last thought as her mind drifted off was that it was four days to her birthday. Then she'd be eighteen. An adult. And everything would change.

Everything.

5

SPECTER

The next day was a cacophony of fiddles, training seminars, and chatting with strangers. Crystal had looked for Glenn during the morning buffet, but missed him in the bustle of bodies around the platters of grits, eggs, toast, and other vittles.

Just after the mid-morning break, Crystal spotted Glenn as he slipped behind a door into a seminar teaching double-stops and the Chicago shuffle. She measured how to get closer to him without appearing too forward. Waiting for a moment when she wouldn't be on his heels, she cracked the door to peek through. She watched his entrance, as several girls seated with fiddles on their laps looked up and followed his advance with their eyes to the first row of the class, which was full. As he glided like silt on marble toward the front, a youngster in a black shirt turned, raised a hopeful face, and offered Glenn his seat— taking the one behind him—so Glenn could be on the front row. The instructor stood up from where he had been seated on the edge of a table top, openly beamed and nodded to Glenn. Power and control — definitely someone others wanted to be near.

Seeing no other chairs available, Crystal silently shut the door and hurried to find another, less-crowded seminar.

Twice more that day, Crystal spotted Glenn, but he was always surrounded by a group of musicians who seemed to fawn over him. From across the room, she'd heard him playing, and he was excellent — maybe the best one there. He showed off some five-note rolls to some listeners and demonstrated how to do them. Annoyed, she decided to distance herself. She wasn't into playing those kinds of games; if he wanted to be the "Big Mon on Campus," let him. She was there to learn, not to be impressed by some guy. At least, she hoped that attitude could convince her to take the mature approach.

At lunch, groveling and giggling girls pushed their ways to his table. Crystal noticed him trying to catch her eye by waving and motioning her over to where he dined. He pointed to the chair next to him, his eyebrows raised. She smiled a fake cheerleader grin and waved *hello* back, pretending to have misunderstood his gesture. Hurriedly, she looked away so he wouldn't try again, filled her dish, and found a nearly invisible table in the corner.

As she sat alone, her face intent on her plate of macaroni, a gentle presence flowed over her. She looked up to see a slight girl with shoulder-length brown hair that was so fine it lifted in the draft across the room. The girl introduced herself as "Elinor," and in a shy voice asked if she could sit at the table.

Crystal looked around. Except for the smaller table she was at, all the other tables were full and bustling with instrument cases and excited musicians chattering about the seminars and various music-related affairs.

Crystal smiled warmly and indicated an empty spot across from her. Elinor slid her petite frame into a chair and pulled a strand of hair from in front of her face. She looked up and offered "Thank you," in a demure voice.

Over lunch, they talked about books they'd read, their favorite fiddle tunes, and techniques on some of the harder pieces. By the end of lunch, Elinor seemed less shy and Crystal knew she'd found someone she genuinely liked. They decided to meet again for dinner. It turned out that Elinor's cabin was only two doors away, so they could visit each other easily.

As they were bussing their plates, Elinor whispered, "Have you seen the feral boy?" She looked around to be sure no one had heard her.

"No. What do you mean?" Crystal looked around, too, though she wasn't sure why.

Elinor giggled. "I don't know. I shouldn't have said it."

"No, tell me."

"I've seen him in the shadows."

"The boy?"

Elinor finished bussing and stepped out of line. "A wild boy," Elinor whispered as she and Crystal left the dining area.

Crystal paused, measuring her friend, then picked up her instrument lined up with others by the doorway. "Mason's kid?"

Elinor shrugged.

"Maybe it's your imagination."

"Maybe." Elinor changed the subject. "Are you going to Babs Limbs' workshop?"

"What's it on?"

"Transposing on the fly."

"Oh, that sounds good. But I think I'll stick with Darrell Angel's. He's doing improvisation and I really could use some work there."

"See you later, then."

That night, Barbara decided to go to bed early and wanted the lights out, so Crystal was left with visiting her new friend Elinor, going to bed, or going for a walk in the moonlight.

Elinor answered Crystal's knock with her hair wrapped in a towel and white cream covering most of her face. She explained that one of her roommates had felt ill after dinner and was already asleep, so she couldn't invite Crystal in. Also, since her hair was wet, she declined braving the chill of the evening for a stroll.

Pulling her penlight from her pocket, Crystal decided to explore the area alone. She should be safe enough in the dark if she didn't veer off the trail. After all, they had people up here every year and she hadn't heard of anyone getting irretrievably lost.

The trail was steeper and rockier than she'd anticipated, and before she'd gone three hundred yards, she was panting. Pausing, she listened to the night noises. She was surprised to hear frogs, as the temperature seemed too low for them to be active. She put her palm on the bark of a tree for support and brushed aside a wayward branch. An owl in the distance warned her not to come too close.

Though the night was intense, beautiful, and cold she could feel her passions rising and wished she had the nerve to bring her fiddle up here. She'd always loved playing in the outdoors — particularly making up her own tunes. Connecting with nature in this way fed a private and very personal communication with — the *beyond*.

A sudden crunching in the bushes off to her left

caused her to flick off her light and hold very still. Were there bears up here. Perhaps it was a deer. Or a mountain lion. As she tried to recall what her pamphlet had said about the wildlife, a boy about seven darted across the trail. He was wearing only a pair of shorts and tee shirt, unheeding of the cold. His irregularly spiked hair spoke of home cutting, and his lack of shoes spoke of poverty. Blood drizzled around a gash running around and above his ankle, but he seemed oblivious to it. Who would let their child run around like this?

On the other side of the trail, he stopped and cocked his head as though listening. Then he turned and looked directly at where she was standing, hidden in the shadow of the tree.

"Oh. You silly girl," he said in a voice sounding older than his years. "Your turn is coming." He opened his mouth and widened his eyes in a manic caricature, turned, and took off through the trees.

Crystal's breath caught in her throat, and she had a sudden, urgent need to urinate. What had he said to her? What kind of crazy place was this? The night didn't seem so friendly anymore, and the frogs had quit trilling.

She began the descent back to the cabin, when an abrupt chill stopped her in her tracks. Shivering, she felt in the grip of darkness, as though a shadow from the forest had slithered over the top of her and pinned her to the trail. Her teeth started chattering and the voices began. This time, with the voices, she clearly heard the sound of music. Of bells and clear chimings, tinkles of a fairyland, a dynamic a millimeter beyond her hearing and understanding. It forced itself upon her, and as she stood trembling in the middle of the trail, in the middle of the night, it rode through her bloodstream like a ripple of oxygen bubbles. She fought it with her mind, trying to force it out.

Below the tingling and the light, was a red and burning passion. It bore into her body, and her body flipped in hard jolts: back and forth and back and forth.

"*Uhngh!*" she cried, but could not release herself from its grip.

Then she was flat on her back, looking up at the Milky Way. The moon, almost full. Three days before her birthday. She felt someone, some *thing* enter her, through her cells, through her muscles, into her heart.

She lay inert—aware but unable to move. A pulsing drone began at her toes and moved up her body, inch by inch. It felt as though a steel bar, or rod about two inches wide, was hovering over her, scanning her—probing her body. Each section it passed over felt tingly, mildly electric.

It reached her throat. Panicked, Crystal thrashed, fighting its grip, but her body barely trembled. When it reached her head, her mind went numb. Barely aware of her surroundings, she drifted in a mindless fog, her eyes open, her mouth slack.

6

UNDERTONES

When Crystal came to awareness, she felt dirty,
violated in ways beyond the physical. Her skin
crawled, and it was too cold for it to be from bugs. She'd
quit trembling, but now the frigid hardness of the ground
seeped into her bones.

Standing, she felt light-headed, but not dizzy. Looking
around, she took her bearings, holding onto a tree for a
support. More than the cold ground had chilled her. A
black fear had lodged in her core. Something was terribly
wrong with her. Maybe she had a neurological disease.
Had she had a seizure? Maybe she was turning schizo-
phrenic.

Maybe . . . *maybe she was like the rest of her mother's
family . . .*

That thought scared her the most. She didn't want to
be like them. She wanted to be normal. Regular. A regular
girl who played the fiddle. Having a regular life. Finding a
regular husband. Someone nice. Like her dad. *Or someone*

spectacular, like Glenn

At the thought of the tall stranger, a rush of incongruous warmth sizzled her body. The heat intensified until she no longer felt cold. An area below her belly button swelled with a yearning, as though it had a life of its own.

The rush of feeling after the strange episode was too much. She really wanted to call Tish. She needed to talk. Now. She had to tell someone what was going on with her. Maybe she was too sick to be here. Maybe she should go home. Unconsciously, she ran her hand over her pocket and remembered her phone was back at the camp.

Shaking off her weird feelings and entrapping thoughts, she flicked on her penlight and staggered a few feet down the trail until her feet became steady. About a third of the way down, she thought she heard crunching in the bushes, and this time she didn't stop, but pushed into a sprint. If it was the feral boy, she intended to run past him as fast as she could.

Sneaking into her cabin, she found the day bag containing her phone. Barbara lay atop her bed, still dressed, her book having fallen to the side. She moaned in her sleep and thrashed. Crystal held still. For some reason, she didn't want the girl to know she was getting her phone.

At that moment, she realized how completely freaked out she was. She was going to call Tish at a late hour, probably waking her up, just to ease her own growing sense of apprehension. But changes were happening to her. The nausea a couple weeks before, the voices, the feelings, the music. Passing out—and now the strange paralysis. All of it. Here she was in the camp of her dreams, and she couldn't enjoy it. She felt like a two-year-old admitting it, but not only was she afraid she had a disease, she was homesick for the normalcy and privacy of her own room.

She crept outside again. Afraid to venture to the trail
and risk encountering anyone, she crossed the clearing in
a crouched Ninja pose and headed for the trees on the
other side. It was immediately darker in the thick pines
with barely space to squeeze between.

Backing to a tree wide enough to hide her entire body,
she turned on her phone. The light flashed three times. NO
SIGNAL. Just her luck. She moved about a hundred feet and
tried again. The same response.

Cheesits! It must be these trees blocking the signal.
She'd have to risk getting nearer to the main house.

In Ninja mode again, she swept across the clearing
and sidled up to a bush partially covering a window in the
dining area. At least, no one would be inside the house in
this room to overhear her. She turned on her phone again.
NO SIGNAL .

"What are you doing?" Wanda stood two feet behind
her and appeared to be looking over her shoulder.

Crystal literally jumped a foot off the ground. Her
hand flew to her chest and she laughed out loud as she
faced Wanda.

"Oh! You scared me to death!"

"Ah, honey. Sorry. I didn't mean to spook ya'."
Wanda smiled with her lips, but her eyes stayed steady.
"I've been looking for you. So, you're trying to call out?"

"Yeah. Just wanted to talk to my girlfriend." Crystal
shifted. *Looking for her?* She didn't want to tell Wanda why
she was calling out. Mainly, she was embarrassed — it
would be hard enough to explain it to Tish. But somehow
Wanda was making her feel guilty for trying to call
outside the camp. Why should she feel guilty?

"Honey. We're all your girlfriends here." She gestured
toward the camp. "At least the girl ones of us."

Crystal nodded. "I know. You guys are great. It's
just — well this is my birthday week and — " Crystal's

mouth was going overtime to her own horror and amazement " — and I just wanted to, you know, touch bases."

"Your birthday? Your *birthday*? I'm so glad you let us
know! We always love it when someone has a birthday
here. We like a reason to have a shindig — outside of the
regular performance ones, I mean. You have heard about
those, right? We have one midway through the week, then
the grand finale. Ya' know, the big one. We have a band
scramble and put folks into groups. It's fun."

Crystal nodded affably, the false grin on her face
making her jaws ache, her body tensing with desire to get
away.

Wanda took her arm. "Hey, let's go in the house.
There's a bunch of us gathering in the kitchen for a late-
night, old-fashioned jam."

"Well, I wanted to make a call . . ."

"Oh, there's no way out here. Maybe if you climbed
the mountain you could get high enough to catch a signal.
Look around. No power lines. We're on generator and
there's no cell service. We're in what you call a 'dead
zone.'"

Wanda continued to pressure her arm as she started
to walk. Crystal smelled a cloying perfume wafting from
the girl, who suddenly seemed much larger — and
stronger — than she. The only way she could get away
would be to wrench her arm free. She wasn't sure she
wanted to be that rude.

"How do you make calls then? How was your stuff on
the internet?"

Wanda quit walking and turned to her with a serious
face. "Cris, my daddy takes care of all that. He's got an
office in town he does all that from. Out here, it's just us
chickens."

Crystal was beginning to feel intimidated, but her
mouth just wouldn't quit.

"But—but what if there was an emergency?"

"What kind of emergency could a bunch of fiddle players have? Broken strings? We've got extras of those inside." The smile came back on and she pressured Crystal's arm again. "Now come on in. You don't look that warmly dressed for out here."

Crystal relented, but a growing uneasiness tightened her neck into a clench. She didn't want to join the jam and she certainly didn't want a bunch of people she barely knew celebrating her birthday when it arrived. In fact, she was beginning to enjoy her aunt's gift less by the minute.

"I'm not sure I'm up for a jam tonight," she said.

"Ah, come on. It'll do you some good. You've been sticking pretty much to yourself and I'd be no kind of hostess if I wasn't fixin' to see you had some fun."

"Oh, my fiddle is in the cabin, though. I'll need to go get it."

"Don't worry about that," Wanda said, still clutching her arm. "We got a whole slew of instruments in the house." So saying, she opened the back door and all but pushed Crystal in.

The house was completely silent.

"They're through here," Wanda said, and opened a door to a room off the kitchen.

The room was unlit. Soft shifting sounds and irregular breathing hushed through the space.

"What the—" Crystal started. Her pulse thrummed cut-time. For a moment she felt entirely surreal—as though she had stepped into a bad horror movie.

A light flicked on. The room was full of people from the camp. All held perfectly still, staring at her with solemn faces, like a photo outtake from *Invasion of the Body Snatchers*.

Wanda cleared her throat. One of the girls giggled then stopped.

Numb, Crystal's eyes skirted over the crowd, her lips parted.

"Well come on, then. Y'all trying to give her the willies?" Wanda's voice boomed out and everyone animated like compliant puppets, then yelled *Surprise!*

Crystal was stunned. Her face involuntarily cracked into a grin, but tears streamed from her eyes. A *party?* But how did they know? She'd just gotten through telling Wanda. How could they have arranged this so fast? After the people finished laughing and congratulating her, they broke out their instruments and began singing and playing.

Elinor came up to her looking guilty. "I'm sorry, Cris. I wanted to tell you, but Wanda threatened me with bread and water for the rest of the week if I told. Here, I picked up your fiddle for you."

"Uh, thanks," Crystal said. She was still staggered. How had Wanda known it was her birthday? Never mind that she had the day wrong. *Dad!* Her father must have mentioned it the night he stayed over. She felt the blood come back into her face, and her agitation lessened. Nothing spooky going on here. Just a birthday party.

She giggled a little. "It's okay, Elinor. I wouldn't want you chained in the dungeon," she said and hugged her new friend. It was then that over Elinor's shoulder she noticed, behind a banjo player, the feral boy reclining lengthwise on the back of the couch, like a cat. He grinned at her, both top and bottom teeth showing, his eyes unblinking. Crooking his index finger, he drew it slowly across his throat.

"*Oww*," Elinor choked as Crystal's grip tightened.

"Oh, sorry. " Crystal continued to stare at the boy as she released her friend. "It's that boy," she whispered. But as Elinor whipped around to see, the child rolled off the back of the couch and disappeared behind it.

"Where?"

"He was on the couch. He's hiding behind it."

"You mean the feral kid?" Elinor's eyes widened.

"Yes. I saw him earlier tonight."

Elinor looked around the room. "I wonder who he is."

"I don't know. But I think he's really creepy. And someone should take care of his ankle."

"Ankle?"

"It's bleeding."

"What are y'all carrying on about?" Wanda's raucous voice broke in as she sidled her buxom form into the private space made by the friends.

Annoyed, Crystal looked at her, square on.

"We were having a personal conversation." She cringed as she realized how rude she sounded, so she lightened her voice. "It was about that boy that's running around here. Somebody should put some clothes on him and take care of his foot."

"What boy?" Wanda looked across the room. "What does he look like?"

Crystal described him as Elinor nodded in agreement.

Wanda's grin erased and her entire body stiffened. Laser-beam eyes blazed directly onto Crystal. "That is not funny. Not funny at all," she said. Then her voice caught and tears welled up in her eyelids. "That's some kind of awfulness to make fun of a tragedy like that." She turned around and strode from the room without speaking to anyone else. Two or three people watched her go, then glanced over with somber faces at Crystal.

Elinor and she turned to each other.

"What was that?" asked Crystal.

"I truly don't know," Elinor said. "I'm about tired of this place. I haven't had one lesson yet that was a challenge, and please don't quote me as I don't want to get that kind of burny look directed at me, but there is something wonky going on around here."

"What do you mean?"

Elinor took Crystal's hand and pulled her through some French doors into a foyer where they could be alone, except for the moose head that watched them from high on the wall.

"There's that boy. And, last night I saw some old man with a limp roaming around the hills. I brought a small spotting scope to look at birds and stars while I was up here, and this old guy in some long black cape . . ." she started laughing, then began hacking, looked up at Crystal's eyes, which were wide on a serious face, and began braying again. The laughter welled up and bubbled out. She couldn't stop.

"What is it?" Crystal, still serious, watched as her friend held her stomach and fought to wind down. Elinor sat on a small couch pushed against the wall.

"I heard myself. 'Old man in a long black cape,' like Dracula is running around here." She laughed again. "What did they put in that punch?"

Crystal forced interest and said, "Well, a cape is pretty strange. What was the old guy doing?"

Elinor flicked her hand. "I couldn't really see. He just seemed to be hiking up some trail in the forest. But I saw him watching the cabins, earlier, too." She giggled. "I've probably seen too many horror movies."

After what Crystal had been through, it was difficult to make light of it. "It might have been a neighbor, don't you think?"

"Probably. Anyway, I don't mean to sound like a lunatic."

Crystal smiled her reassurance. "I don't think you're one. And even if I haven't seen your Dracula, that boy is strange enough.

"Anyway, I really need to go to bed. It's been a long

night and I'm really tired."

Elinor said, "Okay. Oh, and happy birthday."

Crystal left, not bothering to correct Elinor. She didn't want to run the risk of another birthday party in two days.

7

WAXING MOON

As Crystal crossed the gravel and passed the bush she had stood near earlier when she was trying to phone, a shadow stepped out. Jumping back, she raised the hand not carrying her fiddle into a claw and snarled. She glared at the intruder and then grinned stupidly. Glenn smiled back.

"Whoa! No kill, please!" Glenn held his hands up in mock surrender.

Crystal felt herself flush. "Oh! I'm sorry. I'm just tired of getting the *begasses* scared out of me around here." She set down her fiddle, then held her attack hand demurely.

Glenn guffawed. "As long as it's just the gasses and not . . . Hey, I have been trying to get a hold of you ever since we got here," he said. "You're not avoiding me, are you?"

"Yes. I mean, no. We're just taking different classes, I guess." She averted her eyes as she felt his gaze silently scan her, making her feel unnerved.

Her lie drifted in the air between them. Palpable. She remembered dodging out of a class when she saw him inside surrounded by groupies. Basically, he was just too popular and too good a fiddle player for her to be comfortable with him.

"I'd like to go for a walk with you, if you will."

She looked up into large, warm and violet eyes gazing down on her. She'd never been this attracted to someone so quickly and wasn't sure how to manage her emotions. His hair glistened in the gleam of the waxing moon. His skin seemed to glow like an angel's, and she felt her spine draining of will. She felt near to collapse. What if he touched her? Held her hand?

She was going to decline, but this would be the second time. Still her stomach was erupting with uneasiness and her armpits were beginning to moisten. She clamped her elbows to her sides and succumbed. "Sure," her mouth said, devoid of brainpower or consideration.

Then, reaching toward her, he grabbed her lapels and tightened her coat about her throat. "Chilly out here," he said. An edge of collar touched her jaw line, as did his finger. The intimate gesture was all it took. Her voice was gone. Her will was gone. The rest of her melted into a pool of butter.

They started to walk up the same trail Crystal had climbed earlier, where she had encountered the boy.

"Not that way," she urged, so they veered to the left.

"I found this trail last night," Glenn said, and a pang of jealousy coursed through Crystal. He stopped, took both of her hands, and looked into her. "No. I haven't been out walking with someone else."

Crystal sputtered, then coughed.

"And, no. I didn't read your mind." The deepening night whipped around them and the trees groaned. "I'm just highly intuitive."

They walked.

"Have you ever had a Meyer's Briggs test?"

Crystal shook her head.

"Where I worked one summer, we gave them to new hires all the time, to make sure they were in the right job. Mine was about off the charts for intuition. I hope it doesn't bother you too much.

"I'm not a witch."

"Warlock," Crystal corrected, glad her voice worked.

Glenn chuckled. "Oh, so you were thinking that!"

She smiled and relaxed. "My aunt has told me some stuff . . ." Crystal found herself revealing matters she'd told no one, not even Tish. First about her fear of her aunt, the weirdness of her mother's entire family, and then about the strange happenings that had been plaguing her recently. Together they laughed about the *Night of the Living Salad* and her almost vomiting on her aunt. She withheld the event with the boy on the trail and the voices—she didn't want to scare him off entirely. But he seemed to take it all in stride and said she was an "Interesting, not to mention beautiful girl." Then he corrected himself. "Woman, I mean. Now that you're eighteen, you're legal."

Crystal laughed. "Not quite," she said, and confessed that her birthday was not for two days.

He stuck out his bottom lip in a faux pout. "I'll have to wait then," he said. "At least the moon will be full. Auspicious."

Wait? she thought. *Wait for what?* Caught in a bubble of elation, as the night grew darker and colder, she felt lighter and freer.

Glenn glanced at his wristwatch and for an instant, while his attention was away from her, she became aware that she was shivering. Her mouth felt numb and she didn't know how she'd been holding this easy conversation. When his attention was on her, it seemed as though they were in a bright and free cocoon, where all was as it should be. Yet now a blackness surrounded her, and just on the periphery she heard voices buzzing like angry bats. Mixed in with them was a sound of tinkling bells or a toilet running. But when he captured her with his eyes again, the warm and wonderful feeling returned.

"We'd better get back," he murmured. "I have a special happening tomorrow and I need to be rested."

"What is it?"

He looked at her coyly and she let it go. It didn't matter.

Leaning in, he took her chin in his fingers. She knew what was happening, but seemed unable to resist. Her lips pulled together and apart in a natural purse. Softly, he began a kiss that was a minuet, that drew her into his arms and into his heart. When their lips met—even though it was a brief touch—they danced to a music in the wind, in the stars. He pulled away gently and stepped back. He looked at her, surprise registering in his eyes. Then he took her hand.

They were quiet as they descended the trail back to the cabins.

Crystal no longer felt a need to call Tish.

She didn't sleep all night as she replayed the events. She touched her lips, where the kiss still felt warm. Had that really happened?

Then it was dawn.

She was still numb.

♪

As Crystal headed to the house in the morning for a shower and then her first training seminar, Elinor flew across the clearing toward her.

"Wait! Wait!" she called, huffing and puffing. Her

fiddle case was under her arm, which made her run lopsided.

Crystal was happy to see her. After meeting with Glenn, she'd felt a shroud lift, revealing a more joyful and liberated self. She wanted to be more open and friendly with Elinor and everyone else.

"Hi, Elinor. Good morning!" She hoped Elinor was going to the same training. They could sit by each other.

But the look on Elinor's face was one of panic, not joy.

She stood in front of Crystal and panted to catch her breath. "Did you read the pamphlet they gave you?"

"Huh? You mean the itinerary?"

Elinor nodded.

"Of course."

"Yeah, but did you read the *back* page?"

"I'm not sure. I just read about the animals around here and the different trainings scheduled. Why?"

"Look." In the hand not holding her fiddle case, Elinor gripped the schedule. She held the crinkled paper out to Crystal.

Puzzled, Crystal took it from her and smoothed it. She looked at Elinor then turned it over. And stopped.

On the back page was an article of the history of the camp. No wonder she hadn't read it; history was not an interest. Beside the article, was a fuzzy image of the boy, the unkempt boy, that she and Elinor had both seen. The same boy who had twice threatened her. He was fondly referred to as "Beans." And the camp was named for him.

It was an obituary.

Elinor and Crystal stared at each other, stunned. A door slammed somewhere and people began moving across the clearing toward the main house. They lowered their voices.

"Is this the same boy you saw?" asked Elinor.

Crystal nodded.

"How can it be? What do you think?" Elinor set her fiddle case down and took the paper from Crystal to read it again.

"I honestly don't know. I swear I saw him, and he was as real as you or me."

"Well, it says here that he drowned. In some spring runoff, some creek around here. Apparently his father, Mason, was torn up and set up the whole camp to honor him."

"That doesn't explain the cut on his foot. Not that who we saw was him. I mean, it couldn't be, could it? We didn't see a ghost, right? I mean, did the boy you see look solid?"

Elinor nodded and whispered, "Solid." Then she said aloud, "I think so. I'm just not sure anymore. Maybe I was mistaken. This couldn't have been, could it?"

"Maybe he has — had a brother. Maybe the kid we saw is — was his brother."

"Oh, I bet that's it. Of course. And no wonder Wanda got so mad at you last night." Elinor looked toward the house and the people filing in.

"*Cheesits!* I'd better find her and apologize." Crystal looked around. "Uh, oh. Looks like I missed getting my shower. Whose class are you heading for?"

"I'm headed to Laney Lewis."

"Do you mind if I come with you?"

"Sure."

As the girls entered the main foyer, the room went silent. Wanda, who stood with a cluster of students, glared at them, mumbled to the group in low tones, and they dispersed. Crystal had the feeling they'd been talking about her.

"Okay ladies and genties," Wanda boomed to the crowd gathered in the main room, her voice friendly. "Let's get this show on the road!" All the musicians headed off to the respective rooms in the house to attend to their trainings.

"I'll catch up," said Crystal to Elinor, and headed toward Wanda.

But when she called her name, Wanda pretended not to hear. Crystal walked quickly and touched her on the arm.

"Wanda, I'm really sorry what I said last night."

Wanda looked at her dispassionately.

"I didn't know about—about Beans. I hadn't read the back of the pamphlet."

"I can hardly believe that," said Wanda. "Everyone saw it but you. And everyone knows that's what this camp is about. I just think it's cruel to play innocent about it all."

"Honest, I'm so sorry. I was excited to be here and I just didn't read it," Crystal pleaded.

"Well . . ." Wanda softened her look. "I suppose it *could* happen. Anyone can make a mistake."

"Yes, I'm a complete blunderbuss. My mom always says."

Wanda smiled with a crook of her lip. "Oh, okay. You're forgiven."

"Thanks, Wanda," Crystal hugged her. "I guess I got confused when I saw his brother. They do look a lot alike, now that I've seen his picture."

"What are you talking about?" Wanda was angry again. "Beans had no brother. Just me. His sister."

This time Wanda turned and walked away, her shoulders set. Crystal watched her leave, speechless.

Huffing back across the clearing toward her cabin, Crystal decided not to go into the training and to explain later to Elinor. So far, she had missed most of the trainings and was getting zero out of her dream camp. But this had gone beyond uncomfortable. Now the hostess hated her and would be sure to talk about her to the others. Never one to like a lot of attention, Crystal was especially distressed about receiving negative attention.

She was fuming. What had she done wrong? Nothing that she could see.

She needed to get ahold of her dad and see if he could come and get her.

The only thing going right so far was her friendship with Elinor. It was strange how connected she felt to the girl. They almost felt like sisters. She had to admit there was also magical time with Glenn. Where was he this morning, anyway? He'd said he had a special occasion today and didn't tell her what. In fact, if she thought about it, she'd told him almost everything about herself, and he hadn't told her one detail about himself. Zero. Not where he was from. Not even his last name. If she left now, she'd have no way to reach him later. If he wanted to be reached.

Then again, it would take her father eight hours to drive to get her. And that was *if* he could get the time off work. Maybe her mother could come. In between time, she'd find Glenn and make arrangements to get each others' email addresses. It was so hard to believe they didn't have any way to contact the outside world out here. What was up with that?

Crystal returned to her cabin with sand bags beginning to fill her eyes, since she hadn't slept the night before. She dug out her cell. What was it Wanda had said last night? If she got high up on the mountain, she might get cell reception?

She stepped outside the room and looked up at the mountain looming behind the camp. It looked steeper than she remembered it. How far would she have to go up to catch a signal? A vampire of tiredness sucked energy from her at the thought of the climb.

Perhaps if she took a quick nap she could raise enough energy to sprint. *Just for a minute,* she told herself. She lay on the cot and closed her eyes.

It was dinnertime when she woke up due to hunger. Dismayed, she noticed the late afternoon sky out her window had pushed the mountain shadow across the camp. A growling stomach demanded she eat, but the thought of going to the cafeteria for food made her nerves tense and her skin flush. She dreaded running into Wanda again or having the others look at her with disdain. Even the thought of seeing Glenn or Elinor didn't soothe her.

Angry at herself for sleeping so long, she eyed the dimming sky, then rummaged in her bag and found some trail bars. They would have to do. She ripped bites off and chewed fast.

This time, to avoid any risk of freezing, she put on a sweater under her jacket and put on tights under her jeans. Wool socks went over the tights. With her beanie pulled over her ears, her gloves, and coat, she felt like an arthritic Eskimo and hoped she didn't have to run from any animals. But she'd need the warmth. It was cold up there, and she intended to *climb.*

8

WATER NOTES

Crystal pushed her body up the trail—the same one where she'd encountered the child. A mixture of trepidation, disgust and disbelief set her chest into a hard barrier. She didn't believe in ghosts; that was her aunt's domain. If she saw him again, she'd just ignore him or ask him what he wanted. For a moment she mused. If he were a ghost, really a ghost, didn't that mean he was pinned somehow to this ... reality? Her aunt would probably know how to help him—if all the stuff Sarah believed was true—but she certainly didn't.

This time, she'd borrowed the larger flashlight from the cabin, hoping her roommate wouldn't miss it. Her rational sense told her that going alone as far as she intended was foolhardy. But what else could she do? She wasn't welcome. She had to call home.

After about a mile uphill, she began to hear the frogs again. She recalled that last time she had some weird sensations not long afterward. This time, however, she was too angry and resolved to let any such notions deter her. As she paused to catch her breath, Crystal noticed another trail leading off to her left. It was partly obscured by some tall grasses reaching across it, but they were easy to push back. She wondered if it was a deer trail. Whatever it was, it would be a steeper climb, but would put her nearer a high point on the mountain sooner. Maybe then she could capture a cell signal.

Because of the temperature, the ground became scorched with frost and the dirt and rocks were slick. On occasion, she held onto the grasses to help pull herself up. It took twenty minutes to go only a quarter mile, and her breathing was coming in gasps. Deciding to stop for a minute, she removed her cell and checked it. NO SIGNAL. "Of course," she mumbled aloud.

Listening from her position on the trail, she noticed that the frogs had become a chorus. How could so many frogs be out on such a cold night?

Farther up the trail the grasses ceased and more trees cloistered together. Standing near a wide fir, she paused to listen, and then heard the notes. They were high, like bells or wind chimes. They tinkled and crackled in a pattern. She closed her eyes to better hear them, tilting her head back, and saw colors. White and pearl and golden sparks. Dancing and swirling patterns. And beneath them, a dark purple river, blending into an indigo sea.

She began tapping her foot, but she couldn't quite catch the rhythm. The notes seemed familiar somehow, but the name of the tune eluded her—if it had a name.

Her eyes opened. The boy's face was directly five inches away from her own as he hung from a branch by his knees.

She screamed, stepped backwards, slipped and fell, wrenching sideways and sliding on her behind and upper thigh. Pine needles poked through her pants as debris smeared up her leg. The flashlight rolled off the trail.

The boy opened his mouth to show his teeth, then laughed silently.

Remembering her resolve, Crystal scrambled to pick up her light and shone it directly on him. She opened her mouth to scold him, when the boy shape-shifted and became nothing more than moss and branches. The frogs went silent.

It took a few minutes for Crystal to regain her breath and slow her beating heart. She twisted a piece of moss that had been the boy's arm between her fingers. Rough. Stringy. Obviously, she was hallucinating. Again. All the more reason to get ahold of Dad.

The tinkling continued. As Crystal slogged up the trail, she realized she was getting closer to its source. Stepping between some bushes, the view yielded a small creek plummeting down the hill. In the dimness of moonlight, puffs of rising mist gleamed as the stream wound downward. For a moment she stared, mesmerized by the ethereal vision, and found herself drifting to it.

She hunkered next to the water. Removing a glove, she poked the stream — first with a finger, then immersed her hand. *Warm.* How could that be? No wonder the frogs were so happy. She stood, looking upstream, captivated by the mist snake as it twisted ever upward. She followed it.

As the bell-sounds grew louder and the back-beat deepened, more dimension and power emanated from the tones, until a divergence of rhythm and song flooded the forest. Drawn to it, she half forgot the purpose of her walk. She felt as though she were on the verge of a wonderful discovery — some mysterious source of songs amplified from the mouth of the earth itself.

The music intensified into a roar, but a controlled one, as though multitudes of voices were joining in and it was only because of the voices working and harmonizing together, that the tune existed at all.

Stepping from behind a bush, Crystal stood with her legs slightly apart and her hands to her side. About twenty-five feet in front of her, a moonlit waterfall issued over the lip of a plateau, splitting as it coursed over glimmering rocks, and rejoining into a hot pool at its base. As the iced water hit the pool, steam issued skyward amidst crackling and popping. A natural gold and red glow emanated from a bubbling hole in the center of the pool, making it seem like a glowing eye.

Transfixed, Crystal listened to the variations of the water music. The air was vibrant with oxygen. Her lungs begged for the song. Her body yearned to play the music. To *become* the music. She spun the flashlight beam across the waterfall and it lit a crouched and shadowy form on the other side. She stared hard, afraid the form would once again dissolve into leaves and moss. But instead, it motioned at her.

"Go away! Go away!" the person cried.

Crystal moved forward to the edge of the bank and turned the light full on the form huddled on the bank. A thick chain ran from a tree to his ankle. Next to his foot was a fiddle case. She moved closer and shone her light into the face of Glenn.

"Go!" he cried. "Hurry, before he comes back!"

Startled, Crystal lurched. As he shouted for her to stop, she clambered across slick rocks in the stream to reach him, nearly losing her balance.

Sloshing out onto the bank, she shouted, "Glenn! What is going on? How are you here?" Crystal dropped to her knees, grabbed the chain and tugged.

"Ow! Stop. It won't come off. I've tried."

"Oh my god! What has happened? Who put you here?"

"There's no time," Glenn urged. "I can't get free. I can't get free."

"I'll go back and get help!" Crystal jumped to her feet.

"No, wait. You can't. They can't know you found me. *Don't tell anyone!* I don't dare leave. I don't *want* to leave."

"What? Why?"

"Please, Crystal. You have to go. You don't know what this is."

Her voice rose. "I'm not leaving you here!"

"*Shhh.* You have to go. Hurry. I hear him coming." Glenn folded his arms across his chest and feigned sleep.

Crystal stared, dumbfounded, then heard a rustle in the forest down the trail. Gauging the direction, she splashed back across the rocks and took cover on the other side of the pond. Through the steam and mist, she saw a man in a black cape emerge from a trail near Glenn.

Elinor's Dracula! she thought.

"Awaken!" she heard the man say. His accent sounded like someone of German or Swedish decent. He kicked Glenn's bare foot with a leather boot.

Crystal fought to hear his words over the rush of the water. "I have brought your dinner. Bread and water. That is what you get until you—" As he moved so that his back was toward her, the singing voice of the waterfall obscured his words. His arms gestured in the air, as though he were arguing with Glenn. He seemed angry and she feared for Glenn's safety.

Crystal's throat dried and her breath came in little whimpers. Could he hear her? Probably not, over the water music. What could she do? From what Glenn had said, it sounded as though the people who ran the camp might be in on this. What were they doing to him? Could Elinor help her? She thought of Elinor's slight build. A puff of wind would carry her away. And Wanda—she hadn't believed about the boy. So either Wanda wouldn't believe her or she was in on it.

Crystal slipped her cell phone from her pocket. *Please*, she whispered, and pushed the button to turn it on. It gyrated, flashed, and a logo popped up. *Oh, thank you! Thank you!*

The phone had made a musical sound when it connected. The man in the cape spun around, dodging to peer through the steam. Hidden in shadow, Crystal held her breath and covered the phone with her hand so the light wouldn't show. After a few seconds, he turned around again and began talking to Glenn.

She punched at a digit with her gloved finger, intending to dial her area code, but a number popped up on the LED screen and began dialing. *No!* This must be one of the numbers Mom said she'd preprogrammed. Maybe it was to her home.

Crystal squinted to read the buttons, but she could not make out the tiny symbols in the available light. She punched a button to stop it, and a beep sounded, but it kept dialing. Looking over her shoulder, it seemed the caped man had not heard it. He still appeared to be berating Glenn.

Flustered, she put the phone to her ear and turned her back to hide the bluish light glowing from the device, as she moved behind a bush.

The phone rang several times, paused, then was answered.

"Hello?"

"Hello!" Crystal kept her voice low.

"Hello?" Never had Crystal been so happy to hear her aunt's raw voice.

"Aunt Sarah," she whispered urgently. "It's Crystal."

"Huh? Who's this? Speak up. I can barely hear you."

"I can't. Aunt Sarah, you have to tell Dad to come. I'm really scared. They've got Glenn, and . . ."

"Who is this? I can't hear you through all this

crackling. You'll have to call back." The phone beeped again as Sarah hung up.

With a sharp intake of breath, Crystal stared at the phone. She bit it as she pulled off her glove, then attempted to dial again. This time, the phone got midway in the series when the battery indicator began flashing and the phone went dark. Completely dark. She wanted to scream and rage but not attract the attention of Dracula or whomever was over there, doing what? Drinking Glenn's blood? What *was* he doing?

Glenn stood, towering over the man, holding his fiddle case, his head down. The man appeared to be unlocking the chain on his foot. Then, ignoring Glenn, he left through a path in the trees. Glenn followed, his bearing dejected. Once, he glanced back over his shoulder as though looking for her, but he did not seem to see Crystal in the shadows.

Crystal scampered back along the creek, the way she had come. She left her light off until her feet kept tripping on roots and rocks, and branches scraped her face. Disoriented, she turned on her light long enough to pick up the trail again, then turned it off, thankful for the moon.

Where might Glenn and his captor emerge from the forest? If they came out on her same trail, could she avoid them? She tripped over a torn branch and shone her light on it. She picked it up. She could hit him with a stick. Or a rock. But what if the man had a gun? Or a knife? How else could he have captured Glenn? Glenn was tall and looked strong enough, and the Dracula man was short. And old. *Really* old. Could she really hit an old man?

He *must* have had a weapon to capture Glenn. And yet, when they left the forest, Glenn was following him and, it appeared, *willingly*.

Crystal threw down the stick. It would only slow her

down.

Making it back to the main trail, she held her breath and looked up, then down the pathway. She neither heard nor saw anyone. *Not even Crazy Ghost Boy*, she thought wryly.

A sense of freedom found her feet as she took off on the better worn path and soon could see lights flickering below her. She was nearing the cabins. *Safe*, she thought, then remembered Glenn's warning. *"They can't know you found me!"* Maybe it would be better to sneak into camp, find Elinor and — and what?

She wasn't sure what to tell her friend, but she was sure she needed help. Maybe Elinor had a cell phone and they could climb back up the mountain to call. Or maybe she had a car and they could leave.

Staying in the shadows, Crystal sidled up to Elinor's cabin, and peeked in the window, hoping to spot her friend. If the roommate was gone it would be easier, but there the roommate stood, next to a clothes rod hanging wet laundry.

Pushing her face against the glass, Crystal still couldn't see the entire room. With a sigh, she moved to the front and rapped lightly on the door. After Wanda's display, she suspected she was *persona non grata*, but the roommate would just have to deal with it.

A girl with bright red hair, brighter blue eyes, and clothespins in her hands opened the door. "Hello?" Her face grayed when she recognized Crystal.

"Is Elinor here?"

"Do you see her anywhere?"

Crystal looked over the girl's shoulder. Two other girls seated cross-legged on their beds paused their chatter to stare at her. She shook her head. "Do you know where she is?"

"I think she left."

"Left? What do you mean?" It seemed unreasonable that Elinor would leave without even saying goodbye. But then Crystal had not shown up at the class they were to take together. Maybe Elinor had an emergency and had to leave. She twisted her fingers together.

"All I know is that around noon some old guy came to the door and asked to speak to her. I assumed it was her grandfather, and they left together with her violin. Shortly after, Wanda and a couple people came to get her gear."

"They got her clothes *after* she left? Isn't that odd?"

The girl sighed.

"Look, I really don't know, and I'm letting the heat out, so I'll see you later, okay?"

"Yeah, sure." The door shut in her face. Chilled on several levels, Crystal decided to return to her own cabin. She didn't know where else to go or who she could seek help from. Plus, she was really hungry. She might just have to force herself to go to breakfast in the morning and brave the mean stares from everyone.

But she had one more question. Steeling herself, she knocked again.

The girl whipped open the door, anger flashing in her eyes. "What?"

"Sorry to bother you, but do you know a guy here named 'Glenn'?"

"Glenn Wheats?" She gushed a little, even through her rigidness. "Everyone knows Glenn."

"Do you know what cabin he's in?"

The girl was silent for a minute. "You really shouldn't be bothering him. He's not someone you can just go wake up. You're lucky I wasn't asleep."

"I promise I won't wake him up."

The girl stared at her.

"Well, do you know?"

"He's in five-C." She shut the door. Hard.

Crystal stuck her tongue out at the closed door.

She skulked past a few cabins and up an incline to 5C. Once again, she decided to peek in the window before knocking. She couldn't be sure Glenn would have returned to his cabin after he and the old man left and she didn't want anymore rude encounters, if she could help it. But the cabin was dark, with not even the glow of dying embers in the woodstove. She'd have to knock.

After three light knocks, she waited a moment, then tried again. Not a stirring came from within. Looking over her shoulder, she slowly twisted the knob and pushed the door open. It seemed even colder in the cabin than outside.

"Hello?' she asked gently. If someone was sleeping, she didn't want to frighten him. She held her breath and heard silence. Avoiding a glare from the larger light, she unpocketed her penlight and shone it around the room. Both beds were empty and stripped of bedding. No possessions were in the room. He wasn't here.

Had the girl deliberately sent her to an empty room? Taking her leave, she headed to the parking area off to the side of the clearing and tried to remember what car he had come in. Oh, yeah. An Explorer.

Most of the attendees had been dropped off, so there weren't too many vehicles to inspect. It soon became clear that his car was gone. Glenn was gone. Without a word to her. He must have left directly after returning from the pool with the old man. Well, who wouldn't? She was scared to death after what she'd witnessed.

No Elinor. No Glenn. A sense of isolation drew her deeper into fear. What if someone had seen her come back from the woods? Glenn had stressed that no one could know she'd found him. She dared not wait until morning.

She tried to remember if she'd seen any other cabins or houses as she and her father drove in. She didn't think so. She recalled her father commenting on how remote the place was and how many miles they'd gone on a dirt road to get there, after turning off the main highway. What had he said, thirty? She hadn't been listening.

Well, it didn't matter. Cold or not, hungry or not, she was going to have to walk. And she should leave tonight, before anyone missed her.

Hungry! She was smart enough to realize that she could be in real trouble alone in the wilds if she didn't eat. It had been over a day since she'd eaten, except for the trail bars. She would sneak into the kitchen and grab some food to take with her on the road. Starving or thirsting to death didn't sound like a good escape plan.

For a moment, a gray lump of grief pressed in on her chest. *What if she couldn't get out?* She shook her head. If she took time to cry, to console herself, she wouldn't escape. She had to force herself to be brave.

What were they doing to Glenn? He'd been chained like a prisoner. And threatened. What kind of crazy place was this?

Her body took that moment to tell her that it had to go. She wondered if she could hold it until she got away, but the urgency said 'no,' so she headed for an outhouse. Once inside, she felt momentarily safe, and seated herself. With the door locked, no windows, and (hopefully) no one knowing where she was, she could relax. *Oh, yeah? What if a rat grabs you from the pit?* She forced herself to hurry and told her imagination to shut up.

As she cracked the door to exit, she paused. *Cheesits!* She would leave her clothing, but she could not bring herself to abandon her fiddle. It was the one possession she prized above all else. Not a replica of a Strad, like so many students used, hers was an authentic hand-built model by a famous luthier who had been a school friend of her mother's. It had been a gift to her years ago—

probably the finest gift she had ever received. Not to mention, it was her unborn twin, in her mind.

She had to go back for it.

9

PERFORMANCE

Turning the handle a few degrees at a time, she inched the door open and peeked inside. Barbara was snuggled under blankets and a sleeping bag, her mouth hung open and occasional snores gurgled forth. Quickly, Crystal whipped her body inside and shut the door, before the cold air could shoot across the room and awaken her roommate.

Crystal slipped across the floor on the balls of her feet, then tripped over Barbara's shoes. As she stumbled, she slammed the side table near the bed and knocked over the lamp.

Barbara's light glared on and she sat up, angry and frowning. "Why are you being so noisy?"

"I'm sorry," Crystal tried to keep her voice calm. "I'm just getting my fiddle."

"Oh. Are you going to the performance tonight?"

"*Uh*, yeah." The roommate yawned and looked at her more closely. "You're going like that?"

Crystal looked down at herself. She looked more like a bag woman than someone preparing to go to a performance. "Oh, I just came back to dress."

"Wanda was here looking for you." Barbara yawned again but didn't lie back down. "I told her I'd let her know when you came in."

Chills shuddered across Crystal. *They were looking for her!* After Glenn's warning, she couldn't believe that Wanda just wanted to apologize. But maybe she was wrong. She didn't know *what* to believe.

Crystal decided to pretend ignorance.

"Oh, great," she said lightly. "I'll let her know you told me. I'll be seeing her before the performance."

Barbara scowled again, continuing to watch as Crystal went through her bag for her dress.

The ruffle dress felt pretty scant for the chill, but she left her tights and boots on, hoping she wouldn't tip her hand to the roommate. After Barbara snuggled back into her bag, Crystal slipped her sweater into the pouch of her fiddle case to put on later. Picking up her case, she put on her coat and headed out. "Good night," she said.

Barbara snored.

As she stepped outside, the wild boy stood in front of her. "Hey —," she started, but he held up his finger to his lips in a "shush" motion, and pointed across the clearing. Three people were headed her way. He motioned for her to follow.

Her arms stiff at her sides, she deliberated. If it was Wanda coming toward her, she could show the boy to Wanda and maybe vindicate herself. Beans, or whoever he was, was clearly visible and decidedly real looking. Then again, if Wanda was involved in the abduction of Glenn — and possibly Elinor — she'd just be drawing attention to herself.

The boy continued to stare at her, his eyes questioning. He motioned again for her to follow.

"Thanks," she whispered, and ducked down. She followed him to a shadowed area on the perimeter of the clearing, where they both hunkered to watch the people moving forward. They split up and seemed to be looking for someone. Her? Glenn?

"Thanks again," she whispered to the boy. "You were trying to warn me before, weren't you."

The boy looked at her with openness. Up close, his skin took on a translucent glow. It looked silvery and smooth, like porcelain. But he looked alive. She reached out to touch his cheek, and a spark shot from him to her. "Ouch!" she cried. He giggled, soundless.

"What was that?" one of the people called in a loud whisper.

"I don't know. Bobcat?"

"*Shhh.*"

Crystal put her hand over her mouth, stifling surprise, and smiled at the boy with her eyes, no longer sure he was real. *Non-corporeal.* The word came from the same place as the earlier voices. Was it from him? Was she becoming telepathic? This time, though, she didn't feel afraid. The boy's presence was calming, and she felt safe with him. Surrounding him, the air or space exuded a clarity and tranquility. She could see better, hear better. Could he help her somehow? Could he sneak in and get her some food?

"Are you a ghost?" she whispered. He surprised her by opening his mouth in a wide yawn. The yawn was so huge that it seemed to encompass his entire head. When he was done, he rolled his eyes.

Crystal said, "I guess you get that a lot. Huh." On some level, she believed she should be afraid of him. Hadn't he threatened her before? *Or was he only trying to warn her?* And why could she see him at all? Elinor had been able to see him as well. Why them? Why not the others? She felt a sadness, looking at him. What had happened to him? She'd have to figure it out later. Later. After she got home to her own bed, her own house. Though a part of her wanted to forget this week had ever happened.

The people congregated in the center of the driveway and chatted, turned their heads for one last look at the perimeter, then headed off toward the house. If she were to go in to steal food, she'd need to wait until they left, or be very sneaky indeed.

At least she had been able to get her fiddle.

"Can you help me?" Crystal turned to the boy but found only the bush behind which she was hidden. Once again, she was alone.

After waiting for several minutes, lights remained on at the far end of the long house, but the kitchen stayed unlit. Deciding to chance it, she crept forward through the shadows.

Outside the kitchen door, she was met by a pressure around her head, and the familiar flow of nauseating energy. After experiencing the calmness of the boy, it was jarring. She put a hand on a pine log of the wall to steady herself and to wait for the feeling to pass. This time, the voices were back. *Näcken. Her heritage . . . she won't . . . Vingåker . . . release her . . .*

The voices buzzed, then lifted off with the accompanying nausea. This time she'd actually made out some words. But some of the words seemed to be a different language. What was *"Näcken"*? And that *"v"* word? She'd have to find out later.

Crystal moved across the wooden floor in the kitchen toward the fridge. She'd been afraid they might lock the door at night, anticipating raiders, but apparently she was the only one rude enough to break the rules. Oh well.

They'd soon be rid of her.

She opened the fridge door only a crack, so the light wouldn't shine out and be visible from outside. Setting her fiddle down, she prowled through several wrapped and containered packages, which stood in neat stacks.

Probably some bread would be good. Also, fruit would work, if they had any, as she didn't want to carry too much. Most of the containers looked too unwieldy, and probably contained meaty foods.

A pressure moved around her head and tightened into a trapping band. *Someone was behind her.* She spun around, but no one was there. *Weird,* she thought. So much for her budding psychic skills. For a minute she had not doubted her ability. And that was the trouble with her mother's entire family. All their weird powers and they never doubted themselves. There. She had proven it. The so-called abilities were false.

She turned back to the fridge and found an orange. It was small, but she could eat the peel as well.

A throat cleared behind her.

"Is that you, Crystal?"

She dropped the orange and fell to her behind. Her palm smacked the fridge door and it swung full open, knocking over her fiddle case.

This time, there was someone there. Relieved, she saw that it was only Pete, the boy in charge of laundry. But what he was doing up this late, carrying sheets, she had no idea.

"Oh, yeah," she chortled. "*Whoo*! You scared me! Hope I don't get in too much trouble. I was really hungry," she said sheepishly, and grinned her most pleasant smile. She picked up the orange, closed the fridge, and stood. She could charm her way out of this spot.

He chuckled softly. "Oh, don't worry about it. Where you're going, you won't need much food." So saying, he threw the sheet over her head and tightened his arms around her. Wanda had been right; he was really strong.

"Stop, let me go! This isn't funny!" Crystal said and struggled.

"You'd best be quiet," he responded calmly, "or I'll have to gag you."

The thought of having an object shoved in her mouth was horrifying. Crystal still attempted to fight, but she began whimpering.

"Please, please, let me go. I'll do whatever you want." As soon as the words were out, she knew she was lying. If she could get him relaxed, she'd claw out his eyes or do whatever it took to get away.

"It's not what I want," Pete said. "You've been chosen by the Master."

Crystal was silent. A numbing terror swirled in her stomach. What was this? Were they some kind of coven? Was she going to be sacrificed to the devil? She decided that screaming was her only choice. Maybe someone in one of the cabins would hear her. She cut loose with a yodel that would split the ears of anyone nearby, and Pete covered her mouth with his hand over the sheet.

"I said be quiet."

She tried to bite his fingers, but he pushed her down and straddled her, holding one arm down with a knee and the other with his hand. Then he shoved a wad of the sheet into her mouth until she gagged.

"Now I mean it. You've got to go along with this. You won't be sorry. It will be the best thing that ever happened to you."

Was he insane? Apparently so. All cult people would sacrifice themselves for their leaders. Of course they thought she should, too.

Crystal heard other people come into the room, and even though someone turned on the light, she could not see out through the fibers. The panic and adrenalin coursing through her body had her jumping like a cooking lobster.

"Get her instrument," she heard one of them say. *No! Not her violin!* She tried to scream "Let me go" through Pete's hand.

"We'll need to tie her, she's not being easy." Crystal could have sworn that was Wanda's voice.

Hands rolled her over and she felt herself being tied in the sheet at the ankles, knees, and stomach. Then her arms were lashed to her sides.

"I'm not sure she deserves this," said the Wanda-sounding voice. "She's not good enough."

Crystal struggled against the gag and tried to make an agreeable sound. Fine, let her talk and she'd agree that she wasn't good enough and they could all go on their merry ways.

"We'll need to bag her. She could freeze."

Enough light came through the sheet for Crystal to see at least four forms. So a group of them were in on this. Is this what happened to Elinor? And where did Glenn end up? Were they all sacrifices? How did they explain that to the parents when they came to get their kids from fiddle camp? "Oh, sorry. We had to sacrifice him."

Maybe this had to do with Beans. Did they sacrifice Beans? Maybe he hadn't drowned at all—maybe he'd been put on an altar somewhere.

It was becoming hard to breathe. Even though the sheet had a plenty loose thread count, in her excited state her breath came in short, fast pants and the gag was preventing enough oxygen from coming in. Panicking, she thrashed wildly, her voice coming in high whines.

"She's flipping out. Give her something."

"Like what?" A male's voice.

"I dunno. Make her stop."

"Don't you have a shot?"

"Like of what?"

Someone was pinching her arm as she struggled and yelped.

She felt a hand over her face.

"Shut up! Calm down!" Pete's voice.

But the hand was the last straw. Oxygen depleted, she sank into fearful unconsciousness.

♪

She awoke in a cold cocoon, in the midst of a roar. In spite of the softness around her, her back ached from clenching against the frigid ground. A rigid weight ran alongside her leg. No longer restrained, she frantically wrestled against the fabric binding her. She emerged from a mummy bag into the shadows of early morning, still wearing her coat, dress, and tights from the night before. A dawn bird began trilling and ratcheting to wake up the day, as Crystal surveyed her setting. She'd seen this place before. It was the exact spot she'd found Glenn.

Where were her captors? She pushed erect and felt a heaviness on her foot. A metal clamp embraced her ankle and was attached to a nearby tree with a metal chain. The chain had been the cold pressure she had felt in the bag.

A pulse of horror ran through her. Shock erupted from her core and merged with feelings of powerlessness. For once, she wished she *did* have the magic powers her aunt professed to have.

Frantic, she spent several minutes attempting to remove the ankle clamp. Taking off her shoe, she tried pointing her toes really hard, but though her foot cramped with the effort, she could not make it small enough to slide out. Finding a stick, she pushed it through one of the chain loops and pulled hard in an attempt to break the link, but instead the wood cracked and split.

Her body trembled as she looked around.

No captors. *Where were they? Why had they left her here?*

She had to be able to free herself. But Glenn had tried and failed. And he was a lot stronger than she.

Nearby, next to her violin, lay a container wrapped in tin foil. She remembered how hungry she was and decided to risk it. If it was poison, it couldn't change her circumstances much. If they were going to kill her, they'd do it whenever they wanted. Plus, if they were going to sacrifice her, they wouldn't want her dying before their great event.

She opened the container to expose a rice dish and plastic spoon. She used the spoon to dig out the bits of chicken in the dish as she finished the rice.

The hours passed as the chill sun slipped through the shadows of the trees. Slowly, with the music of the water soothing her and no immediate threat, she calmed to more rational thought.

Perhaps their plan was just to leave her here until she died of exposure. *But wouldn't they have taken her coat?*

She cried for several minutes, but with no one to console her, she realized she was wasting time. She *had* to escape. She looked around. What could she use? Sticks. Stones. Her fingernails. But there was nothing to escape with.

Except her own abilities.

She felt sick. The energies that had bludgeoned her, the voices. What if they had meaning? What if . . .

Maybe Aunt Sarah really did have magical abilities. And maybe, just maybe those hideous differences she suspected about her family — that they were connected to magical forces — could be used. Maybe *she* could use them.

She had to try.

She focused her will on her aunt. Her so-called magical aunt. If anyone could hear her psychic cries, it would be her. Besides, Aunt Sarah got her into this. Aunt Sarah would have to get her out.

Forming an image of her aunt, she imbued it with as much reality as she could. She projected the aura of her aunt—smelling her hair, breathing her breath—until she could *feel* her.

Aunt Sarah! she called in her mind. *Help me! Bring help!* She put her strongest intention into the command, pushed it into her aunt's head, and could only pray it worked.

As she sat, trying to think of other ways to break free, the sound of the water began echoing in her mind. She watched the light play on the hot pool and the constant rush of steam and spray from the falls. An internal metronome ticked in her, and she wished she could play it. Play the colors. Play the light and shadow of the falls. Play the tune that tinkled like a thousand instruments. She felt herself drifting into the *nothing zone*, which preceded her playing.

"No!" she commanded herself. "Work on getting free!"

But as the hours passed, and the day turned warmer, she had exhausted her ideas for escape. All that remained were her, her fiddle, and the water. She sat on the sleeping bag, her head in her hands.

Gradually, she became aware of some*thing* else. In the deeper tones of the river, just as the water crashed into the red eye of the pool, she heard a voice. At first, it seemed to be just random syllables, then it crystallized and formed into words. *It called her name.*

She grew mesmerized, lured and hypnotized by the sound. She fought it. Had they given her a drug? She needed to get away! But each tone seemed to glide on a ray of sunlight, carrying her into *elsewhere*. She drifted into a reverie, seeking, wanting it. A passion unborn demanded birth.

She removed her instrument from its case and caressed it. Placing her cheek against the wood, she closed her eyes and felt the vibration caused by the water coursing down the rocks. If only she could play those tones, those vibrations. With her eyes closed she could see it: the colors, the dances, as the water burbled and fell. There seemed to be more colors than was possible in the human spectrum; colors she had not seen before. And, attached to each one was a tone; tones of earth and magic; tones of light and dark; tones that lifted her to heights and carried her to depths. Places that stripped her to the soul and left her naked in the light.

She tightened her bow. Keeping her eyes closed, she drew the hair across the strings. As her mind felt for the magic, her fingers felt for the tones. Like birds, they flew through the woods of sounds and dove into harmonic vibratos. They lifted and soared and plummeted into the infinite fathoms of darkness so profound she could only breathe it, not see it. Then they shattered the existence of being with a beauty so rich it defied imagery. *If this is God, let me be here forever*, she begged.

An energy unlike anything she'd ever felt moved over her. Peering through slit eyes, it seemed the red eye of the pool had opened and begun a frothing, drawing motion. A warmth, as though she were held in the arms of a loving mother, drew her closer to its heart. Her feet found their way forward, her playing flushed into a love song to the water and forest, drawn to the heated rapture of the stream.

It became a living being, then. Calling to her, promising resonances of riches beyond wealth and beauty. Beyond five senses; beyond the fragile and small spectrum of light; beyond scent, touch, and taste. Beyond three dimensions. Somehow, she knew. There were infinite dimensions in each spectrum, and infinite spectrums in the universe. She was called from *beyond*. Where she *belonged*. Where she needed *to be*. She reached the end of her chain and pulled her leg hard. Frustrated, she screamed, pulling harder at the tether, then playing harder on her fiddle. She closed her eyes again to envision it. Perhaps she could *undo* the chain with her music. Suddenly, it seemed possible; everything seemed possible.

But disobeying her will, the ankle clamp held. She screamed again, a deep, inhuman tone of rage and desired release. From all the trapped souls of the eons. *Let me go!*

She heard a slight sound — a sound not of the water. A slight cough or choking sound. Her eyes opened. On a boulder near the water's edge, sat the Dracula man she had seen with Glenn. He was crying.

"Why you stopped?" he asked. "You — you are the one! At last, I find."

Crystal didn't know what to say as emotions flooded her being. Anger, fright, outrage. But those were small, compared to the new awareness and feeling of having been embraced by the universe, by God.

There were no words to say to the man, so she lifted her bow and stood erect. Throwing back her head to feel the air, stretching her being to embrace the space, she joined in the song of the *Näcken*.

With her untethered leg, she reached closer to the water, closer to the source of her power, until the chain was again tight and the clamp on her ankle cutting into her foot. Still drawn, she yearned to get closer. She played over the pool until her fingers bled and her soul was saturated with sound. She played beyond the reaches of love into an ecstasy known by only masters and madmen. When she next opened her eyes, she saw Beans sitting atop a white stallion, who pawed the ground and snorted. Tears ran down his face as he nodded at her, conveying his appreciation of her understanding. She knew why he had drowned. That he, too, had heard the music and been lured by the *Näcken*. But unlike her, he had broken free of his chain and dived into the water to be in the source of bliss.

She was done. She was free. She had played the song of the water, of her life, of the murky and clear elements of her being.

"Keep playing," said the old man.

"Let me go," she said. "I must go to it."

"No. I am Master. You will learn!" He stood and came toward her, and Crystal recognized him from an old photo. This was the secret man. The fiddle instructor with all the wild rumors. He was quite a bit older, but this was Olaf Widmark, who had been rumored to have been taught by the *Näcken* — the water spirit. And like the water spirit, his eyes were filled with a sad longing — for a force or vision he had attained and could never reach again. Relief for his loneliness could only be found in the playing of others who could find and sustain it. Crystal felt a deep empathy with him, then let it go.

"What did you do with Glenn?" Crystal felt brave, untouchable. The water spirit, light, and sound would protect her.

"He would not learn! He could not see! You will learn. You think you know all, but there is more, so much more."

"No. I won't play anymore. Unless you let me go."

"No. You play." Olaf took a step toward her and stopped. "You must learn to open it — the door . . ."

Crystal held her fiddle over the water.

"I'll kill it," she said. Even as she said it, she knew it didn't make sense. To threaten him, when all she longed to do was to – jump in and join with it. Still, as her playing had ceased, she had started to return to her senses. The sensations she had felt still lingered like a dream, but her mind was once again becoming her own.

Olaf's eyes widened. Blood light from the center of the water played over the finish of the violin. Crystal wasn't sure if she meant to kill the violin or the *Näcken*. But the threat worked. He backed off.

"You are tired now. The *Näcken* will sing to you again, and again you will play. Then I'll return." Olaf turned and strode away with his cane, stronger than it seemed he could be at his age. He took the same trail on which Crystal had seen him leave with Glenn.

She found it odd that he had not once glanced at Beans on the white, unbridled horse. Beans grinned at her, and his horse leaped. Water splashed up and sizzled on the rocks as the animal and boy disappeared into the red eye.

Released, relieved, and reprieved, Crystal sat on the earth and bawled — an emotional explosion she could not explain.

10

OPENING

It was late afternoon when Crystal heard the rustle in the forest that implied someone was coming. She had made her decision about playing for the Master. The music — this music — was from beneath the earth, from the stars and beyond. She could understand why Glenn didn't want to escape, why he wanted to play it. Already, she felt changed and knew she would never be the same. The world was a far more mysterious and alive place than she could ever have imagined, and somehow she had tapped into a vein that led to its heart. But if the music had taught her anything, it had taught her freedom. She would not be held captive to play. No matter what he did to her.

Whispering penetrated over the rush of the water.

"Cris! Cris!"

Across the water, beyond the bushes crouched a form and above the scrub oak, a ponytail stuck straight up into the air. Standing, she raised her hand toward the form. "Please. Come. Hurry. Help me get away."

Clearly, in the dying streaks of sun, the chicken-tail hairdo of Aunt Sarah popped and darted between the bushes, then bobbled as she came across the rocks of the stream.

Crystal groaned. Of all people to save her . . .

"Crissy!" Her aunt came close and hugged her until Crystal squeaked.

"Oh, I'm sorry." She pushed Crystal's hair out of her eyes. "What is going on here? I got your call — well, I saw your number on my cell. And then . . . I had an intuition you were in trouble. What is this place?" She looked around at the pool and forest.

"Did you bring Dad?"

"No, I didn't want to worry him in case I was wrong."

"Well, you're not wrong, Aunt Sarah. You've got to get me out of this chain."

"They chained you?"

"Yes, look." She held out her foot.

Her aunt dropped to her knees and began tugging.

"It won't work, Aunt Sarah. We need a chisel. Or a crowbar. Or a key."

"This is crazy. How did you get up here?" her aunt was babbling now.

"That's a story, but how did you find me? How did you know I wasn't down at the camp?"

For a moment their eyes locked. Instead of the flighty, fruity aunt Crystal knew so well, she saw someone serious, someone who knew truths she could only begin to fathom. Crystal thought of the mental command she had issued earlier. Had it worked?

"I have a high sense of intuition," Sarah finally said. "Ever hear of Meyer's Briggs tests?"

"Funny you should say that . . . but — never mind. What are we going to do?"

"You there!" Olaf's voice boomed across the bank to

where they stood. "You, woman. You are not to be here."
He limped toward them.

Sarah puffed like a cold chicken and turned her beak
at him.

"Are you the maniac who has tied up my niece?"

Crystal was astounded. She'd never seen her aunt in
action. She didn't show a feather-weight of fear.

"I demand you release her, *now*."

Olaf shot out words in Swedish. Crystal caught the
word "*Näcken*."

Then, to her utter amazement, her aunt rattled back in
the same language. Crystal watched as he blanched.

"She will play. Now. Or—" He dropped again into
Swedish. Now it was Sarah's turn to blanch. Their voices
rose in pitch and they yelled over the top of each other.
Olaf shook his stick in the air. What was this, the war of
the wizards?

Crystal knew what to do. "Wait, wait. I'll play," she
shouted. Aunt Sarah stepped forward, her hand raised to
stop her, but Crystal cast a significant look at her aunt.
Their eyes locked and held as though a thought passed
between them. As though Crystal had *willed* her to hear.
Sarah stopped her advance.

Crystal lifted her fiddle and drew her bow.

The color of the pool eye was red. The color of her
music was fire. It lit them — even Sarah stood transfixed. It
flowed and danced and reverberated amongst the trees. It
crescendoed — louder — louder — and right at the peak,
Crystal hurled her instrument, her unborn twin, the love
of her life, onto the rocks of the falls. It shattered into
pieces and was consumed in the spray of the pool.

"There!" she shouted at Olaf. "Now you and your
kracken or nacken or whatever can have it!" Crystal
stared — defiant and powerful — stronger than she had ever
felt.

Olaf stood, his mouth open in apparent shock and his cheeks pumping air in and out, as he stared at the place the violin had disappeared. He seemed to crumple into himself and was suddenly only an old man with a dead dream. He looked at her, the anguish of death etching sorrow across his face and into some forbidding, hidden past as he understood she would not be forced. Despite her anger, Crystal felt pity for him and a measure of guilt.

Turning his back, he hunched over his stick and began walking away. He let a key drop on the ground.

Sarah ran over and picked it up. She released her niece and they hugged. Aunt Sarah didn't feel nearly as creepy as Crystal remembered.

And Crystal had received a birthday gift beyond her imagination. She had tapped into her power, and the power of the world.

11

CHANNELS

Crystal shivered in her ruffle dress and tights as they descended — glad she had worn her hiking boots and still had on her coat. Even with her aunt by her side, she did not dare return to the cabin to pick up her belongings, and with her fiddle destroyed there was no reason to head back toward the camp. Sarah and she stole down the mountain, holding their conversation until they could get in Sarah's vehicle, which she'd parked on the road beneath the camp. Even though the old man had let them go, Crystal still feared they might be chased by the horrid camp people.

Once inside, Sarah started the car and turned on the heater full blast.

"I hope you don't mind, but I thought we'd get a motel at the next town." Sarah sat at the edge of her seat, straining to see over the steering wheel down the steep and bumpy road. "I just made this drive in about seven hours, and I'm fried."

She added that after they returned to Ohio, perhaps they should stay at her house until camp week was over. Sarah could call Richard and Emma to say Crystal had phoned wanting her to drive her home so they could talk about the gift.

Crystal raised an eyebrow.

"Yeah. Fat chance, huh?" Sarah grinned with half a lip. "But I don't think they'll contradict me if I say you called."

"Well, you can't tell them what happened, regardless, Aunt Sarah. I don't want Dad coming up here threatening to sue. I don't know how we'd prove any of it anyway. Besides, there's other stuff."

Sarah glanced to the side, but quickly looked back at the road. "I'm sure there is. You know, when I turned, it was a beautiful time, but then, I sort of knew what to expect and I had your mom to help."

Crystal was silent as she mulled her aunt's words. Finally, she said "What do you mean when you 'turned'? My playing was . . . amazing. I still can't believe it happened. But I don't know what you mean by 'turned.'" Already, as they drove away, the imagery was dissipating—the reality of the occurrence moving into a fantasy. The heater began to cook her feet, so she loosened her belt, leaned over, and took off her shoes to dry her socks.

"Oh. Geez, honey. Didn't your mom tell you *anything*?"

"You sound like you're talking about sex or periods. Of course she told me about that. I am eighteen—actually, today."

Sarah nodded. "Oh, I know. And, happy birthday. I guess this was a strange one, huh."

"One I'll never forget!"

"But no, I didn't mean sex, and I'm not sure I should

say too much about turning. I mean, I'm not your mother and it's traditionally her place. I thought she'd tell you before your birthday."

"Tell me what?" Crystal had been so relieved to get in the car and be leaving Beans Camp without being chased that she had begun to relax. Now her stress level started to rise, and it felt like she was being wrapped in a scratchy blanket. As usual, her aunt was beginning to irritate her. Then, in a sudden flash of insight, she knew her aunt held the key to her understanding recent events. But could she really hear it? Was she ready?

"I have to know what is going on. I know I've been awful, and I'm sorry. There's something — *wrong* with me. Something bad. This whole week I've been too mixed up. And how did you know how to talk to that old guy? Was that Swedish?" Crystal's questions were spinning in her head, erratic and fast.

"Wait." Sarah stopped the car and Crystal caught herself against the dashboard. They were on a steep incline and Sarah kept her foot on the brake while she turned to her niece.

"Let me ask you a question. Have you been experiencing like, I dunno, unusual *powers* lately?"

Crystal looked at her aunt annoyed, then laughed. "Like flying? Or x-ray vision? Or maybe just playing my fiddle into some other dimension?"

Sarah continued to watch her, her face serious, which killed Crystal's ability to joke her way out of it. She didn't know if she should be making light of it, throwing a tantrum, or asking to be committed.

"Sorry. That was snarky." For a moment she looked away from her aunt. This was the place, *the place*, she hadn't wanted to go with her aunt. She needed answers, but if she let her aunt in, how would she ever get her back out again? Sarah would know the hidden things. The things about her Crystal that couldn't even face herself. And every time she looked at her aunt after this, her aunt would look at her with those knowing eyes. And she'd never, ever, be able to go back and pretend she didn't know. Because she was starting to.

She did need help to figure out what was happening to her, but she needed a little more time to formulate her questions and to go over in her own mind what had happened. To try to accept the possibility that magic might be real and that she wasn't just crazy.

As though her aunt had heard her thoughts, she sighed. "When you're ready, hon." Releasing her foot from the brake, she continued down the hill toward the town, a warm motel, food, and sleep.

The potential stress of spending the next two days with her aunt was offset by her need to be alone to think, and for the time being, at least, her aunt was giving her some space.

The strain of sleeping in her aunt's spare room under coarse blankets and listening through thin walls to snoring kept her from moving into the deep zone and feeling her best during the day. Sitting on her aunt's porch step wearing an oversized sweater, she hugged her knees and thought about Glenn and Elinor. Had they really just left without saying goodbye? Were they all right?

What she'd undergone violated her sense of reality and her expectations of how she would be treated in life. She tried to be *good*. Wasn't the world supposed to treat her the way she treated it?

And how exactly was her fiddle playing related to the old man and why he would be forcing people to play by the river? Had her aunt been able to see what she saw when she played, or was it all a hallucination? The voices, the feelings, she'd been experiencing. What were they? Would they go away soon?

She was ready—more than ready—to ask her aunt some questions.

She slid like an ice skater in her stocking feet across the linoleum floor in her aunt's kitchen, and asked Sarah to join her in a cup of tea.

Sarah made the tea, adding a pinch of mugwort "for health." Not knowing what mugwort was, Crystal played with the warm cup more than sipping.

"So, are you ready to hear?" Sarah plunked herself into the kitchen chair and shoved a small plate of donut holes and cookies toward her niece.

"Yes, and I have a lot of questions."

Sarah held up a hand. "Before you get into it, I need to tell you some background stuff, or you'll never understand."

"Like what?" She took a small bite of cookie.

"Well, like about Fredrik in Sweden."

"Fredrik?"

"Yes. He's related to us—a relative, so to speak. He was the brother of Olaf's mother. So his blood is in our veins.

"And, he is a wizard."

Crystal scoffed, making her choke on the cookie. "Fredrik is a wizard? And related?" She coughed. "So we're sort of related to Olaf?"

Sarah waited until Crystal cleared her throat before beginning again. Her eyes took on a faraway glaze as she looked into the air to the right of Crystal's head. Crystal peered up to see what was there, but her aunt ignored her, focused on the spot, and started in.

"I believe it was sometime in the late eighteen hundreds or early nineteen hundreds that they all lived in Sweden. Before any of us migrated to America. It was a small town, quaint, cobblestones. You know the type. Back when they really used to dress in caps and pinafores, leggings and hard leather shoes . . ." Her voice took on a floating quality as her eyes continued to focus into the air above Crystal's head. She seemed connected to another place, another time, or some*one* else.

Long ago . . .

Dressed in his long cloak, Fredrik tucked the hand-made book up his sleeve, into the crook of his elbow. The flap of skin tied against the window of the mill house opened a sliver as his fingernail slit it for a peek.

    Outside the stone structure, the townspeople gathered — their backs drawing power from the heavy trees at the forest's edge. His granddaughter had told them of the book he kept; he knew she intended to burn it. They stood, shifting on their feet and in their faces. Their torches, their tools — signs of their healthy labor — now turned to blood lust. Their faces eager and wary, looking like his long ago Viking ancestors. The blood connection ran deep. There was Sven and Benkt. Enar, Solveig, and Greger. And Fisk. He'd thought Fisk was his friend.

    All of them, each of them, without fail, had come to him in secret, in the night, and asked for his aid. Greger for his wife's blood after the birth of twins. Benkt for the failure of his crops. Enar had sows with the foot disease. All of them, needing help. And he had cured them all. Yet still, their children gathered behind him like gnats when he ventured out, throwing sticks and darting behind wagons, yelling "Pigsty! Svinstu! *Pigsty!" Sometimes, he'd whip around and pin them with his eye, move his fingers in the air, and point at them. Then they would run screaming, as he snickered into the front of his shirt. Perhaps he shouldn't have played with them such.*

    Staggering back from the window, he slid the book from his arm to his palm. If they took him, it might fall out of his sleeve. It needed hiding.

    Using a poker, he worked on a stone in the fireplace surround. The mortar was old, and it cracked and crumbled easily. *Puffing hard and fearful breath, he soon managed to pry behind the rock, loosening it. With a final push, he broke it free. Behind was a space, just wide enough. He inserted the book and forced the stone back in. Gathering ashes from the grate, he rubbed his hands over the rough rock exterior of the hidden area to make it blend in with the rest of the mantle then scattered the mortar chips.*

Breathing the air of his sanctuary and drawing in from the forces he could summon, he made symbols; manipulating his fingers into shapes for strength.

He wondered if there were anyone to help him, but even his protégé, whose music was beloved by the town, could not save him. The music passed to Olaf by the Näcken and painstakingly written in his own hand was stolen by the same woman who had raised the people against him. She had burned it in the middle of town for all to see, to prove her innocence, her virtue, and her allegiance to the church. If she would do this to someone like Olaf, what more would she prompt the townsfolk to do to him?

At least the book was safe. Other household goods they destroyed could be replaced. They might kill him, but he doubted it. Too many of them had need of his dark skills. Still.

"Wait, wait. Aunt Sarah. This is some weird stuff, but I really don't get what it has to do with my fiddle playing. Or me. Or us. Or even Olaf that much. If Fredrik was born in the late eighteen hundreds, Olaf would have to be — how old? Plus, I don't get how you would even know this about him unless — unless . . ." Crystal wasn't sure what she wanted to say. Sarah seemed somehow *connected* to the old ancestor. His tale seemed to be coming *through* her. Her voice sounded funny. Could she be *channeling* him?

Her aunt focused on her slowly, as though she were in a dream.

"Just be patient. I'll get to that." She took a sip of her tea, dunked a cookie and chewed. "You got the part of the relative burning Olaf's materials, right?"

"Yes."

Sarah shook her head. "Really a shame that. All original music." She finished her cookie. "Looking back, probably none of it would have happened if Olaf and the Gypsy had not come together."

"Gypsy? What Gypsy?"

"*Shhh.*" Sarah's eyes raised above Crystal's head again, and the whites of her eyes flashed.

Crystal fought the urge to look, this time.

If only Olaf and the Gypsy had not come together. But wasn't it the blame of all the men of the town? They had all agreed. Invite the Gypsies to a war of sound – a betting game. The Gypsies with their famed Faragó, who could dance and play the fiddle with the air of magic and make all swoon who heard him. Pitted against Olaf Widmark. Olaf, Fredrik's protégé. So many had failed to capture the sound before Olaf. But Olaf had been taught by the essence of the river. And his violin had taken on the voice of the true world.

They had met at the edge of the water, near the falls where the Näcken was strongest. This was Olaf's idea. The breath through the forest was chill and the tall pines cast the clearing into a twilight. The men had gathered – some had brought their wives. Olaf's daughter, young Alicia, had carried his cases. Pride in her father had inured her to the danger afoot.

The young woman had noticed a Gypsy girl, about her age, standing near the wagon at the edge of the pool. Alicia stayed at a tree nearby, lest her father need some rosin or some help with his instrument. She had left her new husband at home, begging him not to attend with the other men, more because she feared the clutches of the beautiful and mesmerizing Gypsy girls, than fearing his gambling.

Gathered in their wool cloaks, the clansfolk tucked their faces into their scarves to later claim they were not present, should a neighbor see them.

Faragó played first. His bow struck the strings and drove them into their hearts. It lifted up their lies and truths and shouted to them about their dreams and visions.

Then Olaf. From a dimension outside sound, he sliced the sky with a breath of beauty. Then he dazzled them with a truth so brilliant some fell to their knees in tears.

Angered, Faragó jumped in playing over the top of Olaf. Then the two began warring. Faster the music went, harder the sound became. The two men, fixated on their playing, did not notice the color arising from the deep of the water. It bubbled upward and shaped into a red pool. As their tones merged and blended, creating harmonics that shrieked and battered, a crimson thread ascended into the air then broke into a prism of light that erupted through the forest. Still they played, their eyes and instruments bludgeoning each other with sound. A substance like thin ice shimmered in the air over the falls. The fiddlers did not notice as some townsfolk ran in horror from the area while others fell prone in prayer.

Still they fought, their bows zinging with white energy and their passions fierce. Then the icy shimmer burst open and screams ripped across the clearing. The Gypsy girl and Alicia, held numb in a light beam, were lifted across the water, directly into the center of a spiral energy hole swirling upward toward the infinite. Too bright to see in, Olaf dropped his fiddle and shielded his eyes, screaming his daughter's name. But the Gypsy girl and Alicia had disappeared – been swallowed by the force beyond, conjured by some dark magic and the notes of the violins.

Olaf dropped to his knees, praying and crying. Faragó stood motionless staring at the place color had appeared and now throbbed with the grief of the frigid night air and stunned faces.

And now they had come for him, Fredrik, for knowing the secrets of magic, that in another time would be called science.

"What? What? Aunt Sarah. This can't be true. I just don't believe in people being lifted up by light beams. What was it? Like a UFO? Beam me up, Scotty?"

Sarah drew her eyes back from the place in the air and shrugged. "How would I know? I wasn't there." Her voice sounded groggy and a little distant.

Forgetting the mugwort, Crystal took a glug of the tea and swallowed hard.

"So you're saying that when they played a UFO came down and zapped up a couple of people, including Olaf's daughter?"

Sarah nodded. "Sort of. I don't know if it 'came down,' or came through. The way it was described was not a UFO. It was like a portal, an opening from somewhere. Like another dimension."

Crystal sniffed then got up to turn off the stove. The tea kettle had run out of water and was starting to burn.

"I just don't know about this," Crystal said. "I'm sorry, Aunt Sarah, but so far this just seems like a wives' tale. And it doesn't explain what's been happening to me."

"I'm not finished yet," said Sarah. "Do you want to hear the rest?"

Crystal thought about it for a second. What did Olaf's family have to do with her? None of this seemed connected to her at all, except that perhaps she and Olaf had a similar experience with the water. But her aunt seemed to think it was related, so maybe she'd get to it. Besides, for the first time, she was honestly interested in learning about her remote relatives. A wizard? *Cheesits*!

"Of course," Crystal responded. "But can you answer some questions afterward? I really have some questions about what's been happening to me."

"We'll get to that. I do need to tell you, though, what happened later," Sarah said as Crystal listened.

Two years later, Alicia wandered into the town — dazed, confused, and unremembering. Though it was September and frost had chafed the leaves and crops in the morning, she was unheeding. Naked, she walked through the center of the street, her feet cold on the cobblestones, seeking her home, husband, and Olaf, her father.

And it was clear for all to see that she was several months pregnant.

Sarah seemed to be waking up from whatever dream-state she'd been in. Her eyes focused, and she looked around the room, then at her watch. "Oh, dear. It's getting late. I told a friend I'd take her to the store. She's almost ninety and I help her out now and then."

Sarah paused and shifted in her chair while her face took on the bland look of the fruity aunt. "You know, I really shouldn't say too much more just now. It's not my place. Your mother should be here."

Crystal was surprised. Other than this weird story that seemed to have nothing to do with her, she didn't feel any boundaries had been crossed.

"Tell you what. Let's hold off a bit until we can get together with your mother. There are a lot of details she can fill in and she might resent my being the one to help you cross." Sarah patted Crystal's hand and, in spite of herself, Crystal felt a gush of warmth toward the aunt who had saved her.

Crystal pumped her bike and pulled into Tish's driveway. She couldn't wait to tell her about the camp, the spooky old man, her surprise party and the ghost boy. For a moment, she lingered in the light of the old days when she would have told her friend most, if not all. But now, she knew she would change the way she spoke. She'd tell her the surface. "Accidentally" dropping and breaking her fiddle. Meeting a handsome guy. Their kiss. Her friend Elinor. But how could she ever explain the intense experience with the *Näcken*? How could she explain her sadness for the old man and her easy acceptance of the ghost boy? There were things she could not share with anyone, except—and she smiled at the thought—her weird Aunt Sarah.

Now, getting back in her regular routine, Crystal was becoming less worried about her experiences, and more hopeful that her life could go back to normal. Or a little better than normal, since she had accepted Aunt Sarah more.

Reluctant to bring up her changes to her mother, Crystal had managed to sidestep her for a few days. Her mother, who seemed so remote. How could she ever understand? Plus, nothing out of the ordinary had happened to her since she'd returned from camp. As though somehow the playing had purged her soul of all bric-a-brac. She felt clean, and except for longing for her fiddle, happier than she had in a while.

Still, there were unanswered questions and she would need to learn more about the abilities she was developing. Seeing into other dimensions? Hearing peoples' thoughts? Drawing forth the *Näcken*? What were these abilities for? Why her? The old man said she was "the one." That she had been chosen. But for what? What was she supposed to do?

Holding her face to the sun, she breathed in the crisp air. Perhaps her best advice to herself was to put it all out of her mind. Go back to normal. *Please! Just go back to normal!* For a moment she allowed herself the old feeling of the safe, happy days of her childhood. Then she hugged her shoulders.

An excited bird had burrowed into her spirit and she sensed those days were done. She was on a personal adventure now — one that would lead her into uncharted areas, where music was alive, creatures sang from water, and people disappeared into portals.

How she was involved would remain to be seen.

PART II

BLOOD

WICKET

1

FREDRIK

Vingåker, Sweden

Fredrik of Now snuggled into his good wool coat and stepped into the mill yard. The crisp air of *Vingåker* carried a twist of decaying leaves, but not more than could be frozen out by the stronger scent of impending winter. He slogged across the terrain toward the windmill then stood and frowned at the broken vane. It lay bent, cracked, and partially burned, amidst the peeling paint and fractured mortar of the tower.

For a moment, in his mind's eye, he looked back to when he was young enough to sustain the repairs. His vitality, his love of life. His skill with a hammer and saw. But even then he had enemies, just for knowing what he knew, and doing what he could do. He watched his younger self working on the mill, repairing the mortar and moving rocks along the stream edge. He smiled at the younger self.

The younger self turned, his face glowing, looking skyward, smiled back and waved at his future self, who was the Fredrik of Now. Fredrik of Now remembered that day well; it was the day of discovery that he could talk to himself across time. Later, he would learn to talk to relatives across time and space as well.

And now, he must retreat again to the house. For his future self had told him that others were coming and he must prepare for their arrival. Several others — people of different types, with different needs. And they each wanted a different magic from him. One of these carried the blood and could be the one to mend the tear in the universes. She was coming for him — and he didn't know what to say.

He peered into the white sky for a last long moment and imagined the stars and planets aligning as he knew they were doing. The time drew near. The time of the Great Change, when the fine dust that held the universe together would yawn. The membrane would stretch, thin, and disappear.

Those on the next plane, who were helpful to humans, would reach forth. And those on this plane who were ready, could embrace the glory and choose to leave or stay. But only for an instant. Then it would close again for another period, as the Snake that Ruled Events reached around and gripped its own tail, to repeat time over again.

He thought of the relative named *Sarah* and her niece, *Crystal*. If the girl truly carried the blood, the tear might be mended.

He had been a middle-aged man when he felt the first concussion of the time rift. The sun had seemed wrong all day, and a sudden spike in its fury combined with experiments being done on the planet, far away in space and time. A fist of force slammed across the earth and twisted perceptions. Then everyone continued, not knowing, not realizing time had slipped. Yet, they were repeating the past.

It would be many times going around the loops of time before he became fully aware of what had happened to cause the Great Event. On that day, he'd felt a force crash against the world and nature, as though a tree had fallen on the windmill. And sure enough, the mill had broken in two.

In his mind's eye, he saw the Snake that Ruled Events begin to consume its own tail. Trapped in a circle going forever around, he then knew the truth of what ruled the world. All the people of the planet were held captive, forever locked in repeating time — unless another Great Change would come. And he was not certain how to help.

Fredrik, and a few others like him, learned to spot the signs of the time-slip before it came. The feeling it evoked became known as *déjà vu*. With each pass, the duration between concussions got closer, the loop of time they lived in before being reborn, shorter. One day they would all be stuck in the same moment — an eternal Now from which they could not escape. Crushed in a single moment of time and space — a black hole of infinity.

Fredrik shook his head as his boots clomped into the house. It smelled of wood smoke and bread baking. He worked his way to his chair to finish his thoughts.

He remembered long ago when the townspeople had decided against the old ways of his magic and come with threats of fire. They sought to burn his book as they had burned Olaf's music. He had held the men at bay with his strong eye and his own threats to reveal their former business with him if they pursued the matter further.

Pulling the book from his sleeve to his lap, he stroked it. Thumbing to the back of the book, he reviewed his script. The title of the section was "The Truth of All Things." His script had started clear and strong, but over the years had become shaky. He was becoming old and wished he had someone to pass the book to. He thought again of his younger self.

Back then, he didn't fear. At that time, long ago, his future self had said he would live through the night, which brought him comfort and courage.

As usual, his future self told him the truth, and his life had been long. But menace had grown in the world, and in this century, especially. And he was getting old in so many ways. His mind wandered.

This time, when he groped for his future self to seek help, when he called to view the wisdom beyond the night of the event that was coming again, no one was there. His future self was gone.

2

STALKED

The red eye of water sprayed violent streams about Crystal and sucked her toward its center with leaden weight. A voice, far off and plaintive, cried to her. Leathery hands of ghost boys dragged at her ankles, pulling her toward the mouth of a huge white horse. The water became tears, which turned into golden butterflies and buzzed around her head. She slapped at them, and little bells tinkled as they shattered. Her violin bobbed in the center of the pool. A black snake tongue reached out, licked it, wrapped about it, and sucked it down.

Crystal thrashed in her sleep and pulled her sheet over her head. Her breathing was shallow, but the agony of losing her instrument ran deep. Her eyes came apart and, glazed, took in the time on her clock. 3:13.

She lay for a minute more, letting the images subside, then allowed a ripping grief to move upward from her belly to her throat. For the first time since she'd returned home, she allowed herself to mourn the loss of her instrument. Recalling her mother's face—stricken and white — when she told her of "accidentally" dropping her violin and breaking it, moved a larger ball of tears behind her eyes. Lying to her mother came hard, but she believed revealing what had happened at camp would serve no good purpose. Outside of her family, who would believe her? Her father would want to sue. But she couldn't prove any of it had really happened and attorneys would cost money.

Tonight she grieved, wondering how she could ever replace the instrument. Thinking back over what had happened, she focused on Glenn, the young man with the violet eyes and dark, curly hair. Her emotions shifted from grief to an intense yearning. Never had she felt this way about anyone. Despite their physical differences, she felt they *belonged* together. If she never moved again, if he took her in his arms and they turned to stone, she would die the happiest person on earth. But he had disappeared. Like Elinor.

Strange. Both of them, gone. Vanished. And she had felt a kindred to Elinor as well. At least she had Elinor's email address to try to contact her. But Glenn. All she had was an accent and, thanks to the rude girl in Elinor's cabin, his last name. Wheeze. Or had she said "Wheats"? Strange enough, but she could search for him on the internet. Maybe she could find him on Facebook.

Stepping into her slippers, she tiptoed into the kitchen and nuked some water for a cup of tea. Picking through the tea boxes, she selected a smooth mint that seemed soothing and might help her to sleep. While she waited for the water, she peeked out at the moon. Already the full was past and it looked like a ball half-deflated. That's what she felt like, as well.

She'd never noticed before, until her aunt pointed it out, that her moods coincided with the moon. She hadn't wanted to think of herself as tied to anything other than herself and God, but she guessed that a person's body could be influenced by outside sources. After what happened with the *Näcken*, she was surprised she'd ever doubted it. But what was the *Näcken*, really? Was it a being or an energy? And *how* had it controlled her?

The microwave dinged. She took her tea back to her room to sip. Turning on the computer, she typed in Elinor's email address and started a letter to her. Two paragraphs in, she looked at what she'd written. It wouldn't do to tell Elinor in an email of the events with Olaf Widmark. She erased her text and typed:

ELINOR. WHAT HAPPENED TO YOU AT CAMP?
YOU DISAPPEARED. PLEASE CONTACT ME ASAP.
IT'S IMPORTANT. CRIS.

After thinking about it, she added her phone number. She really wanted to talk, not email.

She finished her tea and climbed back into bed. She held an image of Glenn's face in her mind and her heart bloomed into a blissful sleep.

The next morning, Crystal climbed aboard her bike and took off across the front lawn. Aunt Sarah was coming over later, and Crystal was hoping to have an excuse not to be around. Even though Sarah had saved her, Crystal needed to recover her equilibrium; she didn't want to have to think about what she'd experienced, or the magic her family seemed to have. She was still uncomfortable with the idea of asking her mother about their family, as Sarah had suggested.

The incident with Olaf, the ghost boy, and the intense music was fading into a dream. Maybe someday she'd want to know her family history and how she tied into her ancestors, but not yet. She'd changed her mind. Right now, she wanted life to go back the way it had been, so she could deal with normal problems. Like getting a job.

There were few jobs to be had in their small town, that was for sure. Even if she managed to beat out the other recent graduates and land a job at one of the restaurants in town, or even the movie house, the eight dollars an hour would barely pay her gas to get to and from work. Much less give her any extra to put toward a new violin.

As usual, Tish looked fantastic when she arrived, and they took off on their bikes for the mall. Once inside, they shopped around the stores, never intending to buy. It was just for fun. Then Tish headed toward the food court and Crystal tailed behind her, watching her friend's tall form swish through the crowd like a queen.

Her attention went back to Glenn, as she thought how good Tish would look with him — both of them tall and regal. A sudden jolt of jealously danced over her heart and she shot beads of anger at Tish. Realizing what she'd done, she grinned to herself.

"What's funny, girl?" Tish turned to look at her. "And what you doing back there? Get up here where we can talk."

"I just can't quit thinking about Glenn," she said as she moved forward. Her shoe rubber caught on the floor and squeaked as she tripped.

"Well, I can't quit thinking about Jason, either. These men. They make me so mad."

"I wouldn't call them men, though I guess Glenn is. Glenn. Glenn."

Tish laughed. "You just like saying his name. Too bad you didn't get his number or email. I'm not even sure I should believe he exists."

Crystal looked stricken. "What? You think I would lie to you?"

"No, I'm not saying that. I'm just saying that you've been maybe a teeny bit jealous since Jason and I got together."

"I'm not jealous. And you're not together."

"I meant, in my mind." Tish laughed again. "Hey, let's get an Orange Julius."

"Oh, I can't. I've gotta save for . . ." Crystal trailed off. She hadn't told Tish about her fiddle. It would lead to too many questions.

"For what? Hey — look. Quick. Let's get in line." Tish jumped ahead to hold a place, then turned to Crystal as she caught up. She tightened her lips and talked between them as though she were a ventriloquist. "Don't look now, but somebody's watching you."

Crystal swung her head around. "Me? Where?"

Tish's nails dug into her arm. "I said *don't* look. There's a pillar off to your right, behind the pizza place. There's some pale guy with a face like a manikin. He keeps watching you."

Crystal pretended to drop an item and looked up. Just moving out of sight around a corner, was the back of a someone wearing a black trench coat. He glided on feet that barely seemed to touch the floor.

She laughed. "Very funny, Tish."

"I'm not kidding, girlfriend. I saw him before when we were looking at purses. I thought he was suspicious, and then he followed us and was there when we got out of Victoria's Secret. And here he is again."

The grin slid off Crystal's face as her solar plexus constricted. Having been captured and forced to play for the *Näcken* had been traumatic enough. She was ultra sensitive to threats.

Tish looked around. "Is he still there?"

"No, he skedaddled."

"Did you get a look at him? Do you know him?"

"I didn't see his face. And no, I don't know anyone who would be traipsing around on a day this warm in a black coat. Do you?"

Tish's hand went to her hip. "You're right. That is odd, isn't it?"

The girls ordered their drinks. They sat at a bistro table and watched the crowd as they sipped.

"Who do you think it is?" asked Tish.

"Honestly, I don't have any idea. I can't think he was really following me. I mean, why would he? I'm a no-body."

"You are not a nobody," Tish admonished. "How dare you talk about you like that?"

"I didn't mean it that way. I just meant, I'm nobody special to attract a man in black."

"Do you think it was?"

"Was what?"

"A man in black? You know, like *Men in Black*?" Tish's cheeks stretched with good humor. "*Ooh.* Maybe you're not really Cris at all. Maybe you got turned into an alien in that fiddle camp and they're coming to get you."

"Ho ho ho. Very funny." But Crystal didn't think it was funny. After her camp experience, she did feel a little like an alien. Despite trying to force herself back to normal, an internal awareness had shifted and would not let her enjoy the old innocence.

Her mother was chopping lettuce when Crystal returned home that afternoon. Crystal said "hello" and headed toward her room

"Company for dinner," her mother called back.

"Who?" asked Crystal.

"Your Aunt Sarah."

"I thought she was coming earlier."

Her mother raised a brow. "Is that why you got back so late?"

Crystal didn't answer. *Cheesits.* Her stomach twisted a little. Aside from listening to her aunt cackle all through dinner, she fully expected Sarah to stare at her with knowing eyes and prompt her to open a conversation with her mother. Sarah had left a message on her cell phone once, urging her to do just that. Crystal hadn't returned the call.

Oh well. At least it was just salad and toast, so she could eat fast and get out. She could tell her mother she had to practice. Remembering her fiddle's fate, she groaned. That wouldn't work. She'd need a different excuse.

She still couldn't believe her fiddle was gone forever. She needed a plan to get a new one. But, no job. No money for college. And, though she had earned high grades, the only scholarship for which she was eligible demanded that she pay her own room. The logistics were beyond her. She'd toyed with the idea of attending a tryout in New York for one of the Broadway musicals. She didn't enjoy orchestra music—she was best at improvisation and playing from the heart—but she would have done it for work, if she could pass their stringent tests. Now, however, with her fiddle shattered into a million pieces in the Appalachians . . .

Her mother's voice carried down the hall. "Cris *please*. I need your help."

Crystal returned to the kitchen to set the table.

The doorbell rang and Crystal crossed the living room to open the door. As she neared, it opened on its own, as her aunt stepped inside. She wiped her feet on the entry rug, calling "Helloooo?"

"Hi, Aunt Sarah. Mom's in the kitchen," said Crystal, who moved to close the door all the way.

"Hi, dearie," said her aunt to her back as Crystal stood staring outside.

A black van idled across the street. The windows were tinted and Crystal had the feeling someone was looking at her. Strange. She knew everyone on the block, and no one had a black van. It revved and pulled away from the curb. Stepping onto the porch, she watched as it motored to the stop sign at the end of the street and sat there for several seconds. Involuntarily, her legs carried her down to the sidewalk. She watched the van signal and turn right.

Her stomach tightened, and Crystal placed a hand over it. She stepped back and bumped directly into Sarah. "Oh, sorry!"

"What was that?" asked Sarah.

"Don't know. Probably the wrong house."

But Sarah looked at her with those wise eyes that Crystal remembered from their time in the forest. She didn't want to see her aunt's eyes, just then. "Let's go eat," she said lightly, and tripped up the steps to the house.

Her aunt caught up to her and gripped her arm. "Are you being stalked?" she asked, without a note of humor in her voice.

"Of course not!" Crystal wrenched her arm free. "Don't worry, Aunt Sarah." She strode toward the kitchen, fighting down hysteria. This couldn't be happening. She was a normal girl living in a suburb in Zanesville, Ohio. Situations like this didn't happen in their town. Especially not to her.

Her aunt entered the room behind her, wearing a small frown.

"Hi, Emma," Sarah said to her sister's back then turned her gaze to Crystal.

Emma turned around. "Hi, Sis. Ready for dinner?"

Crystal busied herself with napkins. She watched out of the corner of her eye as her mother became aware of Sarah staring at her with intensity. Crystal put the salad on the table.

The sisters looked at each other, and a silent message seemed to pass between them.

"Oh, no," her mother said softly.

Sarah didn't answer, but she returned to staring at Crystal.

Crystal stopped her activity and looked from her mother to her aunt. Both stood completely still, focused on her, unblinking. Heat ran up her spine and the back of her neck pulled taut. Under their gazes, she began to tremble. *Why couldn't they just leave her alone?*

Her mother stepped forward and Crystal saw a power in her eyes she'd never seen before. Instead of the distant and two-dimensional person Crystal considered her mother to be—the clerk, the gardener, the woman who made their dinner—Crystal saw someone who knew more than she revealed and who had depths Crystal had never wanted to see before.

"We need to talk," Emma said in a commanding tone. Aunt Sarah nodded.

Crystal paused. A wisecrack might deter them, but nothing glib would come. Why was she so dreading this conversation? The bridge of her nose pushed up, and tears burned her eyes. *Please don't let things change.*

Her aunt and mother took her into the living room, where she sat on the brocade chair that had belonged to her grandmother. She felt guilty, as though she had been hiding a terrible secret.

Emma had just seated herself next to Crystal, when her father came in the back door and called out "Anybody home? I don't smell any cooking!"

"In here, Richard," said her mother.

Her father entered smiling, looked at the group gathered on the couch and chairs, and then his face went serious. "Oh. It's time?"

"I'm afraid so," said her mother.

"Yes. Past time," said her aunt. "They've been following her."

Shock moved Crystal's mouth into an *o*.

How did her aunt know that? And who were "they"?

"Who is? Aunt Sarah. What do you mean?" Perhaps a few more minutes of innocence would turn back the hands of time. Perhaps she could go back to being seventeen. Perhaps even sixteen. Anything but eighteen—an adult—who was destined to—*what*?

Forces that had been pressing at her these past weeks formed in the air, a nebulous shape of sounds and lights. A *knowingness* that was deeply a part of her. Her aunt and mother watched her, then turned to her father.

"Richard," said her mother. "This is just for us gals." Her voice was soft and gentle, and Crystal watched in amazement as her father turned eyes of complete love and devotion to his wife.

"Yes, my queen," he said.

Crystal would have laughed aloud, if everyone weren't being so serious. *Yes* MY QUEEN? Was he messing with her? Who were these people? Maybe they, not she, had been turned into aliens while she was at camp.

Her father looked at Crystal, compassion in his eyes, and left the room.

"It's time we told you about the family," said her mother.

"About who you are." said her aunt, nodding.

Crystal's mouth tightened. As much as she craved answers, she wanted to scream. Pressure shot to her head as the room spun in a haze of gray. Her stomach turned the same way as when her aunt had tried to foist Tarot card readings on her.

"Emma, I told her a little family history on our way back from camp," said Sarah. "And you should know . . ." Sarah cast a guilty glance at Crystal. "Olaf was there."

"*Olaf*? Why didn't you tell me?" Emma's voice cracked as she fought to keep from raising it. "How could you put her at risk that way?"

Sarah fidgeted. "I didn't know he would be there. And I thought this was between you and Crystal. I promised I wouldn't be the one to tell." She flushed.

So her mother knew Olaf, too? A strong need to understand overcame Crystal, at the same time her emotions warred against hearing any more. The entire fabric of her life to this point was shredding like old stockings. Her family kept secrets—from *her*. Secrets that had put her in danger.

"Wait! What do you mean somebody is stalking me? Who would be doing that?" Crystal held out her hands. How could they be sure the people in the van were watching *her*? Maybe they were all just paranoid. Who were these people? They certainly didn't seem like the family she'd known a month ago.

"Oh, honey," her mother's voice was soft, sympathetic. "It's a long story."

"Yeah," said Sarah. "They're black ops." She nodded emphatically.

"*Shhh!*" Emma nearly spat the hush.

Crystal's eyes widened. *Black ops?* She'd heard the term on television. On some spy show. What kind of craziness was this? First Olaf—now black ops? What was going on?

"Mom?" Crystal fell silent, her lips parted as her breath came fast and shallow.

Her mother ran a hand across her forehead then placed it on her daughter's knee. "Cris, now I don't want you to worry, but what your aunt says is true. Our family has been in hiding for various reasons, and you need to know about it."

"Don't worry?" Crystal stood up. "You've got to be kidding me! Mom . . . they're *stalking* me? And we're *in hiding*? And you say 'don't worry'?"

"It's—Cris. It's about you . . ."

Crystal's father called from the kitchen. "Emma! There is some company at the back door!' His voice sounded strained.

Her mother and Aunt Sarah locked eyes.

"I'd better go talk to them," her mother said. "Stay here," she said to Crystal, and left the room.

Crystal looked at her aunt's serious face and giggled. Could it get any weirder? After a couple of minutes, when her mother didn't return, Aunt Sarah went to join her.

Holding up her hands, Crystal shrugged, slipped down the hallway, and peeked around the corner of the doorway. The backs of her aunt and mother were visible, and she could see a slight woman's figure dressed in a black dress with a high collar through the back screen. Another figure stood to the side, not quite discernible.

Even though her mother was speaking softly, Crystal could sense the tension in her voice as she said "You have no right to come to my home. Olaf can come himself. If he wants Crystal, he'll have to deal with me."

She tried to hear what the woman responded, but couldn't. She slipped back into the living room before her aunt or mother noticed her.

What did her mother mean, if Olaf wanted her he'd have to deal with her? Was she for sale? Was this more of the madness like the "queen" episode, and the black ops? *Was her mother planning on giving her to Olaf?*

Panic slapped her into motion. There was *no way* she was going anywhere with him.

Leaving by the front door, she checked and saw no van, so she strode briskly down the steps and toward the end of the street.

An uncommon anger overtook her as she walked. If the family information was so important, why couldn't her mother have put off the company? She stomped up the street. Could she even trust her mother? What had her mother's words meant? *"He'll have to deal with me . . ."*?

Crystal's anger blended with true terror — a shock and horror that landed on her back.

Echoing down the street, her mother's voice called to her, but she kept her face forward, then began to run. A car motor slowed behind her — she was in the center of the street. She veered and kept running until she reached a field between houses on the cul-de-sac.

Her nose stuffed up and tears streamed down her cheeks. She hated this. Hated what was happening to her. And hated her mother — and her aunt — and her father for calling her mother "queen." She needed air, space, freedom from her family.

Setting off through the field, her internal compass set to Tish's place. *Her* family was normal. And Tish would understand. Crystal would tell her everything she'd been holding back so Tish would understand what she'd been going through. Tish would let her spend the night. She was eighteen, after all. She no longer had to ask permission.

She bludgeoned between the bushes growing wild in the field and entered the brief expanse of forest on the other side. Trails crisscrossed between the trees; this was a popular place for dog walking. She'd take the left trail to the next street over, then cut through the neighborhood to Tish's place.

As she walked, she calmed, but embarrassment held out a bony finger. An image of herself throwing a tantrum and running away from her mother assailed her. Wrestling it down, she said aloud, "I don't care." Anger rode her like a clutching monkey.

Seating herself on a granite rock under a fir, she rubbed a scratch on her arm. They had no right to be violating her reality this way. It was her world. She'd been good her entire life. Why were they doing this to her?

A crunch on the trail behind her made her tense; if someone was walking a dog they'd see that she'd been crying and she'd feel a need to explain. Sometimes she hated trying to be polite. She used the back of her arm to wipe her eyes.

"Crystal," came a raspy voice.

She flipped around to see an old man in a cape. He looked very familiar. In fact, she'd never forget his face as long as she lived, in this or any other life. Olaf Widmark.

Without hesitation, she screamed.

3

LIES

"Crystal! Stop that!" The old man's voice held disdain but carried power nonetheless.

Shocked by his tone, as though he'd thrown cold water on her, she first went silent, then made a grueling sound in her throat.

"You keep away from me!" she voiced in a guttural pitch. Her feet splayed out and she prepared to rise.

"Crystal. Stop. We must talk."

"No! I'm not talking to you. You kidnapped me!" She stood, stepped back and looked around for a rock to hit him with.

Someone called out their door, "You kids shut up out there!"

"Can a great-grandfather kidnap his own great-granddaughter?" he said calmly, his hands raised toward her, palms up.

Crystal stared. "Wha — what do you mean? You're not my great-grandfather!"

"I am your mother's grandfather. Olaf Widmark."

"My mother's maiden name is not *Widmark*. It's *Angstrom*."

Olaf sighed and looked into the forest. "So, that is what she told you, eh? That is how she runs away."

"Well I don't blame her. You probably chained her up, too!" Even as the words were out, Crystal sensed she was missing the mark. Her words rang untrue, even to her. With the behavior of her mother earlier that evening, could she have been lying this whole time—Crystal's whole life—about who she really was? And Olaf—to be her great-grandfather he would need to be at least eighty. Well, he did look at least that. Or more.

"That was for your protection. So you would not fall in."

"Fall in? What do you mean?" She spotted a rock near her shoe and picked it up. It was small, but it might give her fist enough strength if she had to fight him off. Like brass knuckles. "Fall in what?"

"The *Näcken* would have had you, as he had the boy so many years ago. And as he had others in my country before that. And, as he would have had me."

"I don't know what you mean," Crystal blurted. It seemed she had split in two. Part of her knew he told the truth, and she could not deny it. The other part truly believed that if she could deny it hard enough, it would become a lie.

She dropped the rock, spun, and began running through the trees. She heard no one following her. Glancing back, she saw the old man standing calmly, watching her. He shook his head.

She slowed and turned. He still didn't come toward her. He must have been with those people who came to the house, seen her run off, and followed her.

She wouldn't believe him, he was crazy. They all were crazy. They were making *her* crazy.

The *Näcken*. What did he mean by that? That was the word he had used when she played. That was the word the voices in her head kept using. *What was the Näcken really?* Dare she ask him? Could she go back?

No! What would Tish do? *Run!*

She ran until she was on the next street over. Then she ran, her lungs aching, until she reached the end of Tish's street. Then she sat on the lawn at the house next to Tish's while twilight crept across the sky. Adrenalin rushed through her body like sixty-fourth notes. But in the midst of it, a calm place warned her. *You must learn this*, it said.

There seemed to be forces inside and outside compelling her. She breathed, feeling as though she were playing a game she already knew the result of and was just pretending she didn't know.

Her panting abated, she stood and stared up the street. Why hadn't he followed her? She was scared, yeah, but what was he trying to tell her? *Cheesits!* Unsure what to do, she made a decision toward what Aunt Sarah would do, and confront him. Though her legs felt wooden, she headed back up the street and into the patch of trees, hoping to find the old man again. She would demand answers.

But when she got back, he was gone.

Crystal returned home and sneaked in the back door. Once in her room, she crawled into her bed and pulled the covers over her head. In this one spot, she felt safe, as long as no one entered her room.

Once, she had seen a teenage slice 'em-dice 'em movie about the parents and everyone in the town turning into aliens. She felt that way now. She had nowhere to go, no one to turn to, and the people who had raised her and loved her all of her life had undergone some sort of personality shift. Her mother — she'd always wondered at the meek persona and wished her mother had more of a backbone — suddenly she was a commanding *queen*. And her father — always the stable, nice guy with a level head. Suddenly he was a fawning pawn to her mother. And her aunt — well, she had always been peculiar, so no change there.

But Crystal had changed, too. She didn't dare spill her guts to Tish. Tish was into science and had long outgrown pretending or imagining. Would Tish even believe her? To Crystal, the events on the mountain at camp, the passionate playing to the *Näcken*, that part, at least, had been real. It couldn't have been just in her mind. Could it? The sounds had been all around them. The colors. Sound could do that — penetrate realities. Couldn't it? Vibrations. Weren't they used scientifically? Just because a thing was not built of matter did not mean it wasn't real. There was energy. Vibrations. Tones. Even love. Maybe Tish *would* believe her. Was it worth risking their friendship to find out?

Suddenly angry with herself, she thought of Glenn. Why hadn't she thought to ask Olaf what had become of him? How would she ever find him? Should she have called the police when she got back from camp? She'd seen him leave with Olaf, and it seemed willingly. But had he gotten away all right? It seemed erratic, irrational, but she wondered if she found him, if perhaps somehow she could find safety with him.

She glanced at the twilit sky outside her bedroom window. It was late enough that her parents might be in bed. Or maybe they were waiting up for her. She listened, and hearing no one moving in the house, she crawled from her bed and went to her computer.

Turning the sound down so no one would know she was home, she logged on. If she looked up all the states where people lived who might have an accent like his, and did internet searches, she might find him. She didn't have the money for *People Finders*, but with luck she might find a Facebook photo and track him that way. She opened Google and typed "Glenn Wh—" when an icon in the corner of her screen flashed. She had a new mail.

A message from ElinorJ@horsespals.com popped open and Crystal scooted forward.

> HI CRIS! OMG, SO GOOD U WROTE! I COULDN'T REMEMBER YOUR ADDRESS. SORRY FOR TAKING OFF WITHOUT TELLING YOU. LOOOONG STORY. NEED TO TALK. I TRIED CALLING EARLIER, BUT YOUR MOM SAID YOU WERE OUT. CALL ME!
> ELINOR

She'd left her number under her signature.

Crystal rushed to the handset by her bed. She lifted it up, but changed her mind. If her parents happened to look at the living room phone, they'd see a light, know she was using it and was back. She wasn't ready to get into it with them.

Remembering her cell, she began a quiet search for the charge cord. She found the charger in her closet still in the box. How long did it take these to charge? Last time it had run out. Plugging the charger and phone into an outlet under her window, she lay on the floor between her bed and the wall, where she couldn't be seen if someone entered the room, and punched the *on* button. The phone lit up and told her she had twenty-seven minutes of phone time remaining. "Yes!" she whispered.

Elinor answered her cell on the second ring. They greeted each other, with Crystal speaking in hushed tones.

"Why are you whispering?" asked Elinor.

"Ellie, there is some stuff going on—I'm hiding in my room. I need to talk, but I don't want my mom and dad to hear."

"Me too! You wouldn't believe what happened to me. How are we going to get together? Do you drive?"

Crystal knew that Elinor lived in Granville, at least an hour from her house. "I don't have a car. Maybe I could hitch."

"Oh, no. Don't do that. It's too dangerous."

"Nothing could be worse than what's going on."

Elinor was silent for a moment. "Don't you have some sort of train or bus out there?"

Crystal remembered that there was a shuttle that went to the airport in town. It would cost about fifteen dollars — which would just about clean out her kitty from her last babysitting job.

"Can you pick me up at the Columbus airport?"

Elinor agreed and they planned. They also agreed to erase the emails so anyone snooping wouldn't know where she was.

Crystal hung up, feeling sorrowful and scared. Her neck tensed with feelings about leaving her mother and father in a state of worry. But she was eighteen, right? She didn't have to tell them where she was going. Still, in her mind she was sneaking out in the middle of the night and violating the trust that bound her family together. She was *running away from home.*

4

TRUTHS

Crystal bounced on the seat in the rear of the shuttle. Her book bag, containing a change of underwear, pajamas, her makeup kit, and purse was tucked under her arm. She wished she'd brought *Split River* to read, but she had to content herself with watching traffic lights out the window.

As she neared the airport, she wondered what her parents would do when they discovered that she had not returned the night before. Or maybe they'd figure out she'd come back since her purse would be missing. Her heart hurt from worrying about frightening them, but she needed to get away from them. She needed to talk to someone who was not them, *about* them. She consoled herself with deciding that she'd explain it all later, and because they loved her they'd understand. Then she could finish the conversation with her mother.

The reflection in the glass partially obscured a vehicle driving in the blind spot of the shuttle. In her haze, it took a few seconds for the thought to penetrate. The van was black with tinted windows. Crystal pushed closer to the window to try and see through the tint but could not see anyone. She could, however, see the front license plate. Washington DC. Curious. Why would anyone from DC be in their podunk town?

A chill ran through her. She'd assumed the van on her street had belonged to Olaf. And maybe it did. Was he still following her? With his accent, she had trouble believing he'd be from Washington DC, though. And her aunt had stated the *black ops* were following her. What the heck?

Deciding it was a coincidence—there had to be millions of black vans in the world—she turned her attention to the airport, looming ahead of the shuttle. She couldn't wait to see Elinor and tell her the rest of the story about the ghost boy, her kidnapping, and the strange events since.

When Elinor pulled up in a red BMW Z4 roadster, Crystal broke into a wide grin. The girl's spindly shape was dressed in steam punk; the spiffy car was incongruous and reeked of money. She popped out of the car and hugged Crystal.

"Sorry—I hope I'm not late," she said.

"Not at all. We just got in." Crystal admired the little car. "Is this yours?"

"Oh. My father. He's always travelling around and he tries to make it up with nice gifts. He really doesn't know who I am, though."

"I think he knows who *I* am," Crystal laughed. "What would you rather have?"

"A truck, I think. A small one, you know, so I don't pollute. But I like trucks. Then I could tow my horse."

"You have a horse?"

"Oh, yeah. Wait'll you see him."

They put the book bag in the trunk and got in the car. Elinor revved and peeled out like a pro.

"You sure don't drive like this isn't your car."

Elinor chuckled. "Do you want to go to an all-nighter and talk before we go home? I don't want my family to overhear us," she said.

"That sounds super."

They pulled into the parking lot of an all-night chain restaurant, to Crystal's dismay. But, she guessed the rot gut coffee could suffice. They weren't there to eat, anyway.

After the waitress had seated them and taken their orders, Crystal turned to Elinor with wide eyes. "Tell me now; I can't stand it anymore. Where did you go?"

Elinor turned somber, brushed aside some strands of overly long bangs, and said, "Please don't think I'm lying. I haven't even told my mother about this as I don't think she'd believe me. But look." So saying, she reached down and pulled up her pant leg, then pulled her sock down over her ankle. A red and purple bruise, rimmed in yellow, surrounded the tender skin.

"Whoa!" Crystal said. She pulled down her own sock and showed Elinor her own ankle. Bent over with their legs sticking out of the booth, they both looked up at each other wide eyed. The waitress moved within range and stood off to the side looking at the girls' legs.

They quietly pulled up their socks as the waitress rolled her eyes and set the coffee on the table.

"The old man?" asked Elinor.

"Yes. You, too?"

Elinor nodded.

"But how did you get away? My aunt showed up and got me out."

"I played for a while and he got mad and said 'You are not worthy!' I could barely understand him with his accent. Then he unlocked me and took me to my car. Wanda was standing there next to my luggage—they'd already packed up my stuff! I was afraid to say one word. I just left. I was terrified! I'm sorry, but I didn't even think of getting ahold of you."

"Similar with me. Except my aunt showed up and they talked in some language—Swedish I think—and he let me go. Oh, but that was after I broke my fiddle."

Elinor's fist hit the table. Their coffees bounced and sloshed. "What! Your fiddle broke?"

"No, I threw it at the waterfall and killed it." Crystal's face crunched together as she tried to joke through fighting tears.

"That's so horrible! I'm so sorry."

Elinor seemed to instinctively understand what losing the fiddle meant to her.

Crystal shifted. "That playing—did anything strange happen to you?"

Elinor was silent as she thought. "There was a period I felt connected . . . or I had some kind of energy . . . but then it was just me out there playing for some pervert," she said.

Now it was Crystal's turn to be quiet.

"Why? What happened to you?" Elinor asked.

Crystal did her best to relate the experience, her aunt showing up, and the strange events of her family since she returned home.

"I've pretty much run away," she said, and could not prevent grief from shadowing her voice.

"Well I don't blame you. I'd be freaked if my family suddenly changed like that. Did Olaf really say he was your great-grandfather?"

"Yes—but he couldn't be. Plus, he's way too old. He'd have to be a great-great-grandfather, I think."

Elinor stirred a cream packet into her coffee. "So when did all this start?"

Crystal thought about it for a minute. "I think the

night I was chased by a big head." She regretted telling, the second she said it.

Elinor looked up sharply, her face breaking into a grin. "A big head?"

Crystal protested. "When you put it that way, it sounds stupid." She wanted to change the subject.

Elinor laughed. "Did it chase you around your house, or what?"

"No, outside. Down the street."

"You're serious, aren't you." Elinor's smile dropped, and she was silent for a moment.

"So did it just hurtle through the sky like a cannon ball, or what?"

"No, it was stretched out . . . elongated and distorted. Really huge. Like as big as a house. And there was black energy wiggling all around it."

"Uh, huh." Elinor stared at her.

Crystal's embarrassment grew.

Then Elinor asked, "Was it a friendly big head?"

Crystal laughed. "Yes, sort of. It looked just like my friend, Tish."

Elinor tapped her spoon against her cup then looked up and yawned. "Well now what? Where do we go from here?"

"I'm not sure. Can I stay at your place tonight? I really have nowhere to go and I can't take the thought of seeing my family right now. "

"Oh, of course. That's a given. I already told my mother I was having company."

Crystal looked around. "Doesn't she mind you being out so late?"

Elinor looked at the table and ran her finger through some initials someone had carved in the top. "No. She doesn't," she said simply, which told Crystal all she needed to know about Elinor's mother.

When they left to get into Elinor's Z4, Crystal noticed a van parked on the far side of the parking lot.

"Elinor—remember that van I told you about?" she whispered.

Elinor looked. "We'd better hurry. I don't know about you, but I'm not in the mood to be tied up again."

The girls took off running and Elinor used the automatic door opener on her keychain to unlock the doors before they reached the car. The van engine had started, but it had not yet pulled away from its parking place.

"Maybe it's a coincidence," said Elinor as they hurried into the car.

"That's what I keep telling myself, but I keep seeing the same van."

"Are you sure it's the same one?"

"Let's get a look at the license plate and I can let you know."

Elinor backed out the car as though they were leaving and drove slowly toward the exit. The van lights came on and it pulled out of the slot. Elinor turned the small car in a quick u-turn and headed straight for the van.

"Elinor!" shouted Crystal. "What are you doing?"

"Getting a look." The roadster shot forward and jarred to a stop nose-to-nose with the van, where Crystal couldn't help but see the plates.

"Yep. Washington DC," she said. "Now let's go!"

"I want to get out and thump his turnip!"

Crystal glanced at her little friend and laughed. Here was someone else she had underestimated. The small, geeky-looking girl was a tiger in disguise! She liked Elinor even better.

"No, let's go," she said. "They might have guns." She nodded toward the two shadowy forms seated in the front behind the glass.

Elinor whipped her car around in a fast three point turn. "At least they know we know."

"Yeah. For whatever good that will do. Do you remember the number? Maybe we can find out who they are . . ."

"No, I was letting you get that." Elinor looked vexed.

"I was just looking to see if it was Washington DC." Crystal pursed her lips. "I wish we had talked before you drove up there," Crystal continued.

Elinor ruffled a bit but kept quiet.

They zipped through the back streets until they caught a main thoroughfare, with no sign of the van. Elinor followed the freeway, looped around, and headed toward Granville.

"They're probably too chicken to follow us," said Elinor as they took an exit.

"Yeah. Thanks for scaring them off." Crystal hoped she hadn't offended her friend.

They pulled into a wooded and moneyed section of the city and Elinor slowed down. She touched a device on her dashboard and a tall, iron railed gate opened before them. The Z4 crept forward over brick inlay toward an elegant stone mansion at the end of the drive.

"You live here?" Crystal was awed.

"Yeah. I don't look the type, do I." Elinor giggled. "It's my way of being a rebel."

Good disguise, thought Crystal.

They entered through a side door which led through a long corridor to a staircase sweeping toward some upper floors. "That's where my mother lives," said Elinor, "and my father when he's home."

"What does he do for a living?" Crystal took in the marble opulence, crown molding, and chandeliers.

"Oh, you know. Father stuff." Elinor was blasé. "I've taken over the east wing. Well, not all of it, but a couple rooms are all mine. Come this way."

She led Crystal past tall mahogany furniture to a door leading down another hallway. Then they entered into a room that seemed as large as Crystal's entire house. At the far end was a king-sized bed and computer system. Scattered throughout the room were Disney characters the size of children. "My friends," Elinor said, grinning.

"Huh. You didn't look like a Disney sort of person."

"Oh, they're my baby toys. I just couldn't part with them. You'll be glad to know I no longer have tea parties with them, though."

Crystal looked askance at her friend. What did she really know about Elinor?

An overstuffed chair and couch were at one end of the room and Elinor told Crystal she could sleep there. "I hope you don't mind; I could give you a spare room, but I thought we might want to talk some more tonight."

Crystal nodded her assent. The huge house was intimidating enough. She'd rather be in her friend's room.

"I'm not going to wake up the maid, but I'll get you some spare blankets," Elinor said, and left the room.

Crystal took the opportunity to peer through one door, which led to a bathroom larger than her bedroom at home, with both a shower and a Jacuzzi tub, and through another door that led to what appeared to be a music room. A stunning gilt mirror gleamed from a floor-to-ceiling inset at the back of the room, reflecting back her astonished face and multitudes of musical paraphernalia.

Elinor came back just as Crystal was peeking in.

"That's not the music room," she said. "That's just my practice space. Sometimes I like to get up in the middle of the night and play."

Crystal nodded, impressed. One wall held cases for several instruments. "These are all your violins?"

"Yes, but my Vincezno is in a locked cabinet in the

music room. I hardly ever get to play it."

"Wow. I mean *wow*. Do you play other instruments as well?"

"Oh, I play a little guitar and piano, of course. Everyone in our family plays piano."

Crystal looked puzzled.

"Oh, my word. You don't know, do you?"

Crystal stared.

"My father's name is Stone, but my mother's last name is Goldberg. You know, of Goldberg pianos? You've heard of them?"

Crystal was too tired to react strongly, but she felt a jolt of envy. What a family to be from! And here she thought she and Elinor had a lot in common.

"Don't get too impressed." Elinor grinned. "I'm really just me, and it's hard to live down the name."

Crystal's eyebrows lifted. She hoped this new information wouldn't change their relationship. Elinor was, after all, the same person. But she'd felt more comfortable thinking the girl was just a talented geek. Maybe her thinking needed adjusting. It really must be hard to have a famous family. She'd never know.

She glanced at the clock. 3:13. They'd been up nearly all night. Snuggling into a comforter, Crystal curled up on the couch in Elinor's massive bedroom, and was instantly asleep.

She awakened to the smell of eggs Benedict and bacon. A maid, dressed in a tea dress and hairnet, had set a tray on a stand next to the couch. She heard the shower running and knew that Elinor was already up. Looking at the clock, it read a few minutes past eleven.

She stretched, thanked the maid, then looked at the tray. It was happening again. An aura of gray surrounded the food, and it smelled like dead organic matter to her. A glass of freshly squeezed orange juice on the tray seemed bathed in a bright and sparkling light. Her body craved the juice—not for the vitamins, but for the *life force* it contained. A quick look at the maid's retreating form revealed a purplish pattern near her lower back and Crystal knew an old injury affected her spine. A bright pattern glowed around her midsection, and light blue that retreated into indigo near her throat. Crystal knew, without knowing how, that the woman had left words unsaid and if she didn't say them, she'd become ill.

After Elinor came out, Crystal took her turn in the shower, but had to put on her same clothes. Elinor invited her to the music room to show her some other instruments.

When they stepped into the hall, they were met by her mother, who was on her way upstairs.

The woman was tall, elegant, and had a perfectly clear aura, surrounded by a tight shield of silver. Crystal couldn't read her at all, but she had the distinct feeling that the woman disliked her on sight.

"Good morning, dearest," she said to Elinor. "And who might this be?"

"'Morning, Mother. This is Crystal. Crystal, my mother."

Crystal raised an eyebrow at Elinor's formal use of her name. Still, she held out her hand. The woman ignored it but nodded and turned to Elinor. "Your father will be arriving this afternoon and I want to be sure you'd be home for dinner. He's bringing someone from the Agency. At half past six."

Elinor's mother glided away.

Quiet type, thought Crystal. *And snooty.*

They visited the music room, which held a Goldberg grand piano, a case containing not only the Vincezno violin, but a more valuable Stradivarius, several guitars, a cello, and some rare violas.

"Do you play viola?" Crystal asked her friend.

"Yes. I actually enjoy it better than violin, but my mother preferred I play violin."

"I'm surprised she let you come to fiddle camp. I mean, it's *fiddle*."

"She'd heard that Olaf Widmark would be there and she wanted him to teach me. I'm not sure, but she might have twisted his arm somehow to get me a chance with him. If she only knew what his methods were!"

"Why didn't you tell her?"

"I'm not sure what she'd do. She'd probably think it was my fault. Already she thinks I'm not good enough and that's why he rejected me."

Crystal looked at the instruments with admiration.

"I don't believe that. I heard you play and I think you're great," Crystal said. "I'm not sure why he liked my playing — and I can't really say he taught me. Other than leaving me by the water until I was so bored I played out of sheer misery." Crystal smiled slightly. "But I'd been having such weird things happen and when I played, it was like I was — I'm not sure how to explain this — but I was *playing the water*. I was *playing the trees and the colors of the world*. Not like imagining them, but somehow reaching into their substance."

"Well, I'm envious. I'd like to be able to play like that."

"I'm not sure it's such a great gift. You feel *everything* that you play. This new ability came with my other birthday 'gifts.' And the alien parents. Maybe you're lucky just to have normal parents."

Elinor's eyebrows lifted. "Normal?" Both girls laughed.

After the tour, Elinor and Crystal drove into town to visit the local music stores and try out instruments. Elinor was especially anxious to go to Waltons, as she had her eye on more than an instrument there.

"His name is Mark," she told Crystal. "I always go in there but I never make a purchase. At least with you there, they might be fooled into thinking I'm legitimate and not just ogling him."

Crystal knew the feeling. If she had even a clue where Glenn was, she'd be all over it—even if it took the rest of her meager baby-sitting money.

As they entered the store, Elinor fixed her attention on a fiddle on the wall near the front of the store. Crystal asked Elinor if she'd met Glenn at the camp.

"No, not really. He was always surrounded—you know what I mean? Plus, I didn't really want to play with him. His music was . . . different. I'm classically trained and his was, I don't know, old world. Different." She took the fiddle and bow down, tightened the bow, and drew it. "Did you hear that?"

"The frog?"

"Yes." She dropped to a whisper. "That's why I don't buy from here."

Crystal nodded.

"Oh, hey. Talking about 'different' music, I have one ticket for a concert tonight at the hall by the university. It's supposed to be Hungarian music. I could get another if you'd like to go."

"I'd really like that—but honestly, I barely made the fare to get here. I'm going to have to call my parents for money to get back."

"Don't worry about it. I get an allowance that I rarely spend. I'd love to treat you. Here, I'm going to call now."

"But I didn't bring a change of clothes . . ."

"It's casual. You're fine. Or you can borrow a dress."

Elinor pulled out her cell, dialed, and ordered the extra ticket.

Crystal watched her and thought about being gone all

night. She felt a sense of remorse realizing her parents would have worried about her all night.

"Elinor," she said, "May I borrow your cell for a minute? I think I'd better call my folks before they send the police looking for me."

"Are you sure you want to?"

Crystal sighed, then nodded. "I think I'd better."

When she called she was surprised to find her mother's voice normal—which was almost creepier than when she didn't sound normal, now that Crystal knew she had some other personality. Her mother seemed relieved that she had called and that she was with a friend. Crystal didn't tell her where she was, but her mother asked her to let them know when she wanted to come home. No pressure. Amazing.

Crystal felt a lot lighter after speaking to her mother—almost as if she were out in the world with her parents' approval. Not that she needed it, she reminded herself again.

She became excited to go to the concert; she'd always wanted to listen to real Gypsy music. She'd tried playing some, but the pieces were too difficult and the cadence all over the place. She had decided she just didn't have the knack for it. Or the soul.

After Elinor had ogled Mark for a sufficient time, they left and journeyed to the waterfront, where they had coffees at an outdoor cafe. Elinor told Crystal she was auditioning for the University of Rochester, and was assured she'd get in, by her mother's generous contributions and her father's standing—whatever that was. But when she asked where Crystal was going to college, Crystal could not hold back the tears.

All day she had felt a part of Elinor's world—carefree, full of possibilities. But now the hard truth came home. She loved music. She was impassioned by music. It was in her soul. It *was* her soul. And she not only didn't have an instrument, she would never, ever be able to afford college—even a community college was out of the question. She'd applied for a part-time clerk job at the local college, and if she got it, she might be able to go to school by adding the money to some grants. Maybe. But not where her music could really excel—like the University of Rochester.

After consoling her friend, Elinor drove them back to the house so they could prepare for dinner. They showered and reapplied their makeup in front of the mirror, giggling at the faces each other made trying to get eyeliner on.

Crystal asked about the company Elinor's father was bringing.

"I don't know—I never know," said Elinor. "And I know better than to ask."

"What do you mean?" Crystal was truly puzzled. Everything about her family was open—well, at least she had thought so until recently.

Elinor assessed her while holding her hand and mascara near her cheek. "I'm not really sure who all these people are. They all seem a bit—unusual. But then, I'm not sure what my father does all day, either."

"What does he say he does?"

"He says he works for his country—whatever that means. Father's work acquaintances are off limits to family discussions."

Visions of a hit man conjured in Crystal's head. After her recent encounter, she didn't need anymore spooky thoughts so she changed the subject to eyeliners.

Elinor explained that when her father was home, they dressed for dinner—not formal, but a cut above regular clothing. Since Crystal had no change of clothes, Elinor asked her mother for a dress to borrow, since Crystal was closer to her mother's size. Her mother indicated one of four closets in her storage dressing room and stated that "some little thing in there should suffice."

Crystal's face pinched with embarrassment. She was really beginning to feel out of place.

After seeing what Elinor was wearing, she selected a simple black silk dress that probably cost more than her parents made in several months. She hoped that Elinor's father would forgive her tennis shoes, as her feet were too large to borrow any pumps.

Elinor grinned when she saw her friend. "You actually have a shape!" Then she saw the Nikes and told Crystal not to worry. She put on some hiking boots and thick socks, so they would look like a couple of punk kids when they entered the dining hall.

Elinor's father was late arriving, so they delayed dinner. Periodically, Elinor poked her head from the library, where they waited, and checked her cell phone for the time. At last, they heard the greetings in the main hall indicating her father's arrival with the guest.

Elinor's mother, already seated at the table, raised her eyebrows and pursed her lips as the punksters entered the dining hall.

"Ellie!" called her father. "Nice to see you."

Elinor strode to where her father was seated at the table head and gave him a perfunctory kiss on the cheek. "Hi, Daddy. Nice you're home." She looked at the visitor, who was seated to his right.

"This is Mr. Aiken, from work."

Elinor acknowledged him, with a rehearsed smile, limpid handshake, and a nod.

The man was dressed in formal attire, sported a closely manicured hair cut, and wore an unreadable, smooth, unremarkable face. His hands were polished and refined, and his voice baritone as he said "Nice to meet you." A nowhere man.

Crystal still stood at the doorway, uncertain of where to sit or how to respond. Elinor's father turned to her. "And who have we here?"

Elinor motioned her in. "Daddy, this is my friend Cris. She's a violinist also."

Her father scanned Crystal , his eyes alighting on her shoes. He looked up and away. Elinor nodded toward a chair for Crystal to seat herself.

A maid entered the room and fluffed a dinner napkin onto Crystal's lap.

"Thanks," she murmured.

She caught the eye of the maid, who acknowledged her with a brief tick of her lip, then proceeded around the table to decant soup into each crystal bowl.

"Another violinist!" said Elinor's father. "We do seem to have a lot of them. Tell me, Cris—is that short for 'Christine?'"

"Crystal."

"I see. Tell me, *Crystal* . . . *er* . . ."

"Carson," said Elinor. "Her last name is Carson."

Her father retrieved a small notebook from his breast pocket and made a point of writing down the name.

Crystal's stomach lurched.

"Tell me, Crystal," he started again. "Where have you studied?"

Crystal's voice cracked into pianissimo. She cleared her throat so that she could be heard. "I — um — haven't — I'm — um — self — "

Elinor jumped in to save her. "Crystal was trained by Olaf Widmark."

A bombshell dropped at the table. Even the maid stopped in her tracks. Crystal caught the cold, gray gaze of Mr. Aiken. The set of his jaw twitched into an ice sculpture.

Then Elinor's father smiled and everyone relaxed. "Well, you must be one talented young lady." He continued to the maid without pausing, "Raynell, would you see that the bread is oven fresh tonight? You know I like it fresh."

Crystal glanced at her friend with gratitude and fear. In the presence of these people, she felt as though she were wrapped in a dirty washrag and sitting on a heap of garbage.

Elinor's eyes begged her to get through dinner and still be her friend.

Crystal faced her soup. It was a light tomato, that glowed with a clear golden tone, with live shrimp. She watched their legs moving and spiking against a pearl onion and parsley. Her vision cleared, and there was tomato soup. Only. *She had seen all the way to the base of the soup and the agony of the dying creatures.* Her stomach thickened with disgust and horror; she knew she could not eat it.

She got past the soup by crumbling some crackers and pretending to sip from a spoon. When the maid came with the next course, she was ready. Some sort of conversation drifted among the adults. It seemed light and friendly, but Crystal realized she was picking up the subtext and innuendoes of those present. Like a TV drama in which she and Elinor were quiet—good girls—and the adults were playing games right before her eyes.

Her salad arrived and Crystal was delighted to see the bright energy emanating from it. It was fresh, had been raised in a garden with love. It had been grown with the purpose of human consumption and it was fulfilling its purpose. It was a *happy* salad. She smiled at her internal thought and munched away.

Elinor's mother and Mr. Aiken were eyeing each other

sexually. As her gaze skirted over the woman, Crystal read that she was accustomed to having affairs and had no moral issue with them. Crystal read Elinor's father. He didn't care what his wife did. He was with her for some reason connected to his work. Their relationship was complex, and Crystal could not read it fully.

She glanced at Mr. Aiken to feel his aura. He looked up, as though he'd felt her touch, and a bolt of energy shot from him, causing her to choke on a lettuce leaf. She coughed, covering her mouth with her napkin. All conversation at the table stopped until her hacking ceased.

"Are you all right, dear?" asked Elinor's mother.

Crystal wiped her eyes. "Yes. I'm sorry."

"No problem, dear. We're all family here." Her face retained the polished veneer of a smile without using her lips. She glanced at her husband and Mr. Aiken. Then at Elinor.

Elinor blanched.

A side door opened and the maid pushed in a cart laden with fare. A smell of death and horror clung to it like a dark honey. As Mr. Aiken's noticed the tray, his aura constricted into an excited whirl of red and silver threads, dancing around. Hungry snakes.

"Mother. I'm sorry, but Crystal and I have tickets for the concert tonight, and I'm afraid we'll be late if we stay all through dinner. May we be excused?"

The woman looked at her daughter—her canine hanging just below her top lip and poking into her bottom lip. A wolfish grin played at the corners of her jaws. She was in control, knew it, and enjoyed it.

Mr. Aiken cleared his throat.

"Oh, all right. You don't mind, do you, dear?" she asked her husband.

"No. We'll see you tomorrow, Elinor." He turned to Crystal. "Good night, Crystal *Carson*."

Crystal's legs felt weak as she pushed back the chair from the table and stood up. Elinor took her by the hand and they hurried down the hall, across the foyer, and out the front door.

"Are you all right?" Elinor asked as they climbed into the car.

Crystal nodded.

"Did you get enough to eat? I'm sorry I pulled you away so quickly."

"Yes—I'm fine." She thought about the idea of eating the rancid mass of dead flesh that Mr. Aiken was preparing to enjoy and almost retched. Would she ever get over this aversion? Maybe she should just tell people she was vegetarian until her stomach decided to be more compliant. She thought of her aunt. Did this problem run in their family? Her aunt was always harping about being vegetarian, and she rarely—if ever—had seen her mother eat meat if her father wasn't there. In fact, now that she thought about it, her mother even made tomato sandwiches, avoiding meats and cheeses for straight vegetables. This could be a physical problem that her family shared. Funny they'd never talked to her about it. They must all be deformed. Or malformed. Eating meat—pieces of dead bodies—was natural. Wasn't it?

5

CONCERT

No one paid any attention to their style of dress as the usher showed Elinor and Crystal to their seats in the concert hall. After the tension at dinner, Crystal was reticent and just looked forward to listening and drifting for the evening. Even if she couldn't play now, she could still enjoy and appreciate the gifts of others.

While Elinor left her seat to visit the ladies room, Crystal admired the grand hall, ornate lighting fixtures, and milling audience. Elinor had traded her third-row ticket to obtain two seats next to each other, even though they were near the back of the auditorium.

Crystal bowed her head slightly at the person next to her and wished the seatmate would not have worn perfume. A quick glance at the woman convinced Crystal that she had a growth in her uterus of which she was unaware. Not sure how she knew this, she wondered if she should broach the topic with her — to give the woman a heads up. Even if the woman thought Crystal was intrusive, she might think about it later and get checked

out. Then again, Crystal had been through enough drama
the past while, and if the woman reacted poorly, it could
ruin the evening. Crystal simply wanted to go into a
dreamy reverie with the orchestra.

She decided to remain quiet, not really trusting this
seeming new ability of hers to read people, anyway. It
probably had to do with a low iron count in her blood, or
some other chemical imbalance. Or maybe it was like the
voices—unexplainable and not quite believable, even to
her.

Looking around the performance hall, she delighted
in the sound and flavor of the attendees. All had come to
experience beauty; no matter their walk of life, they all
had that in common. The sounds of the orchestra tuning
up issued from behind closed curtains.

As Elinor returned, Crystal opened her program, just
as the lights dimmed. The audience quieted and the
curtain parted in glorious yards of velvet to reveal the full
orchestra.

Crystal's heart lifted as the audience began their
applause. The orchestra members rose and began applauding as the conductor made his way across the front
stage. The audience stood, clapping.

Elinor stopped mid clap and stared at Crystal.

Crystal stood wooden, staring at the stage. She
squinted.

"It's not, is it?" asked Elinor.

Crystal's gut was wrenching. He looked so much like
him, but no.

"No, it's just another old man." *Not Olaf.* "But they do
look a lot alike, don't they?"

Elinor nodded and resumed clapping as the girls
watched the conductor accept the applause. Everyone sat.
After the usual coughs and sneezes, the conductor turned
to his orchestra, which sat as they moved bows, horns,

mallets, and hands into position. As the conductor raised his arms, the players struck a chord, and the universe bowed to the beauty of the music.

Crystal closed her eyes and watched the tones dance in color and event. She drifted into a dreamy semi-sleep and connected with a different world, where life was known and pleasurable, and drama existed to heighten sensuous experience.

During the intermission, Crystal took a peek at her pamphlet and read the conductor's name. He was a guest from Hungary, whom she had not heard of before. Marcus Hegadu. She was practicing saying "Hegadu" when Elinor corrected her pronunciation.

"It means 'violin'," said Elinor.

"What? I thought it was his last name."

"It is. Apparently, in Hungary they are named after what they do sometimes. His family must have been violinists or conductors going way back."

"It says here that a 'Bela Weisz' will be performing a solo Gypsy violin. Oh. That sounds wonderful. Thank you so much for bringing me!"

"You're welcome. After what we've been through, we needed some good times. I've heard that Bela isn't much older than us and he's very good. I haven't heard him before either, so this will be a real treat."

The audience murmured to silence as the lighting dimmed to black. Then a flood of undulating dark purples gleamed across the stage. Silhouetted front left, a Gypsy crouched on a barrel holding a fiddle. The conductor turned to him and raised his baton.

The violinist began to play, his silhouette stretching skyward until he stood, still backlit by the stage lights. A slow, lugubrious Hungarian tune flowed from his fiddle like a groan of sorrow.

Crystal closed her eyes and followed the notes

through woods, across deserted plains, and was tossed into the fire pit of passion. Her eyes jerked open as the house lights brightened, then began a kaleidoscopic gyration — tossing prismatic hues all over the seats.

The fiddler leaped from the barrel and ran to the edge of the stage. His black costume, banded hair and spangled fabric mask added to the thrill as he jumped from the stage and ran through the aisles into the audience. The audience applauded wildly and cheered, but the fiddle was miked, so the music continued to fill the hall over the noise with robust yearnings and ancient longings.

He got to within twenty feet of Crystal before he turned and headed back to the stage. She bobbed her head trying to glimpse him between the standing audience members. She stood up, applauding wildly with the rest of the spectators.

Elinor pinched her arm in a fierce grip and looked at her, wild-eyed.

"Did you see? Did you see?"

Crystal was grinning openly, tears streaming down her cheeks.

"Huh? What?" she said, annoyed at Elinor for breaking the spell.

"It's Glenn. It's Glenn!"

Crystal stopped grinning. "What?" She craned her neck to locate the virtuoso, but he had returned to the stage.

Now with the regular lighting, she could see the curls reaching down his neck having escaped the band, the slim, sinewy form, and the elegant hands curled about his instrument.

The conductor gestured to the star, then added his claps to the applause, waiting until it died down. Glenn lifted off his mask, bowed, and strode from the stage. The audience applauded wildly, then reseated themselves with reluctance.

"What are you going to do?" Elinor whispered.

An angry *shhh* whipped the back of her head and Crystal stare silently at the black curtain where he had disappeared. Had she misread the program? She opened it while Bach's *Air* filled the hall with a gentle elegance, a dichotomy to the wild night with the Gypsy. Scanning the pages, she found the reference. Nope. Definitely read "Bela Weisz."

Had Glenn lied to her about his name? He must have. Lied to them all. Except the last name. Unfamiliar with Hungarian, she had been thinking "Wheeze," not "Weisz." She thought about his star quality. No wonder he exuded such strength and confidence. He was a world-class fiddle star! She'd never studied Gypsy or Hungarian fiddle, and didn't follow who was who, so she hadn't guessed.

How odd he would be in the Appalachians for a fiddle camp. Unless he had been there for the same reason as Elinor. Maybe that was why he was reluctant to escape from Olaf. He *wanted* to be trained by the man. No matter what it took.

Still, he had lied to her about his name. Perhaps her feeling that he was a soul mate was all in her head. A soul mate wouldn't lie, would he? She wouldn't. Tears sprang to her eyes. "Excuse me," she whispered and stood.

Elinor let her squeak past, as did the others in the row. She barely registered the glares and expressions of annoyance as their emotions came toward her, deepening her sense of wrongness and loss.

She went to the ladies room and fixed her makeup with some tissue. Looking around the room, she tried to brighten her face. But an internal bell clanged. This was her one chance to find him. Well, maybe not, now that she knew his name. But maybe she could meet with him.

Tonight. She needed to learn the truth. Was their encounter before — the specialness of her feeling for him — all in
her head? Or did he share it, too? And why had he used a
fake name?

She left the room and headed toward the back wings.
She had learned long ago during stage performances of
her own, that if you behave as though you belong, the
guards don't stop you. She put on an aura of belonging
and power and strode to the guard without stopping. She
nodded to him, as though he were doing her a service. *It's
all in the attitude.*

Striding down the hallway to the dressing rooms, she
glanced left and right, hoping to find some indication of
where she was headed.

A young woman pushing a cart of instrument cases
moved down the hall toward her. When she got close,
Crystal asked in a casual, offhand manner, "Have you
seen Bela? I forgot which room he was in." She smiled a
conspiratorial grin.

The girl grinned back. "He got a private one. Eleven-
B."

Crystal heard the thunder of applause even here in
the back stage area. The performance would soon be over.
She hoped the members stayed on stage long enough for
her to find her way.

The door numbers were nowhere near eleven. They
were in the hundreds. Coming to a chart on the wall, she
studied it. *Darn!* She'd need to go over two halls and up
one level. She hoped the girl knew what she was talking
about.

As she climbed the stairs, the orchestra members
flooded from the stage. Crystal was swept up in the drain
of people and caught in the uphill flow.

When she reached the top floor she focused on the
numbers on the doors. A man blocked her way. "Excuse
me," she said to his chest, and stepped to the side. He

stepped the same direction. She laughed a little and looked up.

And fell into those violet eyes. And went down, and down.

They stood for a moment, staring at each other, then a psychic swell enfolded them. His warmth flowed over her like a gentle river, and carried her to places where they were alone, just the two of them, with rocks and trees and unencumbered nature.

In her imagination, she felt herself swept into his arms. Then he turned her to him, and she trembled as they kissed. Not like they had at the camp — slowly, briefly. They kissed like lovers who have known each other for all their lives, for all their lifetimes. They embraced until their skin felt like it melded into one vibrant animal, and still they kissed. They dropped to the sand of a beach on a golden world far away — their embrace feeling like the horizons of the universe.

"It's so good to see you," he said, shattering her reverie. Once again she stood in the hallway. "Would you like to come in and sit down?" Standing a couple feet away from her, looking demure and innocent, he opened the door to the room.

Jolted, Crystal shook off the vision, certain that he had felt it, too. Remembering his "high intuition," she smiled, embarrassed, weak, and completely overcome.

"Thanks." She seated herself on a couch.

"Did you like the performance?"

"It was wonderful, Glenn. Or Bela. What is your name, anyway?"

He chuckled. "Depends who you talk to. My grandfather likes to call me 'Bela.' My mother named me Glenn. You can call me Chuck."

"Chuck?" she said, confused.

"Just a joke." He winked. "Can I get you some

Perrier?"

She nodded and watched as his lithe form moved to a small fridge in the room. When he returned, he sat next to her on the couch, and stared at the floor for a few seconds. Setting the bottle down, he looked up from under long lashes, into her, and took her hand. "You feel it, too, don't you." It wasn't a question. He played with her fingers, feeling them.

She nodded. Then she felt silly. Yet true. They were engaged in something . . . magical. The room moved in a harmonic of their combined energies and a tone, like a celestial orchestra, moved them together.

Part of her was screaming. *Too fast! Stop! Too fast!* But again she felt drained of will. It seemed *right* and time felt short.

Their lips travelled through light-years, across time and space, and met in the middle with a rush of thunder. Yet when they touched it was as light as a spider web — a gentle brushing. As they moved apart on the couch and stared at each other, Crystal still felt connected to him, as though their hearts had become one. As Glenn took her hand, a wash of ancient seas drew them into each other. His eyes lowered to their hands.

"Stop that! Now!" A voice shrieked through their love. Torn from the dimension they had flowed into together, Glenn abruptly released her and Crystal jerked up into a stiffly seated position.

"Girl. You go now! Bela!" The conductor stood before them, his stocky form a mass of gyrating energy to Crystal's eyes. A burn coursed through her, whether from embarrassment or fear, she could not tell.

She looked at Glenn for direction.

"Wait, Grandfather," he said. His voice was like smoke. He walked to a table, picked up a pen and jotted on a small piece of paper. Returning to her, he slipped the paper into her hand. "Call," he whispered.

She turned and walked past the conductor, who stared at her as though she were a pustule. When she reached the door, she turned to see him one last time. He watched her with rapture. His aura was golden. The conductor stood between them, his arms folded.

Closing the door behind her, Crystal felt her body explode into a multitude of emotions: joy, pleasure, fear, desire, grief, loss, radiance. But above all, she *knew*. She had daydreamed of feeling like this, of having this connection with another soul. She was stunned and overjoyed.

He was the one.

He was *the one*.

6

BEHIND THE FLAME

"Thanks for waiting for me," Crystal said as she climbed into the Z4.

"What else was I supposed to do?" Elinor didn't seem miffed. She seemed excited. "So tell me. Did you find him?"

Crystal pushed on her cheeks to wipe the monkey-grin off. "Yes. I am just stunned. I really can't talk about it yet. I'm just so — so —"

"In love?" Elinor beamed at her friend.

"Oh, yeah. Oh. Wow. Yeah."

The girls hugged each other, then Elinor started up the car. "Well, I'm happy for you. I'd so love to be so in love."

Crystal allowed herself to float for a moment, then turned sober. "This won't be easy," she said. "That man — the conductor — is his grandfather. He walked in on us."

"Oh, no!"

"Yeah. And he wasn't happy. But Glenn, or Bela, or whoever he is, gave me his number. So at least we'll get together again. I hope." She became aware that she was still holding the crumpled paper in her hand. She folded it and slipped it into her purse.

They drove in silence, Elinor beaming in the balm of late summer air, and Crystal floating in a dream world with Glenn.

As they pulled into the drive, headlights approached them, so Elinor pulled to the side to let the car pass.

She and Crystal gawked as the black van with the DC plates pulled alongside and stopped. The tinted window whirred as it opened and it was Mr. Aiken's voice that greeted them, "Nice to have met you both. I hope you had a good evening." The window went back up and the van drove on.

Shocked, both girls' mouths opened as they stared at each other.

Agitated, Elinor paced the floor of her room. "I swear I've never met him before. I can only think that my father is having me followed."

Crystal was seated cross-legged on the floor. She'd removed the borrowed dress and slipped into her jammies. "Why was he in *my* neighborhood, though? You weren't even there."

"I don't know. Unless my father somehow found out you were my friend and put him onto you." She fisted her hands and turned full toward Crystal. "I am so pissed off! How *dare* he? I am seventeen. I'm almost an adult. He has no business having me followed. No wonder I don't have any friends. My parents are too frigging nuts!"

Crystal felt a twinge of compassion for Elinor. She guessed that money didn't really change problems that much. She had the same complaints about her own family.

"Well, let's not worry about it. In fact, if we see the van again, now we can just wave and say 'Howdy do!'"

Elinor's mouth relaxed and she seemed to calm. "Well, it is better knowing who it is. But I'm going to ask my father why I'm being followed. And you. That's so unfair to spook you like that."

Crystal agreed, but didn't say it aloud. On the up side, it meant her mother and aunt were wrong. The van wasn't black ops or after her. She'd be glad to tell them.

"Anyway, Elinor, I had a wonderful, wonderful night and I'm so grateful you took me to the concert. But I do have a question . . ." Crystal trailed off.

"What's that?" Elinor paused in her pacing.

"Can we sneak down and raid the kitchen? I'm starving!"

Elinor laughed her agreement, and the girls planned their raid.

Later, Crystal lay in bed with a shaft of moon streaking across the room, feeling excitement and contentedness. She listened to the cat-purr breathing of her friend — her *sister* — and knew her life would be better now. She'd turned a corner.

After breakfast, Elinor took Crystal to the practice room and let her pick out a fiddle. They tuned up, and Crystal was surprised to see that Elinor didn't use a tuner. "How do you do that?" she asked.

"I have perfect pitch."

"That's amazing."

"It's a bit of a curse. For example, in that orchestra we listened to last night, I could hear the sixth fiddle was slightly flat in almost all of his intonations. It was driving me batty." She scowled.

Crystal ran some scales to warm up and noticed the loss of dexterity in her fingers from not practicing. How long would it be before she couldn't play at all? She felt better, though, when Elinor stared at her mutely, then said, "Wow! You play with so much passion. Even your scales. No wonder Olaf chose you."

Crystal couldn't suppress a smile. The only other person to ever comment on her passion was an orchestra teacher, who said her technique was too melodramatic and would never fit in group playing. Crystal had felt demeaned and had relegated herself from then on to playing alone, feeling the music, and seeking the higher bands of joy she sensed outside of the spectrum.

"Hey, let's have some fun," Elinor said as she put on some slippers. "Light some candles. I'm going to get my Vincezno from the conservatory. I'll be right back."

Several candles in silver holders were strewn about the practice room. *Elinor must practice this way a lot,* Crystal thought. Not a bad idea — mood practice. A silver-plated lighter stood next to one of the candles and Crystal used it to light the wicks.

After several candles were glowing, Elinor still wasn't back. Crystal backed up toward the door and surveyed the room. It felt a little out of equilibrium, somehow violating her sense of the artistic. Glancing around the room, she sized it up, then picked up a thick, rose-colored candle and moved it closer to the ornate mirror that had so bedazzled her when she first entered the room. The mirror returned the light and helped to balance that side of the room.

Crystal looked in the mirror at herself and thought she looked a little better than she had. She pulled some pale strands of hair along her jaw to accent it. Then she noticed a dark patch in the mirror, adjacent to where the candle sat on a small shelf beneath the glass. "Oh, no," she murmured, hoping the heat from the flame hadn't damaged the glass somehow. Quickly, she separated the candle from the mirror, setting it back a couple of inches and inspected the glass. The mirror seemed normal. She moved the candle closer, and the patch reappeared. Peering into the patch she could see shapes in the mirror. *Through* the mirror. On the other side. It appeared to be the arm of a couch.

Elinor whisked in, giggling, her violin held close to her chest.

Crystal was seated stiffly in a chair. Where had Elinor really been? She eyed the honest and cheerful face. Was it a ruse? Was she in some kind of game?

"Sorry I took so long. I had to sneak it past my mother. She doesn't like it out of the conservatory." Elinor stared at Crystal who attempted, but failed, to smile.

"What's wrong?"

"I saw your mirror."

Elinor glanced up at the mirror. "Yeah? Okay. I thought you saw it when you came in."

"I mean, I saw *into* your mirror. I didn't mean to snoop."

"Huh?"

"Your two-way mirror." Crystal couldn't restrain herself and blurted out, "Were you spying on me while I looked at your instruments? Didn't you trust me?"

"I don't know what you mean. Two-way mirror? That's just a plain old mirror."

"Look." Crystal stood, a rod of anger welding her spine, and lit a flame in the lighter. She held the flame close to the mirror.

Elinor set down her violin and moved closer. She peered behind the flame. The dim, partial form of a room with chairs and a small couch was visible in the patch. Metallic devices and recording equipment stood on a table aimed toward the mirror. She stood back.

"Lord! I don't believe it. I never knew it was there!" She turned to Crystal. "I swear, I didn't."

The look of horror on her face convinced Crystal.

"Why would they be spying on you? Would it be your parents?"

"Who else could it be? I mean, my father had that mirror made special and installed in my practice room. He said it was to practice my performance stance. It had to be him. I don't know what to say. Please don't think I knew about this."

"It's okay. I don't. I'm sorry." Crystal hugged her friend.

"I'm going to have to have a long talk with my folks. Now I have two issues to confront them about. I'll wait until you leave though. It might get messy." Elinor took the lighter from Crystal, struck a flame, and peered again into the hidden room.

Elinor offered to drive Crystal home, and she accepted, rather than calling her parents. She put the top down on the car and they let the wind whip their hair into knots as they sped across the countryside. "Just like Thelma and Louise!" Elinor shouted and Crystal laughed aloud. Somehow, being boisterous helped to dispel the unsettling energy that had accumulated with the discoveries at Elinor's house.

Apprehensive of the initial confrontation with her own parents when she returned home, Crystal felt better having Elinor at her side. Having gotten some space, discovering there was no black ops after her and— best of all—having met up with Glenn had lifted her spirits, but she still needed to fix her relationship with her parents.

She was ready, _hungry_ to learn about the family, her budding abilities and to hear whatever her mother had to say. Chagrined about her earlier blowup, she looked forward to making up with her parents and Aunt Sarah.

As they drove up to her house, Crystal's embarrassment grew. After three days basking in the opulence of Elinor's home, she felt self-conscious at the meager state of her own. Her friend seemed to sense this, as she said, "Golly. A regular, nice neighborhood. You don't know what I'd give to be just regular." Even if it wasn't true, it made Crystal relax.

"Mom, Dad. I'm home," Crystal called as they entered. The house was silent.

Elinor followed her into the kitchen while she checked the fridge for a sticky. No note. Why would they leave one? They weren't expecting her, after all. Crystal looked in the back and noticed both vehicles were missing, so her mother must have gone somewhere.

Pulling open the fridge, she assessed nothing edible — except living dead things — so she and Elinor headed to the garden, where they pigged out on fresh tomatoes.

Elinor left soon after, with hugs and a promise to keep in touch. Crystal watched her go with a tinge of sadness. It had been fun pretending she had a sister. She'd wanted to introduce Elinor to Tish, but there didn't seem to be time that particular day.

When she returned to her room, it looked like a foreign land. How could it have changed in such a short time? Lying on the bed, she thought of the events of the past month. Had it only been a month? In just a couple more weeks school would start and she'd do what? And she was in love. Even if she could get a job at the community college, how would she ever go to school while she was so in love? How could she think? She didn't even want to think. Or learn. Outside of being in love, all she wanted to do was play her fiddle — if she had one — and that was just to express her love.

Watching the dust motes, she drifted off, and was awakened by the gentle hand of her mother.

"Sweetheart," she said through a mist, "you need to

wake up." She stroked her daughter's hair. "I love you so much," she said.

That seemed odd. When was the last time her mother had told her she loved her? Crystal stretched and opened her eyes to an empty room. *Weird to dream about my mother,* she thought.

The tomatoes were gurgling in her stomach, so Crystal decided to get some ginger ale. When she walked into the living room, however, her aunt and father were seated in silence. An air of dimness pervaded the room, despite the translucent curtain billowing a cool and sunlit breeze through the air.

Self-conscious, Crystal stood awkwardly, her attention on her feelings as she mentally stammered over what to say about her absence. Aunt Sarah stood and embraced her. Surprised, Crystal stepped back and noticed that her aunt's face was red and tear-streaked.

"Oh, lord," Crystal said. Somehow, it seemed her aunt's mind had joined with hers. "Mom — ?"

Her father looked up at her and stood, but before he could walk over to her, his hand went to his face. He pinched the bridge of his nose and began sobbing. Aunt Sarah tried to hug her again, but Crystal went to her father and put her arms all the way around him.

"I'm sorry, Squeaky," he said with a thick voice. He was using her baby name again. "Mom's gone."

"Oh, lord," she said again. Tears gushed from her head — it felt like her throat, her eyes, her sinuses and her heart were spewing hot liquid. "What do you mean?" Then anger filled her as the room spun. "Dad, what happened?"

"She got a job — she was on her way to work. The car — she stopped at the stop sign at a railway track, and started across. The car — that old car — died. It was one of those old crossings on a back road near Baxter street — you know, where they don't have automated guards. The people behind her kept honking at her—trying to warn her so she'd get out. To run. She probably thought they were angry at her, since she just kept trying to start the car. The train . . . hit." Her father looked down at her, sincerity in his eyes. "It was instantaneous. The car exploded. She didn't suffer. Not one bit. Not one little bit." With those words, Crystal knew better.

Releasing her father, she found her way in an internal darkness to the brocade chair she loved so much. She looked at her mother's matching chair and broke into fresh tears. A horrible moaning gushed from a place in her midsection.

"Honey, I'm so sorry," said Aunt Sarah and patted her arm. "So sorry."

It occurred to Crystal that Sarah was probably hurting, too, but just then it was more than she could do to salve her own grief. She left the room and returned to her bedroom, where all there was to console her was the cocoon of her bed.

Even in the protection of her room, shock sandblasted her. It must be her fault. If she hadn't run away — perhaps her mother was upset. Somehow she had caused it. She had rejected her mother and now her mother would never know how much she had *loved* her.

Now, more than any time in her life, her hands craved the feel of her violin. The one thing that understood her totally, needing no words, that could conceptualize beyond human understanding. Because she didn't feel quite human anymore.

7

HIDDEN IN BOXES

The funeral for her mother was a blur of sorrowful faces. At the reception in her home afterward, Crystal deftly avoided the tables of food and sought the calming effect of her friend Tish as much as she could. She wondered what it would be like without her mother's cheerful "good morning," and seeing her back hunched over the vegetables in the garden. Already, it was becoming overgrown; the tomatoes had outdone themselves and ripe, luscious fruits were spread on the ground as well as wrapping heavy heads up the fence.

As people milled around, Crystal made her escape, and found her way past the peach tree, into the garden. In a blue suit purchased for the occasion, she crouched next to the garden, her back curled as she had so often seen her mother's. She began pulling weeds—at first timidly, through a haze of tears. This was her mom's domain and she wasn't sure she belonged. But then, moved by a desire and longing to do something, anything, for her mother, she began ripping weeds in great handfuls and flinging them behind her. Dirt showered over her shoulder, across the bun clip holding her hair.

"Are you okay?" Tish stood solemnly watching her, then kneeled next to her.

Crystal looked up, her face emblazoned with grief, mascara streaking her cheeks into rivulets. "It's all my fault, Tish. I was so mean to her."

Tish hugged her friend, then released her.

"I never even said goodbye. A closed casket, Tish. You know what that means?"

Tish was silent, gazing at the ground. Seconds passed. "You missed one," she said, pointing down. Crystal looked at her horrified, stared down at the weed, then emitted a mournful laugh. Once she started, she couldn't stop. Tish alternated between laughing and trying to be somber, which set Crystal to laughing harder. She sat on the ground and continued until, like an overstuffed balloon, the air just ran out.

Weakened, she realized the earth below her seat was making her skirt wet, and she'd need to traipse back through all the people to change. Tish extended a hand and helped her to rise.

"Look, girl. I'm here for you. And you can stay with me whenever you want." The friends hugged and released as Sarah came through the back door, tiptoeing along the brick steps toward them. As she passed the peach tree, she frowned, looked at the tree, and continued onward.

"Uh, oh," Crystal said under her breath.

"Steady," Tish said between her teeth.

Sarah watched the girls through eyes darkened by loss of sleep, sorrow and blue eye-shadow. Her hair was matted and Crystal wanted to fluff it for her, but the idea of touching the grease bomb made her fingers curl inward. In spite of her aunt's having saved her, she could not get over her revulsion, nor could she understand it. What was it about her aunt that so destroyed her serenity? As though just asking provided an answer, her vision shifted slightly and she saw an oily tendril of congealed blood reaching from her aunt's heart to the back of her neck. The vision was capped by the peach tree behind her writhing with the shadow of wormlike shapes. She blinked, and it was gone.

"Girls, the visitors are leaving, and I thought you might want to say goodbye." She looked pointedly at Crystal, as though to say "And you should be taking more responsibility."

Crystal bristled. She didn't care about these people, most of whom she didn't know, anyway. In fact, now that she thought about it, who were they? She'd assumed they were friends of her father's from work, since she knew all of her mother's friends. And the way they stood around . . . all dressed in black, somber and quiet. Well, it was a funeral. But an occluded thought niggled at the back of her mind. She'd been too grief-stricken to notice before, but now she wanted to get inside quickly and take another look. What was it about these people?

"I'm sorry, Aunt Sarah," she said. "I'll go in right now. Thanks for telling me."

Sarah looked at her as though she knew her true feelings, and sighed.

The girls walked briskly up the walkway, when Tish paused near the peach tree. Fingering one of the ripening fruits, she turned to Sarah. "It won't be long now," she said. "The tree is really loaded."

Sarah looked at the fruit, her face questioning.

Crystal stared at her friend as though she had stuck her head in acid. "Don't do that!" she snapped.

"What?" Tish's eyes jerked toward her.

"I'm sorry." Crystal calmed. "The fruit is — bad."

Tish scrunched her eyebrows. "Well I love this tree," she said, "I'd live in this tree if I could." She released the peach in a huff. Sarah stepped behind her, watching

Crystal with concern.

Ignoring them, Crystal turned through the door and entered the living room as the last three guests were departing. Her father stood on the far side of a table that had been set in the center of the room for casserole dishes and platters of snacks brought by the visitors.

She watched as her father hugged one of the departing women as he murmured, "Thank you." Another stood near a man Crystal didn't recognize, awaiting her companion.

Crystal took a close look at the women. Both had long hair pulled into knots on the back of their heads. No makeup. And both wore identical high-collared black dresses, hosiery, shoes, and beads. That was what had been bothering her in the back of her mind. All of the people who had come to her mother's reception were dressed the same, as though they'd been cut from the same mold.

Crystal watched the women leave, their crisp steps in tandem alongside the man, their arms linked.

"As though they just dropped in from another planet," said Sarah, also watching them depart.

Crystal jerked and whipped around to her aunt. "I wish you'd stop that," she said.

"What?"

"Reading my mind." Her aunt smiled, but Crystal was serious.

That evening, Crystal's father called her into the kitchen to join in a family meeting. Crystal still had not come to terms with the "different" father who called her mother "my queen," even though, except for the grieving, he seemed back to himself now.

All of them were exhausted from the day, and looked at each other across the table with sympathy and concern.

"Doing okay, Squeaky?" Her father's voice was soft. Crystal nodded.

Her father took her hands in his. She looked at the subtle wrinkling of his skin and felt a pang of nostalgia. "I don't want you to be upset by what I'm about to say," he said. "Your mother would want it this way. There was some insurance. Enough, once the policy comes through, that we can pay for you to go to school. To college."

Crystal was stunned. Emotions broiled inside. She sensed her father was trying to please her, to get her to see the silver lining, but her mother was *gone*. She couldn't think about college now. If ever. It was *blood money*. She didn't know what to tell him, so in a meek voice, she said, "Thanks, Dad."

"There are some items—of your mother's—that I wanted to talk to you about."

"Oh, Dad." Crystal looked downward, her heart sliced with fresh pain.

"I'm sure she'd want you to have them."

Sarah's eyebrows raised as she looked at him.

He nodded.

"If it's her jewelry—I don't want—I mean—"

"No, it's a couple of personal items she kept in a cedar chest. From when she was a girl. They were special to her."

"Oh." Crystal was silent as her father scooted his chair backwards with a screech on the linoleum and left the room.

When he returned, he was carrying two instrument cases. One was an old case that looked as though it was made of alligator hide. The other was a rectangular case, made of old leather. Pieces of the fabric had worn through, exposing a wooden undercase.

"This," he said placing the cases on the table, "was your mother's when she was a girl." He pushed the foremost case across the top toward Crystal, who didn't touch it. Her fingers curled in her lap as fresh tears began running down her cheeks.

"You should open it," Sarah said.

Like an automaton, Crystal pulled the case toward her and unclasped the locks. Because the case hadn't been opened in many years, the top and bottom were partly sealed. Crystal tugged to free it. As the jaws of the case widened, the smell of old varnish and rosin wafted out. A violin gleamed dully in the kitchen light. It was a pale gold tone, with a sleek neck and slender body.

Crystal let out a breath. "It's Italian," she whispered.

"If I recall, it's a *Guarneri del Gesù*. I'm not sure what that means or if I'm saying it right, but I think you're right and it is Italian. Your mother was very proud of it."

Crystal didn't dare touch it. The instrument was as rare as a Stradivarius. Her mother had kept it secreted all these years, when selling it could have brought them a fortune. "But why? Why didn't she ever tell me? I never even knew she played!"

"Your mother—there were traits about her family— Sarah? Would you tell her?"

Crystal fought telling them she didn't want to hear. A few days ago she would have screamed and run out. Then she had returned home hoping to hear, but from her mother, who was now gone. And now, in the midst of this—it just felt like the wrong time and she wasn't sure how much more she could take.

She looked at her father, whose face had grown older overnight.

"First, show her the other one," Sarah said.

Her father set the other case on the table. Crystal stood and stepped around to open it. Inside was a highly polished and ornamented instrument that lay gleaming like a focused eye.

"Oh, my word. I can't believe it." Reverently, Crystal lifted it from the case. "It's a devil's fiddle."

"A what?" asked her father.

"A devil's fiddle. A Hardanger. They're—incredible."

"Do you know how to play it?" he asked, eyeing the eight strings and elaborate inlay.

"No. I've never even seen one in real life before. They're used a lot in Norwegian and Swedish folk music."

"Well," added Sarah, "if anyone can play it, you can."

"I'm not sure. It has multiple harmonics and overtones. Did . . . did Mom play it?"

Sarah was quiet, then pursed her lips before answering. "Your mother was amazing. When we were children, she had a reputation, you know, back then. Where we lived, she was reputed to be in league with the devil. Our family has this . . . air . . . about it that goes way back. There were abilities that ran in the family. Magical, some people said. You know about Fredrik. It was he, they say, who taught your great-grandfather to play by chaining him to a stump in the forest next to a waterfall. He wouldn't let your great-grandfather return until he learned to play from the *Näcken*."

"What is this *Näcken*? I keep hearing that word."

"It literally means 'naked.' It's from our Swedish mythology. *Näcken* is a magical being who lives in the water longing for someone to play fiddle with. Sometimes he'll lure children onto a pony, and when the pony is full of children, he calls it into the water and drowns them, to keep them with him."

"That's a terrible story!" Crystal couldn't help but think of Beans.

Sarah looked at her unperturbed. "It's old world. Anyway, my grandfather listened to the *Näcken* playing and learned from him. Then, when the *Näcken* heard him playing, he became so enraptured, that he tried to pull my grandfather into the water. It was only being chained to the tree that saved him, but he limped after that. And, he became a famous fiddler in our region of Sweden, since he was trained by the *Näcken* himself."

Crystal's heart was beating hard. She didn't dare openly question her aunt in front of her father, who didn't know about her having been kidnapped by the old man. Nonetheless, she peeked at her father to see him distracted by his tea and ventured, "The old man?" Her aunt nodded.

So Olaf Widmark truly was her great-grandfather! He had spoken the truth.

Crystal sat in silence while the impact of all her aunt had said hit home. As of that moment, there could never be normalcy again. Her dreams of a light and free childhood, unencumbered by drama and weird were over.

The woman who had disappeared — been abducted by the beam of light — was her grandmother. That made the baby she'd had — her mother? Really? And that made her — Crystal fought to accept it. Her stomach jumped with nerves, while a sense of truth blazed through her mind. That made her one-quarter of whoever, or *whatever* had impregnated her grandmother after she passed through the light.

"We need to talk!" Crystal whispered urgently. This time, she was ready to understand — to really listen.

Sarah nodded and said, "Finally!"

After Crystal took the cherished instruments into her room, she and her aunt walked to the wooded area near the house.

"Your mother was an amazing player, but our father was afraid of staying in the village and ran away with us both to America. He made her promise never to play in public. It about killed her — she was like you with the violin—but she did it out of respect.

"Afraid of what?"

"I was only fifteen at the time, and your mother was eighteen. I was too young and scattered to notice all the details, but my father was terrified we would all be killed. And later, after what happened to my mother, he was afraid Olaf would find us."

"What happened to your mother?"

"Let's sit here," Sarah said, indicating a fallen log. After they settled, she remained quiet, then began again. "My mother was removed from the house the night we escaped. I think that was what made my dad take the rash action of running away with us to America."

"Removed?"

"Taken. Some townspeople—I'm not sure who as I was asleep when they came. Or she might have run away herself that night. I've heard it a couple of different ways."

"*Cheesits*, Aunt Sarah. Could you please just tell me straight?" Crystal's twisted her fingers together. "I don't get it. Didn't your dad tell you later?"

"Wow. You are an impatient one. I'll get to that." Sarah furrowed her forehead, then continued. "We moved to Virginia, I went to school, graduated, and got a job. Your mom met your dad and you were born."

"She met him where you worked, right?"

Sarah smiled as she stared into the air near a tree.

Crystal looked, but could not see whatever memory Sarah was enjoying.

"Yes. Your dad worked with me. They literally bumped into each other one time when she came to pick me up. It was sparks at first sight."

"I know how she felt." Crystal stopped and flushed, realizing she'd let her new romance slip out.

"Oh? Do tell?"

"Never mind," she said with a grin. "Tell me more

about the family. What about this wizard, Fredrik? And how did Olaf—I mean your grandfather, I mean *my* great-grandfather—come to be here?"

Sarah cocked an eyebrow at her niece, then stared at sunlight filtering through the leaves as they rustled in the treetops. "It gets complicated. Suffice it to say that Grandfather Olaf came to find us. Because of her talent with the violin, he never wanted your mother to escape.

"Townspeople had come after him and Fredrik. Cattle had disappeared and they blamed our relatives. As usual. Anytime anything went wrong, they believed it was us.

"Even though Olaf wasn't directly involved in magic, many had witnessed him with the Gypsy and the resultant portal light show when the two played together, so he was blamed as well. Also, since no one knew who the father of your mother was they were talking about . . . demons.

"Your grandmother was terrified—they were coming for her. She grabbed her fiddle and ran to the stream where Olaf and the Gypsy had opened the shining portal all those years before. She knew what to do.

"She played desperately over the water, calling to the other side to save her. Olaf ran after her, but it was too late. As he cried out for her, the *Näcken* took her to the other side. He saw the light as she disappeared."

Crystal was silent. "So Olaf's daughter *willingly* went to the other side of this portal? The townspeople didn't kill her?"

"That's what some people said." Sarah brushed dust from her shoe and shifted on the log.

"What about your father?"

"He wasn't Emma's father. Your mother and I were actually half-sisters. When our mother ran out with her fiddle, my father packed up us kids and ran out the other way, bringing us to America. He didn't want anything to do with the trouble brought down by the Widmarks.

"Olaf spent years searching for us. When I saw what he had done to you at the camp, I knew he had systematically searched all over the country."

"But why? Why was he doing this?" Crystal had twisted her hair into a tangle around her finger.

Sarah stretched out her legs in front of her. "After his daughter — your grandmother — was taken the final time by the *Näcken*, he went berserk with grief and blamed himself for ever opening the portal to begin with. He was determined that one of us in the family could bring her back by opening the portal again.

"We heard from friends in Sweden that he tried to open the portal again by himself for years. When that failed, he tried to get the Gypsies to help, but they refused him.

"Finally, he believed that since your mother was half from the *other side* that she could do it. *We* were not sure what he was in league with and were afraid of him. We've been in hiding our entire lives. Now that he's found us, what will we do?"

Crystal erupted, "But, Aunt Sarah, you have to tell me. *What am I?* If Mom was half whatever, then I'm quarter. I need to know, *what's on the other side?*"

Sarah took a ragged breath, her eyes filling with tears, and looked up at her niece. "Oh, Cris. I want to, but I just can't tell you all of it right now. There has been too much. I mean with your mom and . . . I should have told her about what happened to you at camp. Maybe she would have shared all of what she needed to sooner."

Sarah began weeping. Cris shifted next to her on the log and embraced her aunt. She saw Sarah as a middle-aged woman afraid of getting old, who still needed magic to feel whole. Her aunt needed time.

As it was, Crystal was spinning with her own

darkness from the loss of her mother, and her own confusion at her own identity with new, uncharted abilities. *What was she, really? And were the powers she'd been experiencing to do with her magical family, or a grandfather from beyond the portal?*

But they all needed time to heal.

She stroked her aunt's hair as she wept. Learning more about the family would have to wait.

But if Crystal had her way, she wouldn't have to wait much longer. Couldn't wait much longer. What had her aunt said?

Now that he's found us, what will we do?

8

CHASING SHADOWS

Crystal didn't sleep well that night. The violins sat propped up next to her desk, and as much as she ached to play, she could not yet bring herself to touch them. She longed to call Glenn, but was embarrassed to have him hear the depression and grief just under the surface in her voice. She wondered if he was thinking about her.

At 3:13 she awoke to a buzz near her ear, and she swatted as though a mosquito had come in the room. But nothing was there. Annoyed at her lack of sleep and being woken up, she rolled out of bed, put on a robe to abate the chill, then turned on her computer.

While it was loading, she padded on bare feet into the kitchen to get some water. She could hear her father's voice, soft in the living room, speaking to someone.

Nearing the door, she paused to listen. He was laughing. She couldn't believe it. He actually sounded happy. "Yes. I love you too," he said. Bile and rot flooded her stomach. Who was he talking to? Aunt Sarah? Were they having an affair? Crystal decided to confront him right then and there.

She walked into the living room. From the faint light coming through the curtain from the streetlamp outside, she could see the shaded form of her father sitting at a side chair near the phone. No, wait. It wasn't him at all. The curtain ruffled, and the vision—that had seemed so solid—was gone.

It was happening again. She was seeing and hearing things. She really did need to talk to Sarah again.

She stopped in the bathroom on the way back to her room. The nightlight flashed red, then blue, then gold as she washed her hands. She looked up at herself in the mirror over the sink, thinking she seemed unfamiliar. Turning to the full-length mirror, she dropped her robe and stared at her body, wondering what parts might be alien, if what Aunt Sarah said was true.

Her eyes seemed too large. Hadn't schoolmates mentioned that before? Someone told her once that they flashed blue "laser beams." She'd laughed at the time, but now she wondered. She ran her hands over her arms. Her skin felt almost too soft, as though her pores were smaller than other peoples'. Her breasts looked normal, but what about her legs? She was the only person she knew who did not have to hem new jeans. Her legs were long enough to fit. She scanned her willowy form but saw no other abnormalities.

What abilities might she possess, provided by some alien DNA? Could she levitate?

Closing her eyes, she willed herself into the air. When she felt sufficiently high in her imagination, she opened her eyes, to see herself still standing on the floor.

When she returned to her room, the system was up and an email from Elinor was flashing. It said: LET'S TALK TOMORROW. IT'S IMPORTANT—ABOUT MY FATHER AND MOTHER.

The time stamp was from yesterday. It was way too early in the morning to contact her. Elinor was a late riser, so she'd wait until after ten. She wrote back, apologizing for not responding sooner, explaining about the death of her mother and her need for some time to heal.

The week had pushed her into a pall of gloom, and the idea of seeing her friend was mildly uplifting. Maybe she could get Tish and Elinor, and the three of them could have a day together. She'd call Tish early.

She finished her tea and went back to bed, wondering about the vision of her father. As she drifted off, she thought it had looked so real. Almost like a movie, *or a residual energy pattern.* She jolted awake. Where had those words come from? Then her lids became heavy and she slept. Blessedly, she dreamed of Glenn, or Bela, or whoever he was. Not really a dream—more of a feeling. His energy was all around her, blending with hers. Melding through and into the heart of each other, together, somehow, somewhere.

By the time she arose, it was nearly nine. Crystal hurried downstairs, made some toast, and drank some apple juice. This was her dad's first day back at the clinic, where he worked as an attendant, so she'd be alone for the day. She would have time to think about school, what school she wanted to go to, and to contact her friends. Maybe Tish and Elinor could help her come to some decisions.

Crystal decided to call Tish first. They chatted for a minute, and decided to get together at ten-thirty.

Sitting on a chair on the back porch, she stared out at her mother's garden. So much had happened in a short amount of time. Out there, somewhere, was Glenn—probably wondering why she hadn't called and thinking she didn't care. Springing to her feet, she rushed to her room and found the paper he had given her at the bottom of her purse. Taking a deep breath, she picked up the phone and dialed.

It rang several times. Then she heard the voice capable of melting her even through the phone line.

"Hello?"

Crystal was silent for a moment, just floating on the vocal timbre of his word. Then, "Oh, hi. This is Cris. You know. The girl from camp."

He laughed. "Cris! I was so stupid that I didn't get your number. How are you?"

Crystal explained what had happened and accepted his condolences.

The conversation shifted to more mundane topics, and while she talked to him, Crystal felt they lifted into a space together, some private mental or spiritual place where they had no bodies, and yet she could clearly see his face as if he were with her. As she basked in the glow of him she was surprised to *see* the energy fluctuate, break into red and orange hues and become erratic. An instant later, she heard a man's voice say "Bela. Time to practice. Now."

Glenn's voice dropped to a whisper "I want to get together with you. Where can we meet?"

Crystal couldn't think. He lived in Ithaca—a state away. Getting there would be difficult.

"I'm not sure. Call me back when you can. On my cell phone." Just before they hung up, she quickly gave him her number.

Sudden adrenalin forced her feet into a prancing dance down the hallway, into and around the living room. Then she jumped into the air. *I did it!* she exalted. A momentary guilt that she should be so happy under the circumstances threatened to bring her down, but she forced it aside. Grief had buried her for days. It was time to see a little light.

She carried the adrenalin to her bike, which she

mounted for the trip to Tish's, excited to tell her about the conversation with Glenn. Seeing Tish might help to lift the weight of the past few days that had been pressing down and it was nice to have a good circumstance to report.

Crystal had peddled midway up the street when Elinor's Z4 zipped toward her. She held up her hand, and the tiny vehicle screeched to a stop. As the window rolled down, she dropped her bike and jogged to it.

Belying her petite and perfect features, Elinor's face looked grotesque. Huge circles spread like grape jelly under her eyes, and her cheeks had puffed out like she had eaten too much salty Spam. Uncombed, her hair had ratted into a mouse nest and her breath oozed out.

"*Cheesits!*" Crystal couldn't help herself. "What happened to you?"

"Oh, Cris. Let me pull over."

Crystal returned to her bike and rolled it over to the car. She laid it down, then climbed inside, next to Elinor.

Elinor peered at her and pulled her lips into a grimace as she tried to smile. Her eyelids had risen like dough, to where only little red slits remained. "I look like heck, huh?"

Crystal nodded. "Serious heck. What is going on?"

Elinor took a breath, snorted, and looked out the side window. "My mother and father are sending me to live somewhere else."

"What? Why?" Her throat went dry.

"There's more. They're going away. Back to 'the Agency,' from what I understand."

"Huh?"

"They said they aren't my parents and that I'd have to go live in a foster home now."

"What? What? A *foster* home? What do they mean they weren't your parents? They can't do that, can they?"

"Apparently, they can. They never were my parents."

Elinor put her hands over her face. "I can't believe it. They never told me. I'm almost eighteen. I'm just going to run away."

"But wait. I don't get it. If they weren't your parents, who were they? And how did they get you?"

Elinor opened her lips to speak, but glanced in the rear-view mirror. "Oh, no! Here come their minions! Put on your belt!"

She peeled out.

In the side mirror, Crystal spotted a black van hurdling up the street toward them.

Zipping down an alley, tires squealed as Elinor forced the car into a sudden one-eighty and sped back the other direction.

"Speed is twenty-five!" Crystal squeaked.

Elinor ignored her. They passed the van on their way out of the neighborhood.

"They've been following me!" Elinor screamed over the engine's revving. "Which way to the freeway?" Crystal pointed and looked back over her shoulder to see the van stopping and attempting to turn around on the narrow street.

"I think they're trying to take me back. Or put me somewhere. After I fought with my father he called someone."

"Elinor, you're scaring me! Don't get on the freeway. Let's go to my friend's house. They won't find you there."

Elinor kept going, her foot hard on the gas pedal.

"I mean it! I don't want you driving like this! Turn right at the next street and we'll cut back."

Elinor did as she was told, and Crystal guided her to Tish's house.

When they got there, Crystal sprang from the car and ran to the door. Tish came out, smiling at first, but Crystal hurriedly explained that they had to hide Elinor's car. Tish didn't ask for further explanation. She opened the garage door and motioned Elinor to drive her car in.

With the car concealed, the three girls slinked into the house though the door in the garage.

"Is your mom here?" Crystal whispered to Tish.

"No. Her sister's getting some wisdom teeth pulled and she's with her for a couple days. Why? What's going on?"

Crystal shook her head.

"Wait," said Elinor. She walked through the dining area to the living room and peeked through the curtains, turning her head both ways. "Seems to be clear," she finished.

Tish looked at Elinor, then at Crystal. "Tell me. What the hell is going on?"

"Oh, sorry," said Crystal and introduced the friends.

Elinor said "hello" and shook hands. Her attention went to scrutinizing Tish's head.

Tish stared back, patted her hair, then ran a nail through a tooth.

Elinor continued to stare.

"What? What you doing? Is my head bad?" Tish snapped at Elinor.

"Oh! Sorry. No. I was just zoned." Elinor looked away.

Crystal checked with Elinor, then caught Tish up to speed on what had happened with Elinor's parents.

They went into the kitchen and sat at an oak table. Tish got them each a soda.

"But what I don't get," Crystal said turning to Elinor, "is why they're all of a sudden saying you're not their daughter. That's so horrible! And who are these people who are after you?"

"When my father and I were fighting—you know, about the two-way mirror and that man who follows me—

he mentioned a Project Pegasus connected to the place he works. I Googled it and found some interesting info — mostly from conspiracy theorists."

"You've gotta be kidding me!" Tish looked surprised and extra interested as she grabbed some cookies from the cupboard. "This calls for girl food!"

"Yeah. Seems this whole time I was some kind of experiment, and they expected me to develop some sort of abilities. When I failed, I guess it took them a few days to complete the paperwork —" Elinor's face darkened as her throat caught, " — and then it was over. Me. The experiment. Just like that.

"And Cris, I think this has to do with you." Elinor lowered her head and rounded her shoulders like she was going to cry again.

"Me?" Crystal sat back in her chair. "Why me? I mean, we didn't meet that long ago."

Elinor raised her face. "You know that thing that happened to us at the fiddle camp?"

Crystal nodded.

"What thing? What thing happened?" Tish shoved a plate of cookies onto the table and looked to Crystal. "You never told me anything happened."

"It's too weird, Tish. I didn't want to tell you because it was too hard to explain."

Tish looked hurt.

Crystal and Elinor glanced at each other, and Elinor nodded. Crystal proceeded to tell Tish about their kidnapping, Olaf and the chaining, and the forced fiddle playing.

"You should call the police!" Tish said when she was done.

"We talked about that, but it would just be our word against theirs. And — some of these people are scary. At least, the ones following us," said Elinor.

"So why are they following you?"

Elinor sighed. "I'm not sure. But when I failed the test—the violin test given by Olaf that apparently Cris passed—the place my father works quit considering me a candidate for *whatever* they planned on using me for."

"What? A fiddle test? This ain't making any sense at all." Tish stood then sat back down.

"Yeah. To me neither," said Crystal. "And I hadn't told you, Elinor, but Olaf is my great-grandfather. I just found out. My family thinks he was coming to get me. Or to get my mother before—you know. But nothing could possibly connect me with you, or your dad, or his agency. What do they do there, anyway?"

"I'm not sure."

"Well, what do those online conspiracy guys say about it?" asked Tish.

"They seem to think it's some sort of black operation." Elinor's voice trembled.

"*Pshaw!*" Tish grinned. "What do you mean? Like those guys that go around in black helicopters?"

"No, like some guys who monitor people in this country with PSI."

Crystal's gut wrenched. She knew that PSI stood for "parapsychology," and much as she didn't like to admit it, having a large dose of her family's psychic ability did explain a lot of her strange occurrences of late. And hadn't her aunt said the black ops were after *her*? Not Elinor. *Her.*

"Well, in spite of what I've read," said Tish, "I don't exactly believe in all that stuff. Then again, I'm going to be a scientist, after all, and need to keep an open mind. One man's magic is another man's science. Or woman's." Tish rubbed her arm. "Plus, I believe in God and don't think he'd want us messing around with it. If it's true. Unless He created it. God, that is." A burgundy red flushed across Tish's cheeks.

"But anyway. What do they want with you? Are you psychic?" Tish put her hand on her hip. Her attitude was not lost on Crystal. Apparently, by Elinor's sudden reticence, it wasn't lost on her either.

"No," answered Elinor quietly. Her eyes shifted.

"You?" Tish looked at Crystal.

"Not that I know of — though I've had some unusual happenings lately." Crystal took a deep breath and assessed her friend of ten years. Already Tish had expressed offense that she had been left out of the loop.

Making the decision to divulge all, Crystal explained about the strange voices she'd heard, being chased on her bike, the energy visions and her aversion to meat. Then she took a deep breath and told Tish all about the *Näcken* and her feeling connected to nature and some other dimension when she played her fiddle.

"Oh, bizarre," Tish said. "And those visions . . ." She turned to Elinor "Is that why you were staring at my head?"

Elinor nodded, sheepish.

Tish looked off for a moment.

Crystal counted the seconds, believing their friendship was dissolving. She knew she sounded out of her mind.

Then Tish spoke again. "Remember when we were talking about HAARP that one day?"

Crystal nodded.

"What?" Elinor raised her eyebrows.

"People who mess with sound waves to change weather and control peoples' minds," Crystal said to her. Even though a building sense of hysteria made her want to laugh, Crystal's stress kept her mouth turned downward. She hoped Elinor would just take the information in stride.

Tish continued, "What if you've got some sort of

power—you know, human bodies do put out electromagnetic waves. What if somehow you are able to *organically* manipulate sound waves like those black ops folks have been trying to do with machines?"

"Like how?" Crystal asked.

"Well, I don't know. I don't know all of what they do. But it seems this all centers around sound waves." Tish crinkled her nose.

"My father doesn't work for HAARP," Elinor said. "He works for some guy named Irving."

Tish's jaw dropped. "IRVing? Your daddy works for IRVing?"

Elinor nodded.

"Hah! That's it then!" Tish looked triumphant.

"What do you mean?" Crystal played with her fingers as she became impatient.

"IRVing means 'Institute of Remote Viewing'."

Crystal put her hands on either side of her head. "That tells me nothing. Remote *viewing* has nothing to do with sound waves. Does it?"

"No!" said Tish, grinning.

Elinor and Crystal looked at each other, their eyes bulging.

"Well, then so what?" Elinor held out her hand.

"Oh, you guys. IRVing deals with all sorts of research that can be used for warfare. They started out as a branch of the CIA. Of course, I'm just speculating, but I can see where they'd use sonics to create earthquakes in hostile nations, maybe using remote viewing to target the spots." Tish spoke quickly, excited.

"I don't think so, Tish. It sounds too far fetched. They don't sound at all related." Crystal's mouth twitched as she tried not to patronize her friend. "But you could be right."

"Maybe," Elinor said. "But for now, we just don't

know for sure, do we?"

The three girls looked at each other.

Elinor shrugged.

"What I want to know," asked Crystal, "is what this has to do with playing the friggin' fiddle? And Olaf? And me? And you?"

Elinor turned pleading eyes to Crystal. "I don't have all the answers. All I know is that I failed and they didn't want me anymore."

Crystal reached across the table and picked up both Tish's and Elinor's hands. "I'm sorry. I didn't mean to upset either of you. I guess what we need to know is, what do we do next?"

"I wish we had an adult to talk to. I mean, not that we're not adults — sort of," Elinor said.

Tish snickered, then Elinor continued, "Anyhow, if we had, you know, somebody who knows the ropes and would believe us."

Crystal stayed silent.

"Well, for now, why don't you two just stay here with me? Mom won't care, and we have a lot to figure out," Tish said.

Crystal ignored her statement and ventured, "I do know someone who would believe us. And someone who could maybe fill in some blanks." She released their hands.

"Who?" Elinor and Tish said at the same time.

"My Aunt Sarah," Crystal responded.

Aunt Sarah. It kept coming back to her.

9

A Lot of Money

"Well, let's get her over here. I can't stand this anymore. I am stressing out." Elinor's hand shook as she reached for her soda.

Tish and Elinor both stared at Crystal, who was busy fighting down a lump of her own stress.

"Okay. I'll call her. But you have to know that she's — really different. I mean, Tish, she *does* believe she's psychic, and she won't talk to us if you ridicule her."

"I'll be good. But if she's psychic, shouldn't she know how I feel, anyway?"

"It doesn't always work that way."

"And you know this — how?" Tish grinned at her.

"Wait," said Elinor, rising from the table. "Look, before we get your aunt over, I need to get to the bank. I refuse to go into a foster home or wherever they had planned for me. I need to get my money. I'm running."

"So, what bank do you need to go to?"

"City Federal."

"There's a branch about a mile if you cut through the neighborhood." Tish indicated the direction with a nod. "We can walk."

"No, that'll take too long and if that van is still around, they might see us. Do you have a car?"

"No, my mom and I share, but you could take my bike." Tish raised her eyebrows in question.

Elinor thought about it. "Okay. Do you have a book bag I could use? Or a backpack? And can you draw me a map for the back streets?"

Tish looked at her, puzzled. "Sure. Do you want one of us to go with you?"

"No, that will take too long. And two on a bike is a little too cozy."

"I'd go with, but my bike is back on the street," Crystal said.

"It's all right. I'll be okay. I hope." Elinor's brows crunched into a worried face.

With Elinor on her way, Crystal called her aunt and asked her to come to Tish's house. She then took some time to tell Tish about Glenn.

Tish watched her face, which seemed to be glowing with rapture, while Crystal talked about him. They both broke out into a grin.

"Well, girl. You've certainly been busy," Tish said.

Crystal heard her aunt's rattle-trap station wagon pull up and peeked out the living room curtain to be sure it was her. A blouse of shiny orange, gold, and black assaulted her eyes. Sarah had left in a hurry, as evidenced by her still wearing pink bunny slippers. Yep. Her aunt. No black van lurked up the street that she could see. Nonetheless, Crystal ushered her aunt in quickly, then gave her an uncharacteristic hug.

They retreated to the kitchen table, where Tish offered Sarah a soda.

Sarah declined. "Some herbal tea, if you have it. Now, what's this all about?" she asked Crystal. Her head tremored slightly, which made her high ponytail bobble a bit.

"There's a lot to tell, but I need to know more about what we were talking about the other day. You know, about our family."

"Why? What's going on? Has something else happened?" Sarah didn't wait for Crystal to respond. "Damn. I knew your father needed to get us out of here. Ever since Olaf's minions showed up at the house."

"What does Olaf have to do with it? And the van that is following me?"

"The van?"

"With the DC license plates. Like one that was at our house."

"DC? Oh, no. The Agency. It's got to be IRVing."

Crystal and Tish exchanged glances. "How do you know about them?"

"How do *you* know about them?" Sarah demanded.

"Elinor's dad works for them."

Sarah sat stunned, her mouth open. Her hand moved to the side of her cheek. "Oh, lord. This is worse than I thought."

"What? What? Would you please tell us?" Tish begged.

"You're Elinor?" Sarah asked turning to Tish.

"No. I'm Tish, remember?" Tish looked at Crystal and rolled her eyes.

"Oh, yes. I think I met you before. Who is Elinor?"

"She's a friend. You haven't met her, but she'll be here any minute. I met her at the music camp."

Sarah was silent. "She's coming here?"

"Yes."

"She'll be followed. We don't have much time."

"No, we already shook them off."

"Don't you believe it." Her aunt's daggers were more intended for the Agency than her niece, but they struck Crystal, anyway. "That's probably how they found out about you—by following her. We had been very careful.

"Okay, here's the story," her aunt went on. "IRVing is where I used to work, and where Richard worked as well."

"No way Dad would work for a war place."

"A war—? Oh, I see what you mean. Later on our work was used for locating targets and was used in war. Yes. But I'm sure he didn't know it when he became involved, just as I didn't. It was a branch of the CIA and they are very good at 'storefront' organizations. What is Elinor's father's name?"

"I don't remember."

"Well, I'll ask her when she gets here."

"Maybe we should wait for her. Should she hear this?" Crystal asked.

"Uh, I don't know. A lot of it is *family* stuff, you know?" Sarah glanced askance at Tish. "Then again, if they're after you—all of you?—probably. I just hope there's time."

"Time for what?"

"To explain it. Cris, you know there's something going on, something big, right?"

"Well, I don't know about big, but it's sure been strange." She glanced at Tish who was watching them converse. Her attention seemed fixated on Sarah's ponytail.

"It's big. Bigger than you could know. And it goes back generations," Sarah continued.

"Oh, the family, again. What is it? How does it tie in with the IRVing agency?"

The back door opened, and a panting Elinor

clambered in. The full book bag slung across her shoulder weighted down her side, so her stance was lopsided. "Made it," she croaked. She saw Sarah at the table and stopped. Pretending casualness, she removed the book bag and tucked it under the sink.

"Did you see anyone? Were you followed?" Sarah demanded.

"I don't think so." Elinor again stared at Sarah.

Crystal introduced them, but noted to herself that the energy in the room shifted and felt off. It seemed her aunt and Elinor were eyeing each other with sidelong glances and mistrust.

Crystal let Elinor get settled in a chair and caught her up on her aunt's story. "We were just getting to the part where the family figures into all this. Right, Aunt Sarah?"

"*Um hmm,*" Sarah said, then looked directly at Elinor for a few seconds.

Elinor became visibly agitated, rose and said, "I need to use the restroom," as she left.

Sarah took a deep breath. "When I graduated high school I wanted to go to college. We didn't have much money, so I looked for any way to find income. One day, I saw an advertisement. The Psychology Department was performing PSI tests on kids and would pay fifty dollars. That was a huge amount of money back then. What I didn't know was they were helping the Agency to locate potential PSI practitioners.

"Well, being young and stupid, I decided to show off my powers. I knew our family had the traits and I had played with them. Just games, you know."

"What do you mean 'games'?"

"Oh, like I'd be with a bunch of friends at a diner and say 'Hey. Watch that guy. He's going to scratch his ear.'" Then I'd *will* a tickle on his ear and he'd scratch it. My friends thought it was a riot."

"How did you do it?"

"I had more training than you have." Sarah continued, "At any rate, I strutted my stuff, took my fifty dollars, and had a good titter about how dumb these people were.

"Then the Agency moguls showed up at my house. We didn't know who they were, but they offered me a job *and* college tuition. I was on cloud nine. This was a top-secret facility — and at the time I thought it was benign. I was too naive to know they were working on weapons of mass destruction."

"What? What? WMD? How can that be?" Some spit sprayed out as Crystal stammered.

Sarah looked into the air over Crystal's head. "Using our powers of remote viewing to locate targets to take out, and the like. Locating witnesses so they could off them. Off course, I didn't know what they were doing with the information. I just was having fun exercising my powers."

"That's like what I said!" Tish was triumphant. She bit a cookie, which hid her grin.

Crystal frowned. "And my dad really worked there?"

"Yes. But don't go thinking bad thoughts. He's who helped me to get out. He wasn't a subject, he was a monitor. You see, the Agency doesn't let you leave if you have . . . talent. But after I lost my baby — " Sarah's face hardened. "Anyway, your dad helped me by convincing them that I had lost my powers because of my grief. And it was pretty true at the time." Sarah looked into some past and her features grayed.

Crystal cleared her throat, picked up a cookie, and chewed at the edge in little bites. "What does all this have to do with me and Elinor?"

"I'm not sure about Elinor — except that you said her father works for IRVing — but I was stupid. When I filled out their entrance forms, I blabbed it all. They wanted to know about our family, our background, our *mythos* as you will. I told them about the—" Sarah looked at her askance, "—the *Näcken* incident, which I thought was just a fairytale. Well, they were very interested in that, and wanted to investigate the vortex I had described. I'm sure now they were hoping to turn it into a weapon."

"So why me? Why now?"

"You've had—shifts, changes happen recently, haven't you."

Crystal paused, unwilling for Tish to hear this, but knew she couldn't wait for a convenient time. She nodded.

"And some of those changes involve knowing what people are thinking, right?"

Crystal nodded.

Tish interjected. "Hey, whoa. I don't want anyone knowing what I think." She put her hands to the sides of her head as though to stop her thoughts.

Crystal laughed. "Don't worry, Tish. It's sporadic. I never know when it's going to happen."

Sarah ignored her and continued. "And visions. You've had visions, right?"

"Not recently. Plus, I don't know if they're visions," Crystal replied. "I'd call them hallucinations. Does our family have something wrong with it?"

Sarah smiled a wry grin. "Oh, come now, Cris. Look to yourself. You *know* what it is." She watched Crystal unwaveringly as Crystal let go of pretense and blanched.

"Are we—are we *witches*?" she whispered.

Sarah laughed out loud. "Witch—gads, no wonder you've been so freaked out. Of course we're not witches."

Crystal sighed and grinned, embarrassed. "Whew!"

"We're wizards."

Crystal's eyes bulged and now it was her turn to laugh. "Yeah, right."

"No, we are. In our family, going back generations, we are. You know, now that I think about it, the lines are kind of blurred. Some people might mistakenly call us witches, though we don't practice Wicca in any formal sense."

"Well I don't practice it at all. So why am I having these things happen? And what does it have to do with IRVing?"

"Oh, lordie. I suppose with your mother gone it does fall to me.

"Do you remember when I told you about us coming to America?"

Crystal nodded.

"That was to get away from the townspeople. They wanted to kill your mother. This gets weird."

"No kidding." Tish's eyebrows had gone up at the word "kill."

Sarah began playing with her ponytail as she continued. "You know about Olaf being trained by the *Näcken* and the rest about when he played with the Gypsies and the vortex and all that."

"Yeah, and that the town's people got mad because of a UFO attack. And my grandmother was taken and so was some other girl. Right?"

"Oh, no. And it wasn't a UFO; I *told* you that. You need to pay better attention. They got mad because of what happened afterward. After they found out about the strange effects of the opening. The *eye*, the locals called it. The after-effects began to be apparent."

"What after-effects?"

"Some good. People who were ill got better. Cows produced more milk. Cancers cured themselves. But then other changes made the townspeople question. Like over a period of years, people weren't aging anymore. Well, they did, but very slowly. Once people got over the thrill of it, they were freaked out. It brought all the religious superstitions to the forefront."

"It seems that if there were a town with really old people, it would be in Guinness World Records."

Sarah stood and yanked her purse strap up and over her head. "You're just going to have to take it on faith for now. I'm sensing that we must get out of here. Now. I'll have to tell you the rest later."

"Wait, Aunt Sarah," Crystal said. "We need to know what to do."

"Get your friends. We'll take my car. Hurry." Sarah strode through the kitchen to the front door, with Crystal following her. Tish stood back, out of the way.

She opened the door, looked over her shoulder, and repeated, "Hurry!" as she stepped through the screen door to the porch.

"Guys!" Crystal called over her shoulder.

Sarah stepped back in, slammed and locked the front door, fear in her eyes. "They're here! Quick! Get out the back!" she screeched.

10

CAUGHT

Elinor reentered the kitchen just as the three burst in from the living room. She did a zigzag dance toward the sink, where she had stashed the bag. She started to open the cupboard, then abandoned the plan — saving the seconds and choosing a quick exit toward the back door instead.

"Come on!" shouted Crystal, and they all piled outside.

Tish was first around the corner of the house, and was immediately forced back, struggling against a man with a crewcut who held her arm high behind her back with his hand over her mouth. The other three halted, started, and looked for exits, when the man said, "Do what I say, or we'll hurt her."

Crystals hands fisted in an automatic response. She felt like a cat getting ready to spring.

They all stopped and stared. The man's angular jaw and muscled arm said he meant it.

"You can't do this," said Sarah stepping forward. She put on her best evil witch's eyes, but the man seemed immune.

Two more men came from the house behind them, and one, a tall, red-headed man, held a pistol.

"All of you," he said, "into the van."

"You can't do this." Elinor meant it. "My father is the director of IRVing."

"Yeah." Crystal stepped forward, her stance challenging, though her knees felt weak.

The two men looked at each other and grinned.

"We know who your father is," said the one holding Tish.

Crystal wanted to scream, to alert the neighbors, but she was not sure what the men would do. Would they shoot all of them? Break Tish's arm?

Elinor gripped Crystal's hand and held it so tight her fingers pinched. Crystal had to yank it away.

"Come on, girls," said Sarah, puffing up. "They'll have to let us go. The neighbors are watching."

The man holding the pistol looked around at the closed curtains and quiet yards of neighboring houses. He grimaced and jerked his gun toward the van.

The four were herded into the back of the van where a grid separated them from the driver. A single bench lined one wall, and all four girls squeezed onto it. Surveillance equipment lined the other van wall. The gunman entered behind them and crunched down on a stool near the door.

"Strap in," he said.

The women did as they were told.

Crystal noticed a glass panel sliding across the back of the driver's seat. Then their guard reached into a compartment, pulled out a small, rubber mask and, just before he placed it over his mouth and nose, said, "Nighty night."

"Huh?" Sarah peeped as a cloud of gas hissed into the van.

Crystal held her breath as long as she could but eventually succumbed and inhaled a lungful.

When Crystal came to, she was on a cot in a brightly lit room, unrestrained. The room was gray with cement flooring. Nothing broke the solid expanse of walls except a panel with buttons next to the door.

She stood wavering, feeling groggy, and dragged her eyes through the drug to look at her friends. Lined up on similar cots, they still slept.

Going to the door, she ran her hand over the flat surface. No knob or handle protruded. Apparently, the panel opened it. She pushed one of the buttons and a single tone rang out.

Startled, she jumped back, removing her hand from the panel. If the captors were unaware she was awake, she didn't want to alert them. Unlike at Elinor's house, no two-way mirrors were evident. She scanned the room for cameras or listening devices, but saw now. However, she didn't trust that they were not hidden.

Going to Sarah, she knelt and shook her aunt gently. "Wake up."

"*Hunngh*?" her aunt groaned. "What's it?"

Crystal kneeled next to her aunt.

Sarah sat up, rubbed her head, and looked around. Her ponytail was half out and, with an automatic gesture, Sarah pulled out her elastic and fixed her hair back into another tail. "Oh, brother," she said.

"Where are we?" Crystal realized she was whispering—not wanting to awaken the others or alert their captors.

"I'm not sure."

Crystal surveyed the room again. "There's a panel by

the door. There's no knob."

Sarah's face grew taut. "Oh, crap. The Annex."

"What is it?"

"The place they were building when I left the Agency. I went exploring before they were done. I wondered what all the rooms were for."

"What do they want us here for?"

"Not sure. I'm not sure. Some of these were designed to keep people *in*."

"Against their wills?"

Sarah got up and walked to the door. "Wake up the others," she said, and began pressing along the edge of the door. "But be quiet."

Crystal glided to Elinor's side. "I can't believe you worked for these people," she said low over her shoulder to her aunt.

Sarah shot her a look.

Crouching next to Elinor, Crystal shook her gently, then moved to Tish.

Tish groaned and sat up. "What the hell?" She rubbed her head. "Where are we?"

"We're at the Agency we talked about."

Crystal's head swam with information. She'd never even heard of remote viewing, all this sound wave stuff, HAARP, until recently. If they were after her, maybe she could convince them she any abilities she had wouldn't work and they'd let them all go.

A minute later, Elinor became conscious as well.

Sarah, Tish and Crystal sat on the floor by Elinor's cot.

"Look," said Sarah. "We need to figure a way out of here. I remember some of the layout of the building, if we can get out of the room. But there are cameras in the halls and I don't know how much this place has changed since I worked here. If we can get out, we'll have to run — maybe in different directions to confuse them."

"You worked here?" Elinor was surprised.

"That doesn't matter now." Sarah's shoulders jerked as though she were embarrassed.

"Hey, wait," Elinor said and fished in her pants pocket. Her face fell. "They took my cell."

"What do they want from us?" Tish's voice turned high and panicky.

"*Shh*. I'm sorry, Tish," said Crystal. "You really have no part in this. I guess we shouldn't have gone to your house."

"My mom will call the cops when I'm not home and she sees my bike!" Tish pouted.

"Or my bag of money," Elinor said softly.

All three stared at her.

"Your what?" Sarah asked.

"The bag I put under Tish's sink is full of hundred dollar bills. When I came in and saw Sarah and I didn't know . . ."

"Where did you ever get that much money?" Tish jerked away from her as though she oozed criminality.

Elinor turned to Crystal. "I told you I never spent my allowance. If we can get out of here, we can use it to escape and go far away. I was planning to go . . . anywhere."

"We'll think about that later," said Crystal. "There's an electronic panel over there that seems to be the only way out. Tish, you're the scientific one of us. Can you figure out how to open the door?"

"Gads, girl. I'm just a high school grad. I mean, I've had basic electricity and all that, but this is probably over my head. Now ask me a question about basketball . . ."

Crystal sighed. "Have a look anyway, would you?"

Tish went to inspect the panel.

"Look girls," Sarah turned to the others. "If we can't escape, you have to pretend to cooperate. Just don't—

whatever powers you have—don't let them learn the extent. Even if we're trapped here for a while, if they don't think our powers are very good, they'll eventually let us go."

"Powers? What powers?" Elinor seemed genuinely confused.

"*Shhh.* Do you think this room is bugged?" Crystal looked around.

"No. I was here when they were building these rooms. I'm pretty sure we're in one that was just to be used for storage. I guess they didn't know where to put us."

Tish returned. "I can't figure that thing out. It makes a bunch of beeps, and that's all I know. I'd have to know the combination."

Crystal groaned. "Can't you short it out like Scotty on Enterprise?"

"I can't do it, Cris!" Tish said, her voice angry. Her eyes betrayed her fear, however.

"I'm not sure that was Scotty." Elinor said softly, trying to remember.

"It doesn't matter. We'll have to play along then, until we see our chance. If even one of us escapes, promise to come back with help for the others." Sarah was adamant.

They all promised.

11

PERFECT PITCH

A tall woman with broad shoulders and an old-fashioned suit entered the room a few minutes later. She was accompanied by two guards, who took up station on either side of the door.

"My name is Wynn and I'll be your escort. We thought you might be hungry."

"How about we need to go to the bathroom," Tish sniped.

The woman shot her a stone stare, then said, "Follow me," as she clopped across the floor in green pumps.

Stopping at the doorway, she hid the electronic panel with her body, and punched in some numbers. The door popped open.

Crystal noticed Elinor's lips moving, as though she were cussing.

The guards followed the group down the hall toward the food galley. As they shuffled down the hall, a nausea overcame Crystal and she heard a voice in her head. Some of the words were garbled, then she heard . . . *I've got to call before five or she'll be gone . . .*

Spontaneously, Crystal turned, looked at the guard behind her, and whispered, "You better call, then."

The guard jerked, stared hard at her, and his jaw clenched. Crystal felt pressure across her scalp as he tried to shut off his thoughts to her.

"The head is over there," Wynn said to the group. "One at a time, and a guard will accompany you."

"Not inside!" Tish retorted. She stomped off toward the room, a guard on her heels.

In the cafeteria, the group followed Sarah's lead, and ate sandwiches in silence. On occasion, they cast furtive glances at each other. When they had finished, they were escorted down a gray corridor to another interior room. This one contained four chairs in a row. The only ornamentation in the room was a large mirrored panel on the wall.

Without discussion, in a *gestalt* connection, Crystal sensed that the group intuited it to be a two-way mirror, so all remained silent.

After a few minutes, the door opened smoothly and an elegant man Crystal recognized as Elinor's father entered.

"Crap!" Elinor squealed.

What felt like a ray of energy slammed against Crystal and dragged her attention to Sarah. Her aunt's skin turned pale with hard red spots on her cheeks and forehead. Hatred, grief, and fury peeled from her like decaying skin, as her fingers gripped the side of her chair in a vise. The intensity of her aunt's feelings set Crystal's gorge to rising and she was certain she was going to be ill.

The man stopped in front of the group.

"You asshole!" Elinor shot.

He smiled with a professional, success seminar face.

"Now, honey. There's no need to be rude. You'll upset your friends."

Sarah was breathing hard, and glanced at Elinor. "You know him?"

"Meet . . . *my daddy*," Elinor said. Her voice was taunting, teasing and heated. "Or, should I say, my *former daddy*."

Now he stood before Sarah. "Oh. And this would be . . . yes. Hello, Sarah. You've changed — a bit." He eyed her hips and seemed to be measuring her excess weight.

Sarah's forehead flushed and small beads of perspiration dotted her upper lip.

He reached out a finger and stroked her cheek. She jerked her head back to rid herself of the flange.

"So nice to see you again," he said.

He moved in front of Crystal. He studied her momentarily, but said nothing. Then he set his gaze Tish, who managed to give him the big chill she usually reserved for very rude punks.

"Well, ladies. As most of you know, I'm Raymond Stone, the director of this facility. I'm sorry to have brought you here in this manner, but it is a matter of national security."

Silence.

"I'm sure you'd all love to help your country, wouldn't you?" He assessed the group, folded his hands, and began pacing in front of them.

"I do apologize for the accommodations. They're temporary, of course. We had a number of new recruits come in today, and they had taken all the rooms before you arrived. I'm sure some bunks will be empty by tomorrow." He smiled at Wynn, then turned back to the group.

"You'll undergo some tests and, if you pass, you'll be immediately released. If you don't pass, we'll work with you until you can easily do the training routines. In the meantime, if you need any particular supplies, just let me know. And just relax. It will all be over soon." He smiled, showing a charming dimple, glanced once more at Elinor, and left the room.

"Asshole!" Elinor spat. Crystal, Sarah, and Tish jerked and stared at her. "Don't do what he said. If you pass the routines, they'll lock us up here."

Sarah swallowed and her voice came out hushed. "She's right."

Crystal suspected they were being watched through the two-way glass, so she shook her head and nodded toward it. They returned to silence.

One at a time, guards took each of the girls and ushered her out. When it was Crystal's turn, she looked at her aunt for reassurance, and her aunt nodded.

She entered a gray, dimly lit room and was seated in a cold, metal chair facing a panel and screen. A young man with marks on his temples and a tattoo of a dragon running up his arm, cleaned spots on her skin with alcohol. Electrodes were connected to spots on her head, her heart, and her wrists. When the youth left the room, a voice spoke over an intercom, asking her to respond to a series of images on a screen by pushing buttons on the panel.

The images seemed of random events, but her choices on the buttons in front of her were a triangle, a circle, a rectangle, and a star. She watched the images and, without trying to determine the purpose of the test, randomly punched the buttons. Sometimes, she'd push a different button than she had the impulse for, just to mess up. Couldn't they guess that trapped people would be uncooperative? What could they hope to gain?

Next, she was taken to a room lined in metal, except for one wall. A short woman sat on a chair next to her, facing the wall.

"Dearie," the woman whispered. "Try to do what they want and they'll let you go. They run these tests on a lot of kids."

Crystal glared at her, then said, "What do they want?"

"You're supposed to draw what you 'see' in the room on the other side of this wall." The woman handed her a tablet and a pencil.

"See?" The wall was solid.

"You know, visualize." The woman stared at her with clear, green eyes behind thick glasses. Fine gray hairs rose and fell as a pulse at the side of her creamy white temple pulsed in a one-two rhythm.

Crystal imagined stabbing her with the pencil and running out, but the woman looked so sweet, so *sweet, like a kindly old grandmother.* It would never — *do — to — hurt — her* . . . Crystal felt herself floating and the image of stabbing the woman disintegrated before her eyes. She *melded* with the woman. To hurt her would only hurt herself. She felt captured in the energy of the woman, controlled by her. She stared at the tablet and began to draw.

Fiddler extraordinaire, she had never passed first grade when it came to drawing. She drew a room with a chair. On the chair she drew a stick-figure girl she shaded in to be black. She made her hair spiky like Tish's. Next to the girl on the chair, stood a man, and on the other side of her was a woman. She drew a tie on the man.

She moved out of her reverie and the lights in the room brightened. A panel slid back between the wall and a window, and she saw Tish sitting on a chair. Next to her was a man with a green tie.

"*Oooh.* You did well!" The short woman sounded giddy she scrutinized the drawing. "What color is the tie?"

"Green. Now will you let us go?"

The woman laughed. "Oh, no. I lied."

"But—but I didn't even get it right. I show a woman in the room with her."

"Look at the woman you drew."

Crystal looked at the stick-like figure with her hair in a pony tail and the plaid shirt, and realized she'd drawn herself in the room, from the angle she had been, when she was *seeing*.

"But, you've got to let us go. We have people looking for us!"

The woman left the room.

The man wearing the green tie grinned at Crystal through the glass as Tish looked at her wide-eyed and shrugged her shoulders.

A stocky man in a lab coat and two guards escorted the girls back to the room with the cots. Sarah immediately sat on the edge of one.

When they were sure the woman wouldn't be back in, Elinor motioned for them to gather around Sarah. Turning to the group, she said "I got the code."

"What code?" Tish looked surprised.

"Yeah, what?" asked Sarah.

"To the panel. It's E-flat, B, A, A, F-sharp."

"How? What is she talking about, Cris?" Sarah looked perplexed.

A light dawned on Crystal. "She has perfect pitch! The panel is in tones."

"So," said Elinor, "we only need to find out which button is which tone before they know we're messing with the panel. I can open the door, then . . ."

"Then, run like Hades," Sarah finished. "And, look girls, if this works, I can't run fast. I'm too fat. I'll be a decoy."

Crystal was stricken. "I'll stay with you then."

"No, you especially. You've got to get out of here. There's more to tell, but it will take too long. There's an event and someone waiting for you—you've got to get to Sweden. You haven't accepted who you are yet, but the answers are there for you. For all of us and for all of humanity. And time is short."

"What time? Sweden? All of humanity?" Crystal's skepticism radiated from her. "Look, it's past December twenty-first, two-thousand twelve, and nothing happened. Wasn't some big event supposed to happen then? How can I believe this?"

"*Ungh!*" Sarah held her palms up and her face flushed as she made fists. "Crissy! There's one person who can explain it all. The wizard I mentioned. Fredrik."

Sarah sighed. "Look, just run. If they catch me, they won't keep me long. I know how to fool them. But go. Try to get out. And if you make it, promise me. You need to go to *Vingåker*."

"All right! But let's get moving!" Crystal's emotions churned like fathomless water in a red-eye pool. She wouldn't abandon her aunt, but she could let her think she would. If she got out, she'd get help.

Sarah eyed Tish. "Did I hear you say before that you played basketball?"

Tish nodded.

"Here's what we'll do. I noticed a janitor's closet outside in the hall. I'm going to get a broom or mop handle and go right. Can you leap high enough to knock the cameras in the hall out of alignment?"

"I'm not sure." Tish looked up at the ceiling. "How high is it out there?"

"I think the hall is only nine feet high. If you can jump that high, they won't know which of us went left or right. It won't work for long, but we can screw up their vision."

"I've got enough adrenalin to shoot me fifteen feet high right now."

"Good. Then you girls go left. These rooms aren't encased in metal, so that tells me we're on the first floor. If we were lower down in the facility, we'd be getting headaches from the microwaves by now. We're in the older section, so look for a wooden door or a door with a wooden frame. Those always lead to the outside."

Crystal grabbed her arm.

"Wait—get me a broom, too. I can hit them with it!" Her teeth were bared.

"They have guns, remember?" Sweat beaded on Sarah's brow.

Crystal let go of her arm. "If we get out of here, you have to explain *everything* to me."

"I will. Just let's get out!" Sarah's voice cracked on the last syllable and a rash of red spread up her throat.

They all huddled around Elinor as she approached the panel.

"Stop breathing on me," she chuffed. They stepped back.

She ran her fingers lightly across the nine-digit panel, not even stopping to register the tone. She was accustomed to picking up tunes quickly.

"Get ready," she said.

The girls crouched like sprinters in front of the door.

"One, two, . . ." She popped the tones from the buttons and the door swung into the room. They all burst into the empty hall.

"Which way?" Tish whispered.

"Left!" Sarah said and took off to the right.

Tish ran to her right.

"Your other left!" Crystal and Elinor shouted.

Tish turned, following Elinor and Crystal. The cluster of girls ran down the hall. A camera trained on them, and Tish leaped into the air, whacking it with a fist.

Sarah reached the janitor's closet and pulled a package from it.

"Wait! Elinor! Take this with you!" she called. She sent a plastic-wrapped parcel skidding along the hallway and Elinor picked it up.

"Why? What is it?"

Sarah ignored her. "Go, girls!" They ran.

A honking siren shattered the otherwise silent hallway.

Tish, with her longer legs, sprinted ahead to a tee in the hallway. "This way! I see a door!" She sped down the hall.

Elinor and Crystal pell-melled behind her, but couldn't keep up.

When they burst from the door, they saw Tish struggling with a uniformed guard. Without thinking, Crystal threw herself at the back of the man as Elinor swerved right and caromed off the side of the building into a bush, pulled herself up, and ducked further behind the hedge.

Another guard rounded the corner and grabbed Crystal. The guard easily flipped her from his partner's back and chuckled, "Fire brand!" He grabbed her by the shoulders then captured her wrist in his palm. He twisted it up as Crystal squealed.

The other guard held Tish in a similar restraint.

Tish gnashed her teeth and tried to bite the guard's hand. He held her head back, cracking her neck.

Fury and indignation flooded Crystal, and tears burst from her eyes. She was angry at her tears for making her seem weak, and angry she had been caught again. At least Elinor had made it out. With luck she could get to a phone quickly and call Crystal's dad for help.

The honking, blatting sound ceased, then four armed guards thundered past them out of the building, apparently in search of Elinor and Sarah.

The guards forced Crystal and Tish into the building and down the hallway. Partway, two middle-aged women in lab coats joined them.

Both women had hair rolled into tight dams above their ears, like the 1950s coifs, and the paleness of their faces made Crystal's look like a Hawaiian native's.

Tish's fists clenched as she stage-whispered "I'll take Tweedle Dee."

"Shut up," said the guard, and twisted her arm further. She squealed.

"Hey," said Tweedle Dum. "Don't do that."

Crystal's head hurt as though she had been slugged, and a heavy weight, like a rubber blanket in the air, pressed down on her. Her neck tensed as though she were being dragged in two directions by a rope tightening about her throat. She looked over her shoulder, past the guard's muscled arm, and saw an image of herself run naked across the hall and through the wall.

What the hell? She shook her head, certain she'd suffered a concussion in all the shenanigans.

12

DARK CAVERNS

The chill of the tiled floor reached through Sarah's bunny slippers as they slapped down the hall. Spying another camera, she angled the broom handle and swung. She missed. Trying again, a piece of the wood splintered, but did manage to knock the camera slightly askew.

The end of the corridor dropped into a ramp, carrying her downward toward a heavy door. Putting her shoulder to it, Sarah was able to push it open to a dimly lit basement area, full of pipes. She allowed her eyes to adjust for a moment. Outside of the hum and clang of equipment, she seemed to be alone. The air smelled chalky, and twice she suppressed sneezing. Someone could be down there with her. She worked her way among the pipes and mechanical controls toward another wall.

At last she reached an elevator. Instead of numbers, it bore an epsilon symbol. Her knowledge of Greek was limited, but this one she knew. It seemed impossible that she was on Level 5, since the building had changed — she couldn't be sure. Maybe it meant the elevator went to Level 5.

This section of the facility was just being built when she had left nearly eighteen years ago, and outside of knowing they planned a number of underground passages and rooms, she didn't know their uses or layout. She eyed the button and wondered why this elevator didn't call for using a more secure key-card. She assumed this was an older part of the building that had not been retrofitted with new gadgetry.

As she entered the elevator, a siren began honking. Twenty-odd buttons on the wall panel, each with a Greek symbol, indicated the height, or depth, of the facility. Sarah breathed hard and her thoughts spun. In the olden days, a side door on level two opened to a patio where they could take smoke breaks. With luck it was still there. She'd try to get there, then hit all the buttons, so they wouldn't know where she had exited.

She pressed the beta symbol. The doors paused, dinged, and, as they drew together, Sarah saw a man in a lab coat running toward her with his hand above his head.

"Oh! Hurry!" She yipped and punched the button multiple times, rapidly. Just before the doors shut, she thought she heard the man call her name.

A light came on above the zeta symbol. Someone at a low underground level must have flagged the elevator before she punched to go to level two. As her stomach rose, she knew it was descending.

Midway, the elevator clanged, jarred to a stop, creaked, and began moving sideways.

"What the hell?" Sarah held onto a railing for support. Whatever track the car was on must have been rusty, as a hard scraping accompanied the motion.

The elevator stopped again, and continued downward. No lights came on to indicate floor passage. It stopped.

Sarah was about to push the beta button again when the doors opened. She could no longer hear sirens, possibly due to her depth in the facility. Scooting to the back corner of the elevator, she lowered her face, hoping to not be recognized as an escapee.

Three teens wearing either lab coats or hospital gowns, she wasn't sure which, approached. Sarah watched from under long bangs as the closest youth moved woodenly through the opening and held the door, waiting for the others. Their eyes were glazed, and one of them trembled as though he were an elderly, infirm man, as he made his way along the hall.

The outside hallway itself drew her interest, as it was rounded, as though a boring machine had carved it out, melting the sides into glass, and then scraping a flat floor. Sarah's eyes rose and her head followed. The area gleamed as though coated with obsidian, and metallic sparks flicked in a dull light.

Too late, she saw the form moving behind the youths, as though driving them.

Instinct splattered adrenalin into her cells before her mind could grasp what she was seeing. Part of her reasoned that she was seeing a very tall man dressed in metallic armor. Probably someone from the Society for Anachronism — just playing with the kids. But the part of her that knew better, the part that urged her to run with all her might, said she was looking at a being nearly eight-feet tall and that it wore no clothing at all. What a portion of her mind saw as armor, she now realized were scales.

And the eyes that looked coldly back at her, that bore into the soft orbs under her bangs, were covered by a thin membrane. The nicotinic film pulled back, exposing yellow eyes with a silver, vertical slit where there should have been pupils, above a face pinched into lizard-like features.

Part of Sarah must have run, because the part remaining felt instantly weak and devoid of defenses. Her jaw dropped open and a tiny mew issued from the back of her throat, so far away that it could have been from a distant planet. Her arms turned to rubber, ceased to hold her erect in the elevator, and she slid along the wall like putty. Dropping to the floor, she gurgled, screamed in a whisper, and wet her pants, while the three youths stared blankly forward, seemingly unaware of her.

The elevator doors came together, the rubber insulation pushing into a single line. A tick. A shift.

A silver-gray claw wormed its way through the rubber. The door groaned and opened. The creature moved toward her. It reached out a clawed hand larger than her head and pointed a device at her. A low tone hummed from the apparatus.

Air rushed from her throat in a single hysterical attempt to scream, but no sound accompanied it.

The creature dragged her from the elevator car.

Lights out.

♪

The guards left, while the two women continued escorting Tish and Crystal down the hallway. They came to an elaborate elevator door, coated in a glistening copper. Tweedle Dee, whose badge identified her as 7482, swiped a card in a slot and after a few seconds, the doors opened, showing a metallic-lined interior. The other woman, wearing badge number 222, entered first and stood with her arms folded.

"Here, put these on," said 7482 as they entered. She offered the girls two folded silver bands. The girls watched as the Tweedles opened their own versions and covered their heads with them.

"Tin foil hats?" Tish stifled a hysterical giggle.

"They're to hold back the electromagnetic forces. Microwaves. You know, EMFs. If you don't want headaches as we descend, you'd best use them," said 222.

"Why are you doing this to us?" Crystal's voice felt very far off, as though she were disconnected from her body. "Just let us go. We won't tell."

"That isn't the way it works," 222 actually smiled at her. "I know you're scared, but don't worry. It's totally safe."

222 and 7482 exchanged looks that gave Crystal a jolt of fear. *They were lying.* She didn't know how she knew, but she possessed certainty that what they headed toward was deadly. And, in a flash, she saw the hundreds before them who had already died, in a confusion of frequencies, energetic swirlings, and, the most grotesque, having been dragged through some *place* by some *force* and returning in the middle of walls, ceilings, ships, and with body parts buried in the earth.

The girls put on their hats, but even with the alleged protection, Crystal felt her teeth rattling as they descended in the elevator. A resonant, low hum pervaded every aspect of the walls, the air, and became louder the farther they dropped. 222 and 7482 seemed unaffected, while Tish seemed unaware of the sound.

Crystal's hands went to her head and she closed her eyes, attempting to block out the rumble.

"Uh oh," she heard 7482 say. "Looks like we have a natural Level Five."

Crystal opened her eyes to see 222 nodding. "Should I give her another cap?"

"I don't think that will help. Let's just get them into the Dark Room. The shielding is better."

Crystal wanted to ask questions, wanted to make demands, but it seemed that with every pulse of the tone she became weaker.

They left the elevator and walked down a dim, narrow hallway. Pressure and a sensation of pervasive terror accompanied them.

"Don't fight it, honey," said 222.

Crystal recoiled. The woman seemed to be oozing a colorless slime through every pore. Receiving her attention felt like being covered in diarrhea.

A minute later they stopped at a room with a tall and solid metal door that looked similar to a meat locker's. 7482 pulled the handle and told Tish to enter. Tish looked with fear at Crystal, whose eyes filled with tears. Crystal's gut told her it would be the last time she would see her friend.

7482 followed Tish into the room and a light came on automatically. Wires coiled all over the walls in between speakers. The floor was padded. Straps emerged from the center of the floor.

As 222 closed the door, Crystal glimpsed a man in a jumpsuit strapping Tish to the floor on her back. She expected her friend to punch and try to run, but she just lay there, unresisting. Perhaps Tish was feeling the effects of that low droning as well. A new shade of fear enveloped her, seeing her feisty friend so docile.

222 opened the adjacent room for Crystal to enter. This one contained a small television screen, two chairs, writing paper, and a pen chained to a small desk. Metal shielded the walls, ceiling, and floor. A silver skull cap was attached to a portable arm near the chair at the desk.

Crystal stared at it with a sense of dread and deepening horror. She couldn't quite remember what—it felt a bit like *déjà vu* — but it seemed she had seen that cap before and knew what it could do. *How could she know anything about it?*

It was as though all her senses, all her family gifts, were being triggered in this place. Familiar feelings and places—the walls, the halls, the strange people and twisted events—they all combined to shift her into a perceptual rent—a tearing of reality, of space and time, and of who she believed herself to be. This place was wrong. Bad. And she was trapped. *Again.*

Warnings screamed from the voices that she had heard before. Before the events at the camp. In the garden. The voices that now seemed angelic in their intent, compared to what she was undergoing.

Crystal began panting.

"Easy girl," 222 said "This won't hurt a bit."

Liar! Crystal thought, struggling to control herself. She sensed that if she even spoke she'd lose strength. Although unaware of what they had in store for her, she knew it would take every skill she had to stay alive.

A firm hand on her shoulder shoved her into the seat. 222 swung the skull cap around and lowered it over her head. She tightened screws tightly onto Crystal's scalp and Crystal yelped and grabbed for her head. The woman slapped her hand, grabbed her chin and said, "Don't give me trouble." She then turned on a monitor behind her.

Touching her ear, she spoke into a microphone. "We're ready in here. Are you set?"

"Just let me get into the monitor station. She's down," came over an interior speaker.

"Okay, call when you're ready."

Crystal's breath came in fast spurts, and her heart sped up. Her senses seemed to be magnifying in the tight room. She heard a small voice come through 222's earpiece.

"Ready. Sending the warm-up to Level 2 *now.*"

The television in front of Crystal came in just in time to see Tish on the screen, lying flat on the floor. A yellow light pulsed across the room, intensified, and flashed. Tish closed her eyes, thrashed on the floor, and screamed.

Crystal's hands turned to claws as she reached for the screen. She screamed, too.

13

SHATTERED CRYSTAL

Something snapped in Crystal, and she turned away from the television monitor. She looked *through* the wall at Tish thrashing in the forces that rifled her body. Focusing beyond her eyes Crystal slipped into energies at a molecular level; a sense of depersonalization intensified, similar to the effect she had felt earlier, when she had drawn the figures in the room next to her. Her anxiety ratcheted up in intensity as Tish screamed in anguish

"Help!" Tish's screamed gurgled and became a shriek.

7482 turned a knob. Crystal wasn't sure how she could see 7482, but without thinking, she hurled spikes of fury and fear at the woman, who looked into the air as though she sensed a gnat. She turned the knob again.

"Now, it's up to you to stop the waves," 222 said to Crystal.

It was like a game to them! Crystal was sure of it.

"Wha − t? I can't−" Her head felt as though someone were pounding it with a salami and her mouth felt larger than her face. Her humors felt stretched and her skin fluid as though her fiber were becoming *distorted.* And, as she watched Tish, that is exactly what was happening to her.

"You need to keep yourself centered. You can *will* whatever you want, but do *not* let yourself be drawn into your friend's situation—or you'll both go over."

"Over where? Where?" The pulsing, the pounding— Crystal felt she had to scream the words to be heard, yet her voice came out in a puff.

"Watch."

7482 turned the knob again, and waves of color became visible to Crystal.

"You can see them, can't you." 222 watched her closely.

"All those colors. What are they doing to Tish?" Crystal's voice floated from her mouth, sluggish, in time with the pulsing electromagnetic forces.

"I can't see the emanations like you can," said 222. "They're caused by the acoustics. They'll open a tear, soon, just watch."

"No! Let her out of there!" Crystal felt as though she were jumping up and down, but she sat demurely at the station and spoke in a calm voice.

7482 turned the knob again and a charcoal, throbbing mass engulfed the room. Tish's body liquefied and spread throughout the molecules. A scream tore from her throat as it stretched into a smear of energy and blended with the dark vibration of the EMFs. A final audible thought ripped from her, projecting into Crystal's mind. *"Help me!"*

A red and black vortex opened up in the room, swirled in concentric circles, and drew Tish's elongated and misshapen form through the vertex. It was impossibly larger than the room and clearly not contained in the same reality.

Tish simply disappeared from her position on the floor.

Sudden brightness flooded the television screen.

Numb, Crystal stared at the spot where Tish had been.

"Now," said 222. Her voice was matter-of-fact. "It's up to you to bring her back."

"What? How? How?"

"You're a natural. You need to tap into your powers and summon her. *Draw* her back into being."

"Where is she?" Crystal continued to stare. Her voice was soft, as though every emotion had been drained from her. She felt larger than her body, completely compliant—as though she had been drugged.

"She's on the other side. Or in a different time. We're hoping you can find her."

"Me? How can I? Why would you think this?"

"Just take a look. Close your eyes. Remember what you saw, connect with the resonance and frequency, and *follow her*. Then bring her back."

Crystal stared at the television, dumbfounded. What kind of insanity was this? She had no idea what they were talking about. It wasn't even similar to what happened to her when she played her fiddle. And she didn't have a fiddle now. What could they expect from her?

"Please, please. I don't know how. Please bring her back." Crystal started crying.

222 laughed. "Oh, honey. We don't use that human emotion and reaction around here. It's just wasted energy.

"We'll take you back to your room, now. You think about it and we can try again later. Just remember—if you don't bring her back, no one can. So you'd better try." 222 stood and escorted an unresisting Crystal back to her room.

♪

Sarah lay in darkness as a slow gray dawned, drawing her into wakefulness. Pressure held her in a fixed position, flat on her back. Her eyes opened and she became aware of a hard, plastic shell encapsulating her body. Fighting to move and realizing she was restrained, she yelled from a hoarse and raw throat.

A form, distorted through the plastic, came over and peered down at her. It looked like a lizard in a lab coat. She must be hallucinating. She heard a hiss, as a slightly medicinal smell rushed into her tomb from vents in the side. She was instantly asleep.

A voice sounding like waves on the shore reached inward to her. *Sarah . . . saaarrrahhhh. Plleeeaase wake up . . .*"

"No . . ." she said. She felt good. Floating. So sweet, this space.

"*It's 7.83 Hertz,*" came *the Voice That Knew All.*

A tick, a change in pressure. She could move, she stretched and farted. Her eyes opened. A stranger's face. Her mouth opened to scream. A hand clamped over her mouth. She pulled against it with her hands, under her control now.

"Sarah. *Shhh.* It's me. James." Earnest gray eyes peered into hers. "Me. Your friend."

Sarah quit struggling. James? Who was he? He looked vaguely familiar. Her head swam with fractured images.

"Be really quiet—we only have a few minutes before the next shift starts and it took me a while to find you. I can get you out, but you have to do exactly what I say, okay?"

Sarah nodded and James released her mouth. "Here, let me help you sit up. You'll be groggy for a few minutes." James assisted her to sit.

Sure enough, her head spun and she spewed vomit onto her lap. "Yuck," she mumbled.

"Never mind. Here, put this on." James handed her a

metal sheathing for her skull, like the one he wore. "It helps to defray the EMFs down here."

"Why am I in a bassinet?"

James stifled a surprised smile. "It's a birthing chamber. Apparently, they figured you had escaped from here."

"Birthing?" Sarah looked around the room. It was cavernous. Clear plastic containers shaped like coffins stretched far in either direction. Each container she could see held a nude human female body. Some were obviously pregnant.

She realized she, too, was nude. Her hands flew up and covered her breasts.

"Here," said James. He handed her a lab coat. "It was all I could get without it appearing suspicious."

He helped her out of the container.

"Now, let's get the heck out of here."

Still groggy, Sarah followed him through the maze of apparati. They ducked and crawled periodically as cameras rotated to monitor the area. The floor was cold and Sarah missed her bunny slippers.

At the exit, James swiped his card and the door opened silently.

Once in the hall, James yanked her flat to the wall, and led her sliding along the smooth surface to another door.

"Where . . .?"

"*Shh.*" He held his finger to his lips.

She followed blindly, but as her mental haze thinned, she watched him on edge. Who was this person? Why was he helping her?

A memory of the tall metallic-looking being crossed her mind and fear burbled through her blood. She just wanted out.

They slipped down a dim hallway and came to an outer door. "You probably don't remember this, do you?"

James looked at her, hopeful.

Sarah shook her head.

"They completely wiped your mind." He shook his head and Sarah though she saw tears in his eyes. "This is how we used to sneak out for our rendezvous."

"What? When I was here?" Sarah searched and could find no memory of this man or any rendezvous.

They stepped through the door into a dark tunnel, lit by small red lights that glowing across the ceiling. They came to a sleek, metallic train with no windows.

"This one is for the visitors. They are light sensitive." James looked over his shoulder. "This will get you out of the facility. They aren't using it now, but the train runs on an hourly schedule. When it stops, just depart. There will be a few steps. Go up. He pushed a button and a door hissed open."

"Where am I?" Sarah's voice came in a whisper, her head still in a dream.

"Archuleta Mesa in New Mexico." James looked at her with reassurance in his eyes. "Don't worry. You'll get home.

"Our baby... I never saw you again." James embraced Sarah, and she let him, welcoming the warmth of his body. "I thought you'd died," he said.

"Our baby?"

He reached into his pocket and handed her a key, along with some bills from his wallet. "When you get there, it's the blue Toyota on the second row, fifth car up. I'll find you again. I promise. We have a lot to catch up on, after all these years."

Sarah's need to escape overrode her confusion. Taking the key, she bade her benefactor goodbye—his eyes were *so familiar*—and went through the door.

The train felt as though on water with no turbulence at all. Sarah sat stiffly on a seat that seemed built for a child.

The vehicle whispered to a stop and the door opened automatically. Sarah stepped out, noting the stairway to a landing above. Her hand on a railing, she drifted slowly upward, wondering what lay behind the door at the top.

The door was steel, and the handle a bar. Afraid, she faced it, unsure what would happen once it was open. There might be more creatures on the other side. She was barefoot. Would she need to run?

Sarah peered down as the train hummed then left the station. Unless she wanted to stay in these underground tunnels, she had no choice.

She turned the handle. The door groaned as it cracked open so she could peer out.

A flood of sunlight blinded her and she squinted. Then she breathed clean air.

Stepping out onto a patch of grass, she took in small shops and a clean street. She turned to view the structure from which she'd come. A small, ornate tower loomed above the doorway, with the words *Pagosa Springs, Colorado*.

Crystal lay for three days on her cot, too upset to eat. Occasionally, a shadowy figure would come in with a tray, leave it, and return later to pick it up. On the fourth day, no one came at all.

Crystal pondered what had happened to her and her predicament. It all seemed related to her violin playing and what had occurred with Olaf. Somehow, whatever *force* she had tapped into appeared to be of interest to this strange organization. They seemed to think she could bring Tish back —*but from where?* They had given her no instructions. The place seemed half-baked, not like a tightly run government facility. Perhaps the energy waves being emitted by the machinery were affecting everyone — staff included.

She looked at the silver beanie they had given her to wear. It seemed high-tech, inlaid with wires and multiple layers of super thin metals. But it still looked like tin foil. Did they really think these devices would prevent waves as powerful as those she had seen?

She guessed that no one had escaped, or they would have come for her. Right? She didn't want to die. She wanted to bring Tish back. But how?

On the fifth day, a teenager with a pierced nostril, red and black hair, and breasts jutting from the top of her low-cut blouse dragged another cot into the room. She scratched her head with black, painted fingernails, popped a bubble in her gum, and said, "Hi. I'm Sheila."

After setting up her cot, she plopped down and turned her full attention to Crystal.

"You're Crystal, right? I seen your ol' man out there the other day."

"Huh? My dad?" Crystal didn't want to talk to the girl, but this was news she needed.

"Yeah. He came in asking for somebody who had quit years ago. Then he asked about you. They denied you were here. There was nothing he could do." Sheila scratched her head again, pulled something out with her fingernails, and looked at it. She flicked it down.

"I'm supposed to get you up to speed. I've been here a while."

Crystal stared at her, blankly.

"Hey, it ain't so bad here. It's a roof, you know. Before this I was just on the streets of New York. And hungry. I don't know what your deal is, but here they will feed you — though I hear you haven't been eating — and all you have to do is their stupid experiments. Listen to, like, music and stuff."

Crystal sat up.

"My friend disappeared."

"Oh, yeah. Well, some do. One time they tried to bring someone back and got a cave man."

"How? What are they doing?"

"I dunno. Word is this has been going on for a long time. Back when some ship disappeared and then reappeared with people stuck in parts of it."

Not sure how safe it was to talk to this girl, Crystal still said, "Philadelphia experiment. I heard of it before."

"Yeah, well, they kept practicing. They've built a bunch of these places around the world. They mess with weather, time travel, inter-dimensions, and the like. Some people say they even talk to aliens." Sheila giggled, a high, raucous sound. "Yeah. Like I'd believe *that*. Anyway, it don't matter. They treat ya' okay here. You should eat. You look sick."

Crystal nodded. Her father had come. He wouldn't give up. She'd need to be strong until he returned.

And maybe, just maybe, she could figure out how to tap the . . . wavelengths or whatever . . . and bring Tish back.

14

GOOD IS BAD

Sometimes being a wizard was a real pain and Fredrik was feeling it then. It pressed in on him as though the very air was laden with depressed spirits crying out in agony. Projecting what he hoped was invisibility — it had been a long time since he'd used these skills — he crossed the boundary to his neighbor's field and slogged through it to the forest. He let down his mental shield and wove among the trees, pausing to inhale the strength they offered. Asking the tree first, he broke free a dead branch, which he used as a walking stick to climb down an embankment to a clear stream.

Mist curled along the still water in the morning light, then skipped playfully across the burble over some stones, unaware of Fredrik's misfortune.

He groaned and ran his hand up and down along the stick. He was rewarded with a splinter, which served to remind him why he was there.

In the night, he'd felt the woman with the funny hair scream to him. He'd been drinking his soup and was not prepared for any vision, so he'd had but a moment to comprehend. She had cried out, then gone into a darkness he could not reach. He'd felt a shift, a *tearing*, in the fabric of the world, and had known something had gone terribly wrong. He continued staring into the void, awaiting more visions, but none came. When he turned back to his soup, it was cold.

Today, all day, the world was slightly off, as though color was a shade darker, sound just a tad scratchy, every feeling a bit unpleasant. This was beyond him. He believed it concerned the young woman he had seen through the eyes of his funny-haired relative, but wasn't sure. He'd come here, to the water, home of the *Näcken*, to try to contact her. If she was truly the one to bring change, the water spirit might find her. Water was everywhere.

He stood before the stream and watched as a spring sent secret water gushing in from the side. Accustomed to looking for signs, he realized this was his instruction in how to reach her. Indirectly.

Under the mist, a light from rays that had sneaked through the leaves and hidden under stones, darted like sprites. He focused on the light, drawing it together, and sought the feel and flavor of the girl, wherever she was in the universe. His feet grew rigid and cold as both hands gripped the walking stick. His eyes grew wider without blinking as they fixated on senses beyond . . . Soon his nose ran in the chill of the day and mixed into his mustache.

A jay watched him from a tree, then grew brave and shouted a warning at him. He jerked and, for an instant, *saw* the girl curled on a cot in a gray room. In that moment, he felt her misery and confusion. Then he was pushed away by what appeared to be spikes of energy emitting from the building she was in.

He mustered his strength. There would be but one

chance to penetrate the energetic barrier and send her a message. Only one image could be forced inward to her.

When he was done, he sat on the wet clay and stroked his beard, exhausted. Would the girl get the sign? And if she did, would she understand?

♪

Glad for the darkness, Crystal allowed her tears to run down her cheeks, back across her ears, and into her hair, which protruded from the mandatory foil hat. She lay with her back pressing against the hard cot, and a light blanket pulled to her chin. Sheila's easy breathing kept the room from being soundless.

Weeks had passed since her father had come looking for her, and Crystal was still trapped. Since they had lied to him, what else could he do? What if he couldn't figure out how to get her out? But worse was the guilt that ate at her insides about Tish. *Where was she?*

They seemed to think she could free Tish from wherever she had gone. But they wouldn't or couldn't tell her how. They just kept putting her through their stupid training routines. Today they had her shouting commands at an ashtray. And every day they had her looking through walls. They kept sticking her with needles, plugging her into electrodes, and monitoring every magnetic wave her body or brain produced. She was trying to be compliant. She truly wanted to help Tish. And she truly wanted to go home.

Thinking of home brought a new gush of tears, which she just let flow. She tried mentally shouting to her aunt, like she had at Beans camp, but was met with what felt like a purple-black membrane. Whatever energy field surrounded IRVing, it prevented thoughts about the outside world for any meaningful duration.

Crystal had learned that 222 was her monitor and was in charge of training her. She'd become afraid to go to sleep at night, because many times during their instructions, 222 would attach electrodes to her head then turn on equipment to induce a sleep-like state. In that state, she was easy to control, weak. Her monitor would give her commands designed to force her to use her powers. Didn't they think she would if she knew how?

They used sophisticated equipment to copy her own natural brain waves and body electromagnetic waves, enhance them, then curl them back toward her, to help her project. And though some of the tests seemed fruitful, the important one, the one that would bring Tish back, eluded her. They said she wasn't trying hard enough. That she had to force herself.

Tired of crying, she allowed herself to drift toward sleep. A sudden image, accompanied by a burst of adrenalin, shot into her consciousness. She saw a face of a man, hairy, unkempt, with kind blue eyes expressing compassion. The image was replaced with that of a cow.

The black and white cow stood in a field, perfectly content. The cow was perfect. A *good* cow. A stream bubbled nearby.

That was it.

Crystal was alert, though she had no idea what the vision meant. It had a different feel from the images that she encountered through her trainings. This one had come from *outside* and, she felt, was directed toward her, probably from the man, to relate information. It didn't seem like she was remotely spying, reaching toward the cow as a target. More like the cow had targeted *her*. Was the man someone her father had hired to contact her using telepathy?

A *cow*?

The next day, Crystal dragged her hand along the cement wall leading toward the training rooms. Sheila walked next to her, dragging her feet as though she hadn't received enough sleep.

"Hey, are you okay?" Crystal asked.

Sheila turned red-rimmed eyes toward her. "I must have let my purple shield down."

A lanky boy holding a furless animal with a twisted head hurdled by them. "Moooove!" he shouted. Crystal looked after him

Sheila ignored him. "I put up a purple shield at night to keep the voices from coming in. Don't you?" She looked up at Crystal. Salt residue lined her eyes.

"No. I don't know what you mean."

"Let's stop for a minute. I feel like I'm about to keel over." As Sheila leaned against the wall, Crystal noticed how thin her legs were as they protruded from her hospital gown.

"Look at us," said Sheila, glancing down the hallway. A group of teens shuffled toward their designated rooms, their eyes on the floor, or off into space. "We look like a bunch of cattle." She gripped Crystal's arm. "You won't tell anyone if I tell you, will you?" Her eyes looked feverish, pained.

Crystal shook her head "no."

"I'm going to get out of here. I've been planning it. Everything they do, what they tell us is good, isn't. So they feed us. Keep us warm. So *what*? Look at us." She surveyed the deathful group. "I'd rather be dead than be like this. And the problem is, what they do to us here, you *can't die*."

A voice shot down the hall.

"You girls hurry up! Your monitors are waiting." A short man with wiry hair and folded arms strode toward them.

Sheila rushed her last words. "They say the hats keep us safe. They don't. You have to imagine a purple shield around yourself." She squeezed Crystal's arm, then released it, and headed toward her room. "Buzz off, pig," she said to the man.

Crystal watched her go, sensing a weakness about the girl, and feeling Sheila had gone crazy. She strengthened her resolve to get out, but still didn't know how.

As she entered the room to where 222 awaited her, Crystal wondered about the purple shield. Could it be that some imaginary structure in her mind could actually protect her? Well, why not? Didn't what 222 did to her, and forced her to do, have to do with her mind? What did she really know about electromagnetic fields? Nothing! Purple shields were as good as the next *woo-woo* thing.

222 looked up as she entered. The squat woman had set up the equipment, and was busy chewing gum.

Odd, thought Crystal. *Like she's chewing her cud.* What were all these cow references? Crystal sat on her stool.

222 proceeded to swipe some spots on her head with alcohol. She then attached electrodes.

With eyes closed, Crystal caught an image of a cow udder being cleaned and pumps attached. Is that what they were doing to her? Milking her? But if so, for what? Her life force? Her animal magnetism? She laughed and her eyes popped open.

222 glared at her.

Crystal couldn't concentrate. She'd moved from Level Three to Level Five during her stay, but could not see beyond a roiling black mass that stood between her and Tish. If only she could get there! Just listen to the sound of 222's voice. It would guide her. It was for her own good. It was. . . .

Crystal drifted upward. A slice of light had opened before her. She moved into a meadow. She watched as a cow, a clean, beautiful cow, enjoyed the fresh grass. Here came its master. He led her into a barn. The farmer ran his hands over her sides. She liked the gentleness of his hand and the murmur of his words. Such a kind man to take care of her. To feed her. To love her. The tool cut into her throat and she dropped to her knees. Why was she getting weaker? She looked at the man with a question, and for the first time saw the truth: hunger. All the love, all the care, was so someday the cow could feed his belly. He seemed to take no joy in the act. He simply accepted it.

Crystal slipped back through the light.

"What was that?" 222 demanded.

"I don't know. I couldn't see," Crystal lied. But she knew. She could not be complacent. She could accept no comfort as true. It was all a lie. And she would never escape by doing what they told her to do.

After she passed her last experiment, 222 took her to a room surrounded by sound projection equipment and a large screen. When she turned on some of the equipment, the screen lit up with colors representing the sounds. She then asked Crystal to manipulate the waves.

That night, Sheila did not return to the room. Crystal extended feelers but could not perceive her anywhere in the complex. Beyond that, of course, was the EMF wall of impenetrability.

She waited until the sensors began a midnight hum, which she'd learned from Sheila were designed to keep the children asleep, before she slipped off her foil hat. Immediately, she was assaulted by the EMFs coursing through the building.

As Sheila had suggested, she imagined a purple pyramid around herself, to prevent the waves from entering. She held the shape for about ten minutes, and noticed she was becoming more alert.

A small monitor near the ceiling flashed red, on and

off.

No one could help her but herself. She needed to draw power from herself. But where was it? For weeks they had been drawing power from her, for whatever reason. Milking her.

She needed strength, or she'd end up like Sheila. Could she somehow call her energy back? Draw it into herself from wherever they had sent it?

She wanted herself back! She could try something new. Different — beyond what they'd tried to teach her. It had never been attempted — at least on level five.

Keeping her eyes closed, she ran her perception across her body, across herself, and sensed what she felt like to others. It was an odd sensation, as though she were looking at herself from the outside. Then she extended her feelers outward, seeking the residue *of herself.* A blast of heat assaulted her, then she felt the cool warmth of her own essence. She centered herself and drew it inward, calling it to her. Her personal magnetic force was embedded, it felt, in the very space and time of the building. As she drew it in, she felt a strengthening, a power returning to her.

Using what she knew about acoustics and playing the fiddle, Crystal listened, and then — with her mind — duplicated the wave. Using her will she created new nodes in the visual image of the wave, increased the frequency, and changed the pitch.

Her heart raced faster. She had locked into an area beyond the third dimension; beyond the fourth. She knew this instinctively. And she knew what to do.

222 would be proud, but Crystal wasn't about to tell her what she'd discovered. She placed her hands over her chest, folded them, then began generating a single tone in her mind.

She followed the tone to the origins of sound, and

matched it with some waves she had encountered in the building. Then she *turned* the wave. Flipped it inside out. A sudden shock engulfed her, and she was swept up in a deep purple thrust of tones, energies, sounds, vibrations, and batterings that could not register on any of her five senses. A pulse of fear, then she tightened her will to resist. She focused with iron strength toward the image of herself. Without warning, she was ripped from her bed and a horrible pulsing vortex opened in the wall.

Standing tall, feet spread, she inhaled to the bottom of her lungs, held it, then stepped through.

Still in the vortex, she slid through the wall. As she crossed the hallway, she glanced to the left and saw, to her delight and amazement, as she, Tish, and the Tweedles made their way down the hall, as they had her first night at the facility. She watched the incomprehension on her own face as the past Crystal looked up to see her crossing the hall.

She had done it. She had walked through matter, energy, space, and time to *the past*.

Fighting to hold her position, Crystal waded through the walls as though they were made of thickened water, until she found herself outside near Elinor, who crouched hiding in the bushes. Her body felt whipped as layers seemed to solidify into the space.

"Stay in the shadows," she whispered. Elinor's head jolted upward.

"Cris! How did you get out?"

Crystal was hit with a wave of *déjà vu* as she settled into the past timeline. It felt slightly different, mildly twisted, yet for an instant she knew what would come next. Then her eyes unfocused and confusion riddled her thoughts. She swung her head back and forth.

Elinor looked toward a gated entry looming at the end of the driveway, but Crystal made signals to go to the back of the building, instead. Moving her hand to make the gestures felt like picking up a hundred pound rock.

"*Shhh*. We'll need to hurry." To her, her voice sounded foggy, down a tunnel.

Elinor stared as Crystal moved from behind one of the shielding bushes. Her jaw dropped and she choked, "Gads! You're naked!"

15

THE FUTURE IS THE PAST

Crystal looked down at her body and saw it bluish in the light. It made no sense to her, and didn't seem to matter. Her mind felt mushy, soft and pliable. She felt as though she'd received a concussion: images and sensations dripped and slid through the air around her.

Elinor's grip tightened on the parcel Sarah had tossed at her earlier. Becoming aware of it, she ripped open the plastic bag and a lab robe fell out. "How could she have known?" Her voice squeaked. At no answer from Crystal, she said "Quick! Put this on!"

Crystal donned the garment and used the Velcro to close the front.

As they darted from bush to bush, guards burst from the building and spread out, drawing stun guns. The girls scurried to the side of a large lilac and sized up the fence.

Three of the guards had headed toward the front of the building at a run, but one began poking the foliage with the end of a cattle prod.

"Can you squeeze through?" Crystal whispered.

Elinor eyed the bars. They were roughly six or eight inches wide, but her petite frame just might make it.

"I think so," she said, and stuck an arm through two bars. She angled her shoulder, twisted her face, then torqued her pelvis. Pulling her leg, she was free. She was on a cement embankment housing a flower bed, approximately five feet above a sidewalk.

"Now, you."

"I can't. My boobs won't make it."

"Try, Cris. They'll squish."

Crystal followed Elinor's example, but, sure enough, her breasts hung up on the bar. Reaching her hand over, she squashed one, then the other.

"Ouch!"

"*Shhh!*"

"Wait." Crystal backed out and stood erect. "Elinor. I need you to run. I can't explain more now. But I need you to run about five blocks up, until you come to a bar called Harry's Place. Wait for me there."

Crystal's arms felt as though ants were running through her veins. The sensation began spreading through her midsection, nearing her heart. Her face was becoming numb and she was seeing from her periphery, rather than her eyes. It was difficult to speak, as she said, "Go! Don't look back!"

Elinor's eyes captured Crystal's for just a moment and an understanding passed between them. Without another word, Elinor turned and ran. She didn't look back.

Removing the garment, Crystal dropped it between the bars, outside the fence. Now the sensation had spread through her entire body.

Crystal faced the building. The structure appeared to have been a large church at one time. By the ornate towers and windows, Crystal guessed it to have been Catholic. In front of the church were gardens which still held finely manicured fall roses. To the right was a parking lot, half-full even though it was evening. A large radio tower jutted from a smaller and newer building to the left of the building. Toward the rear, several microwave towers reached into the night sky.

Crystal felt herself becoming *fine*. As though the bubbling sensation in her veins had thinned her into discrete molecules. She broadened and felt the ground flow *through* her, as she flowed *through* the earth. Around and between the particles of composition. Buzzing energy. A sensation of an underground facility leaking swirls of electromagnetic waves. At the far end, at the lowest level, she sensed the unique energy signature that she knew was Aunt Sarah, or Aunt Sarah's residue, and perceived a pulsing light array that she knew instinctively meant a room of bio life-forms. Crystal attempted to call out, but only a shift and tumbling in energy occurred.

At that moment, Crystal lacked a centricity, a locus, yet felt as though she existed as all things and individuals she pervaded, simultaneously.

"Hey, you! Girl!" the guard pointed at her with his prod and broke into a run toward her.

She realized what would happen next. Again facing the iron fence that stood between her and freedom, she concentrated. Then, her mouth opened, showing her teeth in a smile not unlike that of the Cheshire cat, her molecules sped up, and she disappeared into a flow of sounds, colors, and sensations.

And she shifted through the fence.

From where she had been, oscillating concentric rings rippled outward.

A soundless concussion raised the guard into the air and tossed him, unconscious, on the grass.

On the other side, she *willed* her body to reassemble. She picked up the lab robe and put it on.

She stood in an aura of calmness, willing her body to remain outside the remaining guards' awareness. She watched as they systematically scoured the yard, prodding through the bushes and roses. One of them looked directly at her, and his eyes slid off her form as though oiled, not registering it.

Crystal shifted her attention down the street and saw Elinor running. Just behind her, she focused and drew herself together, forming a center. She still felt as though she pervaded the material world around her, but she had more a sense of self as concern for her friend drew her inward. A heaviness, as of molecules joining to molecules, structure to structure, overrode her sensation of being in control of all around her. The world around her seemed to *twist* and she felt centered. Whole. Human. Except for the pounding confusion. *What had they done to her in there?* And Elinor was right. How had she gotten free? Already she was losing her memory of events.

Catching up with Elinor, they continued onward toward Harry's Place.

"We'll use the phone in Harry's," Crystal said. Her voice sounded as though she were echoing in a dream, but was beginning to feel more real.

"I don't have any money. Do you?" Elinor then eyed the lab coat Crystal was wearing and giggled nervously.

"No, but someone might let us use their cell."

Energy spiraled through Crystal, then settled into a gentle pool around her. She felt a melding — a merging with the environment. Still shaken, her mind shifted and settled to her current locale. Already the past — what had been the future — seemed to be correcting into *balance*. Into *now*. As it did, she was forgetting, something important.

Tish? Something to do with . . . someone . . .

They sidled up to the building and Elinor peeked inside. "Seems okay."

Crystal swung her head back and forth checking for pursuers. "Hurry!" Though her word was urgent, she felt drugged, as though she were watching herself from a far corner of her head.

They slipped in.

Two men played pool, while a third sat at the bar eating. A woman tending the bar was busy wiping imaginary dirt from the counter as they entered.

"Hey, you girls look too young to be in here." She took in their disheveled appearance and turned her nose up.

"We need to use a phone," Crystal said. Images slicked across her mind, future events, slipping and disappearing as she spoke. She felt like a sighted person who was losing her vision. What happened with Tish, sliding into a past that never happened.

"Phone's out. And you've gotta have shoes to be in here."

"Do you have a cell we could borrow?" Elinor spoke up.

"No. I ain't got one of those. Now you'll have to get out before the cops show up."

The threat wasn't lost on Elinor and Crystal. They stepped outside and surveyed the area. Besides a couple barely-lit store fronts, the industrial region was closed down for the night.

"She's going to help us," Crystal said and reentered the bar. Elinor trailed behind, eyebrows raised, feet ready to dash.

Crystal approached the bartender and looked her square in the face. "We need your help." The woman started to object, but a wave passed from Crystal to her. To Crystal, it felt like a *pulling* of the woman's will—her consciousness—and an appeal to her inner sense of *rightness*. The woman swallowed, and her voice softened.

"Yes. Come, quickly," she said, and ushered the girls into the back room. "You can use the office phone." The bartender left.

"How did you do that?" Elinor looked wide-eyed at Crystal.

"I'm not sure. It just seemed—*true*." Crystal couldn't explain her feeling that she was in two places—almost two people: one with powers, who was fading as the minutes ticked, and one just a scared girl beginning to shiver in a lab coat.

Elinor shook her head. "Boy, this is getting weirder and weirder."

"Yeah, well now who do we call? The police? Your dad? Ha ha. My dad? We've got to get the others out of there. And if it backfires, they'll have us again."

Her own statement bothered her. Who were 'the others'? There was Aunt Sarah . . . and . . . who?

"Yeah, my father is out." Elinor huffed.

"I don't know what my dad can do. Maybe we should call the police."

"Or maybe your dad *and* the police. Then, our bases are covered."

"Here, let me." Elinor snatched the phone and punched in 9-1-1. After a moment she rolled her eyes. "I'm on hold."

Crystal was silent, then said "Wait."

"What? What is it?"

"What my aunt said. That I needed to get to Sweden, before some event happens. Usually I'd just ignore her, but if I stay here to talk to the police and my dad, I might not be able to get there, you know what I mean?"

Elinor nodded.

"Hang up."

Elinor did as she was told.

"I don't even know how I'll get there," said Crystal

"I have that money, if we can get back to Tish's house."

The feeling returned that she had a concussion and was losing her memory. "And leave them?" she asked.

"No," Elinor responded. "We can call from the airport. Your father can tell Tish's mom. Alert him and the police and take off before anyone can catch us."

With the memory of Tish fast fading, a strange embarrassment overrode her, and Crystal decided to hide her astounding memory loss. She changed the subject.

"One more thing." Crystal looked wistful. "I need to tell Glenn. I don't want him to think I've abandoned him, again."

"Okay. But we'd better hurry. Those guys might be doing a house-to-house." So saying Elinor used the phone to call a cab.

Barely glancing at the driver, the girls climbed into the Checkered Cab, seating themselves on a lumpy seat with their hands held over their noses. The back seat fabric smelled of spilled booze, sodas, and worse from rowdy patrons. Telltale smoke residue hid in nooks and crannies — signs of another age when smoking in public places was legal.

While they were riding through the back streets, Crystal realized she'd need to return home to get her passport from her parents' papers. "Not to mention, something to wear," she said looking down at her front. "And what about your papers?"

"Oh, I came prepared to run — that's why I went to the bank," Elinor responded. "I brought my passport from home, but I had to withdraw my savings."

"You brought your passport?"

Elinor patted her chest. "Put it in my hidey bra. Made for traveling."

"Where were you going to go?"

"Wasn't sure. Maybe Mexico. Maybe," she looked sideways at Crystal, "just to your house." She half-smiled. "Whew. This has all been a lot."

"Yeah."

"Hey, you girls." Elinor and Crystal looked up, surprised to realize the cabbie had been listening to them.

"Oh, oh," said Crystal softly.

"Look. You seem like nice kids." The cabbie's brown eyes flashed in the rearview mirror. "I might have heard a bit of what you were saying. And I need to tell you, there's a black van been following us for about a mile."

Elinor and Crystal jerked around in the seat to see out the back window.

"Oh, lord! What can we do?" Elinor sounded panicked as she kneeled on the seat.

"Who are they?" said the cabbie soothingly.

"Bad men," said Crystal.

"Old boyfriends, huh?

"No! They're a horrible group from the . . ." Crystal jammed an elbow into Elinor's side to shut her up. Elinor clamped her lips together.

"Ah. Yes. I know about that group. I've had other kids get out before." He peered at them again in his mirror. "Do you kids even know where you are?"

The girls stared dumbly at his eyes in the mirror.

"Well, you're in Arlington, Virginia. My guess is, we ain't going to make it to Zanesville with them on our tail.

You want me to lose them?" The cabbie's voice was soft, but his manner held power.

"Yes!" both girls echoed.

"Can you?" asked Crystal.

"They don't call me Invisible Larry for nuttin," he said, and pushed his foot to the floor.

The girls held onto the front seat as the cab whipped through the streets. It peeled around corners, up alleyways, and shot onto the thoroughfare. White-knuckled, Crystal turned to catch a glimpse of the van still behind them.

Ahead was four-lane tollbooth leading across PA-43 Bridge, and the cab was forced to slow.

As it crept up to the stall, a tall woman leaned out of the booth to take the payment.

"Oh, hey, Larry," she said, "How's it going?"

"Time to get invisible. Can you hold him?"

She looked up and scanned the other traffic backing up in the lanes. "Which one?"

"The van. Black one. DC plates."

She nodded. "Looks like he's in Bert's lane. Hold on." She punched a number and spoke into the phone. The girls watched as the man in the next toll booth looked over at them, nodded, and turned back to work.

"Have a nice night, Larry," she said as she passed his change to him. They covertly shook hands.

After several miles, the girl's relaxed. They still had not seen their followers. Elinor's head dropped onto Crystal's shoulder and during the five hour drive, they both fell asleep.

When they finally arrived at Tish's, Elinor hurried in the back door, retrieved her bag, then returned to the cab.

It was nearly eleven when they pulled in front of Crystal's home. The lights were on and her father's shadow paced in front of the living room curtain.

"You'd better come in. It will help me to explain," Crystal said.

The cabbie grinned broadly at the hundred dollar tip, and waited for the next leg of the journey. Crystal held her breath as she stepped up to the porch and entered the door.

To her surprise, her father was right there to grab her in a bear hug.

"Cris! Where have you been? I was so worried."

Crystal motioned Elinor inside and closed the door.

"Dad, you'd better sit down," she said.

16

THE PAST IS THE FUTURE

Crystal sat in the brocade chair talking fast, and told her father everything — all she could remember. Her future experience at IRVing had faded into a nightmarish blur — most of which seemed unreal, and segments seemed to have been wiped from her mind.

He was completely quiet until she finished, and then he said, "We always thought this day might come. I hoped it wouldn't — I'm a practical man and I don't like to believe in fairy tales. But your mother told me when you were born about the myths, and the family traits. She made me memorize the name of a man you might need to see — she said he would mentor you. Fredrik. I think he's also called *Svinstu* or some name like that. He'll teach you about the coming events."

Now it was Crystal's turn to be dumbfounded. "What events? Aunt Sarah mentioned an event as well. What is it?"

"Oh, honey. You mother had wanted to tell you about this. It's an old myth, but had to do with the reason her family escaped to America."

Elinor interrupted, her speech fast. "Cris, can I use your computer for a minute?" Crystal nodded and Elinor moved in jerky, quick motions as she headed down the hall toward the bedroom.

Crystal held up her hand. "No, wait Dad. We don't have time for this. There's a cab out there and we've got to go . . ." She stood.

"This is important, Cris. Send him off. I can drive you."

"No, I . . ."

"I insist." Her father looked at her with strong eyes.

After Crystal sent the cab away, she returned to the living room, but remained standing.

Her father spoke quickly. "Sarah might not have gotten to the part about your grandmother. Olaf's daughter. She was a young, married woman at the time. Your mother said that when the portal opened up, a strange energy came out—"

"Sarah said that." Even with her memory being splotchy, Crystal remembered this.

"Did she tell you that your grandmother and a Gypsy girl were *taken*?"

"Taken? Yes—to some other place."

"And that she returned pregnant?"

"Yes. So it's true, Dad? Mom really was the daughter of something on the *other side*? Is that what you're telling me?"

"I'm just telling you what she told me."

Her stomach lurched. This was her *father* confirming Aunt Sarah's wild tale about her origins. "So that makes me—something else too? Like what we are is not human? What then?"

Richard shook his head and put his arm around his daughter. "Honey, I just don't know for sure. I'm only telling you what she said. I do know you're a hundred percent my daughter."

Crystal pulled back from his arm. "What ever happened to the Gypsy woman?" she asked, breathless.

"Some people said she was stoned out of camp. Some people said she gave birth to a monster. No one knew for sure. The Gypsies moved on. But it doesn't end there.

"Your grandfather had witnessed a miracle. Even after his daughter's abduction and your mother's birth, he wanted to open it again. He wanted to see inside the portal — to that other world. His daughter told him she had met people on the other side who revealed the importance of the portal. They showed her amazing secrets. Olaf went in search of the Gypsies, hoping he'd find one to help him open the *eye*. Then, when she went back to the other side, he was more determined.

"This ties into IRVing, so this next part I know first hand."

Crystal stepped back. "Dad, wait. This is taking too long. Those folks from IRVing could be here any minute. "I've got to get dressed. We have to leave."

"You're right. What am I thinking." He ran his hand over his head and took a breath, then reached behind him and parted the drapes with a finger to peek out. "Go get dressed. I'll meet you and Elinor in the car." Crystal squeezed her dad's hand and left the room.

She headed for her room, mortified. *She was not human. Not human.* Her body began trembling and she dropped to the floor in the hallway, pressing her back against the wall.

Shaking uncontrollably, her mouth opened to a silent scream as tears streamed down her face. As the car started for warming outside, the sound brought her to herself. She crawled up the wall until she was standing, and held onto it while she made her way to the bathroom . She used the toilet, then looked at herself in the mirror. Still looked like Crystal. Except for the bags under her eyes and her pupils looking like pin pricks. Cupping her hand, she drank some water from the faucet and splashed some on her face. She glanced in the mirror again, shook her head, and sped out of the bathroom toward her room.

She rushed into her room and dragged some clothes from her dresser. Pushing her violins toward Elinor, she asked her to take them out to the car.

Elinor came back in after a couple of minutes and found Crystal sobbing on her bed.

Seating herself on the edge of the bed, Elinor put her hand on her friend's back. "Oh, Cris. I'm so sorry. I know how horrible this has been for you. Me too."

Crystal sat up, her head looking like a flattened tire. "I'm sorry. For all intents and purposes, you lost your parents today." She laughed, a low, mournful sound. "I guess we're both a couple of basket cases."

Both girls looked at each other and attempted to smile.

"Do you still want to go to Sweden?" Elinor glanced at the computer-generated boarding passes in her hand.

Crystal ran her hand down a lock of her hair and then rubbed her shoulder as though she'd been punched. Was this what being an adult was like? Making critical decisions when you were too stressed to even think straight?

"We've got to do something. I don't know what this is all about, really, not at all. But there are people after us and it seems that facing this down is the way we'll find out. Maybe if I do go to Sweden — talk to this Fredrik guy — we'll figure it out. I don't know what this has to do with my playing. I mean, I'm decent, but I'm not *that* good." For an instant, Crystal wished Tish were around with her science brain. Maybe she could explain how sound waves could cause strange events to happen in the air, out of the blue with her violin playing. Then her mind jerked away from thoughts of Tish.

"I do know, though," Crystal continued, "that I want to call Glenn. I know this is bad timing, but I —I feel strongly about him. And I'm not sure why, but I *sense* there's something important about him that ties him to all this."

Elinor looked at her with kindness. "Maybe you just don't want to run off and leave him. Call him. I'll take your bag and tell your father you're almost ready. Oh, and Crystal?"

"I know. I'll hurry," she said.

Crystal dressed, then phoned Glenn. At first, he was delighted to hear from her, but when she said she was leaving, he sounded distressed.

"No! I don't want you to go. I want us to be together."

Stunned at the openness of his words, Crystal tried to keep her heart from trembling. That familiar feeling of warm intensity flowered over her body, sapping strength from her voice. "I really need to go. You know what happened with Olaf in the woods. What you don't know, is he's my great-grandfather and I was able to achieve what he was looking for in a student. And it ties in with other strange events in my life. Unbelievable things. There's another man in Sweden that I have to go meet, who can explain it all — or at least, so my father says. And, I don't know when *or if* I'll be back."

A pause on the other end of the line left her feeling dizzy with loss.

"Then I'm coming with."

Hope and adrenalin pelted Crystal. "Oh, no. I mean, can you? Really? Aren't you supposed to be on tour?"

"No — the season finished. My grandfather would be

annoyed, but . . ."

Seconds ticked by. Crystal thought about the forceful old man and the domineering manner he had with Glenn. She heard a intake of breath on the other end of the phone.

"I'm coming," Glenn said at last.

"But Glenn. We're leaving this morning. On the two-thirty a.m."

"If we hang up right now, I might be able to get a seat on the same plane."

Crystal sprang into the air and knocked her desk coming down.

"What was that?"

"Oh, nothing," she said nonchalantly as her hand patted the top of her head.

"Okay. We'll talk later. And Cris?"

"Yes?"

"I —really am looking forward to seeing you."

"Ditto," Crystal whispered and hung up. This time she almost reached the ceiling when she joy-jumped.

Elinor peeked at her from behind the back seat as Crystal entered the passenger side of the car. As soon as she strapped in, her father handed her a passport and a thick envelope.

"Oh, Dad. I don't want your cash."

He embraced her neck with his hand. "I don't want my little girl running off into the world without a way to come home."

She remembered about the insurance money.

"Now," he continued as he pulled out, "I'm telling you the rest of the story.

"When I was working at the agency, they were doing all sorts of experiments. After some initial successes with mind control techniques, opening portals to other dimensions and one-way time travel, they were like kids at Christmas. It was all a new toy to them.

"Your grandmother had said those on the other side warned that humans were not mature enough to be toying with the forces they'd found—but arrogant us, we didn't care. The government agencies believed they had found a way to control minds using directed electromagnetic waves, and they were looking at war tools. They were targeting people and causing cancers, embedding negative commands into their psyches, and basically learning to manipulate or destroy anyone they wanted at any time. It was the perfect, undetectable weapon system. Terrible stuff.

"In the early fifties, natural and IRVing-induced events coincided and there was a rift—a horrific tear in the fabric that separates the dimensions. It ricocheted, unleashing chance waves of various natures that are harmful to all biological life.

Crystal gripped the edge of the seat and dug her nails in. As she heard the word "rift," a deep agony held her immobile. Her mind shot to Tish, but then slid away like oil, leaving her feeling dirty.

Richard scanned the stressed features on his daughter's face. "But it's not all bad. Part of Olaf's urgency to reopen the portal was not just to get his daughter back, but because of what happened after the portal opened up."

Elinor piped up. "What? What happened after?"

Richard glanced in his rearview mirror and scanned the traffic.

"The event IRVing caused loosed many of the illnesses on our planet today.

"During Olaf's playing, a vibration came out of the portal—whether sent by people on the other side, or just a natural occurrence, we don't know. Yet somehow, the vortex that opened with Olaf's playing negated the harmful effects on everyone present. Even though the radius was not that extreme, like a ripple on a pond, it continued outward. To those nearby, it *restored* the vibrancy of cells. It cured diseases. It renewed everyone.

"Your great-grandfather Olaf was born around the turn of the twentieth century. Think about it, Cris. He's way over a hundred years old."

Crystal inhaled sharply. On the edge of her subconscious she had thought he looked *old* yet he was so alert and agile. She hadn't thought it through. She took that moment to count.

"And Mom? If he is over a hundred, what about Grandma Alicia and Mom?"

"I know it's hard to understand. And your mother would never tell me her age." Wrinkles worked across Richard's brow. "But Olaf became obsessed with opening the vortex again. He believed if it could be sustained, it could heal everyone on earth. And of course, that made it of interest to IRVing and some other organizations."

Crystal thought about telling her father about Olaf's methods in trying to open the portal, but didn't want to upset him.

"But Dad, why is IRVing after me? What do they want?"

Her father cast an eye at her then turned back to the road. "Oh, Cris. Come on. With what you know, can't you see how they would want to use you? Opening portals to other dimensions, for starters. And once word gets out, it will be more than just IRVing. How about the pharmaceutical industry?"

"What?" said Elinor from the back.

"I'll explain later," Crystal said over the seat.

Her father continued, "The pharmaceuticals would never allow a free worldwide cure for most diseases. And if opening the portal truly does that . . ."

"Dad—why would you ever work for a place like

IRVing?"

"I didn't know what it was, at first. It takes a long time to figure out what's really going on. When I did, I first helped Sarah to get out. Then I intentionally violated policies and committed actions to make them think I was unfit, so they got rid of me. They didn't know how much I knew by then, so I just laid low."

The three drove in silence for a few minutes while Crystal mulled over what her father had said.

Finally, she asked, "So why now? Why, after all these years, must I go to Sweden now?"

"That's where Fredrik comes in. Your mother told me that an important event was coming, and only Fredrik knew why it was of critical importance to the human race. Fredrik refused to tell anyone except the one who could open Olaf's portal. And right now that looks like you.

"I received a call from . . . relatives in Sweden, and Fredrik said the time is soon. Within a few days. I'm sorry to be cryptic, sweetheart, but I don't know what it is."

This time Crystal said nothing.

Richard pulled into the drop-off lane at the Columbus Airport and killed the engine, while Elinor climbed out with the fiddles. He reached across the seat and took Crystal's hand in his.

"Your mother is—was—astute. She always said it might fall to you. That you would be the key. She believed in you."

"Key? Key to what?" Crystal's voice trembled.

"To open the door, Cris. The door to the other side. Your mother believed it would be better than—what they've done to us here. Whatever IRVing did, the door is locked. The blood you carry in your veins has positioned you. You're like a—key to a little door in a big door—a *wicket*. If you can convince those on the other side to open the little door and look through, maybe they will open the big door and help us cross over."

"Dad." Crystal's voice came out in a whisper. "I'm not going to help people to die. This isn't some kind of cult suicide is it?"

Elinor began pacing next to the car and looked at Crystal pointedly.

"I'm sure it's not. Your mother would never put you in harm's way. Your visions at the water, the pull you felt, the fact those evil bastards are after you. Honey, just get to Sweden. Don't worry about Sarah and Tish — I'll pull some strings to get them out."

"Dad?" Crystal barely held back tears. "I really do love you."

"I know, Squeaky. Be safe. If you run into any trouble, I'm always here for you."

Crystal slipped out of the car and hugged him again through the window. She and Elinor each picked up an instrument.

"Oh, Cris?" She turned to her father. "Fredrik's information is jotted on the envelope."

The moon was nearly full and streaking high over the airport. She faced the lights and crowd, then turned to watch her father drive away. Somehow, she felt it would be the last time she ever saw her home. Her neighborhood. Her dad.

A stranger awaited her in a distant land — some relative named Fredrik. The plane was waiting. The sky.

And Glenn.

PART III

CRACKING

SKY

1

FLOATING ON AIR

A September rain began pelting the plate glass
windows at the Columbus airport. Crystal became
aware that her deodorant had worn off, and caught a
couple of uneasy glances from Elinor. With an eight hour
flight looming, she had no real way to clean up, unless she
used the tiny bathroom in the plane.

Glenn had missed catching the same flight, so she
hoped she'd have time to shower before his plane arrived
in Sweden. Uncertain if her cell phone would even work
in a different country, the best they could do was arrange
to meet at the same hotel.

Elinor had rented a suite for them to stay at a
Radisson. Crystal's eyes had bugged out at the price, but
Elinor didn't seem fazed. Nor had Glenn flinched when
she told him where they were staying and how much it
would be.

Sudden tiredness laid over Crystal and she fought
down some nausea. The crowded airport, too much like

sweet candy and Christmas shopping, choked her with an empty, hungry feeling. She realized they hadn't eaten since lunch at the Agency, but several establishments with various airport style foods awaited them. She determined to skip salad, for once. They lucked out and found a Middle Eastern place with warm, pungent soup and a good vegan menu.

"What are you thinking about? Glenn?" Elinor asked.

"No. Being a vegan."

"*Ha*! Well, the lambies and cows will thank you, I'm sure."

Crystal was unable to explain how she'd come to this. She hadn't consciously decided to change her eating habits—it was just part of what was happening to her. It added to a sense of *purification* that she was undergoing. As though she were purging and needed to be clean, inside and out, for what lay ahead. She nodded as if in agreement with herself.

The cleansing of her body added to her sense of spiritual and moral strength. Internally, she shifted toward a knowing. This was *right* for her. With the acceptance, an internal door opened: there were other actions she could take to increase her strength and power. And for what lay ahead, she'd need every bit of energy she could muster.

Resolved, she let her mind relax. "I'm really tired. You?" She ran her hand over her face and covered her mouth as she yawned.

"Yes. I got us a room with two king beds so we could each roll around if we wanted," Elinor grinned.

Crystal chuckled. "Sounds like a fun night." She focused on some curried lentils. "Do you think they'll come after us?"

"Who—the IRVing people?"

Crystal nodded.

"I don't really know. I mean, are they CIA? They can leave the country, right?" Elinor looked around the restaurant, then craned her neck to peer up the hallway where clusters of people milled. "I sure hope not."

After stuffing themselves to the gills for the first time in what felt like weeks, Crystal and Elinor boarded the plane and strapped in.

As they began taxiing down the runway, Crystal looked out the small window, feeling a sense of loss and stress. *Alien.* The word kept flashing through her mind and she wanted to talk about it with Elinor, but tiredness pushed her into a deadening but uneasy sleep, where she chased herself through crumbling buildings.

Crystal's last sight was of the diminishing airport, until she awoke hours later while landing at their first stop. She stretched and looked at Elinor, whose head also bobbed against the seat as they landed. They had flown the entire distance without even taking off their seatbelts. Crystal started to stretch again, then remembered her promise to herself that she would clean up in the head onboard the plane. Quickly, she lowered her arms.

"Do we have to get off?"

"I don't think so at this stop, but I'm going to walk around and stretch my legs."

"I'm going to the potty," Crystal said. "Are you hungry again yet?"

Elinor grinned. "It'll be a few days."

The girls went their separate ways.

In the little room, Crystal managed to use some paper towels and clean up a bit, glad that Glenn hadn't caught their flight and seen her in this condition. For the first time, she began wondering what she could wear when they arrived at the hotel and she met with Glenn.

To scrub her face with the plane's soap, she used her elbow to keep the water running. Her hair was a greasy tangle. She was going to give Americans a bad reputation in Sweden, if she couldn't do better than this. She found a clip in her purse, and tied her hair into a knot at the top of her head.

Pushing her way out of the room, she bumped into a man waiting to enter. Her heart flipped and she stepped back, as she saw the black trench coat he was wearing. Cold blue eyes atop a ruddy complexion burned into her.

"Excuse me," he said in perfect English with a Swedish accent.

She breathed, relieved. "Excuse me," she said. On her way back to her seat, she noticed two women wearing identical clothing — black dresses with high collars — sitting behind and across the aisle from her and Elinor's seats. One of the women looked up shyly, then hurried to lower her eyes. An indefinable characteristic of the women, or the way they were dressed, nudged at her, but Crystal couldn't think what it was.

Returning to her seat, she watched for the blond stranger, to see where he was sitting, but didn't notice him exit the restroom. She told Elinor about the incident, and both decided to err on the side of paranoia. They began to scrutinize everyone.

A few minutes later the plane boarded. As straight-faced people worked their ways up the aisles, the girls counted twelve suspicious people in black trench coats. "I thought Swedes were all blond," whispered Elinor as she noticed the variety of people. Finally, they looked at each other, laughed, and decided black coats must be a Swedish style.

"Either that," said Crystal, "or they sent the entire Men in Black agency after us."

The girls relaxed. The first-class seats that Elinor had purchased allowed them the extra leg room on the large plane, but nonetheless, by the time they reached their destination, their buttocks were flat and they were eager for some walking.

As the plane tilted on its descent, the sparkling city of Stockholm loomed before them, like a cache of pearls on black satin. They both were excited to find their room in their lavish hotel.

The girls retrieved the violins and Crystal's single bag from baggage claim, before catching the shuttle to their hotel. On the way, Elinor stated that she intended some big-time shopping, as she had zero clothing with her.

"Plus," Crystal said, "if we are being followed, we should disguise ourselves some."

"I don't want to dye my hair." Elinor pulled out a strand and looked at it.

"No, but we can get hats at least."

Elinor laughed. "Yeah, or mustaches."

Crystal dug around in her purse, locate the envelope her father had given her. She counted five thousand dollars, all in hundreds. She definitely could afford a change of underwear.

It was cooler in Sweden than their autumn coats could withstand, so heavier coats went to the top of both their lists.

When they arrived at the hotel, Elinor moved forward to claim the room keys, then Crystal asked the clerk if Glenn had already registered.

The clerk checked, but he wasn't there.

"What do you think?" she asked Elinor.

"He did leave later than us, didn't he? Give him some time."

Crystal smiled, but her heart dropped; what if he couldn't make it at the last minute? What if his grandfather found out and stopped him?

"Could you tell me what time he's expected?" she asked the clerk.

The desk clerk scanned the log and said "He's coming in on a later flight and should be here in about four hours. Would you like me to check and make sure it's on time?"

She shook her head.

Crystal couldn't decide if she was tired, hungry, or needed to work out at the hotel gym. She felt like a cloud following her own body around.

After showering, the girls made a mad dash, first to the hotel's bank to exchange some currency, then to the clothing stores.

When they returned, Crystal checked with the desk, but Glenn still had not shown up.

"Could you make sure his flight is on time?" Crystal asked.

The young man checked the computer, frowned and said, "I don't see . . . Oh, yes. I'm sorry but Mr. Weisz has cancelled his reservation."

They availed themselves of a late-night dinner in the hotel, and then returned to their room. Crystal was tired and moody; disappointed that Glenn had not come.

She sat on the bed and pulled out new strings she'd purchased and set about restringing the instruments. Elinor volunteered to help her, and with both of them experts, the task was finished in a short amount of time.

Elinor settled into reading brochures with titles like "Swedish Etiquette" and "Welcome to Stockholm." Jet lag had taken over Crystal's legs, and after putting on snuggly pajamas, she wobbled to the bed and climbed in.

♪

"Cris. You need to wake up."

This time, it was not her mother's voice she heard, but Glenn's.

He stroked her hair. "Come on," he whispered. "Wake up."

She ran her hand across her forehead, but only her

brow was there. *Oh, no! Not again!* she thought. Pushing at her eyelids, her eyes creaked open to see Glenn's face staring down at her with a look of adoration.

"Hi," he said softly.

"Oh, Glenn! I thought you might not make it." She held open her arms and Glenn wrapped his larger, stronger ones about her as she sat up. They embraced for a moment, enjoying the flavor of their hearts, but Crystal kept her head turned for fear of morning mouth.

"Traveled all night, and just got here. Rather than check in, I thought I'd look you two up and see what the plan is." He stroked her hair again, making Crystal realize she probably looked like Medusa's twin. She glanced over at Elinor who sat on her own bed watching them, with a wide grin.

"Excuse me," Crystal said, and wriggled out from under the covers. She high-tailed it to the bathroom to fix herself up, from where she listened to Elinor and Glenn talk.

"I've been looking at a map," Elinor said, "and I think we can catch a train from here to *Vingåker*. I'm too leery to test their road rules by renting a car. I found a bed and breakfast we can all stay at there, while Crystal locates the person she's supposed to see."

"Sounds like a plan. When I saw I wasn't going to meet your flight in New York, I cancelled the hotel reservation and took a later flight. I managed to get some sleep on the plane, so I'm ready to go—" Glenn paused. "Almost ready. Do you mind if I use your shower?"

Elinor laughed. "Just as soon as Cris is out."

♪

They sat at a small table in the hotel room and made themselves instant coffee while Elinor got dressed. Crystal couldn't stop herself from stealing looks at the tall, handsome guy who seemed as drawn to her as she was to him. *He'd flown halfway around the world to be with her!* And, he'd seen her with her morning uglies and still seemed to like her.

He smiled at her between sips, seeming more shy than she remembered.

All ready, the group headed for the train. Crystal stretched her shoulders as they tensed. She felt surrounded by people and pushed by the crowd.

"How did your grandfather take it that you were coming with us?" Crystal asked Glenn.

He stopped as they were getting ready to ascend stairs to the train. "I didn't tell him."

"Uh oh."

"I left a note. You don't know my grandfather. He's — hard."

Crystal felt like she knew the type of man he was. Old country. Like her great-grandfather. If the two of them ever got into a battle, she wasn't sure who would win.

"Did you tell him where we were going?" Crystal asked as they made their way down the narrow aisle.

"Not exactly. Just the country. But Sweden is a big place. Don't worry. He's not going to send the police. That's not something people in our family would do."

They found their seats and squeezed in. Crystal had only been on one other train, but here the seats seemed smaller. *Europeans sure are used to packing a lot into tight spaces,* she thought. Crystal and Glenn sat together, with Glenn on aisle side, so he could stretch out his long legs. Elinor was in the seat in front of them. A large woman with pale skin and white hair sat next to her, but did not greet her.

Crystal and Glenn talked about their ordeals in the mountains with Olaf, then Crystal set about catching Glenn up to date on the events since then.

The large woman next to Elinor turned around and hissed "Silence!" Shocked, Crystal and Glenn made wide eyes at each other and grinned, but spoke more quietly.

After she and Glenn ran out of talk, Crystal tapped Elinor, who was crunched against the window, "Hey, let's go in the observation car with the fiddles," she whispered. "We've got a while."

Elinor agreed.

Holding cases before them, the three of them moved through the train to the observation deck and found a table to sit at. They laid their cases atop it and, as they opened up their instruments, they gazed out at the countryside as the train chugged through a wooded area.

"Oh, my. Look at that," Elinor said.

Sunlight streamed through the trees and shimmered into a translucent verdant glow. The three stopped what they were doing and gazed out at the landscape as the mesmerizing rhythm flowed around them.

"No wonder composers have been so inspired by this part of the world," said Glenn.

Crystal thought of her great-grandfather, and his fame. She had not really considered his point of view, and wondered at what had driven him to find her for training. Obviously he was attached to music the same way she was. According to her aunt, he had felt the *Näcken*. He had been *trained* by the *Näcken*. And, like her, he had seen wonders through dimensions. Could it be that, on some level, he had meant to give her a gift? Perhaps one that was the most beautiful to him? Another part of her mind screamed at her. *He kidnapped you!* And he had his own selfish reasons: to bring back his daughter from the vortex. *But, maybe, because he was from the old world, maybe he just didn't understand . . . ?*

"Come on, girl. Let's set up." Glenn rosined his bow and picked up his instrument. Its black varnish gleamed in the light.

Crystal shook off her reverie. She lifted the violin her mother had left for her and wondered what notable violinists had used it before her. Would she feel their presences? She thought of her lost fiddle, and felt remorse. People who didn't play could never understand the personality of an instrument. But her twin was gone. To her, the loss was a death.

She held the fiddle under her chin and ran the bow across the strings. She quickly tuned the strings and tried again. Her fingers flew up an A-scale and back down. The bowing was perfect; the instrument more balanced than the sun. She realized she had been holding her breath.

"What do you want to play?"

Glenn looked ready — charged.

Elinor had not opened the Hardanger.

"Aren't you going to join us?" Crystal asked her.

"I haven't played one before. I'm afraid I'll sound terrible. All those extra strings and harmonics. I'd rather wait until I can practice alone."

Crystal shrugged and returned the fiddle to her chin while Elinor seated herself to listen.

"Let's play in D-minor," said Glenn. He struck a chord, playing two strings at the same time, and folded in on a sensuous and slow introduction. As he worked up steam, Crystal angled in, with a high soprano and, staying on the upper strings, played counterpoint to his melody.

"Hey, good improv, you guys!" Elinor called over the music.

But their eyes had met, and energy was flowing, so they didn't acknowledge her. Power began building between the instruments, between their music and the intention of the notes. The tune was completely made up, but a fire began to ignite. As Glenn's passionate Gypsy music radiated sonorous tones and darkness, Crystal's instrument complemented it with fast, light notes. The effect was eerie, almost discordant, and chilling.

Passengers began to gather to listen, and several squeezed into nearby booths to watch. The couple continued unaware, totally trapped in a universe they were creating. Through their instruments, they were talking, speaking truths they could not express through their human voices. Truths for which there were no human words. As Crystal's bow played staccato, then long, extended bows, Glenn's instrument went for the jugular.

It snaked into a world of shadowed beauty, where the daylight yearned for the night, a perfect merging, to rest. Crystal battled with the spears of light — fighting the resolution of the inevitability of the forces. They were the wind, the sea, the immortal stars.

A passenger shouted *Oj herregud!*

Colors and lights flowed from their instruments. Some light with effervescent vapors, some thick and neon, carrying those present on a wild Disneyland ride. If they had been fated to join the car, they were affected. Emotions long buried released, compelling Crystal and Glenn to play them, as though they were notes written on the skin of the universe. They played the hearts of those present: the sorrows, the joys, the thunderous and beautiful days, the damning and miserable sadnesses. They crescendoed, then Glenn tapered off in a diminishing drone, quieting to nothing. Crystal rose to a high *D* and sent the final note into infinity.

She was panting as they finished. Perspiration flowed from Glenn's face, though ice crystals had left twinkles on the windows from the chill in the car.

Complete silence enveloped them, as though all the passengers had turned to stone, emotionally depleted. Then, thunderous applause broke out. Some of the reserved Swedish people openly wept. Others cried out for more.

Embarrassed, and stunned, Crystal hastily replaced her violin in the case, as did Glenn. They avoided looking at each other, afraid of what they'd see in each other's eyes.

"Wow! *Wow!*" Elinor repeated as she picked up the Hardanger. "*Wow,*" she said again, as she followed Crystal through the train.

Glenn continued past his seat. "Excuse me," he said. "I have to, you know." He headed toward the rear of the train where the restroom was located.

Elinor sat in his seat and turned to Crystal, who fought trembling, but failed. "What was that in there? Did I really see that?"

"I need some water," said Crystal, and got a bottle from her bag. After taking a swallow, she said, "That was like what happened up on the mountain with Olaf. But with Glenn . . . Oh, Elinor. I don't know what's going on. That was just so — incredible. Something about Glenn. I mean, I don't know him that well. How could we play like that? I mean, it's unreal."

"We could all see it. It *was* real. But what were you doing?"

The train lurched, and began slowing.

"Oh, what's that?"

"I don't know." Elinor glanced out the window as the train stopped. "Maybe its a route stop. But, seriously. Tell me. What did it *feel* like?"

A tremor went through Crystal at the recollection. "I can't describe it. Like every cell in my body was charged with . . . electricity, or light. I didn't feel quite . . . human."

Elinor laughed, but Crystal was frowning.

"Oh, hey! What the *f-*?" Elinor peered over Crystal's shoulder and through the window outside. "Isn't that Glenn's case?"

Crystal turned in time to see a man in a black trench coat put an instrument case into the trunk of a sleek car parked near the tracks. Then the backs of three men moved into view. One was a short, gray-haired man. The other held his hand on the back of the one in the middle, wearing a blue parka. The man in the parka looked over his shoulder at the train.

"Oh, my god. That's Glenn!" Elinor pushed out of her seat, squeezed past a woman in the aisle and headed toward the exit.

"Rude American!" the woman sniffed at her.

"So sorry!" said Elinor .

Crystal also pushed past the woman, then past Elinor. She continued forcing her way down the narrow aisle.

"Wait, wait, Crystal! We don't know what —" Elinor grasped for her, but she pulled away.

"It's his grandfather! He's being taken!" She kept her eyes on the exit ahead.

"Wait, Crystal. Stop!"

Crystal reached the door and turned tearing eyes toward her. "We've got to do something!"

"We can't stop a bunch of men, Cris." Elinor took a quick breath. "Cripes, how did his grandfather know where he was? Maybe he's one of IRVing's people."

The train chugged into motion.

"No, I won't believe it. We've got to get off." She pushed at the side door of the train, but it was locked. "There's got to be a gadget — like on the cowboy shows — that you pull . . ."

"Cris, stop and listen to me." Elinor touched her friend's shoulder and this time Crystal was openly crying.

"I can't just let them take him away."

"We can't help him. What would we do? Beat up the men and run off in the forest with him? We have no way of getting him out of here."

"We can ask the conductor! We can tell the conductor!" Her words were frenzied, hyped with fear.

"All right. I'll go get one. Stay here. Don't try to open the door. Do *not* open that door. Promise me, Cris."

Crystal nodded, then looked outside at the trees whipping past and wondered how badly she'd be hurt if she jumped. It seemed like she should be able to just go *through* the door. A wave of *déjà-vu* scraped over her and then subsided.

Elinor squeezed back into the car and up the aisle while Crystal sat on the floor near the door with her head in her hands. A few minutes later, Elinor returned with a porter.

"He wouldn't let me talk to the conductor, but he says he can help."

Crystal looked up at the kind eyes of an elderly man dressed in the white and blue uniform of the train company. "Please," she said. "Our friend was taken at that last stop by some men. They are really bad men and they're trying to kidnap us."

The porter glanced at Elinor, who rubbed her forehead and moaned "Oh no."

He cleared his throat and said, "I'm sorry miss. But it's been a long time since we left Stockholm. If your friend was taken, we can file a report at the next station."

"No," said Crystal. "I don't mean in Stockholm. I mean that last stop. Just now. Wherever we were. That's when they took him."

The porter cleared his throat again, and his eyes shifted from Elinor to Crystal. "Ma'am. I don't know what you mean. We have made no stops since Stockholm."

Elinor and Crystal looked at each other. Crystal stood, her voice growing high and loud. "What do you mean, no stops. We *just* stopped. Just a few minutes ago."

"Yeah!" Elinor bristled. "Right before I got you." She

clenched her fists.

The porter stepped back from Crystal, fear crossing his face. "I'm sorry ma'am. I can't help you." He turned his back and hurried up the aisle.

"What? What?" Fury seared through Crystal.

"*Shhh*. Cris, try to breathe. Please." She grabbed a pole to keep from falling as the train staggered across the rails.

Crystal's heart was thrumming in her chest and her hands were balled and hot. "I can't believe this. How could he just *lie*?"

Elinor shook her head.

The girls returned to their seats.

"What are we going to do?" Crystal attempted to keep her voice low.

Elinor parted her lips to talk, but the woman in front of them turned around and pinned them with a steely gaze. "You girls. Stop talking. There are those of us who want to be in peace."

Elinor dropped to a whisper and cupped her hand to aim the words at Crystal. "We'll be in *Vingåker* soon. Once we get settled in the bed and breakfast we can discuss it. What can we do now, anyway? Jump off a moving train?" She picked up her friend's hand and held it tightly. "Can you wait until then?"

"Do I have a choice?" Crystal asked.

The train continued to wind upward through the forested region as snow flurries whipped against the passenger windows and great grey clouds bruised the daylight into night. At last they felt a lurch and heard the squeal of brakes as the train rolled into the *Vingåker* station.

2

RUNNING IN PLACE

The girls stood in the gravel next to the departing train, then stepped up the cement stairs to the *Vingåker* station, a long, coral-colored brick building, well-kept though aged.

Two kilometers from the station, the B&B Elinor had reserved would welcome them, according to the directions online. The snow had begun falling in earnest, and large flakes settled in their hair. Each girl pulled out a beanie and bundled up in her coat.

Crystal looked around. "Where're the taxis?"

Elinor sighed and set her suitcase on the tile entry to the station. "I guess they don't have them here. The town only has about eight hundred people. But it's only a mile or so up the street to the B&B. I say we hoof it."

Crystal eyed the two instrument cases and their luggage.

"I'll carry the Hardanger," Elinor said.

"I don't like the instruments getting so cold," Crystal said.

Elinor scoffed. "Them? What about us?"

Crystal agreed. Both girls pulled on their new gloves and wrapped woolen scarves about their throats. Then they helped each other to strap a fiddle case on their backs before setting off on foot.

They found themselves on a cobblestone street lined with small shops. Smoke issued from chimneys, and store lights twinkled, sparking a cheery, gingerbread village effect.

Crystal trudged, head down, lost in thought about Glenn. Elinor tugged on her sleeve.

"This place is really cute," Elinor chirped. "It looks like a town out of the seventeen hundreds."

Crystal looked up at the stone shops and wooden porches drifted with snow.

Elinor continued, "I bet they get some good skiing up here."

"Probably everywhere in Sweden."

"Do you ski?"

"I'm sorry, Elinor. I can't think about skiing right now. I'm freaked about Glenn."

Elinor nodded in sympathy. The girls continued in silence, and soon had left the shops of town behind. They trailed through along a dirt road past open fields dusted in snow, broken only by the skipping tracks of a rabbit. A fir forest swaying in a breeze lined the perimeter.

"Elinor, look at this," Crystal said and pointed. Through the flakes, a rosy glow emanated from a house up a long side driveway, about a quarter mile away, nestled at the edge of the forest. A sign at the road read: AKE OCH LAGE SÄNG OCH FRUKOST. "This must be it."

"It looks like a Christmas card!" Elinor stood still, seeming bedazzled. "I feel like we're walking into a fairy tale."

"Let's just hope there's no wicked witch," Crystal murmured. "Hey, my Nikes are soaked. How are you doing?"

"What were we thinking? Why didn't we get boots?" Elinor kicked some snow from her toe.

"I didn't know it snowed here in September. Let's watch it up the drive. We don't want to fall and hurt the instruments."

Elinor looked at her askance. "Hey look." She pointed ahead, to where someone rode toward them on a snowmobile. "Modern conveniences! Yay!"

The man pulled up, introduced himself as "Ake," and offered them a ride on the snow machine.

He clambered off to help with luggage, and Crystal stared openly at his huge, Nordic form.

Partly due to his size, he could only take one girl at a time, so Crystal remained behind, trying to pronounce his name. "Oh-AH-kay," she tried several times. If she really had Swedish blood, it hadn't come as far as her ability with the language.

After Crystal's ride, Ake escorted them into the manor house to check in. The old place was as neat as her grandmother's linen closet, and smelled like cookies. "I know there's a witch here somewhere," Crystal stage-whispered to Elinor, who elbowed her.

The proprietress was introduced as "Lage," Ake's wife. It became apparent that her English was not as good as her husband's when she said, "You girls need see the room, then to put on new clothes, yes?"

They nodded and smiled, and were led to a small cabin, adjoined with another. Both cabins shared a single bathroom. The room itself held a set of bunk beds.

"This is the double room?" asked Elinor.

"Oh, yes. See? Two beds." Lage nodded and surveyed the room with pride.

Elinor and Crystal looked at each other and smiled with their eyes.

An invitation to dine in a half hour was gratefully accepted, since the girls planned to be out before breakfast. And because Lage insisted that after their travels they were hungry, whether they were or not.

The girls unpacked while discussing what to do about Glenn. "If we go to the police, they might arrest us. For all we know they're in cahoots with IRVing," Elinor stated.

"What else can we do?" Crystal's voice was strained. "He was obviously taken against his will."

Elinor was quiet for a moment as she picked lint from the coverlet.

"What? What are you thinking?" Crystal's voice was uneasy.

"Look, Cris. Don't get mad at me, but that's not what I saw."

"What do you mean? Didn't you see that guy's hand? He was holding a gun or weapon." She plunked into a small wooden chair.

"Maybe he was. But it looked to me like he had his hand on Glenn's back, friendly like."

"Do you mean you think Glenn was going *willingly*? Without even saying goodbye to us?"

Elinor was silent, and her face was pinched. She kicked off her shoes and set them next to Crystal's, drying by a small heater. Returning to the bunk, she began rubbing her foot.

"Well, do you?"

"I don't know, Cris. It's possible. I mean, how did those people even find him on the train, unless he called them?"

"They're black ops. They know everything."

"His grandfather was with them. Is he part of IRVing, too?"

"You're implying Glenn is part of them? Part of IRVing?" Crystal's face got hot .

"No. I never said that."

Crystal stood up and began pacing. "I won't believe it. There's something . . . special . . . between us. And if he was in cahoots with them, I would know. I would sense it. And why didn't they come after us? Wouldn't he have helped them get to us?"

"Look, I really don't know. I'm just guessing. I shouldn't have said what I said. But I am afraid to go to the police. We don't know what they're like around here. And remember that porter? He claimed the train hadn't even stopped. How are we going to prove Glenn was even with us?"

Crystal's frown deepened. "That porter could have been bought off. The police could interview the people on the train who heard him play."

"And they'll do that on our say-so?"

Now it was Crystal's turn to be silent.

"Then I don't know what to do." She sat on the bed and buried her face in her hands. "Maybe you're right. Maybe he wasn't forced. What if he just wanted to—leave? I'm sitting here having a big romance all in my own head?"

Elinor put her hand on Crystal's shoulder.

"No. No. I'm sure I'm wrong. I'm sure he was forced. You're right. He really seems like a decent guy. Look, I—" Elinor's words were broken off by a knock at the door and the announcement of dinner.

"We'll talk later," she said as they prepared to leave the room. "Now remember. Look them directly in the eye.

Try a bit of every food offered. And if they make a toast, the ladies put their glasses down before the men."

"What *are* you talking about?"

"Etiquette, *ma chérie*. Swedish etiquette."

♪

The girls were ushered to a large wooden table with colorful dishes set. The room smelled warm, of wood heat, baked goods, and herbal teas. Taking her cues from Elinor, Crystal waited quietly with her hands on the back of the chair as Ake settled himself stiffly at the head of the table. Then the girls sat down. After laying covered platters in the center of the table, his wife, without preamble, said grace. Lage then held out her hand for the plates, which were broad, clay bowls. As each was passed to her, she heaped mashed potatoes, lingonberries, and fish onto it and passed it back, in a clockwise manner.

At the end of the table, Crystal was dismayed to see that some juice from the fish had spread across the bowl and mixed with into her lingonberries and potatoes. While the others were served, she stared into the bowl.

She saw the fish swimming in a nearby brook and felt its playfulness as it darted among the stones. Then she felt its shock and horror, as the very food designed to give it life caught in its throat and tore into its gullet. Then she saw Ake, his eyes alight, pulling in the fish, as it struggled for its life. Amidst his joy, in a supersonic vision, Crystal caught the terror and scream of the fish as it realized it would be killed. She felt the drop into survival mode and the realization that it was pregnant. She felt the horror as a rock came down on its head, once, then twice. And then, she felt the flesh bleed out and begin to decay.

Crystal stared at her plate. Could she force herself to eat after witnessing what, for all intents, appeared to be the murder of an innocent? A residue of unhealthy energy surrounded the fish, and Crystal knew it was the energy she would be consuming — not the meat. That she was inherently *energy* and the consumption of matter was merely a formality to appease a third-dimensional body. She wasn't sure how she came to this awareness, but it felt *right.*

Elinor gave her a hard look. *Eat it!* she seemed to be demanding.

Crystal took a forkful of the potatoes at the far side of the plate — those that had not been touched by the fish.

Dinner conversation was to the point; the host and hostess directly asked the girls about their business in Sweden, particularly, their town. They expressed delight when Elinor said they were musicians, and they asked for a performance after dinner. Both Crystal and Elinor agreed, though they were exhausted

Turning toward Crystal, Lage said, "So how you come to play violin?"

Hoping to create a better connection with her hostess, she shoved the fish around in an attempt to make it look somewhat eaten, then Crystal said, "My relative from here played fiddle. He passed down the talent in the family."

Lage clapped her hands. "Did you hear, Ake? Her relative was from here."

"Oh?" Ake looked at her with interest. "Was he a Soderburg?"

Elinor perked up and opened her mouth to speak. She missed Crystal's tense look and subtle shaking of her head. "No. Their last name was Widmark." Elinor grinned.

Without hesitation, Ake's fork clattered onto his plate. His head morphed into a blustery red hue. "*Vidmark!*" he shouted, then stood, his cheeks puffing in and out as though he were preparing to blow out a hundred candles on a giant cake. His forehead crimson, he stormed from the room, seeming twice his size, which was already bigger than anyone Crystal had seen outside of a football game.

Lage went quiet, her face chiseled steel as she glared at the girls. She tugged at the lace on her collar.

"You bring this shame to our table?" she said quietly. "Demon eggs." Then she stood, picked up her and Ake's plates and left the room.

"No, no. I—I'm sorry," Crystal pleaded toward her retreating back. "I don't know what—" She looked at Elinor with questioning.

Elinor shook her head, her eyes wide. "Let's go," she mouthed silently.

The girls rushed through the chilled air, across the slick walkway, back toward their cabin.

"*Cheesits,* Elinor. I wish you hadn't mentioned the Widmark name," Crystal said as they entered the room.

"I'm *sorry.* But I don't get it. I thought he was famous here."

"Yeah, but not good famous like in the States. You couldn't have known this, but over here my family was thought of as demons for the way he played his fiddle, and that whole *Näcken* business."

"Wow. And we're over here to meet the man who trained *him*?"

"Yeah."

"*Uh*, why again?"

There was no heater, except for the tiny electric one, so as they talked they brought pillows onto the floor, slipped on their pajamas and robes, and huddled around it, holding out their hands over it as though it were a campfire. Once again, they set their shoes around it to dry.

"You heard what my dad said?"

"Part of it . . ."

Crystal felt sheepish saying it aloud. "Fredrik's supposed to train me so I can use those abilities I told you about."

"Like the telepathy and interdimensional fiddling whatever?"

Crystal nodded.

"I hope his methods are better than Olaf's."

"Me too. He's also supposed to explain some event I'm supposed to be part of. You don't have any information it, do you?"

Elinor rubbed her feet to warm them in thick socks. "Me? How could I?"

"Did you ever overhear your dad talking about it ?"

"An event? No. And apparently, he's not my dad. In fact, now I wonder if tomorrow is really my birthday."

"Your birthday? Why didn't you tell me? I could have bought you a gift." Crystal was relieved to have a happy occasion to discuss.

"Well, we've been pretty busy. Plus, like I said, who knows? I mean, if they weren't my parents, who were? And when was I really born? I wish there was Wi-Fi here. I'd like to do some milk carton searching for the year I was born. Maybe I was stolen!"

"I'm sorry, Elinor, but no matter who your folks were, you can be my sister." The girls smiled at each other.

A hard knock at the door brought both of them to their feet.

Elinor, in red flannel pajamas patterned with puppies, walked in her stocking feet to answer. She glanced at the clock. Eleven forty-five.

"Who would be coming this late?" she whispered.

When she opened the door, arctic wind blustered in, sending a few flakes along with a chill across the room, and siphoning off the little heat they had stored.

Ake stood on the porch like an ice sculpture, then stepped back from Elinor as she answered. Snow swirled behind him.

"We have discussed it. In fifteen minutes," he said, "I will drive you to the street and you will be on your way. Lage says, or I would not do even this."

"What? What?" Both Elinor and Crystal groaned.

"Here is your money." He held out cash to her, and Elinor took it as a reflex. "It's better you go. We'll not have the Widmark blood darkening our door."

"Wait," Crystal implored stepping forward. "We don't know your town. Where do we go? You can't just throw us out. Please!"

"You leave this town and never come back. We run away your relative long ago, and we run away you, too." Ake's features remained hard as he glared at her.

"Fifteen minutes." The door shut.

Both girls' jaws dropped.

"I can't believe this! We could freeze out there!" Elinor's cheeks flushed in anger.

"I don't want to be here if they hate the Widmarks that much. It doesn't seem to matter to them that I'm only partly related. They might come and kill us in our sleep!"

"Where do we go, then?"

"Back to the station?" Crystal rubbed her arms that felt like cold, dead flesh.

"What if it's not open? I don't think this little town could have a train that runs all the time."

"Maybe for the tourists that come through. Besides, what other choice do we have?"

They looked at each other, real fear in their eyes.

"We'd better layer, then. Really. Put on everything you own. I don't want us to freeze to death. There are some candles in a drawer over there. Normally — well, it would feel like stealing — but lets take the candles and some matches. Maybe we can find some shelter and use them to light a fire." Crystal began dressing.

"I don't even want to ride with him. What if he takes us out and whacks us! Anybody that would send two innocent girls out alone . . ."

Crystal started laughing.

Startled, Elinor frowned at her.

"Innocent girls." She laughed. "I haven't felt innocent for at least a week."

"This isn't funny." Elinor refused to budge.

Crystal calmed down, embarrassed at her tendency to laugh when she was afraid. "You're right. It's serious. Let's get dressed, fast, and leave before he gets back. I doubt he'll follow us."

"Yeah. And just for that," Elinor hissed, "I hope all his plumbing freezes." This time both girls did laugh. A kind of high, hysterical pitch.

♪

Wrapped with every stitch, the girls waddled like Gummy Bears through the snow around the cabin, and began the trek back down the driveway. Ski treads from the snowmobile had made slick tracks, but the rest stood with several inches of snow. The girls walked in the snow for better traction.

"My shoes weren't dry and my feet are freezing," Crystal lamented after a few minutes. "They're starting to go numb."

Behind them, they heard the snowmobile as it neared their cabin.

"Maybe we should have let him give us a ride to the road. I can't walk through the snow like this." Already, Elinor was panting with the effort. "Plus, I'm afraid this strap on the fiddle is going to break because of my thick clothes."

Crystal looked at the hump-backed friend, barely finding her face through the cap, coat, and packs. "Maybe you're right. But what should we do? Go back?"

"No, but if he comes after us, I'm going to accept a ride."

"What? And leave me?"

Elinor brushed flakes of snow from her lashes. "Maybe we could find out where that Fredrik lives and go there. This town isn't all that big."

"Go to someone's house in the middle of the night? A complete stranger?" Crystal tried to hold it in, but she crouched on the road and started bawling. "I should never have listened to Aunt Sarah and my dad. I'm—I'm just a kid. We don't belong here."

With effort, Elinor crouched next to her and tried to put her arm on Crystal's shoulder, but because of the sweater and heavy shirts under her coat her arm stayed stiff.

"Look. First of all, we're not kids anymore. Not after recent events. I don't think I've ever met anyone as brave as you. Plus, we're involved in something—amazing. Cris, *you* are special. And I promise to try and help you get to where you're going."

Crystal stopped crying and wiped her tears with the back of a gloved hand. "You're right. The training and event are too important."

The rumbling of the snowmobile grew louder as it neared.

"What do we do now? Get a ride, or hide?" Crystal sniffled.

"I don't think he'll kill us, or he wouldn't have offered us a ride.

A sudden *zing* whipped past Elinor's face.

Shocked, Crystal rocked backwards and slipped onto her back. The fiddle broke her fall and the solid case pushed her onto her side, where she floundered like a rolled potato bug.

"Run! Run!" Elinor screamed and stood up. Seeing Crystal rolling around, she grabbed her friend's sleeve and helped her to stand erect.

"Over here," Crystal cried, and both girls waded stiff-legged into the field. The air had cleared enough that they could see the snowmobile moving up the drive toward them, with Ake driving. Lage balanced a rifle on Ake's shoulder, raised it, and shot off a round.

Elinor shrieked as she dropped into a drainage canal obscured by the snow drift. Crystal helped her up and they scrabbled up the far edge of the ditch. They lit out across the field, the crisp snow pulling at their feet.

Crystal breathed fire into her lungs as she glanced over her shoulder.

A hard thud and scream of a revved motor shocked the night air as the vehicle hit the trench bank and capsized. Ake continued to rev — trying to back out, but one of the skis was broken. Lage climbed from the back, rubbing her arm.

Crystal and Elinor forced their stiff legs halfway across the field, before collapsing into a heap. They lay, breathing through their open mouths, gasping for air, like a couple of fish.

"I think I wet my pants," Elinor finally panted.

"I—hope—it doesn't—make you—freeze," Crystal said between breaths.

Both girls laughed—raspy, painful croaks, almost inaudible in the frigid air.

After a few minutes, they arose. Ake and Lage could not be seen, and the snowmobile behind them was a black blob, still in the ditch.

"I can't believe this," Elinor said. "I guess they walked back. Where should we go?"

Crystal looked across the broad expanse of snow. In the far back, black woods stood shrouded in white and tapered toward some hills. Adjacent to that area, sweeping to the right, they knew the town lay, though no lights were visible.

"Thank god it quit snowing. At least we have a little light." Crystal looked up at the moon which reflected off the snow through billowing clouds. "What time do you think it is?"

"Around midnight or later. Why?"

"Chances of our finding a place to stay are pretty slim, but if we hike back to town, we can use the phone book — if there is one — to find Fredrik's place."

"Wow. I can't even imagine what the Widmarks did to make those people want to kill us."

"Yeah, well, I think I have an idea from what Sarah told me. But that whole 'demon eggs.' That would have been funny if — "

"They weren't shooting at us." Elinor stood and looked at Crystal. "You look like a Southpark kid. You know, that cartoon?"

They set off toward the road. Midway, they encountered a cottage in the pines with lights on. The curtains were pulled aside and a silhouetted head bobbed back and forth, as though trying to get a better look at them.

Elinor held onto a post near the drive for support, as Crystal went alone to the door.

Crystal looked back over her shoulder, took a deep breath, and knocked.

No one responded.

Removing her gloves to make her knock louder, she rapped hard on a small window in the center of the door. Some wind whistled around the edge of the property, and tossed her hair across her face.

No answer.

"Look," she mumbled. "I know you're in there." She decided to use the straightforward approach.

"Please," she called aloud, "We're freezing out here."

Silence. Crystal looked back at Elinor, who shrugged her shoulders.

Crystal heard a creak on the other side of the door and expected someone to open it, but instead a voice rasped out. "Go away, Widmark!"

"I'm not a Widmark!" Crystal screamed, and kicked snow at the door. She stomped to where Elinor stood.

"The grapevine works fast around here."

"Poisoned well. Come on, let's go."

It took the girls about forty minutes to get back to town. After traipsing up the street, they spotted an old-fashioned phone booth in front of a curio shop. As they both squeezed in the booth for warmth, they shut the door and the light popped on. Crystal grinned. "Feel like Dr. Who?" she asked her friend.

The thin phone book held seven numbers, for *Fredrik*, but none that had *Widmark* as a last name. A compact map of the area showed several landmarks, the town hall, the nearby creek, an old mill. But no street names.

"People must just know each other here. All the addresses are just rural," Crystal noted.

Elinor shifted. "All I can say is this Fredrik Widmark guy must be bad news to have everyone so upset."

"Great. And he's the only person here who might be friendly to us."

"Yeah, and you know what else? Even if we had his phone number, I don't have any Swedish coins. Do you?"

Crystal thought about it. Did she get any coins when they went shopping? "I have some somewhere, but I don't know one coin from the other."

The girls stepped into the overhang of the shop near the booth, and plopped on the stone entry with their backs to the doors. A small amount of heat seeped out along the door crack, which provided welcome warmth to their frozen hides. Lighting one of the stolen candles, Elinor dripped it onto a stone in front of them, more for the reminder of heat than any actual output. Huddling together, they managed to fall asleep.

They awakened to stiff backs and blessed sunrays, which caused icicles formed in the night before to drip sparkles onto the steaming walks. The candle was a mass of hard wax.

A tall woman hovered over them with a serious, but not unfriendly look. She spoke to them in Swedish.

Crystal shook her head and said "American."

"You spend the night here?" the woman asked incredulously, in English. Without waiting for an answer, she stepped over them, unlocked, and opened the door. "Well, come in," she said.

Inside, the proprietress heated coffee and gave the girls pastries to eat. Crystal was relieved that she didn't ask them why they had been huddled in her doorway, as they now huddled near her heater. Soon, Crystal asked if she could use the bathroom, where she removed and repacked some of her extra clothing layers. Elinor followed suit.

When Elinor exited the restroom, Crystal was munching on a cinnamon bun and staring out the window, across the street.

"What are you looking at?" Elinor whispered.

"Those cult women we saw on the plane. I remembered some women at my mother's funeral dressed like that. They also showed up at the house the day I ran away to your place. And now they're here. Do you think they followed us?"

Elinor looked across the street, where the two looked in a store window, but occasionally glanced over their shoulders at the shop Elinor and Crystal were in. "I'm not sure, but I don't want to get shot at anymore." Elinor watched them for a moment. "They look kind of Amish." She took a bite of a cheese pastry. "But, more importantly, how are we going to get to Fredrik's?"

"Please keep your voice down." Crystal turned to the proprietress. "Thank you. How much do we owe you?"

"Oh, I enjoy your company. Please to come again."

Elinor patted at her friend's back. "Well, not everyone here hates us," she whispered.

"That's because she doesn't know who we are."

The girls stepped outside, comfortable in just their coats, and glad to see that much of the snow was melted or melting.

It seemed an impossible decision to Crystal. They'd come so far, and yet they couldn't learn where Fredrik was without risking life and limb. And did she really have the right to put her friend through this? She felt responsible for Elinor's being there. It was up to her to make the right decision.

"I've decided you should go back," she said. "I have to go on, Elinor. This might sound melodramatic, but it is clear that this is my *destiny*. But we almost were killed last night and I can't put you in this kind of danger. The people here are too hostile to my relatives — and if Olaf did anything to them like he did to us, I can see why."

"I don't agree." Elinor stood rock still. "I think we both need to find Fredrik and find out what we came here to know. If we go back, we'll face black ops, maybe your great-grandfather, and still not completely know what this is all about. I don't want to go back. I have nothing to go back for."

"Sorry. I didn't think of that. I just feel like — this is all my fault and I don't want you getting hurt."

"Oh, so you want you to get hurt?"

"No. I don't want to get hurt, either. But, I guess you're right. Somehow you're as mixed up in this as I am, and if you go back, you *still* won't know about the event or Fredrik , or why IRVing wants us." Fractured mental images splattered through Crystal's mind. Half-remembered notions, from some other time or place. Focusing on them made her reel. *Was she seeing the future? The past?*

"You. They want you."

"Okay — *me*." Crystal sighed. "But, we still don't know how to find Fredrik's place." She rubbed her temples.

Elinor looked thoughtful. "Oh, wait! Got it! Post office. They'll be able to tell us. And isn't there a law against post office people shooting customers?"

Crystal grinned. "Good idea. Let's try it."

The post office was the building adjacent to the train station. A few minutes later, they were back where they started from. They entered a second door in the long brick building and saw a waiting room similar to what they were used to in the states. A woman behind the counter spoke to them in Swedish. Elinor stepped forward and responded in English, at which point the woman immediately switched to English.

"I love these multilingual people!" Crystal said. The woman smiled.

"I'll try something different," Crystal said to Elinor. "My dad said he had another name. "

She turned to the woman. "Do you know a *Svinstu*?"

The woman covered a smile with her hand, then said "*Svinstu* . . . you mean to say 'pigsty'"

Crystal raised her eyebrows at Elinor, then turned again to the postmistress. "No. I mean Fredrik. Fredrik Widmark."

The woman's lips flattened into a line.

"There is no Fredrik Widmark in this town," she said.

"Oh, there has to be," Crystal's voice took on a shrill, complaining tone. "We've come all the way from America to see him. And my father said. He even wrote it down."

A whistle blew, and the building rattled as a locomotive pulled into the station.

Raising her voice to be heard over the incoming train, the woman said, "Let me see the paper."

Crystal set down her luggage and instrument, then rummaged in her bag. She produced the envelope her dad had given her with the money in it. While surreptitiously removing the cash, she glanced at what he had written. Blushing hard, she stood up.

"I'm so sorry. His name isn't Fredrik Widmark."

Elinor slugged her arm. "What? What?" Her mouth hung open.

"Sorry." Crystal raised her brows. "It's Fredrik *Lindroth*, not *Widmark*."

A word that sounded like *aieee* shot from the post mistress's lips. Her skin whitened and her pupils dilated. She whipped around to search through a file in a cabinet, and, with a trembling hand, drew a quick map on the back of a town flyer.

"This is how to get there," she said. She stood stiffly, fear oozing from her. "And tell him — you watch out for the drunken moose. Tell him I tell you that."

"Oh –uh- thank you," Crystal said. She was amazed at the woman's degree of fright. She wasn't certain she could answer more questions.

The girls left. Crystal mouthed "drunken moose" to Elinor, who rolled her eyes.

"I'm going to kill you!" Elinor's grin was wide, but her scorched cheeks said fury. "We almost got shot because you told me the wrong person?"

"No, I was talking about my great-grandfather before, like you said. Olaf Widmark. I assumed Fredrik had the same last name."

"But we've been looking all this time for the wrong guy."

"No, right guy, wrong name. Let's look at the map."

They both scrutinized the drawing, then turned south up the street. Two figures had been heading in their direction, and quickly made an about-face.

"Oh, my word. It's those cult women again," Crystal said.

"What? Are you serious? They really are following us?"

"I don't know, but let's high-tail it."

"*Crystal! Crystal!*" A voice called from behind them.

They turned back toward the train station, to see a familiar figure stumping toward them toting a shocking pink overnight case.

"Aunt Sarah?" Crystal stared. "I don't believe it!"

"I'm so happy to find you!" Sarah panted, catching up to Elinor and Crystal.

"How did you?"

"You know, powers." Sarah grinned. "Hey wait." She held up a hand. "Do you hear that?"

Both girls listened. "No," said Crystal. "What?"

"Nothing. Truly, nothing." They listened . . . no birds, no traffic, no sounds at all.

"Spooky." Sarah shook snowflakes from her bangs.

Elinor and Crystal rolled their eyes at each other.

"No really, Aunt Sarah. How did you find us? You just got here?"

"Yes. I had to come. When I talked to your dad, I couldn't believe he—hey, where's your rental car?"

The girls looked at each other. "They don't have them here," Elinor said.

"Oh. Too small, huh? So where are we staying?"

The girls were quiet, and looked at each other again.

"What? What? What's going on?" Sarah covered one exposed ear with her hand to warm it.

Crystal caught Sarah up on the night's events. Sarah listened attentively, but seemed unconcerned.

"So, it looks like you're just now heading to Fredrik's place?" Sarah grinned. "I haven't seen him since I was a tyke."

"You know Olaf *and* Fredrik?" Crystal asked.

"Of course. This is my home town. Well, let's get walking. I can't wait to have some of his mom's pudding. That is, if she's still alive."

The troupe headed up the street.

♪

After pausing once for Sarah to change her shoes, they made the three mile trek up a small hill to a dirt road winding back down to a mill.

"Are you sure this is it?" Elinor looked up at the broken blades and paint peeling from the windmill. A couple acres away, a rambling country house tucked behind overgrown bushes, spoke to years of no upkeep.

"Yeah, pretty sure," said Sarah. "But I, for one, don't want to walk up the dirt road. Or mud road. I think I have a blister. Let's cut across the field. It's shorter and the snow's mostly melted. We can walk on the weeds and save our shoes."

"The ground's kind of soggy still," said Crystal. "Plus it's somebody's orchard. What if they shoot at us?"

"Yeah." Elinor's reluctance to be shot at again revealed in her tone.

"It's Fredrik's place. He's not going to shoot. Come on!" Without waiting, Sarah stepped over the bottom rail of a collapsed wooden fence. After a few seconds, Crystal and Elinor followed, picking their way through the muck.

Midway across the field, Sarah said, "Hey look. There are still some apples on the trees."

"I'm surprised the snow didn't freeze them all off last night," Crystal said.

Sarah pulled one down and took a bite. Immediately, she spat it out. "*Blech*. Fermented. I guess that's why they're still here."

They continued on their way, until Sarah paused to remove her shoe to inspect her blister.

"What's that?" Elinor asked and all three stopped. A slushy, crunching sound came from the far end of the orchard.

"Oh, lord. Maybe it's those cult women after us!" Crystal clenched her fists. "I'll take the skinny one. You and Sarah take the bigger one." She moved in front of them, facing them.

"What? I'm not fighting anyone!" Elinor screeched.

Both Elinor and Sarah raised their faces to Crystal.

"Well I'm not running anymore!" Looking over Elinor's shoulder, Crystal inhaled a sharp breath. Her lips moved silently for a moment, then she shouted "Run!"

Spinning around, her feet slogged through the mud in a slow-motion sprint across the field.

Glancing back, she saw Sarah and Elinor look behind them. Across the field, a moose was gathering momentum. It would have been faster, but its legs buckled, pitching it to the right, then it swayed to the left. It went down on its knees, climbed back up, and came at them again.

"What am I seeing?" shouted Elinor as her legs stretched out full in a full gallop.

The moose issued a long bray, sounding like a cross between a fox and a fart. Disregarding the mud and her blister, Sarah sped forward to cut in front of Elinor.

Sudden gunfire from the direction of the house sent Crystal to her belly. "Get down!" she screamed.

A man wearing a flannel shirt and baggy pants, with white hair flailing in many directions, ran toward them from the house. Again, he shot a rifle into the air. "Bad moose!" he cried. He shot again.

The hairy pursuer shook its head, fell again, and arose, to lumber off in the opposite direction.

Crystal climbed to her feet and the three stood in a line, staring at Fredrik. Crystal's front was coated with the smelly orchard ooze, and mud streaked her face and hair. Sarah held a shoe in her hand, with her foot embedded in mud to her ankle. Elinor glared, holding a rotten apple as a weapon.

"Welcome!" said Fredrik with a wide grin. He opened his arms. "We've been expecting you!"

3

GHOST AT THE MILL

After inviting them in, Fredrik inhaled their fragrance. The three clomped across a stone porch and through a large wooden doorway.

Crystal felt thrust into a different century when she entered Fredrik's home. Shadows from candles and lanterns haunted every corner in the tight, furniture laden room. Unseen presences flitted about, darkening the interior here, causing laughter there. Sardonic and multi-hued voices played around her consciousness. She could not breathe.

Crystal stared at the man. So this was who she had traveled across the world to meet. A wizard, according to Sarah. And yet, except for the impossibly blue eyes which measured her with a bright twinkle, he could have been any elder living on the street, clothed in convenient garments designed for warmth rather than style. His moustache cascaded over his lips, giving him the appearance of having no mouth — just a beard. When he spoke, his whiskers fluttered slightly. Crystal wondered how he ate without getting whiskers in his food, then had the distinct feeling he was *reading* her.

A wave of *déjà vu* pushed over her. Why did it feel like she had done this before? That events just kept repeating themselves? She sneaked another peek at him. It felt like she *knew* him.

He called a name and a stout woman emerged from a back room. She was dressed in a pauper's gown and wore buckled shoes. A pinafore rode atop her dress, and a banded white cap covered most of her hair, which appeared to be in a braid on top of her head. The shyness clinging to her aura, combined with her dress, made her seem like someone who had stepped from the remote past. Fredrik treated her cordially, not like a servant, but she still seemed subservient to him. He introduced her to the group as Greta. She curtsied. They spoke a moment in Swedish, and the woman motioned to Crystal.

Crystal followed her into a room that seemed set up for bathing, although there was no toilet visible. A single claw-footed tub sat in the middle of the room, and against the wall, a wood stove with kettles on its surface. The woman poured the water from the kettles into the tub, which was already partially filled with water, then turned to a sink with a single-handle pump, and refilled the kettles. She set these back on top of the woodstove.

She said something to Crystal in Swedish. Crystal responded that she didn't speak Swedish. Greta shook her head. So here was a rare exception, someone who didn't know English.

It seemed apparent from her manner that Greta expected Crystal to bathe. A small, warped mirror over the sink told Crystal the worst. Her hair was ratty, her face muddy, and she knew, after sleeping in her clothes, that she probably needed a dose of hygiene. She thanked the woman, then looked though her suitcase for her cleanest dirty clothes. Greta set two coarse towels on a stool near the tub and left the room, shutting the door.

Crystal stripped and, to avoid the chill of the room, immediately climbed into the deep tub. The warm water came up to her chin as she settled in with an "*ahhh.*" The radiant heat, plus the purity of the water felt both calming and invigorating. A large chunk of handmade soap lay in a dish and Crystal picked it up and sniffed it. A clear image of a goat frolicking in a field came into her mind. She then sensed the goat, its udder full and pressing, experience relief as warm hands relieved it of its milk. The goat was happy to provide the gift.

Crystal lathered herself all over. A tall bottle of homemade shampoo, smelling like roses and mint, tingled her scalp. She washed and lay down in the tub to rinse, letting the water come all the way to her face. Then, pinching her nostrils, she went underwater and allowed the heat of the bath to penetrate her pores.

Arising to a sitting position, she reached for a cloth and wiped the soap and water from her eyes. When she opened them, her mother stood at the end of the tub, looking as solid as the golden being had in her bedroom what felt like ages ago.

Tears sprang to her eyes, but she fought shutting them, for fear the apparition would disappear. "Mom. Mom. Oh, I miss you, Mom."

"I miss you too, honey." Her mother's voice was soft, angelic.

"I'm so sorry I was mean—I love you so much."

"I love you, too." Her mother's gaze was open, un-fettered.

"I just didn't know—all this stuff. The family. The powers."

"It was my fault. You didn't receive the training you needed. I was trying to protect you. I thought I could hide you—spare you. I didn't understand, before, that you were needed. That it could only be *you*."

Her mother backed slightly toward the door.

"No, please don't go. There's so much I want to tell you. Mostly—mostly that I love you."

Affection showed in her mother's eyes. "I won't go. Cris, I need to tell you about your grandfather. My father."

"I've already met Olaf. But he's my great-grandfather, isn't he?"

"Ol—yes. He is. But this isn't about him. I'm talking about your real grandfather. My real father. Not the grandpa you knew back home.

"You have met the *Näcken*. Olaf told me. What you didn't know, was my father was from the other side."

"Sarah told me about your mother getting pregnant there. But your father . . . the other side where? Where you are?" Crystal's voice felt weak.

Her mother's brow wrinkled. "This material plane on earth is just one dimension. The *Näcken* is on the border of this place, and guards the door to a different plane of existence. The plane where my father is. And my mother, since she went back." Emma looked into the air.

Crystal fought looking up to where her mother gazed—afraid that glancing away would cause her apparition to fade, like the golden being had. She struggled to not blink.

"I thought I could save you from Olaf—from becoming involved. From all of this. But you inherited more than just our normal family wizardry. Because of my true father, you inherited abilities literally out of this world."

"And that's why they're after me? IRVing and the cult? I'm trying to believe all this, but it sounds like a fantasy." Crystal chuckled. "But I have to believe in something, don't I? I mean here I am, talking to a ghost." She laughed again.

"A ghost?" her mother said and picked up the towel from the stool to hand to her. "You think I'm a ghost?" She grinned, then laughed musically — a sound Crystal knew all too well.

Crystal's jaw dropped. "You're *real*? You're *alive*?" She snatched the towel, sloshed out of the tub, and hugged her mother fiercely enough to pop vertebrae. Then sudden anger overtook her.

"We thought you were dead! Dead! It killed us. Me, Dad, Aunt Sarah!"

"I know." Emma opened a drawer, extracted a boar-hair brush, and handed it to her. "I was trying to save you, like I said. When Olaf found us, he sent two of his followers to talk to me. Remember that day at the house when we were talking and I had visitors?"

"Those Amish-looking women?"

Emma nodded. "They wanted to take you to Olaf. I later convinced them I could raise the *Näcken* and get back Olaf's daughter, my mother. I talked him into taking me to try, rather than you."

"But the witnesses . . . the train . . . and Dad . . ."

"The accident was staged so none of you would know. To protect you — let you have the normal life you seemed to want.

"I did call your father a few days after the funeral, and let him know what was going on. I made him swear not to tell you."

Crystal thought about the strange energy residue she'd witnessed in the living room after her mother's funeral, of her father talking on the phone and laughing. *So, that had really happened,* she thought. But anger still pulsed through her veins. She fought down throwing the brush.

"You could have told me! Dad should have told me! The night I came to Sweden he could have."

"He didn't want you any more upset than you were. You'd been through enough, the way he tells it. He left telling you up to me."

"You shouldn't have let me think you were gone!"

"In case I didn't come back, or *couldn't* come back, I thought it was better if you believed I was dead."

"Never!" Crystal cried, then she hugged her mother again. This time, the tears flowed openly.

She wrapped her hair in a towel, and as she dressed, Crystal calmed. She said, "So what am I, then? If your father is what—an interdimensional being—then what am I? An alien?"

"You're just you." Her mother smiled. "And more.

"I used Olaf's violin and tried to open the door again—but failed. The *Näcken* didn't respond to my playing. An element required to call it was missing in me. Only you have the key. That's why you had to come.

"You're our last hope, Crystal."

The door burst open and an excited Elinor rushed in. She glanced at Crystal's mother, then said, "Cris—we need to run! Olaf and an entire army of men in black just showed up!"

Crystal tossed the brush onto the chair and scrambled to grab her suitcase.

"No, wait! You don't understand," her mother said.

"I came here to meet Fredrik, not be trapped by Olaf and his minions."

"No, that's not what is going on." Emma grabbed Crystal by the shoulders.

"Well then what is?" Crystal tried to pull away.

"Please, can you listen for just a minute?"

Crystal nodded.

"Olaf wants his daughter back, but when the *eye*, the

vortex opens, it heals those in the vicinity. Over the years he's accumulated a following."

"The men in black."

"The . . . what? Oh . . ." Emma chuckled. "Their clothes. I don't know if you'd call them a cult or groupies, but they follow him."

"Why would anybody follow him? He's a horrible man!" Crystal pulled the towel from her hair.

"People believe in him . . . because some of them were present when the vortex first opened. Over the years, their numbers have grown as they added friends and loved ones to their numbers. They want the vortex to open to receive healings. Some hope they can go to the place my mother did."

"So I've come all the way around the world to play my fiddle so some cult and its leader can try to jump into a different universe?"

Emma took the towel from Crystal and laid it across the back of the chair. "But that is only Olaf's goal. That's why Olaf wants you. There's far more at stake."

"What?" Elinor moved to Crystal's side.

"That's what you need to learn from Fredrik."

4

THE CAULDRON

The light was dimming outside as Crystal finished dressing. Together, she, her mother, and Elinor joined the people in the main room. Sarah embraced her big sister, amid Elinor's probing glances at Crystal. Others had come in while they were out. Olaf sat on a horsehair divan near a window. And on either side of him, were the two women in the high-collared dresses who had earlier followed Crystal and Elinor.

While Elinor retreated with Greta for her bath, Crystal went outside to think. The apple orchard was filling with people setting up tents, and cooking over campfires. Several were strewing a thick mat of straw over the mud, creating pathways to walk between the house and the temporary abodes. All the women were dressed similarly to those with Olaf, while the men wore coarse shirts, trousers, and black cloaks.

When Crystal returned to the house, Greta motioned her into the kitchen and, lacking anything better to do, she followed. Although the kitchen was dim, like the rest of the house, it sparkled with cleanliness. Wood fire heated a huge iron stove with yawning ovens, griddle and burners, adjacent to a counter made of tiles. A single metal sink with a pump handle stood at one wall. A small refrigerator was accessible on the far side of a waist-high, butcher-block counter standing in the middle of the room. Open-style cupboards were stuffed with food preparation equipment, cans, and bags containing flour, whole grains, sugar, and other cooking essentials. Streamers of peppers and garlic hung suspended from the ceiling.

Flour had been spread on the chopping block and several mounds of dough were already rising. Greta gestured to the unprepared dough and spoke in her native tongue.

"Oh, I don't know how," Crystal responded. Short of opening a can or making a sandwich, she'd never really cooked.

Greta smiled and held up a finger. She pulled a lump of dough toward her, kneaded it, and folded it into a round. She placed it on a large wooden plank for insertion into the oven.

Crystal took a lump of the dough and attempted to knead it. Her hands became stuck and stringers clung to her fingers as she pulled them out of the lump.

Greta laughed, took some flour from the counter top, and sprinkled Crystal's hands. She then nodded toward the dough. This time, Crystal kneaded as instructed. Soon, she had a rhythm going and shaped all the dough. While she was working, Greta chopped vegetables and tossed them into a huge, bubbling pot.

Crystal noticed that even though Greta was working with meat, she didn't see the dark images she'd come to associate with it. Every item in the room, every foodstuff, seemed blessed with a light of health. She guessed the preparation itself might have made the difference. She stared at a brisket and was surprised to feel the intent of the animal. This animal had *wanted* to merge its life forces with those present. It had wanted to contribute to the health and vitality of these humans. And its contribution would help it to ascend spiritually – to move into a higher dimension. Crystal shook her head, puzzled. How was it that this animal welcomed the contributing as a food source, but another animal would feel murdered? There was so much she didn't know. So much to learn. And yet, for the first time in weeks, in a strange kitchen in Sweden, she found herself genuinely having fun.

All twelve of the house guests arranged themselves at a trestle-table laden with food, while Greta and some of Olaf's people took dishes to the others gathered outside.

Anxious to speak to Fredrik, Crystal could not see him in the crowd. Sarah told her he had retired to his private chambers to make some calculations and would join them later.

Crystal was across and down the table from Olaf, and avoided looking at him. Her mother sat to his side and next to her Aunt Sarah.

Elinor was directly across from Crystal, next to Sarah. Both Sarah and Elinor had fashioned their hair into top of the head high ponytails and, with their short statures and perky natures, looked like twins.

Crystal was delighted to see that she had been given wine. Her mother winked at her. Apparently, this was another Swedish tradition. Several toasts were given and by the third toast, good humor had set upon the room. Sarah chatted openly with Elinor and her sister, Emma, along with including a stranger across the table.

Then Crystal held up her own glass. "To my friend Elinor, for joining me, even though it's her birthday."

"Oh, her birthday!" exclaimed Crystal's mother.

Everyone except Sarah congratulated her, which

brought another toast. Sarah, however, stared at her plate, her voice frozen in a sudden silence.

After dinner, Crystal helped clean up, then joined the rest of the household for conversation. Sarah seemed quiet and sat in a chair on a far wall, but the others chatted gaily about their homes and families.

Olaf entered the room and whispered to Crystal's mother. They both glanced up at her, and then her mother left the room with him.

Finally Crystal rose to go to her room, ready to turn in for the night. She said her 'goodnights', and turned to leave, when her mother reentered and stopped her.

"Cris, Fredrik told me the event will occur tonight," she said.

Crystal looked across the room and noticed several pairs of eyes staring at her. She glanced downward. "Oh, but Mom. I had wine."

Her mother chuckled behind her hand. "I'm not sure it will make a difference to your playing. Anyway, don't worry about it. Do you feel ready?"

"No. I'm not sure. I'm scared."

Her mother hugged her and smoothed her hair. "Don't worry. It will all be okay. I promise you. No matter what happens."

Crystal turned a worried face to her mother. "I only wish that was true."

Crystal snuggled into her coat and slipped outside. Across the orchard many of the tent campers huddled around compact fires. She put on an air of invisibility and slipped into the blacker shadows near some tall birch trees, where she could view the moon and Venus. Frosted air filled her lungs with a preview of the winter, and a scent of pine from the nearby woods.

"Can you hear the song of the spheres?" came a voice from shadows near her.

Crystal jumped, then laughed when she saw it was Fredrik. "Not really," she responded.

He sighed. "None of us can, of course. We weren't built for it. Silly bodies, these. Five meager senses and each of those only use a fragment of the available spectrum. One tenth of our brain in use. What poor, downgraded creatures we are." He chuckled. "Most of us."

"My friend, Tish, said something like that. But she's going to be a scientist not a —"

"Magician?" He laughed deep in his throat. "A wizard? Whatever people think I am, I'm not it. Like you, I am just myself. And like you, I have found a bit of the brain that others don't use. They are so in awe. As we would be, if we heard a monkey speaking."

Comforted by his light and straightforward manner, Crystal decided to broach the topic.

"The people here, around these parts, seem to be afraid of you. In fact, the woman at the post office said to tell you she warned us about the drunken moose. Of course we didn't know what she was talking about when she said that."

Fredrik laughed — a raspy sound from a throat unused to the action.

"Oh, she wants a blessing. People think I'm magic. And I do create effects that seem magical to them. But today's magic is tomorrow's science. And vice versa."

He found an opening in his moustache to take a long draw from his pipe. The smoke came out like mist. He looked at Crystal. "Are you ready for what you must do tonight?"

"I'm not sure what I'm supposed to do, other than play my fiddle. And apparently, a bunch of people are coming to watch. Or dance?"

He laughed again. The east wind chose that moment

to whip around the house corner. Crystal pulled her gloves from her pocket and slipped them on.

In the moonlight, a patch of frost was settling on his cheekbone, but Fredrik seemed not to notice.

"It will be up to you to call the *Näcken* and to open the channel. If those on the other side agree, they will open the door the rest of the way, then the event can occur and some will be saved."

Crystal shifted feeling uneasy. "What do you mean 'saved'? They aren't going to commit suicide are they?"

"Is that what you think." His voice was solemn. "No."

"Well, won't the *Näcken* pull me in? Do I have to be chained?"

Fredrik's eyebrows raised. "No. This time the force will open outward, like a flower. You will need to maintain your stance on the outside of the portal to hold it open with your mind. With your will."

Using her mind this way seemed familiar — and vaguely connected with Tish — but she shied away from thinking about it.

"So when I play an event happens and — "

"No. Your playing does not cause the event." He waved his hand upward, toward the heavens. "There's an alignment — it's strategic for putting sonics and celestial energies in position. The magnetic forces around the planets will help with the . . ."

Crystal's eyes were glazing over and Fredrik seemed to notice. His moustache twitched. "Your playing just opens the door to . . . an escape hatch."

"To where?"

He stopped, gazed at the moon and looked directly at her. "I don't know. I've never been."

"Well, what is the event, then? If it isn't my playing?"

"It will come from beyond." He gestured with his pipe to the sky. "Sol, our sun . . ." He paused as though considering it. His voice sounded pensive when he continued, ". . . is sending a messenger. A messenger of fire. A CME. A small explosion. This is the night of the blood moon—a lunar eclipse—and the magnetic forces must be just *so* when the portal is opened. You must play at exactly the right time."

"But it's night here. How will we see the sun?" Crystal asked.

Fredrik rubbed his forehead with his pipe hand and his whiskers twitched. "We don't need to see it. It is the sun on the other side of the world that makes the moon turn to blood."

I am so not into science, Crystal thought. "And so what if I don't play? Just a bunch of cult members get disappointed. It's not the end of the world," she said.

"Well, actually, it is," he replied.

Crystal cocked her head. "How?" she asked. "My mother said something really bad would happen if my playing doesn't work. What is it?"

Fredrik sighed, seeming to choose his words carefully. He spoke slowly. "Have you felt the sensation of *déjà vu* recently?"

"A lot. Way more than usual."

"That is because time is whipping us back and forth. We keep repeating our lives. And time is itself shortening into nothing. When it shortens all the way, we'll be stuck. Right here. Right now.

"We've tried to fix this before—many times. But some vital component of the energies was missing. Whatever the scientists couldn't manufacture to effect the repair, neither could you."

"What do you mean 'we'? I don't remember doing this before." *Was he blaming it on her?*

"In the long ago—or in the future, it's hard to tell— before time twisted into a dying snake, there was another explosion from Sol. Unfortunately, it was during a time certain people—I believe you know them—from IRVing and another place were attempting *time travel* on a large scale. The energy released by the sun combined with the effects of the experiment and tore a hole in, you could say, reality.

"Time isn't really like a snake. It's more like another room—another dimension. *Time and space are the same thing.*

"The scientists know this, but they cannot repair the breach, so they hide the truth."

"My dad told me about IRVing's experiments, but how do you know about them?"

Fredrik tapped his skull and grinned. "Like you, only a different place. One percent more."

"So what about this portal? What is supposed to happen?"

"I'm not sure, as in all our past attempts, Crystal, in all our past *times,* we have never succeeded. I do know that those on the other side of the portal might be able to help us repair the breach—if we let them in. They can't open the door without a human on this side turning the key."

Fredrik tapped his pipe, then picked up his staff. His fingers pushed it around in his palm as he watched her.

Crystal pulled on a lock of hair in frustration. Surrounded by a cult that believed she could do magic so they could fly away to some other dimension. Still running from a government agency that wanted to use her for a military weapon. And now, the entire universe hung in the balance.

What if her playing did nothing? This wasn't the Appalachians. She didn't know how to *call* the *Näcken.* The *Näcken* had called her. And people only *labeled* it a 'Näcken.' Who or what was it really? What if it was an alien invasion or demons or — what if the crowd turned on her? On all of them?

She looked across the heads and tried to guess how many people had gathered at the tent sites. Perhaps a hundred. What if the townspeople came to stop them? Hadn't they tried to kill her grandmother before? And her mother when she was a girl?

"I'm going in," she said. "My hands are cold. If I'm to play later, I need to warm up." She started away.

"There is more — the reason I am here for you. I am going to teach you a secret known only to magicians and . . . a few others. It will help you with the portal."

Crystal stopped and turned. "Okay. What?"

Fredrik laughed. "Come with me," he said, picked up his staff, and strode off into the night.

Oh well. What's one more weirdness? Crystal shrugged, tightened into her jacket, and followed him.

5

TIME TRAPS

Crystal tried to keep up with Fredrik as he wound through the trees, but his stride was longer than hers and she found herself trotting. Finally, she managed a tug on the back of his coat, catching a whiff of old wool and fireplace smoke.

"Hey — *Hey!*" she called. "Please slow down."

Fredrik stopped and turned, a single-mindedness fading from his face. He seemed surprised to see her.

"Sorry," he said. "We need to hurry. We need to get back before the moon turns to blood. Happenings must be timed, just so."

"Okay, but don't forget I'm back here," Crystal panted.

Fredrik bulldozed through wild growth and shrubs. Even though there was no visible trail, he didn't falter as he bludgeoned through the forest. Occasionally, he stopped, looked over his shoulder, and waited for Crystal to catch up. Then, without a word, he would continue.

Finally, they reached a slick incline and Fredrik waited for her. He held out his hand and said "You go first. I'll help."

"Up there?" Crystal looked up the steep bank. There seemed to be no firm place to put her feet, although there were some bushes to grab onto.

"Yes. It's not far."

Crystal took a step and immediately slid back. Fredrik's hands caught on her backside. With him pushing, she grasped a bush and pulled herself up. They proceeded this way; she would clamber up a bit then await Fredrik, who used his staff to dig into the earth and pull himself upward.

Finally, as Crystal poised near some rocks hemmed in by bushes, Fredrick said "Stop."

Crystal panted as she waited for him to catch up. He pointed to the rock.

"In there," he said.

Crystal looked at the rock. A vague memory skirted across her mind. *Did he mean for her to walk through it?* That should have seemed impossible, but it didn't.

She felt lightheaded from the exertion.

"Go in," he said.

Looking again, Crystal noticed a large, vertical slit in the rock. The crack was angled so a portion jutted out, hiding, from their position, the entrance to a cave.

"Why in here?" she asked.

"I can't risk anyone hearing my secret."

Looking inside the black maw of the cave triggered a memory of her running from a contorted shadow on her bike. Her stomach began jumping. "We don't have to go into a cave. We're pretty far from anyone."

Fredrik looked vexed and glanced at the moon as though judging the time of night. "The cave is lined with minerals that prevent the electronic equipment from penetrating. You know you're being monitored, don't you?"

"What? I am? How do you know?"

"Sensitivities to changes in the atmosphere, barometric pressure, increases in microwaves. All sorts of technology."

He looked at Crystal's face. "Don't be afraid. You have the same type of sensitivities and you'll learn to control them and push them off. But for now, if agencies scan you, you'll probably get really sick. You might even faint."

Crystal thought of the incident at Beans Camp when the metal bar seemed to be probing her and she experienced what she thought was a seizure. Could they have been monitoring her even back then? Maybe monitoring everyone connected with Olaf at the camp?

Deciding to trust him, Crystal pushed her fear into a black dot in her center, swallowed, and stepped over frosty rocks into the mouth of the cave.

Fredrik pulled a flashlight from his deep pocket and switched it on. Crystal jumped and he laughed.

"You were expecting a magic glowing staff?" he asked.

They angled over a rough floor ten feet in, when Fredrik said, "That's far enough." He placed the light on a rock protruding from the cave wall so that it shone between them.

Crystal turned to face him. In the glow of the flashlight, his face looked like a death mask in a fun house. His lips shining through his moustache didn't seem to be quite in sync with his words as he said, "What I'm about to tell you is a secret of the ages. You may not share it with anyone who is not ready."

Crystal cleared her throat and placed her hand on a rock protruding from the wall. It was icy, and she quickly withdrew her hand. "Maybe *I'm* not ready."

Fredrik cocked an eyebrow at her. "Crystal. You are ready, but you make light of life. You dodge your own facts. You see the truth, then you duck back into ignorance. You need to accept what you know, then you can use your abilities to manifest wonders and help a lot of people.

"The event will be the hardest test. You will feel more than you've ever felt. It may kill you if you cannot open to it. And if you fail, heaven help us, it may kill us all, trapping us in time forever.

"The event, if it occurs, is the impetus to the Great Change. But we have no control over that change. It's up to those on the other side and the master of all creation."

Crystal looked away.

"I know that right now you're avoiding a pain that happened — recently. In time, you will need to confront it. I also know what you're thinking; that you just wanted a regular girl's life. But you'll find that the more you help others, the more fulfilled your own life becomes. You *will* attain all those dreams."

Crystal took a step backward. He seemed so kind — so knowing. She could not deny what he said, and yet *she was afraid of the darkness*. Her powers, the unknown, the shape that followed her and landed in the peach tree. And maybe that was her first moment of trying to accept her *fear*.

Crystal breathed. She felt herself quieting in the calm of the cave. Usually, she would have been annoyed at a person for telling her what to think about herself, but Fredrik was right. Her heart knew it.

Plus, she realized he seemed right about the cave. Until they quieted, Crystal hadn't noticed there had been a continual onslaught of spiky energy and voices pressuring against her consciousness, for weeks. Here, in the cave, was peace.

"Are you ready to learn?" Fredrik's voice was respectful, as though she were his equal.

"What happens if I tell a person and they're not ready?"

"They won't understand. They won't be able to do it right, and they'll think you are insane. But if they're ready, they'll grow, and they'll learn."

Fredrik waited.

It was her decision. "All right," she said. "What is the secret?"

Fredrik shifted, and his wool coat made a soft chafe. "There will be two teachings tonight," he said. "The first you will come to know is Will."

"And the second?"

"I'm going to teach you to travel through time."

Crystal couldn't suppress an amused look, hidden in the inkiness of the cave. "You mean, like really?"

"Yes. There are three ways that I know of, and there might be more.

"The way I'll teach you tonight is how to take your essence into the future and into the past and talk to your selves. You can also talk to others, but first you must learn to talk to yourself."

Crystal nodded. She wrapped her arms around her shoulders and rubbed them for warmth.

"Close your eyes."

Crystal did as she was told."

"Recall a time when you were a child of six years."

Crystal zoomed in her mind's eye and saw herself playing on the playground at school.

"Now, project an aura of kindness and love, and talk to yourself."

"You mean in my memory?"

"No, in time. See what is happening."

Crystal was puzzled. What did he mean? She stretched her faculties, but just slid across her recollections.

"Do not use your mind," Fredrik whispered. "This is the secret of *Will*. Use your *Heart*."

A gray sheet stretched into a void—like a movie screen needing cleaning. Crystal had the sensation of flying toward and then into it. It folded around her, creating an embracing tunnel of soothing air. She tried to probe it with her mind, but her intention slid off like water on glass. *Use my Heart.*

Crystal felt for a different part of herself—the part that cared about the young girl of long ago. The part that could follow her and watch after her. The part that loved her.

A brief sensation of whooshing through grayness into light lifted her. Then Crystal watched herself climb the ladder of a super high slippery slide. This was a big day for her when she was six. She'd been afraid of this slide for reasons she couldn't say and she finally had talked herself into making the climb. Getting to the top, she felt pride and fear. Carefully, she seated herself, not looking down. *Just look at the slide ahead,* she told herself. She paused. Could she go?

"Come on, slowpoke!" said a voice behind her. She glanced over her shoulder just as boy with brown hair and missing a tooth gave her a shove.

She began careening down the slide, terror causing her to grab at the edges, which burned her hands.

Crystal of Now felt her terror and fear.

"Wait," said Fredrik. "Do not merge with the self of old. Just be aware of its reality."

Crystal backed off in her mind's eye and felt compassion for the little girl who was her. Her eyes popped open, but she still held the images.

Fredrik was staring at her with intensity, as though he

were sharing her vision. "Now!" he said and thumped his staff.

Crystal of Now grasped the spiritual heart of Crystal of Before and, as though she were made of energy rather than flesh and bone, then flowed clarity, calmness, and love to her. Crystal of Before corrected herself on the slide — her mouth opened into a wide grin. "*Waahooo!*" she cried and completed the ride in joy.

The vision faded, and Crystal stood in the cave in front of Fredrik. "I remember it now," she said. I remember being on that slide and feeling like an angel had helped me."

Fredrik nodded. "Yes. That is the way it is." He looked out the mouth of the cave at the sky as though gauging the time. "Now, we'll work on contacting your future self. You can learn many, many useful magics from her."

Crystal felt as though she was floating as they left the cave. *It was so simple!* she thought. She could slip forward and backward in time, correct events, learn truths. As an added bonus, the protection of the minerals in the cave had rejuvenated her being. Her body felt vital, renewed. Grateful beyond words to the old man, she sometimes held his hand on the trail, which helped her to keep up with him.

She thanked him again as they returned to the yard and he pulled out his pipe. He almost seemed to have forgotten her.

"Fredrik?" she asked.

"Yes?" He struck a match and began puffing.

"When?"

Fredrik held his arm to the sky and pointed with his pipe. "There," he said. "When the moon is there it turns to blood. You must already be playing. Use all your will. You must not falter."

"One more thing," she said. "Where?"

"At the home of the *Näcken*, of course. Where it all began. Just follow the crowd."

Crystal looked at the moon, drifting at about the ten o'clock position. When it reached the two o'clock position, as he'd indicated, she would play, with all her might.

Without a glance back, she left Fredrik to the moon and his tobacco. As she walked away, she heard him chuckle, low in his chest.

Entering the living room, she heard her mother's and Sarah's voices arguing in the next room. After the happy dinner, the room felt voided. No one else remained inside, except Elinor, who sat in a puffy chair, turned to the side, staring out the window.

"What's going on?" she asked. Although she was still floating from her experience with Fredrik, erratic energy in the house began assaulting her. Quite a contrast to the peace of the cave.

Elinor continued to stare and then turned her face to Crystal. "Well, it's like this. Your mom and your aunt are fighting over me. Or rather, what your aunt told me."

"What are you talking about? What did she tell you?"

"Your Aunt Sarah has decided I'm her kid." Elinor dragged her finger through the steam on the window and drew a big frowny face.

"What?"

"Yeah. She told me that since my eighteenth birthday is today, and since her kid died eighteen years ago today, and since my pretend father was an IRVing director, that he must have stolen me. That I must be her kid." Elinor bit a nail, then continued looking out the window.

Crystal glanced at the glass and could not see outside. Instead, her and Elinor's reflections gleamed back in like old paintings. "Oh, that's just wrong. If her baby died, how can she possibly think—"

"Apparently, now she believes IRVing took it — me. She said she never saw the body; they had her in a private hospital. She thinks that because of her connection to your family — and all that stuff she'd told them about the *Näcken* — that they must have kept me for study. And after my parents disowning me when I failed Olaf's test, she could be right."

She looked at Crystal again. "I don't know how much more of this I can take."

"You and me, both." Crystal stared at the floor and tried to make out the content of Sarah and Emma's arguments. She realized she'd meant her words of agreement to pacify Elinor. At the moment she felt she *could* take more.

Since her meeting with Fredrik, she'd felt herself shifting. *Wanting* to learn everything. *Everything*. Life extended so far beyond what she'd ever imagined. And yet . . . energy in the air in the room was scratchy, annoying, like someone drilling teeth with a high-pitched tool.

"Are you having second thoughts about staying?" Crystal asked in a quiet voice.

"I've been thinking about it. 'Course your aunt could go all weird and tie my leg to a tree, if that runs in your family. But I don't want to leave you here with them. Truly. I feel like you're the only person I have left."

Crystal nodded. "I know what you mean. And, Elinor, I can think of worse things than us being cousins."

She pinched her lips together in a tight smile. "I guess I'm staying then." Elinor drew fangs on the frowny face.

"For now. It will be over soon. I promise. I'll just play my dang fiddle, and then let's get the heck out of here," she said to Elinor.

"You got it girl." They fist bumped a soft hit. "You know, Crystal, it would explain why we both could see

Beans. Maybe I do have some of your crazy family blood."

Crystal said, "I'd better go get my instrument and tune up. Fredrik says I have to play at a certain time or it will fail, so I have to hurry. Will you stick with me tonight?"

"Of course. I'll bring the Hardanger, in case you want a backup."

Crystal left her friend, fighting down a growing annoyance at all of the evening's events. Just a few minutes before, the world had been full of promise. Now, the feeling in the air was really beginning to eat at her. They'd come all this way—she for the revelation from Fredrik—which maybe made it worth it, but she couldn't know yet. Learning her mother was still alive was incredible, but the deception infuriated her. She still had no patience for Olaf and could not imagine having the kind and loving feelings for him that a great-granddaughter should. Now her Aunt Sarah was causing trouble with the one person who had stuck by her side.

Maybe there *was* an energy in the air here making her edgier than usual, but Crystal just wanted to play and get out, as fast as she could.

6

TRUST

The moon beamed through a spotted pane in Crystal's room, and she hurried to prepare her violin. Time grew short. Fredrik wasn't visible outside, but some people in the yard were packing up parcels and blankets in preparation for a trek. *Follow the crowd*, Fredrik had said.

Crystal hurried back to the living room with her violin case, but Elinor was no longer in the chair. The lamp on the table by the window was knocked over and the face Elinor had drawn on the glass now had a neck—with a long, jagged line through it.

Crystal paused. Hot chills of fear washed over her, then she felt as though a new muscle stretched in her mind and reached around the room. She sensed a vibration like the one that had been irritating her earlier. It belonged to a time from her past—a time she was hiding from herself.

A slip of paper lay folded on the seat of the chair. She

picked it up.

The note read: IF YOU WANT TO SEE YOUR FRIEND ALIVE, GO TO THE OLD MILL. TELL NO ONE.

Crystal's throat went instantly dry, her mind frantic as she searched for what to do. Aunt Sarah and her mother were in the other room. People were gathering outside. Perhaps they could storm the mill and capture whoever held Elinor. She could not lose another friend! Guilt caused her to reel in a haunted place—she could not fathom losing someone she loved by her own actions or inactions. *That would be a fate worse than death.*

She needed to be smart. She could not afford a mistake. She had to leave—get to the place of the *Näcken.* Her arms folded across her midsection as she closed her eyes. Perhaps her new skills . . . contacting her future self?

Using intention, she calmed her mind to the same quiet place—the *nothing zone*— she entered just before playing her fiddle. *Do not use your mind—use your heart.* Words drifted in from Fredrik's earlier instructions. A power surged through her body. It seemed wrong, she needed to run if she were to be on time, yet . . . Looking out the window, she accepted an inner wisdom that seemed independent of her analytical mind.

She chose to hurry alone toward the old mill.

Crystal left by a back door to avoid the crowd and panted at a trot across the acres. The wind whipped against the abandoned mill, causing an eerie wooing sound through loose planks. Beneath the panes, she sensed people in the mill tower. Somehow, the mill felt *full*, harboring energies that were living.

Numbness overcame her fear, allowing her to force her feet forward. Who could have sneaked into the house with all the people around? Why had Elinor not screamed to draw the others? None of it would matter. Just getting Elinor back alive mattered.

She stepped to the mill door, old and battered from

DEEP NAKED   - 335

the elements. It was open a crack, as though the weather had forever banned it from closing fully. She pushed on it, but it was stuck. Putting her shoulder to it, she pushed harder.

The door fell inward, leaving her in a dim round room full of grinding equipment; a gust from her entrance through the door pushed ancient grain dust into the air. It floated around the perimeter of the dirty windows. Wind still whipped around the circumference, singing a song she would never want to play.

Her hand dragged across a rough millstone as she felt her way forward. As her eyes grabbed for light, she noticed Elinor seated near the window, bound and gagged on an old wooden chair. Moonlight glistened across her eyes. They were frantic — trying to tell Crystal something urgent.

Crystal realized what Elinor meant to say, as hard arms folded about her and a familiar voice said "Gotcha!"

She did not struggle as the man pushed her into a chair and bound her. She seemed to float out of her body. The calm embracing her she sensed as being sent from her future self.

A small lantern flicked on, casting teasing light and shadows across a familiar face as it moved into view. She looked into the eyes of 222, her former monitor from the Agency.

"So. You have no idea how much trouble you caused me," 222 said. She grinned — her gray teeth showing a need for dental care, probably not provided by the facility. "Did you really think you could escape?" 222 smiled, her eyes not masking anger. You should know by now that we have your energy map."

Crystal looked at her, uncomprehending.

222 sneered. "Every body has a unique electromagnetic frequency and with our satellite system we can

pinpoint anyone, anywhere on the planet. You are never, *ever* safe from us. "

Then, as though tired of withholding her rage, she slapped Crystal across the face.

The slap felt in slow motion, yet Crystal's head bounced against her neck, which cracked.

When Crystal didn't react, 222 stared at her hard and slapped her again. "You deserve that for what they did to me. And that's a *fraction* of what you'll get when I get you to the States."

Crystal brought her face back to look at the woman and a worm of fear wriggled through her. *Bad had happened here . . .*

An incident she had chosen to forget. Could not allow herself to remember. This woman was part of it.

But she did remember how much she *liked* this woman. How *kind* 222 was. How she would do whatever this woman wanted.

Even as the thought settled in, she realized circumstances had changed. Her instincts warred within her. Her mind said *run,* yet her body felt calm, and some image pressed at her from a twisted time — a dark place, demanding that she *remember*. The compliant part of her, the malleable part, seemed alert and *conscious*.

In the past — in some past — this woman could control her. *Had* controlled her. To a bad end. A friend . . . badness had taken her friend . . . *Tish* . . .

A flash of memory . . . an ability she used with a bartender in some other time and place — Harry's Place? — moved to the forefront.

Her future self sent energy, daylight, consciousness. No longer would she be a victim of her own weaknesses. *She had powers!*

Crystal felt a sensation of her forehead cracking open as she gripped 222 with her intention. A tendril from an unknown place in her reached out and pried open the woman's mind. And *read* the woman.

222 had once been known as Kitty Storm. Her mother loved her, but not enough to save her from her abusive stepfather . Kitty's mother had, in a fit of rage, taken an iron to her husband's head, then, in remorse born of loyalty to her spouse, stabbed herself with a butcher knife. Three-year-old Kitty watched, sucking on a washrag, from the bathroom door.

She had grown up aching for power, for control of others, and her outlet became IRVing, where her hypersensitivity from post traumatic stress disorder passed for psychic abilities, and she learned to project her will to control and dominate others.

"Kitty," Crystal said, her voice a penetrating wind. The tendril connecting them burrowed deeper. "You are loved. *Loved.*"

222 stopped her advance, her hand again in the air, and stared at Crystal. "What did you say to me? What did you say?" Her face flushed and tightened into a gargoylous mask. She raised her hand higher — this time a fist. "Answer me!"

But instead, Crystal felt for the heart of the woman, and, using the will Fredrik had helped her to locate, projected energy into it — joy that Kitty had never felt in her entire life, love that she could never have known.

Kitty's pupils dilated. Her mouth softened. "Oh, oh," she said. Her fist floated to her side; her hand relaxed.

Crystal smiled with warmth. "You really want to let us go."

"No! The Agency wants you — the vortex! We need it!" Kitty's arms flexed, but her eyes wavered, then darted.

"But you can help them, if you help us," Crystal said — her voice was soothing, calming, hypnotic. "We can't give you the vortex if you don't let us go. We must hurry or we'll miss our chance. You need to let us go."

Kitty seemed wrapped in the cocoon of Crystal's presence, the kindness and love pushing out all disagreeableness.

"*Yessss*," Kitty said, her face glowing with pleasure in the dim light. She motioned the strong-arm with her to release the girls.

Elinor ran from the mill as Crystal turned to Kitty.

"You'll be fine," she said. "You can help us now. You need to help us now."

Regal as a queen, Crystal stepped from the mill, then broke into a full-out run, while Kitty watched with adoration.

7

BEYOND THE SOUND OF MUSIC

In the chill of the night, the bundled people followed the creek, then crunched across frosted birch leaves as they crossed into the neighbor's property. They wound and wended through forest trees in the mist, following the path of the water upward to where boulders sat like sentries, jutting onto the trail and lending structure to an abysmal pool. They pushed to the clearing along the bank, overflowing backward into the forest.

Though there was no large waterfall this time, nor hot pool, the area was reminiscent to Crystal of the Appalachian setting; the water funneled down and over the rocks with a loud tinkling, magnified by the ice along the edges of the stream.

"I still can't believe what you did at the mill, Cris," said Elinor as they walked. "That was just amazing! How did you do it?"

Crystal shrugged and shifted her violin to avoid slipping on the slick trail. "I'm not entirely sure. I think I need to work with these . . . abilities . . . more. They show up when I need them; not before and not after." She walked quickly, talking between pants, glancing at the sky to check the moon's position.

Elinor's eyes were wide, as though she didn't quite recognize her friend anymore. "*Uh*, sure."

Some of the followers had brought folding chairs and some used blankets and coats to sit on between the perimeter trees, on rocks, and along the bank of the waterway. Some set up small propane heaters to comfort the elderly members of the group against the chill.

"What, are they expecting a concert?" Elinor sniped under her breath to Crystal as they maneuvered through the crowd, their instruments held to their chests to avoid bumping people. Elinor still seemed jumpy after her escape from the IRVing people, and her gait was stiff. Poised to run.

A cluster of individuals moved nearer to the girls and Olaf stepped from their midst, hurrying to match Crystal's stride as he hobbled with his cane.

Seeing him triggered Crystal. He opened his mouth to speak, but she glared at him, and his lips drew together. His face softened. Tears welled in his eyes, but he stepped back with the others.

Burning with sudden anger, humiliation, and frustration, she glanced over the crowd. Excitement radiated from them. Their faces were eager, glowing. She didn't know these people; didn't believe what they did. She felt trapped by them — a puppet. They wanted magic from her, and in this chill she'd be lucky if her instrument didn't crack in two.

She hadn't had the time to analyze what the experience in the Appalachians, or even the one on the train, had meant to her personally. That she could use her new powers to open the portal for these people, she could only hope. She could promise nothing.

Arriving at the edge of the water, the people settled into positions for the anticipated events. Crystal took out her bow, tightened it, then began sliding her rosin along the hair.

The crowd noticed, quit murmuring, and some people shushed others. Somber faces watched her as though she held the secret to life itself. Wave after wave of peace and *adoration* flowed over Crystal. She softened with the beautiful energy being projected by the crowd. Elinor seemed to sense it, too, as she cracked her neck, shook her shoulders, yawned, and grinned.

The air split with a *pop* as a rifle shot reverberated over the crowd. Almost as single body the crowd jumped and looked around. Elinor and Crystal whipped their faces to the source of the sound.

Across the stream from where they had gathered, a couple dozen townsmen pushed through the forest and took position behind trees and on boulders. Each was armed, with his face set in a no-nonsense grit.

The one who appeared to be the leader stood on a boulder, legs spread for balance, his rifle held across his chest. Ake, his apparent second in command, held himself erect at the base of the rock.

"You there. You're all trespassing. I'll give you a count of ten to clear out."

Olaf stepped forward.

"You cannot stop this, Bari. This is to happen. You know it."

The leader glared down at the old man. "I do not believe that. We won't allow you to do what you did before—your evil magic. It's over." He shouted to the crowd. "You're on my property! All of you, go home."

The crowd shifted and looked to Olaf who was gazing into the sky, his bottom lip dropped. He seemed to be listening.

Bari ignored him.

"No," said Olaf.

Crystal barely heard him as a sound began ratcheting from the sky.

"Get going! One! Two!" Bari lifted his rifle and shot into the air. The cluster of gunmen cheered as the people flinched.

Two large, black shapes appeared in the sky overhead. Crystal peered up into the ruckus as the forms became clear. Unmarked helicopters circled above the men, low over the trees. Someone in the crowd shone a strong light toward one of the crafts, revealing a man in the passenger side holding a semi-automatic weapon pointed over the crowd.

"Black ops to the rescue!" Crystal giggled at the incongruity of the moment.

The men ducked behind trees and boulders, lifting their rifles toward the helicopters.

"Oh no!" Elinor shouted over the din from the copters. "It's going to be a bloodbath!"

Fredrik stepped from the shadows of the trees and said something to Olaf, unheard by Crystal due to the ruckus above.

Olaf nodded and turned to his followers gathered at the stream's edge. Olaf held his hands up, before him, like a conductor, as Fredrik held aloft his walking stick, then jammed it three times into the air.

Holding up his right palm, Fredrik faced it toward the people, closed his eyes and concentrated.

"But what's this?" Crystal turned toward Olaf's group. As if on cue, they all began a low hum, an *om* of sorts, which fragmented into a split harmonic between two notes.

The helicopter blades struck a rhythmic *whup, whup,* working in tandem. Between the sound from the choppers, the hundred peoples' voices rose in pitch.

The copters rose higher, backing off.

Olaf's entire group radiated the a-harmonic tones, each person issuing two notes at the same time, and creating the resonance of a third.

"Middle 'C'," said Elinor.

Crystal smiled. Her friend and that perfect pitch.

The townspeople shifted in their positions amongst the trees and looked at each other with questioning. As the singing intensified, it became a multi-tonal trill, piercing the airwaves with painful tones.

Some armed men dropped their weapons and covered their ears. Bari aimed his weapon at a retreating chopper, when a *ping* hit a tree near him. He seemed to think better of it and lowered his weapon.

Fredrik stepped forward. "Bari. All of you. You know the event that will take place tonight. What you don't know is that we have found the one to complete the loop. Let this happen. This is not a restarting of the centuries, it is an ending. It is a reconnection with the earth as it should have been."

The throat-singing *om* of the groupies intensified and seemed directed toward Bari, holding him in its grip. He stood numbed, swaying in his stance. He struggled to command the men, but his lips went slack. They looked to him, then each other, and stirred with indecision.

Ake stared across the water at Crystal, then at Fredrik. He looked at the helicopters above and the crowd, then motioned the men back.

Withdrawing, they separated and moved off through the trees. As they left, the choppers pulled up and moved off, as well, their sound diminishing into the night.

As the singers closed their mouths, silence hushed over the woods. The group all focused on Crystal.

Released from the grip of the toning and left alone, Bari climbed from his rock, and, looking back only once, followed his men into the brush.

♪

Crystal removed her gloves, rubbed her hands together, and tuned by plucking the strings. Then, she drew her bow across her string and—nothing. No sound, except a slight, almost inaudible screeching, emitted from her instrument.

Her audience saw her attempting to play and watched, breathless.

Crystal tried again.

No music. No sound. No notes. Not even the sound of rough hair on metal.

"I think it's too moist out here," she whispered to Elinor.

From behind them, her mother stepped forward, a questioning look on her face. Crystal explained what was happening, and went back to her case, and she pulled out a cloth. She cleaned her strings and wiped her bow, then tried again. It was a little better, but still no music.

"Does someone have a heater? Could someone bring some heat?" her mother's voice pealed across the attendees. Several jumped up at once, bringing propane heaters —smiling as they contributed to the endeavor.

Surrounded by five heaters, she and Elinor kneeled on the wet earth and heated the bow hair and violin.

"I'd better warm the Hardanger, too," said Elinor, and opened the instrument case.

Crystal waited a few minutes until her violin had time to acclimate, then tried bowing again. This time, a true sound rang out and the crowd applauded.

"Quiet! Quiet!" Olaf yelled and his group paused in their enthusiasm.

"Cris," Elinor whispered as she stood, "I think there are some IRVing guys over near that big pine."

Two men in black coats stood apart from the others in the crowd, ducked in the shadows, barely visible in the moonglow.

"Well what are they going to do now? Kidnap me with all these people here? Let them. Free airfare back to the States." She smiled ruefully and faced the water.

"Okay, girl," she said to Elinor. "Here I go."

Crystal held her instrument to her clavicle, placed her bow on the A-string without drawing it, and let the feeling from the water and crowd flow over her. Then she lifted the fiddle to her chin.

For a moment time seemed suspended, as the audience members held their breath, waiting. Crystal began pulling the bow hair across a string, in a perfect and even pressure. The pure note intoned for a full minute while Crystal allowed herself to merge with the resonance.

Olaf watched her, eager tears filling his eyes. Each second the tone continued, his face glowed with a greater rapture.

After reaching the *nothing zone,* the first element she felt was the coldness, the absolute chill of their surroundings, and the presence of the trees. So she played those in high octave notes and runs. Her music dove like birds between branches, and huddled against the elements in her core. Then the peoples' emotions began crowding in — beauty, love, peace — then the emotions the peace-lovers did not expect — their suppressed emotions. Hate, envy, jealousy. Hot white fire passion.

As Crystal drew her bow back and forth, the crowd became uncomfortable. Some people arose and left. Still she played the hidden motivations behind their leaving. She played their subtext in undertones.

She found her own emotions triggered by those of others. Emotions she had fought and tried to suppress. Her own fury overrode every note that her bow dredged from the soul of the instrument. Crystal strained to connect with the water, to seek out the *Näcken*, but could not. The water remained a sheet of ice that could not be played.

"Stop! Stop!" shouted Olaf and moved stiffly from the crowd toward her. His cane shook into the air as though to thrash it. "You are killing it—the *Näcken*. It will not come with you so—angry. Get it out. Let go of it or none of us will ever be—" He finished in Swedish, using words she didn't understand.

"Leave her alone, Grandfather!" Crystal's mother stepped forward and grasped Olaf's sleeve. "She's been through enough. She shouldn't have to do this."

"She's the only one who can get my Alicia back. She's the only one who can open the door for all these." He swept his hand over the crowd. "Is she a selfish girl?"

Crystal stepped forward, her fiddle tight in one hand, her bow in the other. She went up nose to nose with the old man. "A *selfish* girl? I'll tell you how selfish I am. I've been put through hell, do you hear me? Hell! I've been kidnapped, chained, chased, restrained, shot at, slapped, and even chased by a drunken moose, and still I'm trying to help you and your—your—minions. And I don't even fully believe this stuff. If this makes me selfish, well, maybe I should be *more* selfish and tell you all to go take a flying fu—" Crystal caught Elinor's look, which was one of mirth. She was covering her mouth with her hand, and nearly doubling over. Crystal stopped herself, and finished "—funky donkey!"

The old man stared at her, then turned to his granddaughter. "What is 'funky donkey'?"

Her mother chuckled, and covered her mouth with her hand, as well. She addressed her daughter. "So, what's the word, Cris? Play or no?"

"It's not working, Mom. I can't seem to do it."

Olaf fairly spat. "You must be *Näcken!* You must play your *self*. Not the other people, until you play *yourself*. The key is in *you*. You must be naked! Your soul must be all the way naked! Deep naked!" Her great-grandfather again shook his cane in exasperation, his eyes rolling.

Tugging her sleeve, Crystal's mother pulled her aside to talk privately. "Cris, I know you have reason to dislike him, but he is the resident *Näcken* expert. Maybe what he says will work."

Crystal was steamed, her breath coming in pants. "I hope so. And of course I'll try. There's way more at stake than appeasing his groupies." Crystal eyed the old man with bitterness.

"Hey, Cris. I'll help!" Elinor chirped, and got out the Hardanger.

Several in the crowd *oohed* when they saw their native instrument.

Elinor joined Crystal, and this time, when she picked up the instrument, Crystal focused on her *own* raw emotions. Her own *material*. She began *larghissimo*, slowly playing bottomless sorrow at the death of her mother. She then shot into *gioioso* then *furioso*, as she encountered her joy and anger at learning her mother was still alive. She played frustration, compassion, amusement, and disgust: emotions connected to her aunt. Her feelings of plaintive sweetness and unreasoned sorrow for her father. For each of her friends she played the beauty and darkness of her own soul that each held captive. And Olaf. The rage, frustration, denial, and yet complete and profound understanding of his desires.

The Hardanger joined in with multi-harmonic over-tones and undertones. In Elinor's capable and inspired hands, it tracked with her across forbidden terrains and beyond azure nights. It supported her in tossing surf and kept her tethered when Crystal soared to the heights.

The audience's faces showed a combination of looks, from perplexed to pleased.

The water flowed *adagio*, but for the crashing of the falls. And the air shimmered with only the frost and heat from the propane burners.

After several minutes, Crystal and Elinor looked at each other and, with that psychic twist known to musicians, wrapped up the tune.

They were met by silence.

Faces, some appearing heartbroken, stared at them, but no one complained. Silently, the believers arose, folded their chairs, picked up their blankets, and walked off, following lanterns in the night.

Olaf sat on a boulder with his face in his hands, and his cane between his knees. His granddaughter, Emma, comforted him as he cried. Sarah sat next to him, and kept stealing peeks at Elinor.

Crystal stared at the water, then her eyes rose to the moon. It gleamed full and robust down on her, its light laughing at its superior place in the universe.

An arm hugged her from the side and she recognized the woody smell of Fredrik before she turned to him.

"Don't worry," he said, and his own eyes rose to the moon. "All is as it should be."

"Is that what your future self said? I failed. Do we get another chance?"

"My future self speaks no more. That is how I know all is well. After tonight I will be Fredrik of Now no longer."

Crystal looked above his beard, into his eyes, but could read nothing there but the light of the stars. He drifted away, his black coat turning him invisible in the trees.

"What was that?" Elinor asked.

Crystal shrugged and shook her head. "Well, I guess that's it. No fireworks." She sighed as she put the fiddle in the case.

"I wonder what was wrong?" Elinor opened the case for the Hardanger, disappointment pulling her lips into a frown.

"I don't know. I did what I could, but I've never tried to save the world before. Something — I don't know what — but some ingredient, felt *missing*."

"Yeah, like the dark underlords or some crazy mythological being. Everybody else seemed to show up." Elinor smirked.

Crystal chuckled. "Speaking of which, where are those black ops guys?"

"Oh, they left when they saw we blew it. Guess they decided you weren't the *one* after all. I wonder how they intended to control the vortex thingy if it did open up." She finished setting the Hardanger in its case, and closed it.

"Humans can be so arrogant," said Crystal, picking up her instrument.

"What did you say?"

"Humans. You know. Those people on this plane."

Elinor looked at her square. "Hey. *Plane*? You're sounding kind of funny."

"Am I?" Crystal laughed when Elinor shuddered.

"It's just me."

"Is it?"

"Of course. Now let's get back to the house and warm up. I could eat a horse."

They started walking through the woods.

"I thought you were vegetarian now."

Crystal laughed.

Someone whistled from behind a tree and the girls stopped.

From the shadows stepped Glenn, holding out his arms.

"Cris. Cris. I'm so sorry. I have to tell—"

Winging back her case, she slugged him with it in the side. He squealed and crouched, holding his hands over his head.

"Wait! Wait!" he cowered. "No kill! Let me explain!"

"You betrayed us! You abandoned me! How could you. Why? Why?"

"I didn't—"

Elinor stood, legs apart, glaring. Her fist was tightened on the Hardanger case. That would make a good weapon, too.

"Let me explain! Please!" Glenn's hands were still up in surrender.

Crystal's jaw tightened as she waited.

"When they came on board, they caught me coming out of the restroom," Glenn continued. "They thought I was on my way to meet you—they didn't know you were aboard the train. I went with them to save you. To let you get away."

"Your grandfather was in cahoots with them! We saw him and you with them!"

"No," Glenn rose slowly. "They came to him to find me—to find you. He thought they were police—he thought he had no choice. They said if he didn't tell them where I was, they'd kill me if they found me. So he told. They figured out that since you had relatives here, they would find me on my way to meet you."

Crystal so wanted to believe. His violet eyes shone

like a cat's in the moonglow and even from four feet away she could feel his heat and presence.

"But why you? If they were after me, why did they want you?"

"When I played, the night you saw me at the performance, they were monitoring. They monitored all violinists who played in a certain . . . zone. And their devices told them that I was capable of . . . doing what you do."

"But you didn't. You failed with Olaf."

"I was trying too hard. I wanted to please *him*. And playing *Näcken*, you have to let it all go. You can have no agenda. And there's something else."

"What?" Elinor demanded, her voice spiked and disbelieving.

"When I came here, I asked where your family was and got a really odd reception."

"Like shot at?"

He laughed. "Almost. But I found out about your history. And mine . . . is similar. Both of our grandmothers were impregnated on the other side."

Elinor's mouth dropped open.

Crystal's eyes widened. How could she not have seen it before? No wonder she was so drawn to him. He was probably the only person on the planet *like her!*

"Oh. My. God." Crystal panted. "Oh. My. God. I'm grossed out. You're—*a relative?*"

Glenn's grin dropped. "Oh. *Sheesh.* I don't know. I sure hope not. Neither my grandmother nor yours knew who—or what— the father was. No one said it was the same man—*er*—whatever." He looked to the side.

A long silence followed, while Crystal and Elinor digested what Glenn had told them. They looked at each other, then Crystal focused on Glenn. A halo seemed to emanate around him— the clean aura that had held her so captive in their kiss at camp.

"It can't be. It would be so wrong. And, I'm so ... attached ... to you." Crystal dropped her case and stepped to Glenn. She reached up and folded her arms around his stomach, placing her head on his chest.

He wrapped his arms around her, allowing his warmth to flow over her.

"We'll get tests. We'll pray. All I know is, we belong together." Glenn tilted her chin up and his lips found their way across the galaxy to hers. The purity of that kiss, though it was as light as butterfly wings, resulted in a connection, an inner explosion that linked them, mind and soul.

Crystal could feel both of their emotions. Their bond went beyond the physical — more than the physical could ever be. Bodies were not even needed on the plane where they met.

Drawing away from each other, she still felt the love of the embrace and knew it would be all right.

After a few moments of amused peeping, Elinor turned and walked back to where Crystal's relatives still waited, to give them some privacy.

"What do we do now?" asked Crystal.

"Well, isn't it obvious?" Glenn asked. He jigged a couple of steps, did a pirouette in the frost, and held up his arms to the world. "We play!"

8

ANGELS OR DEMONS

The trio approached the cluster of family that stood watching them. Reluctantly, Elinor relinquished the Hardanger and stepped back. Glenn struck it up. Crystal glowed as she pulled forth her violin. Like trees afire, they took a stand next to the waterway and the dancing falls.

Fredrik, Olaf, Sarah, Emma, and Elinor stood transfixed, silhouetted against a backdrop of pine, highlighted by the high moon. The two ladies who had accompanied Olaf moved to his side, and each took up an elbow.

This time there was no hesitation — no need to force a connection. Glenn and Crystal looked into each other's eyes and their essences danced around and through each other. As they began to play, their energy streamed into one energy — one being.

An earth shadow crept across the sky and embraced the moon with a pink arm, then kissed it full on the mouth, blocking the golden light. The moon began to bleed.

Crystal and Glenn's eyes caught, and they blazed into a rush of centuries and great universes.

The night cracked open with the beams of a thousand stars. Splintering ice rose from the river, forming a shimmering vortex above their heads.

In joy and light, they played — the Hardanger ringing the tones of centuries, the great arts and accomplishments of humankind — the violin joining in with the beauty and fluidity of life and the passions of the earth. They played, they blended, they intensified.

They knocked on the *wicket*.

The water struck red and shot a fountain into the air. The fourth dimension merged with the vortex, vibrated and, with a loud *pop*, cracked into another space/time.

Still they played. Each dove into the soul of the other, climbed into reaches beyond comprehensive words and lifted each other up. With their hearts on fire, their souls at the apex of human beingness, the clarity and purity of all humankind in their centers, the little door was opened.

Numbed, they ceased playing and watched the portal rip wide into another dimension.

Crystal's personal space expanded, embracing and pervading all feeling and thought of those around her.

The family stood together, without sound. Although they could see pulsating colors and white light that it seemed would fry their retinas, all present sensed that this was only a fraction of what the other universe entailed.

Then, from the center of the roiling mass of lights, a glittery being moved toward them.

"An angel?" Elinor croaked, but no one answered.

The being drifted through the portal toward them, and extended a hand.

Olaf took a step forward. Then another. His eyes, so long angered and blaming, brightened with joy and release of guilt.

"Alicia? My daughter, Alicia?" he cried. He walked forward, stiff and uncertain, when a wash of affection projected from the entity and enveloped the group. All hearts joined into one gigantic pulsing Now of Love and Beauty.

Crystal psychically pulled back, keeping her distance. With her awareness expanded, she still perceived what the others were experiencing, but she resisted being drawn in.

Fredrik had warned her . . . she needed to *will* the vortex to remain open, until the other side had completed whatever it was doing. And as soon as she thought it, the ability returned to her. Her will stretched forth like invisible armor, completely controlled by her love. *Love under Will*, she thought.

When she looked at her mother, she saw her father in an ethereal form standing next to her, holding her hand. And next to Sarah was a man she had never seen. And behind them, ethereally connected, were more faces — people they had known, people who had been kind. It was as though all the beloved people of those present were being invited, by special invitation only, to join those on the other side. Glancing at Glenn, she saw a perfect reflection of herself.

The shimmering being extended her hand, which appeared as a whirling pod of light, toward Olaf, and he lifted a shaking hand in response. Just behind her, a tall, willowy form stood, his dimension shifting in the vortex. At times he seemed to have a large gray head with black eyes. At other times, he seemed to be dazzling energy.

One by one those present stepped into the air and passed through the being that Olaf believed to be Alicia.

Some of those to whom they were connected, the ethereal presences, joined them. As they did so, each dissolved into an essence of pure luminosity.

The last to move toward the portal was Fredrik. His face aglow, he stepped to the line separating this reality from that. He seemed caught in the prismatic and dancing light from the vortex. Then he turned and looked at Crystal.

As he strode toward her, it seemed his feet were wading through air, not touching the ground. Standing in front of her, he reached up his long, flowing sleeve and drew forth a tattered book.

"You're next, Crystal. This will help you to find your way," he said and passed the tome to her.

Crystal took the book, stunned by the magnetic charge it seemed to emanate. She thanked her benefactor and held his hand atop the book for a moment. It felt as though they had done this before. Or many times before. Some long, ancient times ago.

Just before he stepped through the portal he turned again, his beard twitching as he spoke. "One more thing . . . You'll need to learn the other two ways!"

"Ways what?"

"Time travel," Fredrik's voice floated into a diminishing chasm. "If you need me, just call!" He disappeared into the portal.

At last, just Elinor, Glenn, and Crystal stood watching — their faces aglow, their hearts in bliss.

The moon eclipsed blood red beyond the vortex as the alignment of the sun, earth, and moon ushered in the event.

Those on the other side, open to the fourth dimension, initiated the Great Change. They issued a tone beyond hearing, beyond the ability to comprehend with small, human minds. A concussion of interdimensional and subtle forces reverberated from the portal across the world and throughout the material universe. It butted against the tear in the past and realigned some of the space/time fabric in the future. It was just a patch, but it would help. It would prevent the collapse of time into the black hole of Now—a crushing of all living things into a seed of potential—for a while.

The next level of humanity could begin, and those ready would partake of it.

Crystal and Glenn had found the missing ingredient. They had found the key. The factor the scientists could never recreate—the reason they could never master inter-dimensional travel. The component that was needed to transition across space and time. That undefilable, unique, unduplicatable and universal element.

Crystal and Glenn had played to the very heart of it. It was love.

AVAILABLE NOW !!

NAKED WORLDS BOOK II

SKIN SLICKERS

Crystal's Blood Hides a Secret . . .

CRYSTAL DISAPPEARS UNDER MYSTERIOUS circumstances and Glenn must find her before a depraved cartel uses her in an arcane ritual. Frantic, he plunges into strange alliances and teams with risky characters for clues.

An alien threat ties to Crystal's abduction and Glenn spins through time and dimensions to unravel her whereabouts. But when allies turn against him, he's shot off-world to die. Will his paranormal abilities and intense love for Crystal be enough to reach her in time, or are too many lies in his truths?

Angels may not be what you think . . .

ABOUT THE AUTHOR

 Riley Hill lurks in the backwoods shadows where dark moods set the tone for her tales of mystery, fantasy, paranormal, and science-fiction. She adamantly denies being an alien or a walk-in, but refuses to answer questions about being a mutant. At times you may see her sitting atop a large boulder in the Arizona desert, in the hollow of a tree in Oregon, or submerged to her waist in the Mediterranean Sea. But you'll never catch her on a space ship. At least in daylight.

Riley enjoys hearing from fans and can be reached at AuthorRileyHill@gmail.com or through her webpage at http://authorrileyhill.com.

If you enjoyed this story, please leave a review for the book at your favorite online retailer.

Thank you for reading!

SPECIAL TRIBUTE TO OLOF AUGUST WIDMARK

Although Olof played a villain of sorts (Olaf) in this fictional book, he was nothing of the sort. He is believed to be the greatest 19th century fiddler in western Sörmlandsleden, Sweden. He was, indeed, mentored by Fredrik Lindroth and trained by the *Näcken*. A statue was built in his honor. His music and playing were revered in his home town of *Vingåker*, Sweden and the music that survived burning by his granddaughter, Anna, is housed in the Royal Academy of Music. It is said that Olaf was so dearly attached to his violin that when he was ready to pass, he asked for it, and died with it in his arms. The following remnant of music is from his handwritten collection.

Taught by the Näcken

[The] music book contains 199 songs, including 15 polonäser, 7 polkas, waltzes 29, 31 fransäser, 9 marches, 15 kadriljer, 4 canters and 2 angläser. Towards the end there is such Jernbanegalopp and Champagne Gallop and the last pages contain a number of American folk tunes (reels, hornpipes etc). Obviously, the book has been used by both Olof August and Per August. — *Excerpt from Sormlands musikarkiv.*

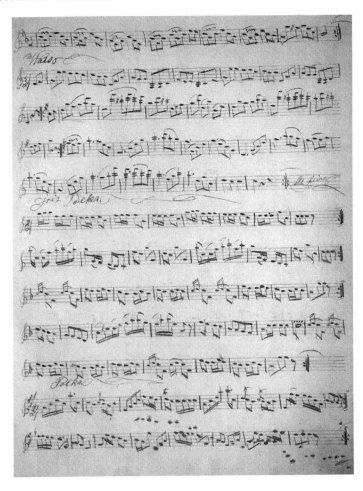

Made in the USA
Columbia, SC
11 August 2018